ANNABEL LEE

"Mike Nappa's *Annabel Lee* is a fast-paced thriller, filled with unexpected twists and peopled by unique and memorable characters. From the first chapter on, I found it impossible to put down."

—Lois Duncan, Mystery Writers of America Grand Master and *New York Times* bestselling author of *I Know What You Did Last Summer* and *Killing Mr. Griffin*

"*Annabel Lee* is compelling, fast-paced, and filled with fascinating characters. One hopes that Mike Nappa's eleven-year-old wunderkind from the title will reappear in future novels of this promising new suspense series!"

—M.K. Preston, Mary Higgins Clark Award–winning novelist, author of *Song of the Bones* and *Perhaps She'll Die*

"A relentless surge of suspense and mounting tension coupled with an engaging mix of characters. With *Annabel Lee*, Mike Nappa skillfully sets the stage for an irresistible series of Coffey & Hill thrillers."

—Jack Cavanaugh, award-winning author of twenty-six novels

COFFEY & HILL • 1

ANNABEL LEE

A COFFEY & HILL NOVEL

MIKE NAPPA

Revell

a division of Baker Publishing Group
Grand Rapids, Michigan

© 2016 by Mike Nappa

Published by Revell
a division of Baker Publishing Group
P.O. Box 6287, Grand Rapids, MI 49516-6287
www.revellbooks.com

Printed in the United States of America

Library of Congress Cataloging-in-Publication Data
Names: Nappa, Mike, 1963–
Title: Annabel Lee : a Coffey & Hill novel / Mike Nappa.
Description: Grand Rapids, Michigan : Revell, a division of Baker Publishing
    Group, [2016] | Series: Coffey & Hill ; 1
Identifiers: LCCN 2015037004 | ISBN 9780800726447 (softcover)
Subjects: LCSH: Private investigators—Alabama—Fiction. | GSAFD:
    Suspense fiction. | Mystery fiction. | Christian fiction.
Classification: LCC PS3564.A624 A85 2016 | DDC 813/.54—dc23 LC record
    available at http://lccn.loc.gov/2015037004

This book is published in association with Nappaland Literary Agency, an independent agency dedicated to publishing works that are: Authentic. Relevant. Eternal.
Visit us on the web at: NappalandLiterary.com.

16 17 18 19 20 21 22   7 6 5 4 3 2 1

For Jan Hummel
who makes things happen!

For the moon never beams without bringing me dreams
Of the beautiful Annabel Lee . . .

—EDGAR ALLAN POE

1

ANNABEL

Date Unknown

Uncle Truck keeps a German shepherd on his farm that'll eat human fingers if you feed 'em to it just right.

I know this because I have seen that dog. And I have seen them fingers.

Truck keeps the dog—house and all—in a chain link cage out behind the big red barn on the property, just down from the winding, dirt-road driveway. The cage ain't very big, but it's long and narrow like a practice track, and it gives the dog a place to run. Except when the dog gets to the end. Then it has to almost stop and put its paws up on the corner of the fence so's it can turn around quickly inside that small space.

Sometimes I think that dog is crazy, runnin' up and down that grass-patched cage. Runnin' like no one is looking. Like it's got to run or else, well, or else it'll go crazy. It ain't the barking kind of dog, though.

I mean, *isn't*. Isn't the barking kind of dog.

9

I am an educated girl. I don't use words like *ain't*, not no more. Not anymore.

I'm not school-educated, no. Uncle Truck says that's a waste of time and taxpayer dollars. But he also says he won't have no stupids in his house neither. That's why I got books all over this place. Any kind of book I want, Truck'll get for me. He says that's my education and I better make the most of it. I don't mind, though. I like books. I like reading. I like that Truck makes time for me to read each and every day of the week, no matter what. I like that at least twice a week—and sometimes more—Truck pulls a language book off the shelf and drills me on German verbs or Arabic phrases or Italian fairy tales or whatever. I like knowing there's something else out there to discover beyond just the acres of this farm, outside the closed-up community of Peachtree, Alabama. And I like it when Truck says I'm real good at learning and a "supernatural" at picking up different languages.

What I don't like is that dog.

It don't bark at me, not ever. But it growls. I can almost feel the rumbling in its throat before I hear it with my ears. Whenever the dog sees me, the growling starts. Sometimes Truck'll tell it to shut-up-mutt and swat it across the nose. But most times Uncle Truck don't even hear it. Most times it's just the dog and me, even when Truck or one of his farmhands is there.

The dog looks me dead in the eye. Never wags its tail. Never moves off its haunches. Just looks at me and growls, low, deep, and regular. It reminds me of some story out of a fairy tale, except the magic here is real, and bad. Like that dog was once an evil warlock vanquished by a handsome prince, and as his punishment, he was transformed forever into a dog that eats fingers and lives in a cage. Something like that.

I make my hands into fists whenever I have to be near that dog.

I asked Truck once why he fed fingers to the dog. He looked

at first like he was gonna laugh. Then he got a serious layer onto his face.

"Just testing the limits," he said. "Nothing for you to concern yourself with, Annie-girl."

"But where'd the fingers come from?" I wanted to know.

Uncle Truck didn't answer.

Kenny, one of Truck's oldest hands on the farm, told me later that the fingers came from a medical research facility in Tuscaloosa, that they was from cadavers dedicated to science and that one of Truck's old army buddies got 'em while he was working out there as a lab assistant after the second Iraq war. Kenny said Uncle Truck knows people all over Alabama, all over the world. And because of that, Truck can't talk about everything he does or everyone he knows to a little girl with a big imagination. But Kenny said he only knew Truck and Peachtree, AL, so he could talk to whoever he wanted whenever he wanted, and that included me.

I like Kenny. But I worry about him sometimes. Even I know it ain't—*isn't*—good to let your mouth run off too much. Truck says that's what killed my parents. I think he may be right.

Peachtree ain't but a fourteen-mile drive from our acreage on the edges of the Conecuh National Forest, so that's where we go to get most of our supplies and to find out the gossip of the world. I saw a man once, down at Kelly Supply store in Peachtree, who had two fingers missing from his left hand. His pinky and his ring finger both was gone down to the nub. Truck was over in the leather section looking at a saddle, so I took a chance.

"What happened to your fingers, mister?" I asked the man.

He looked down, grinning. "Well, aren't you a cutie," he said.

I find grown-ups like that annoying.

I got long brown hair, just enough curl to make it nice, I guess. I got green eyes and a lean, horse-riding frame that older women tell me is gonna turn into a "man-killa" someday, whatever that means. I wear boots most days and a dress on Sundays. But I didn't ask this man to judge whether or not I was cute. I asked about his messed-up hand. Seems disrespectful not to answer a person's question when it's asked straight on at you, so I tried again, pointing at his nubs for emphasis.

"What happened to your fingers?"

This time he raised his hand and looked at it like it was the first time he'd seen he was missing something there.

"Lost 'em when I was about your age," he said. "Stuck 'em under a lawnmower by accident."

"Did you feed 'em to a dog after?"

He cocked his head like he wanted to tell a secret but wasn't sure if I knew it already. I decided not to make him spill something private, so I changed the subject.

"How you gonna get married without having a finger to hold the ring?"

He laughed at the question. "I guess that's a problem," he said, patting his belly, "but first I gotta find me a woman who don't mind that her man eats too much and exercises too little."

I seen Uncle Truck comin' over then. I figured it was time to wrap up.

"Bye, mister," I said. "Good luck finding your woman."

"Thanks," he said. Then he followed my gaze and saw Truck was headed our way. His whole manner changed. His eyes darted all over, looking for exits, and his back stiffened like he wanted to run. He didn't wait around. He turned and walked the opposite direction, around a display of feed grain and then out the door of Kelly Supply. A minute later Truck was standing next to me, looking after the eight-fingered man.

"Who was that?" he said to me.

I shrugged. "Just some man."

"What did he say to you?"

"Nothing," I lied. But I was thinking about Truck's dog.

"Good," Uncle Truck said to me. "Come on, I need to get some rope before we go."

Unlike that eight-fingered man, most people in Peachtree greet Uncle Truck like he's their best friend. Wherever he goes, they call out his name, clap him on the back, and tell stories about off-the-wall adventures. But when Truck ain't looking, I see them sometimes show a little something they don't want him to see. They get this wary gleam in their eyes and fidget around a bit like they's in a spotlight and can't wait to get out of it again.

Afraid.

Makes sense to me.

Truck gets good deals on stuff wherever he goes. The man at Kelly Supply lets him keep a runnin' tab for things he buys at the store. It's listed under the name of Leonard Truckson. He runs up credit in the winter and then pays it off in the fall, after harvest. At least that's what they tell me. I ain't never seen Truck—or Leonard Truckson—pay for anything at that store.

Anybody who calls Uncle Truck "Leonard" or "Lenny" or even "Mr. Truckson" is from out of town. Everybody here knows that he's Truck, period. That's the way it's always been, and I guess the way it always will be.

Funny how he's so peculiar about his name, but that dog ain't got no name at all.

That dog . . .

Uncle Truck keeps a dog that eats human fingers out behind his barn.

I'm afraid of that mean old dog.

But sometimes, if I'm honest, Uncle Truck's the one who really scares me.

2

TRUDI

Friday, August 28

Trudi Sara Coffey brushed a darkened curl away from her eyes and, as was her custom, looked first in the classifieds section of the *Atlanta Journal-Constitution*.

She scanned the personals until the familiar advertisement came into view. It was only one line, easy to miss. In fact, she wondered how long it had been running in the *Constitution* before she'd even noticed it three years ago, by accident, while on her way to the used car ads. It had been running daily ever since, and Trudi now couldn't start her morning without checking to see if its invisible author still had the same message to send out to the world.

Safe.

Trudi had read once about a married couple separated by the tragedy of the Holocaust while trying to escape Poland for America. Before their separation, the husband and wife had promised each other that whichever one of them reached freedom first was to go to America and then take out an advertisement in the classified ad section of the *New York Times*. The ad was to repeat their personal code phrase—something like "love is forever" or "forever is love"—and then add a phone number where the person could be contacted.

The wife had made it out first, just before the end of the war, but was not able to place her ad until August of 1947. Early on, she ran it only once a week—on Sundays—because that was all she could afford. She built herself a new life in America, made friends, converted to Catholicism, became a nurse, and worked for three decades at a hospital in Long Island. But she never married again. Instead she dedicated her life to her work, her church, and her growing circle of friends.

By 1953, she was running the ad daily in the *Times*. Her friends told her it had been long enough, to give up, to move on. Surely her husband had perished as one of the many nameless people in the Nazi concentration camps. She deserved to live her life to the full, to finally be finished with grieving and begin anew with joy. And each time she heard someone say these things, she would smile, say, "You're right, of course you are," and then move the conversation to a different topic. And each month she'd mail in a renewal check to the *New York Times*, making sure her advertisement would continue to appear each day for years to come.

In 1982, she retired from the hospital, was feted with a lavish party, and was presented a gold watch with diamond accents. She settled into her brownstone apartment and prepared to spend the rest of her days reading good books, taking long walks in the park, and generally being grateful for the life she had lived, albeit alone, in her immigrant home.

In 1984, a small news item on the back page of an obscure

newspaper reported that Soviet authorities had decided to shut down several leftover prison camps, relics from their Eastern European victories during and after WWII.

In 1985, the woman answered her phone one afternoon to hear an old man's voice, a tired and nervous accent, speaking on the other end.

"Love is forever."

And the woman knew immediately who it was. Her husband, long thought dead, had come back to life. For her.

In truth, he'd been surviving in a concentration camp in Poland where he'd eventually been forced to cooperate with the Germans in a clandestine weapons program. When the camp was "liberated" by the Russians, anyone found to have worked on the weapons program—prisoners and guards alike—had been swiftly, and secretly, swept into the Soviet Union, trading a German prison camp for an only slightly better Soviet installation in Siberia. He'd grown into an old man there, until finally it was determined that he and his fellow prisoners—those still alive—could no longer harm Mother Russia. He was seventy years old by this time, but he'd made a promise and he intended to keep it.

With unsteady eyes and a body ravaged by decades of discomfort, he traveled to the United States, to New York City. He'd waited a few days in a cheap hotel, working up the courage to hope. Then, after a week, he'd finally bought a copy of the *New York Times* and slowly worked his way through the personal ads until he saw, faithfully printed, his wife's advertisement and phone number. And he'd called her. And, as the story goes, they lived happily ever after.

Trudi thought of that couple whenever she saw the daily ad that read "Safe" in the pages of the *Atlanta Journal-Constitution*. The romantic in her hoped it represented a story of undying love. The bitter ex-wife in her hoped it even more. It would be a terrible world, she decided, if all love was only temporary.

So she looked once again at the four-letter word she'd grown so accustomed to seeing, let a faint grin pass on her lips in gratefulness that it still remained, then contentedly turned back to the front page to begin her day in earnest. Half an hour later, her receptionist (a new hire, but she seemed to be working out okay) buzzed in on the intercom.

"Ms. Coffey," the receptionist said with youthful professionalism, "there's a client here to see you. He doesn't have an appointment but insists that you'll see him anyway."

Trudi turned to the small video monitor situated under her desk, hidden on the left side. The one-room reception area of Coffey & Hill Investigations was empty except for Eulalie Jefferson (the new receptionist) and an older gentleman dressed with impeccable care in a dark suit, carrying a cane. The older man turned slowly and—although the camera in the outside office was well disguised as a lighting sconce on the wall—appeared to look directly into Trudi's appraising eyes. He gave a slight nod toward the private investigator and then turned his attention back to Eulalie, who waited patiently for a response from her boss.

Trudi hesitated. She'd never met this man before . . . had she? The PI studied the gentleman closely for a moment longer, then shrugged. This man was a complete stranger, but something about him tickled Trudi's curiosity. And besides, though Coffey & Hill had enough ongoing contracts to keep busy for the time being, Trudi had no other cases or clients that were pressing for her time at the moment.

She reached over and flipped the switch on the intercom. "Thanks Eula," she said confidently. "Send him in."

The older gentleman paused to review Trudi's tiny office before crossing the threshold into the room.

"Good morning," Trudi said. "What can I help you with today?"

The old man tapped his cane absently on the floor and let a whole breath enter and exit before responding. "Quite a collection," he said, pointing the cane toward the wall of bookshelves behind Trudi's desk. "But I would have expected more in the way of practical manuals and less in the way of, well, pleasure reading."

Trudi let her gaze drift briefly along the books on her shelves. There were several volumes of world mythology, a few books of fairy tales and folk stories. But this visitor had pointed toward the pride of her shelves, the best of her collection. The complete Edgar Allan Poe. Same with Sir Arthur Conan Doyle. Memoirs of Francois Eugene Vidocq. A number of Miss Marple tales, Lord Wimsey, Ellery Queen, and the rest. It was a fine gathering of detective fiction all in one place and, when possible, first editions of the books. Most of her clients barely gave the books a second look, too obsessed with whatever problem or cheating spouse or shady business dealing had brought them to her office.

Trudi wasn't sure whether she liked that this man noticed.

She let her eyes travel slowly back to him, taking in the details. The dark suit he wore was not new but well-pressed and cleaned. It set comfortably upon him, and he within it, as though he wore it or something like it with common frequency. Coat pockets were empty, as best she could tell. No keys in his pants pockets, though she guessed a thick wallet hid behind the drapery of the suit jacket in the rear. She watched his feet rock forward slightly on his toes and realized that the cane was merely a ruse, a prop to disguise . . . what? A weapon? A recording device? She saw his fingers flex round the handle of the cane, noticed clean nails, trimmed and filed, and even through the suit coat made out a deceptively muscular build for an older man.

She stood.

"Thank you for noticing," she said at last. "My guess is that your collection is twice as large as mine. And all first editions, whereas mine mixes in the new with the old. Am I right, Mr. . . . ?"

She watched a grin play at his lips. A slight nod of appreciation.

"You can call me Dr. Smith," he said, easing himself into the ornate metal guest chair across from her desk.

"Really?" Trudi toyed. "That's the best you can do?"

This time a chuckle escaped the old man. He reached into his back pocket to produce a thick, bifold wallet. He flipped it open and laid it on the desktop, never taking his hand off the end. Trudi eyed the identification card inside: *Dr. Jonathan Smith*. Address on the card was somewhere in New York City. She nodded.

"So it would appear that Dr. Smith really is your name," she said.

He nodded amiably and returned the wallet to his pocket.

"But you'll forgive me if I maintain just an ounce of doubt about that, right?" she said. "After all, I have half a dozen ID cards around this place. One might even have my real name on it. But, of course, the rest are all made simply to put people at ease with whatever story I need them to believe."

"I grant you that ounce of doubt," the old man said. Then he leaned in close. "And yes, you passed my test. For the moment, at least."

Trudi nodded, annoyed that he'd even had a test for her to pass. And irritated at herself for so quickly rising to the bait.

"Well, then, Dr. Smith. What can I do for you today?"

"I'm looking for someone."

His eyes wandered through the doorway and toward the storage room across the hall from Trudi's office.

"Missing persons?"

"Not exactly. Though he has been absent for a number of years now."

"Does he owe you money?" Trudi wished she hadn't asked that question as soon as the words came out of her mouth. Anyone with common sense could see that this Dr. Smith had no need of monetary gain. Still, people like him were often prone to insist on recovery of their money—at any cost—so Trudi figured it made sense to ask.

"Oh no, not that." He smirked. "But he does owe my employer something. He stole it, a number of years ago, and it has taken me this long to follow the trail to you."

Trudi tried not to let her eyebrows rise, nor to let her gaze wander away from the old man. Out of the corner of her eye she saw his hand squeeze the cane. *A release button?* she wondered. *Didn't they make canes that hid swords inside them? Or that concealed miniature pistols in the handles?*

"Let's call it missing persons, then," she said swiftly. "Rates for a missing persons case involve a flat fee up front, daily expenses—including travel—and a finder's fee bonus when the case is complete. If, after six months, there's no realistic progress toward finding your missing person, I'll refund half of the flat fee you paid up front. But I'm very good at uncovering secrets, so I don't expect that'll be applicable in this case."

"Oh no, Ms. Coffey, I'm not here to hire your agency." The smile looked almost sincere. "I don't doubt your abilities. I just trust my own more. I've been working on this case for over a decade, and I'm not planning to relinquish it anytime soon."

Trudi ground her teeth. *Another time-wasting moron.*

"So, you're a PI, here in search of professional courtesy or something?"

He stood and removed the wallet again. He pulled a sheaf of

hundred dollar bills neatly out of the lining and dropped them on the desk.

"All I want is information," he said, "and I think that should cover your time, am I right?"

That would cover a month of my time, Trudi said to herself. To Dr. Smith she said, "Why don't you tell me what you want, and I'll tell you whether or not that covers it."

He returned to his seat and now pulled a photo from the wallet. He laid it on the desk next to the money.

Truck, Trudi thought, *what have you done now?*

Dr. Smith said nothing at first but studied her eyes with interest. Then, "I see that you recognize this man. I would very much like to find him. According to my sources, he last surfaced in Atlanta four and a half years ago, and then disappeared into either Alabama or Tennessee."

"Never seen him."

She said it too quickly, she knew.

Dr. Smith let himself relax in the chair. "Detective Coffey," he said, "you'll forgive me if I maintain just an ounce of doubt about that, right?"

"It's a free country."

"Sometimes, yes."

Okay, she thought. *Time to play stupid little girl.* "Well, I don't know this man, never met him. At least not that I remember. Who is he, anyway, and why are you looking for him?"

Dr. Smith didn't respond at first. He made no move to end the conversation, nor did he seem ready to prolong it. He just studied her face, obviously, without fear of retribution.

Well, Trudi figured, silence was a powerful tool in a private investigator's arsenal. So she waited. Wait long enough, she'd discovered, and the other guy almost always gave away something he didn't mean to give. She returned his gaze, trying to look interested and transparent. She pictured butterflies in a meadow, and let that look waft toward the scrutiny of the visiting Dr. Smith.

"His name," Smith said at last, "is Steven Grant. At least that's what it was when I first came to know of him. I'm told that was one of a few dozen names that he used. Uses. Perhaps you know him by a different name?"

Trudi hunched over the picture. Yep, it was definitely Truck. Last time she'd seen him was four and a half years ago, though he'd spent most of the time talking privately with her ex-husband and ex-PI partner, Samuel Hill. The pig.

She shrugged and looked placidly back at the old man, dreaming of monarchs and swallowtails as she grinned. "Maybe he changed his name to Smith."

Dr. Smith chuckled with genuine amusement. He stood. "Well, thank you for your time, Ms. Coffey. I do have other leads to follow, so I'll be on my way." A pause, then, "Please wish your former husband my best when you call him five minutes from now."

Trudi couldn't stop her face from flushing red. She scooped up the cash still on the desk and held it toward the man. "Call him yourself," she said evenly. "We're no longer on speaking terms, as I'm sure you know."

The old man gave a slight nod and collected the money from Trudi's hand. He dropped one bill back onto the desk. "For your hospitality," he said. Then he stepped casually toward the door. "Perhaps we'll meet again under more favorable circumstances, Ms. Coffey," he said at the exit. Then he was gone.

Trudi watched the old man on the reception monitor until he left the office completely. She then switched to the outdoor camera and saw him get into a waiting car, a black Mercedes GL-Class SUV. *Expensive taste*, she thought. The vehicle drove slowly away and out of sight.

Truck and Samuel always had secrets, she knew that. They'd been close before Trudi had met either of them. But what had Leonard Truckson done that kept a trail hot more than four years after she'd last seen him?

"No," she said aloud, "that old man said he'd been on Truck's tail for more than a decade."

Why? What was so valuable that it was worth a ten-year search? And what did Samuel Hill have to do with it?

Trudi waited a full eight minutes before buzzing Eulalie in the reception area.

"Get me a secure line," she grumbled, "then get my ex-husband on the phone. The pig."

3

THE MUTE

The night felt cool, a welcome respite from the dry heat wave that had been lingering for several days over the hollows and meadows of southern Alabama's farm country.

The Mute shifted his weight over the cross branch and settled his legs on the Y-shaped stems that spread out midtrunk from the aged scrub oak tree above the sentry outpost. He knew Truck preferred that he stay inside the cube-shaped, camouflaged building below, but on nights when the air was moving, it felt like suffocating to sit inside that one-room woodshed, blocked from the breath of heaven that swept freely through the knotted oaks and pines at this edge of Truck's farm. Besides, Truck rarely questioned The Mute's instincts. That had been true even before the IED had stolen his voice.

Most people thought that Truck called him The Mute out of cruelty. That it was a sign of power for him to say it, and get away with it, right to The Mute's face. But most people were just as ignorant as they looked. Leonard Truckson had given him that name long before he was forced into silence.

"So, you're the new Special Forces sniper," Truck had said at the army barracks just outside of Fallujah, Iraq. "For a Georgia boy, you sure don't talk much, do you?"

The Mute had just nodded and continued cleaning the rifle pieced out on his bunk. There had been a moment of silence between the two men, and then Truck had stuck out a calloused hand.

"I like men who know how to keep quiet," he said. "I'd be honored to call you a friend."

The Mute had considered a moment, and then taken the hand.

Truck had a different name then, a different cover identity working as a sergeant within the US Army apparatus. He introduced himself and waited.

The Mute had shrugged at the introduction, unwilling to let his own name loose in return at just that moment. Truck had waited a heartbeat or two, then grinned and slapped him on the shoulder.

"I think I'll call you The Mute," he said. "Fits, don't you think?"

The Mute.

Sounded kind of mysterious. Sounded kind of right. He nodded.

Truck had turned to the rest of the barracks then. "This here new boy is The Mute. Anybody got a problem with him gets a problem with me. We clear, soldiers?"

A lackluster chorus of "Sir yes sir" filtered back, and it was good enough.

It took only a few days for The Mute to realize what a gift old Truckson had given to him with that name. Soldiers here had a pecking order, and those with seemingly insulting nicknames were the ones who demanded the most respect. Truck must have known what it felt like to be a Southern boy lost in a whole wide world. So Truck gave him a man's name, a soldier's name. And he became that man, he became that soldier.

A few weeks later, Truck appeared at his bunk just after midnight. He didn't say a word; he didn't have to. The Mute knew what a Special Forces sniper was supposed to do. They left in the dark of night, heading into enemy territory inside restive Fallujah. They returned before 5:00 a.m. hauling a man Truck would only call "an asset."

The asset was bound and gagged, smelling of fear, sweat, and urine, and covered so tightly with a head sack that The Mute wondered how he could possibly breathe inside there. But Truck was unconcerned, so The Mute let it go. Neither soldier had uttered a word during the entire kidnapping; neither had to. Truck was mercilessly efficient, and The Mute knew enough to follow orders even when they were delivered only with eye twitches, head bobs, and hand waves.

They'd taken the asset right out of his bed, so quickly and so quietly that his wife, sleeping beside him, never roused in the night.

The Mute didn't know exactly what happened to "the asset" after they brought him back. Truck pulled their Jeep to a running stop just outside the gates to the camp and, eyes gleaming, waited for The Mute to exit. Then he drove off into the desert. When he returned later that afternoon, he was alone.

Truck never spoke of the raid, and The Mute didn't see any reason to talk about it either, so that was that.

Six days later, Air Force drones blew up two houses in western Fallujah, and the newswires trumpeted that four high-value members of Saddam Hussein's ruling Ba'ath Party had been killed in the attack. The news didn't mention how US intelligence had known which houses to target, but The Mute had a pretty good idea.

For nineteen months, Truck and The Mute made their raids. Sometimes other soldiers would join them; most times they went alone. The official name was Operation Desert Scorpion, but inside Iraq they were just known as ghost raiders, and they became scary bedtime stories Iraqi parents used to keep their children inside and safe at night.

And before long, almost nobody could remember The Mute's real name. Under Truck's leadership and influence, everyone just called him The Mute. He liked that. It felt safe. It felt right.

Neither Truck nor The Mute could have guessed that nickname would also be prophetic.

By the time the improvised explosive device blew up under his Humvee, The Mute had figured he and Truck might go on forever striking fear into the dark places where terrorists hid. And then . . . well, then it was over.

When the vehicle shattered into burning shrapnel beneath him, all he could think was, *Truck's gonna have to find himself a new Mute.* He felt blood gurgling in his throat, felt heat and agony cooking his flesh and paralyzing his mind. He waited to die.

Then a pair of strong, weathered hands appeared from nowhere, pulling him out of the fire, dousing him with water, shouting orders, binding wounds. Cursing at him for being so stupid. Commanding him not to die.

The Mute slipped in and out of consciousness for days he couldn't remember. When he finally awoke for good, Sergeant Truckson was sleeping in the chair beside his hospital bed. The Mute started to say something, felt fire burning in his throat, and realized he couldn't speak. Poetic justice, he supposed. So he lay there, waiting, until Truck opened his eyes and saw him looking.

"'Bout time you woke up," Truck muttered sleepily. "You're too ornery to die. And I'm too stubborn to let you."

After that, people thought it impolite to call him The Mute.

Nurses and doctors started referring to him by his given name, even put it on his discharge papers. Folks on the base called him "Corporal" or "Sir" when they wanted something. Soon he'd be going back to an empty home in Atlanta, just another grunt blown out of the army by an enemy attack.

People thought they were showing respect by politely discarding his nickname. They were really just heaping pity on the wounded soldier who was now, somehow, less than he was before. Only Truck was different. Only Truck treated him like a man. Only Truck called him by the name he'd come to think of as his real one.

The Mute.

Sitting up in this tree on a cool September night, The Mute grinned. Truck had saved his life in more ways than one. And back here in the States, on this lonely farm, hidden away in the shadow of the Conecuh National Forest, he kept saving it.

"A man needs a purpose," Truck often said, "a reason to be more than a man."

The Mute figured Truck to be right on that account. And that was why he hadn't gone back to Georgia after his discharge. It was why, night after night, he manned this sentry outpost on the edge of Truck's farm, waiting for what he hoped would never come. Ready for what he knew would arrive eventually, regardless of what he hoped.

The night was cool. Crickets droned in waves. Leadbelly frogs croaked wet percussion in a distant swamp. The wind sighed lullabies through leaves and trees here in this moment.

It's a good life, he told himself. And he believed it. He was grateful for it.

The Mute leaned his head back into a worn-out groove on the tree trunk behind him.

He smiled.

He closed his eyes.

And dreamed of singing.

He awoke just after 4:00 a.m., the world around him oddly blanketed in silence.

Down below, the sentry cabin was almost imperceptible in the shadows of night. The Mute forced himself not to move, and instead to listen, to understand. He wished now that he'd brought along his M39 marksman rifle when he climbed up this tree, but it remained inside the sentry post below, leaning uselessly against a wall. He felt a little, well, unprofessional, leaving a weapon behind like that, so he decided to make a mental check of his other weapons, just for the discipline of the exercise: a Kahr K9098N handgun with night sights, strapped to his left thigh; a Smith and Wesson knife blade, hanging on a thick metal chain wrapped around his neck and dipping inside his shirt; a .22 short mini-revolver tucked safely inside his right boot.

He reached inside a cargo pocket on his pants and extracted a pair of night-vision goggles, turning the forest an illuminated green in one swift motion.

The intruders appeared almost as silently as the night had become, giving only a slight rustling of dead leaves and crunching of dirt as the sound track for their arrival. There were four of them, each taking a position in sight of one corner of the sentry outpost. They all wore black that bulged with varied weaponry, heads covered with night-vision goggles that obscured their faces. Judging from body shapes, there were three men and one woman, all moving stealthily, all carefully aware to stay out of sight of the four surveillance cameras mounted at intervals around the roof of the camouflaged shed.

The Mute calculated his odds and dismissed his chances

almost immediately. He could take out one for sure, probably two, but they were spaced too far apart. They'd have him in sight and under fire before a third shot could escape his gun.

He thought anxiously about the alarm mechanism wired into the sentry cabin. One push of a button and Truck's main house would light up with warning. But since he was out here, and the alarm trigger was down there, that was another dead end.

The Mute breathed a shallow exhale and let his training kick in. "When you don't know what to do," Truck had taught repeatedly, "wait. Too many men act too soon and pay the consequences for it. Wait, and you'll likely see the course of action make itself plain before you."

So he waited.

Below him on the forest floor, one of the men broke ranks and stepped toward the front of the sentry post, finally letting himself rest in view of one of the four video cameras stationed along the roof of the cabin. A quick wave of his arm and The Mute saw a canister of tear gas fly free. It broke the single window with an impossibly loud *crinssh* that marked a deliberate contrast to the previous silence of the surroundings. The Mute used that noise as cover for an opportunity to shift forward in the tree, letting his legs drop into the opening of the Y-shaped branch on which he sat. He pulled the Kahr from its holster.

As the canister hissed its venom inside the small building, a second and a third man stepped forward, weapons raised. Hot bursts quickly eliminated all four surveillance cameras. And now the woman entered the fray, spraying automatic weapons fire geometrically across the back of the small sentry building, careful to follow rigid lines that rose and fell in crisscrossing stair-step patterns, aiming for insiders who both stood and crouched to avoid the onslaught.

The Mute noticed that the other three intruders backed away

into the darkness of the forest while the woman did her work, apparently intent on avoiding any stray lead fragments that might spring, hot and deadly, from the opposite side of the woodshed.

And then all was quiet again. The woman waved a hand signal, and the intruder closest to her reapproached the cabin. A moment later, he was inside, then back out again.

"Empty."

The Mute heard the voice echo in the greenish-blackness of the night. Where had he heard that accent before? Something to think about later.

"Burn it." It was the woman this time. So, she was in charge of this little night raid. "But be careful of the trees."

They were remarkably efficient. A few grumbled words into a radio, and two Kawasaki all-terrain vehicles pulled into the clearing, each carrying two more intruders, along with a range of supplies. First they bathed the ground around the sentry post in fire-retardant chemicals, then they doused the roof with the same. Next they set firebombs inside the building, watching as the place began to burn from the inside out. It didn't take long. When the walls cindered and collapsed, the fire-retardant on the roof came billowing down into the flame, suddenly reducing the minor inferno by at least half. Fire extinguishers took care of the rest, leaving blackened, smoldering ruins isolated, deep in the heart of his forest.

The Mute felt like his legs would go numb from disuse but still refused to move. As yet, they'd not seen him. He wanted to keep it that way.

The eight intruders now turned away from the sentry outpost and faced southwest. No question where they would go next. Truck's main house was that way.

At last they moved away into the darkness. It was nearly 5:00 a.m. now, and The Mute was finally alone.

He fished a cell phone from his pocket and dialed a number, still waiting.

The line rang once, twice, three, four times, but no answer.

On the fifth ring, The Mute hung up. He cradled the cell in his palms, counting. Fifteen seconds later it vibrated to life in his hands. He pressed "answer" and heard Truck breathing heat on the other end of the line.

"Fade thirteen," his commander clipped, "ready B. Unsafe." Then the line went dead.

The Mute stretched his cramping legs and stood up in the tree. He flung the cell phone into the dying embers that once were his sentry post, reholstered his gun, and slid down to the ground. Inwardly he cursed the pins and needles pricking relentlessly inside his bloodthirsty feet. He took his bearings and forced himself into a jog.

Fifteen minutes later, sounds of the night cautiously returned, crickets and grasshoppers chirruped, country frogs belched, and the wind whispered a new melody. This time, though, no one was left to hear it.

4

ANNABEL

Wednesday, September 2

I hear Truck comin' up the stairs before he ever says a word.

I'm like that, I guess. I sleep solid and good, usually, but when Truck's in a tizzy, it's like this whole house can almost sense it from him—including me. Then I wake up at the slightest creak on the steps, the mildest noise or movement. If I can identify the noise, I can dismiss it and go back to sleep. But if it don't belong, if it's just a little bit outta the ordinary, I'm wide awake and waiting for something to happen.

Something always happens.

Truck stands in the doorway, looking at me. Does he know I'm awake? I'm not sure.

Outside my open window, the night sounds just fine, with crickets and frogs and all them buggy types making a chorus. The air flows cool through my third-floor room, which is a relief. It's been hot this summer. Too hot.

Truck still waits.

What's he thinking 'bout? What's he looking for?

In the darkness I hear him sigh. It's an old man's sigh, like the kind my aged Appaloosa mare gave in the final moments before she passed on two winters ago.

Somewheres I hear a clock ticking seconds away.

"Annabel."

He says my name quietly, like he knows I've been lying here listening to him already.

"What's on, Truck? Something up?"

"Get dressed. Good shoes. Now."

I feel a little awkward dressing myself with Truck standing in my doorway. It was different when I was six or seven, but now that I'm four months away from turning twelve, it just don't seem right. But I learned a long time ago not to question Truck when he's standin' close by. So I do as I'm told, and I'm relieved to notice Truck has enough courtesy to at least keep his gaze focused out my window and away from me.

"Okay," I say when I'm ready.

Uncle Truck looks me over and says, "No boots today. Tennis shoes. Hurry." I know better than to argue.

"Okay?" I say again after the switch, and he nods. The clock on my dresser tells me it's a few minutes after 5:00 a.m., and now I hear a minor commotion going on downstairs in the house. *Truck's boys*, I figure. *Getting an early start on the day's events, maybe?*

"Get your coat," he says.

"It's been near a hundred degrees every day for the past week!"

"Annie."

I get my coat and fold it over my arm.

"What's goin' on, Truck?"

"Quiet, girl. We got minutes only. Just seconds really. You understand?"

'Course I don't understand, but I nod at Truck anyway.
"Good."

He reaches down, and before I realize it, he's swept me up and is carrying me down the stairs. I ain't no baby girl, not no more, and the fact that he's carrying me like a four-year-old sack irks me more than a little. I start to complain, and then I notice he's doing more than just carrying me.

Is Uncle Truck hugging me close? Like something he don't want to lose?

In the kitchen I see Kenny, Rendel, Curtis, and Figgy slamming cupboards and moving furniture.

"They making breakfast, Truck?"

He ignores my question, ignores everyone, in fact. He kicks the back door open and starts jogging into the darkness, headed toward the big barn. When he passes by the front doors and lopes around to the back, I feel myself begin to stiffen.

He's taking me back to that dog.

The German shepherd is runnin' when we arrive. The dog stops the minute it sees Truck, but its eyes are still glowing crazy. I hear the growling start. Truck sets me down roughly, still jogging.

"Keep up," he barks.

"Truck, what—"

I feel his palm flash hot across my cheek, and two hot tears pop outta my eyes before I can stop 'em. I know he didn't hit me hard, leastways not as hard as he could. But Truck has never laid a hand on me in anger before. Not ever. Not even when he was raging or I was awful.

Now his nose is right next to mine, eyes searching. "You got to trust me, Annie." His breath was warm, smelling faintly of tobacco. "No questions. Just follow what I say. Follow what I say or we lose everything. You got it, girl?"

I nod and am embarrassed that two more teardrops leak outta

my face. I wipe the waterworks away and nod again. Truck hates crybabies. And clearly this ain't no time for crying.

"*Ruhig sein!*" Truck shouts at the dog. "*Hinlegen!*"

The animal backs away from the fence and lies down on its belly, head raised, eyes flaming. Teeth bared.

German, I think. *Truck commands this dog with German? Why didn't I ever know that before?*

It bothers me that I can't remember all my German verbs right now. Can't remember any of 'em, in fact. But I don't have time to worry on that, not yet at least.

In seconds, Truck has the gate open and is dragging me inside. The dog watches me. I watch the dog. With Truck here, we're at a stalemate, I guess.

He pulls me toward the beat-up old doghouse. He kicks dirt away from one corner, revealing a lever buried just under the ground. He steps on the lever and, at the same time, pulls up on the roof of the doghouse. I hear hydraulics kick in and watch as the entire structure lifts off the ground like a door on a sideways hinge. A yellow-green glow flickers below, and now I see it for what it is.

Underneath this doghouse is a hiding place, a tunnel dug right into the ground. There's narrow steps that jut inside the tunnel, going downward deeply and quickly to a wide flattened area. From there the tunnel floor ramps around, curving off and down to the right.

"Go."

Truck shoves me so hard I fall down the first three or four steps before I regain my balance. Soon I'm standing at the base of the steps, trying to take it all in, thankful someone thought to install some kind of low-glow lights in patches all the way down the tunnel. Then I hear Truck shouting a command from the top of the opening.

"*Geht!*"

I hear the dog respond, hear its claws digging at dirt and stone. Truck's sending that dog to chase me down here!

I start running.

The air smells wet and dusty at the same time. Running now, I barely notice the dim, round lights spaced out and plastered into the walls. The tunnel is narrow, barely big enough for Truck to fit through frontways, but plenty of room for a smaller body like me. And for a dog. I hope there's nothing on the ground beneath my feet, because I don't have time to be cautious about where I step.

The tunnel keeps making wide loops, winding down, down, down until I figure I must be somewhere between ten and twenty feet underground. It takes only seconds for me to feel claustrophobic in here, only a few steps before I know I'm being buried alive. I don't know what's ahead of me, but I know what's behind me, so I keep running.

Finally the dirt floor levels out underneath me, and the path straightens. Twenty feet down, I see an end. Twenty more feet and I'm standing in front of a narrow steel door. No place left to go.

I hear scraping and scratching behind me and turn back in time to see that dog and Truck headed directly for me.

"*Setz dich.*"

Truck says it breathy, like he too ran down to this confined space. The dog reacts without hesitation just the same, crouching down on its haunches beside my uncle, staring at me eye-to-eye the whole time. Truck steps past the sitting shepherd and stands next to me.

"It's open," he says, and I finally see the space between the edge of the door and the built-in steel frame that holds it in place. I reach out and push. The door is heavy, and it complains against me, barely moving, so Truck reaches over my head and slams it with his palm. It swings wide into the opening, revealing a large, sculpted room, square in shape, with a low ceiling that seems to me to be just about two inches taller than Truck himself. Uncle Truck presses my shoulders, and we both tumble into the big room.

"*Komm her*," he commands, and now my brain starts working better. *Come here*. The dog scampers through the doorway, dashing past me and beginning to sniff at the nooks and crannies in this place.

"A bunker?" I say. "You built a bunker under the doghouse?"

In spite of everything, I see a grin fight its way to the edges of Truck's lips. Then he's all business again.

"You trust me?" he says.

I nod, because I know that's what he wants me to do. But inside I'm not so sure.

"Give me your hand."

I barely move before he takes my wrist, leaving my hand dangling free just outside his vise-grip. He looks at the dog and barks the command again. "*Komm her*."

Come here.

"Truck, wait—" I say, but it's too late. The dog is inches from me, looking at me, then Truck, then back again. Involuntarily, I wrap my fingers into a fist. I feel tears threatening to come again, but I force 'em away.

My uncle shoves my fist toward the open mouth of the dog. I start to scream, but then I feel Truck's hand clap over my mouth and hear his growl close in my ear. "Quiet, Annie. This is important. Trust me."

I think I might pass out from breathing so fast, and apparently Truck thinks so too. He lets loose my jaw and says, "Breathe through your mouth. And hush."

My fist tenses, white-knuckled and cramping, looking plump next to the saliva-soaked fangs of that big, ugly dog. I hear it growling, low like a cicada hum, and watch its long red tongue caress the pointed canine teeth at the front of his jaw.

Truck holds my hand firmly in front of the dog's nose, holds it so close I feel the hot bursts of breath between my fingers as they fly out of the animal's broad, black nose. The dog bares its teeth but stops growling.

I try to imagine what it will feel like to have my hand cut clean off in the dog's mouth. Will its teeth simply slice through my bones? Or will they crunch my bones first, then finally tear my hand off in pieces? Will I pass out when it starts slicing at the flesh of my fingers?

I suddenly feel like throwing up, and then before I can control myself, I do. It's green and watery, just bile left in my empty stomach. Truck ignores the mess. The dog sniffs it once, then also ignores it.

Slowly the seconds tick by, and with every notch on the clock, my hand remains un-severed, hanging in the air in front of this monster's maw. And I see that dog sniffing my hand, eyes locked now on Uncle Truck, asking for permission.

Finally Truck speaks.

"*Prōtos.*"

Not German this time.

Greek?

Is that ancient Greek? Nobody even speaks that language anymore. *Prōtos.* What does that mean? What's Truck doing?

The dog stops growling. It looks confused, if a dog can look like that. It leans back on its haunches and levels a slight whimper, then looks at me again and starts to bare its teeth.

Truck is swift, catching both me and the dog off guard. The backhand that rifles into the animal's snout brings a yelp from the dog, and it tumbles off-balance for a moment. Then Truck grabs the dog's mouth and shoves it up next to my fist again.

"*Prōtos.*"

He says it like a dare, as if he almost wants the dog to argue so's he can hit it again. The animal flinches. Then it paws back away from me and it sits down at attention, eyes alert, no longer growling, no teeth baring, eyes flicking from Truck to me and back again.

"*Prōtos.*" Truck says it quietly now, straight into the dog's eyes. For the first time I've ever heard, the dog barks, a quick snap of its jaw that almost seems like a soldier acknowledging a commanding officer.

I feel Truck's grip beginning to relax on my wrist, feel my blood beginning to rush needle pricks down into my fingertips.

"*Schützen,*" Truck says, switching back to German.

I try to call back my German vocabulary. I know I've heard this word before. What does it mean? Peace? Pray? Why would Truck want a dog to pray?

The animal responds to Truck's command, trotting to the door and lying down across the opening, and then Truck finally releases my hand. I see sweat trickling behind my uncle's ear and down his neck. His hand is trembling, his lips are flat, and for the first time I see that Truck might also be just a little bit afraid of this dog.

"Uncle Truck," I say, but he cuts me off again.

"No time, Annabel. No time."

He's breathing hard. I watch his eyes sweep over the wide-open room and can also see his mind deciding what he has time to say.

"Stay here," he says quickly to me. "No matter what. Even if you're here for days. Or weeks. Stay here. There are enough supplies for four adults to last ten days. With just you and a dog, you should last more than a month. Maybe two months if you're careful. So stay here until I come back for you."

Uncle Truck reaches into his pocket and produces a key. He

points to the steel-reinforced door. "Three dead bolts on that door," he says. "One key. My key. Understand?"

I look at the locks on the door and see that they's the double-cylinder kind. No flipping a switch on these. Got to have a key, whether you're on the inside or the outside.

Truck presses his key into my palm. "When I walk outta here, you lock all three bolts on that door. Got it?"

I nod.

Now Truck makes his head level with mine, eyes boring deep into me, searching. I watch his nostrils flare when he speaks. "Don't open that door for anybody, you got it? Not even me, not unless you hear me say the safe code. You remember the code?"

"Yes."

Ever since I could first talk, on my birthday each year, Uncle Truck would give me a safe code, a catchphrase for emergencies. If one of us said the code, that meant things was okay, that he or she could be trusted. I remember the code.

He nods. "You've studied your German, right? You know German?"

"*Ja,*" I say, and this time he really does grin.

"Good. You'll need that for the dog."

Protect! I think suddenly. That's what *schützen* means. Truck told the dog to protect me? But will the dog still obey that command when Uncle Truck is gone? I shiver in spite of myself.

"Truck, I—"

"Trust the dog like you would trust me. Understand?"

Trust that filthy, finger-eatin' animal? Is he serious?

"Annabel." His voice is urgent.

"Yes, sir," I say out loud. But even I don't believe it. Truck nods at me anyway.

"You'll have to figure out the rest for yourself. At least until I get back."

There's a split second of silence, and I feel the weight of all the things Truck ain't telling me. Then he nods again and stands to full height. A soldier now, ready for battle.

"I've got to go, Annie-girl. What you going to do." It's a command, not a question.

"Stay here."

I feel the tears comin' again. Sheesh, maybe I am just a baby girl after all.

"How long." Again, a command.

"Until you come get me. Until I hear your voice say 'love that was more than love' at me through that door."

He nods. He looks proud. And now I see he might be crying too. Not honest-to-goodness tears, no, but wetness around the edges of his eyes. That's good enough for me.

He don't say good-bye. He just turns and steps into the tunnel, pulling the heavy door behind him until it slams into place. The dog scampers to the other side of the room, away from the slamming door.

"Annabel." I hear Truck's voice from the tunnel, and I jump to obey.

It's short work to slip that key into each of the three dead bolts that decorate this door. I listen to the tinny echo as each bolt turns snugly into its locked position. After the third click, there's the sound of my uncle's footsteps runnin' away from me. I feel my legs getting jelly-like, and forget to care that I'm crying like a bitty baby again.

I turn away from the door and see the dog staring at me, staring hard, waiting.

A low growl rumbles across the room.

5

THE MUTE

Wednesday, September 2

It was well into the afternoon by the time The Mute made it to the main house on Truck's farm, but it was just as well. He surveyed the scene and felt a pang of guilt about the passage of time, but he knew what Truck would've told him.

"Follow your orders."

And that's what he'd done. He still wore the same clothes from sentry duty, but now he was fully camouflaged—and fully armed. The SIG716 sniper rifle felt comfortable across his back, and the rounds of ammunition that crisscrossed his chest felt warmed by his heart. He carried a small pack now as well, filled with just enough dry foods to placate an emergency. Mostly he'd live off the land, hunting and fishing, finding water as needed. He didn't expect to be in full survival mode for too long—maybe a few days at best—but he was prepared for the worst.

Hiding in the thick brush east of the long driveway up to

Truck's house, he felt that this was as close as he could afford to get to the big home. He couldn't take a chance that he'd be seen, especially not now.

He'd have to confirm it with his binoculars, but The Mute was pretty sure that Truck's body was the third corpse in the line of dead men stretched out across the front porch. The black-clad intruders were walking around in the open now, working to clean up the site of the recent battle.

The Mute counted five bodies on the porch, all adult men. He sighed and did his duty, using binoculars to verify that Truck was indeed dead. Amazing. After everything that soldier had lived through, The Mute had almost come to believe he was unkillable. But all dreams die sooner or later, even ones named Leonard Steven Truckson. He gave a silent salute to his commander and then turned his attention to the task at hand.

There were six Kawasaki ATVs in the yard now, side-by-side models like the Teryx 4x4s that could carry at least two people, and maybe a third on the back. At the attack on his sentry outpost, two ATVs had equaled eight intruders, so The Mute figured there should be at least twenty-four fighters on the premises. Apparently they'd hit all three sentry posts last night, probably simultaneously. After almost an hour of watching, he had only been able to account for twelve intruders, and that was a concern until he finally caught a glimpse inside the big red barn at the end of the driveway. It gave him some small consolation that Truck and his men had taken out twelve men before finally losing this battle. Correction. Eleven men and one woman. The Mute saw that the leader of last night's incursion against his outpost was one of the casualties.

Now the remaining intruders were gathered around the ATVs, waiting. The air was warm today, nothing like that cool wind that had blown through the midnight hours before. The

Mute didn't bother wiping away sweat; at this point, he hardly noticed the discomfort. A part of him was tempted to look for opportunities to begin picking off the black-clad fighters, one by one, with his SIG716. But he knew that was just a lazy dream. There were still too many of them to confront directly.

He heard the sound of tires before he saw the black Mercedes GL-Class SUV glide down the long dirt driveway onto Truck's land. The remaining intruders quickly stood, tamping cigarettes out beneath boots and generally presenting themselves as a professional fighting force once again.

When the Mercedes rolled to a stop, the driver exited first. He was Middle Eastern, with an Americanized style. Tall, broad, wearing what looked to be a thousand-dollar Italian suit and shoes to match.

A bodyguard? The Mute guessed. *Wonder what he's guarding?*

Above the Arab's neatly trimmed beard, The Mute could make out eyes that were clear, alert, and busy. He saw them roving the area, checking crevices, looking for threats. There was a slight hesitation while he made a final determination of whether the area was secure, then the bodyguard/driver swept open the passenger door, bowing his head slightly in deference.

A new man stepped out of the Mercedes and gave a quick survey of the scene. He was older, also wearing a tailored suit, brandishing a cane. To The Mute, he looked like a banker or lawyer, not the type to command a crew of mercenaries intent on taking out someone as formidable as Truck. Still, The Mute had learned the hard way not to judge any man by the clothes he wore.

He couldn't hear what was being said but could guess at it. One of the soldiers, German, he decided, was apparently filling the old man in on the results of their raid. The old man asked a clipped question. In answer, the German shook his head, and his lips said something that looked like, "Not here." The old man frowned, gazed toward the red barn, and then stepped away while the other man was still talking. The German followed him to the front porch of the main house, still saying things to the back of his leader's suit coat.

The old man stopped at Truck's lifeless form and looked annoyed. He paused then, and leveled a gaze across the yard. The Mute froze. Was this geezer looking for him? He watched as the man strafed the countryside with his vision and half-admired that the old guy took time to peer at the tree boughs high above his head. If his mercenaries had done that last night, The Mute might be another body spread out on that porch.

Finally the old man turned back to the mercenary behind him. He gave an order, then left that man standing while he and his bodyguard headed back to the black Mercedes.

The Mute started to let his eyes track the old man, but an inconsistency in movement drew his attention. The bodyguard, normally striding just a step behind his charge, took a hitch and hesitated. As he passed by the corpse that Leonard Truckson left behind, he bobbed his chin in that direction.

The Mute saw it happen almost in slow motion. A grimace on the face of the bearded man. A quick pursing of the lips. A wad of saliva flying free, floating through the opposing forces of gravity and inertia. The wet mess landing on its target, dripping down Truck's chin and onto the dead man's neck.

The Mute felt his insides clench at the desecration. He breathed deeply, held the breath, and telescoped his vision inescapably onto the bodyguard's face. He memorized what he saw, the manicured facial hair, the cheekbones, the damp, surly lips, and most especially, the eyes. There would be a time when The Mute would find this man again. He would see to it, make sure that it happened. And when he found him, that man would pay. It was a promise The Mute made to himself, and to Truck.

A moment later the old man and his bodyguard were gone, leaving behind their foot soldiers to handle the dirty work to come.

The German stepped carefully off the porch and made his way to the troops waiting by the ATVs. He waved a hand behind him that clearly included the house and the barn and barked a terse command that was just loud enough for The Mute to hear.

"It is not here. Burn it all."

Scorched earth policy, The Mute thought bitterly. *If this farm is of no use to the old man, it'll be of no use to anyone.*

The black-clad fighters turned wearily toward the job. The Mute noticed several looking angrily toward the red barn where their fallen comrades lay, but no one faltered. Apparently their own men would be cremated at the same time as Truck and his men.

The Mute decided it was time to leave but worried that he was missing something. The good news was that, among all the bodies strewn around this farm, none belonged to a little girl. It was also good news that no child had been turned over to the men in the Mercedes. The Mute figured that was why the old man was annoyed at Truck's death. Only Leonard Truckson would have known where the girl was hidden, and so his death had to be a loss for the attackers.

At the same time, she had to be somewhere nearby. Truck hadn't had time enough to transport her away from here. So where was she? Hidden behind a secret wall in the house? Stashed in a secret basement in the barn? Where?

"Fade thirteen, option B," Truck had ordered. "Unsafe." That meant finding the girl, making sure she was safe. There was a backup plan for that, but that was the hard way. The easy way was the obvious one: Find the girl now and skip to step four or five. But there was no sign of her anywhere. And if he didn't find her soon, he might not even have time for the hard way.

The Mute watched as the intruders made the necessary preparations to burn the buildings here at the main part of the farm. And he worried. Was he letting the hidden child inadvertently become added tinder for the fires? Or was she somewhere safe, somewhere out of reach of these deadly mercenaries?

The first flame took hold on the corner of the main house's broad porch. The Mute noticed that this time the intruders showed no concern for the tree-laden surroundings. When the authorities made a tardy visit to this location, it was going to look like a wildfire sprung out of control. The whole countryside around here might be burning for days.

He felt torn, but when the mercenaries lit up the barn, he finally decided that trust was the key. He would trust that Truck had planned for this, had prepared for it. He would trust that the girl was alive, somehow, and was safe. And he'd be back to make sure of that, hopefully sooner rather than later. But for now, it was time to go. He was going to have to go with the backup plan, and that meant he had someone to meet.

He hadn't done it in many years, but for some reason, The Mute mouthed the words of a short prayer before he slipped away. He hoped somebody was listening.

6

ANNABEL

Date Unknown

I think I might go bat-crazy in this locked-up place.

Or die.

Whichever comes first. At least I won't need no funeral, 'cause I've already been buried deep underground. Truck saw to that for me.

I wonder regularly if that dog'll eat me alive and leave only my bones to be discovered by some future adventurer into the nether regions of Truck's property. But so far I've kept all my fingers, so that's something at least. That dog and I have reached a truce of sorts. I don't bother it and it don't bother me. Works okay, for now.

I got no idea what day it is anymore, or even how long I been down here in this bunker. Sometimes I think it must be weeks already, but then I check the supply shelves and know that can't be true. Too many bland, canned, dry foods still left to be eaten.

There's no clock anywhere that I can find, and my watch is still sitting on the dresser in my bedroom in the main house. So now instead of thinking in days and nights, I think of "wake times" and "sleep times." It's arbitrary, I know, but it helps me feel less crazy cooped up in this empty place.

It didn't occur to me to mark days or nights during that first wake time when Truck locked me inside here. I had other things on my mind, like particularly, a mean, finger-eatin' German shepherd growling low and heavy in my direction.

I was standing at the door, listening to Truck's feet run away up that dim-lit tunnel back to the surface. Across from me, next to the table that was the only freestanding furniture in the room, that dog was trembling beside the table, staring at me, growling, and flashing his dingy fangs from time to time.

Truck had said the dog spoke German. Well, that it understood German. I figured it was time to test that theory, but my memory felt scrambled. Usually I'm real good at languages—Truck says I'm a supernatural, or something like that. But at that particular moment, I couldn't think of any German words except the last one Truck spoke before he left.

"*Schützen!*" I shouted at the dog. *Protect.*

The dog shuffled back and forward again. It let out a quick whimper, then resumed its growling.

I felt stupid. Had I just commanded that dog to protect the table? I breathed in deep and closed my eyes. *I know German,* I said to myself. Then, *Ich kann Deutsch.* It was comin' back to me. I just had to make room for it in my head.

"*Ruhig sein!*" *Be quiet!* I said with my eyes closed. The response was almost immediate.

Silence.

I heard water runnin' somewhere, softly, like a faucet left on in another room. But no growling. No dog at all. I was tempted to keep my eyes closed, to wish my simple command was enough to make that dog disappear. But even my ears knew better than that, so I opened my eyes and saw Truck's mutt standing beside the table, staring at me hard and angry, like it had obeyed, but it didn't like it.

"*Sterbt*," I said—*Die*—just because it was how I felt at the moment.

The dog just stared at me.

"*Sich hinlegen*," I tried, and this time the animal responded, lying down next to the table, just as I'd commanded. But it also started growling again, head raised, still watching my every move with its horrible yellow eyes.

Well, I'd figured out how to command it to "be quiet" and to "lie down." It was a start.

"*Immer noch warten*," I said. *Be still*.

The dog closed its jaw and stuck its chin on the floor. Good. Leastways, this was a smart dog. But I knew that already. Evil warlocks is always smart, ain't they?

I finally took a moment to get a good look inside this bunker that Truck dumped me in, checking out my new home for who-knows-how-long. Judging by the way the tunnel outside wound around and back again, I started thinking I must be directly underneath the big red barn, or at least someplace close to that.

The place was mostly just one big, square room, I'd guess about twenty feet by twenty feet, with what felt like cement floor covered with low, purely functional gray carpet. Round light fixtures like the ones in the tunnel were attached to the ceiling in clusters, providing enough light to make it feel like a normal, everyday room. They wasn't any light switch, though, no way to turn 'em on or off, which made me think they was powered by some sort of battery operation. I wondered how long the batteries would last, and if I'd find any spares down here.

Built right into the wall on my right was two sets of bunk beds, each with a rolled-up sleeping bag on them, and nothing else. Guess Truck didn't figure people would need pillows down here.

At my left shoulder, built into the wall that shared the entry door behind me, was shelves stacked with all kind of supplies. Canned foods, boxed foods, military MREs, along with metal utensils and things like that. On the top shelf, above my head, was a row of books. I made a mental note to look through them books as soon as I could. Truck must've included them here for a reason, not just for pleasure reading.

The only freestanding furniture in here was a big wood table with four chairs around it, set smack in the middle of the room, like it was inviting people to eat dinner or play cards or something.

Except for the reinforced entryway I'd just come through, there was only two openings in the walls of the big room. No doors hangin' on either of them, just open spaces cut out of the walls. One opening was smack in the middle of the wall to my left. The other was about ninety degrees away from the first, situated in the wall directly across from me.

I heard water running again and moved to check out the first opening on the left wall. I took a step to the left, and the dog raised its head. I took a second step, and the dog fluffed out a sigh through its nostrils, then set its head back down between its front paws.

Was that a tail wag?

I decided to test something.

I moved back to the entryway, and the dog lifted up onto its haunches. It flashed its teeth at me, once only, then waited. I stepped in front of the door, and immediately that animal started growling again. I stepped away from the steel door, and the dog quieted itself right down. I walked all the way down the shelves to the other corner of the room, and that blamed dog actually seemed to relax, laying itself all the way onto the floor again. For the first time on this crazy morning, the dog seemed to almost forget I was even there.

I took a quick step toward the front door. Nothing. I took another step, still nothing. Then I got within a foot or two of the tunnel, and that dog sat up quick, growling at me.

"You don't want me to stand by the door?" I said. Don't know why I said it, 'cause I know dogs can't talk. But it made sense at the time.

I walked back down the supply shelves to the other corner of the room, and the same thing happened as before. Dog settled itself down, looked like it was preparing to take a nap.

"You're a pretty smart dog," I muttered. "Maybe you are trying to protect me or something."

I felt suddenly tired and wished I'd walked over toward the bunk beds instead of down here by the supply shelves. I sank down to the floor and stared at the dog underneath the table. It closed its eyes, and that seemed like a good idea to me too. I pulled up my knees and put my head down on 'em.

It was surprisingly easy to fall asleep right then. I guess nearly getting your fingers chomped off, getting sick on the floor, and getting abandoned by your uncle all before breakfast will do that for you. So I slept, right there on the floor, in that cramped corner of the room, putting an awful ache in my neck the whole time but not noticing it until I finally opened my eyes again some hours later.

It was hot when I woke up.

7

TRUDI

It took six full days before Samuel Eric Douglas Hill bothered to return Trudi's "urgent" call, and even then he didn't actually call back. He just appeared in her office on the morning of the sixth day, acting like he still belonged there, pretending nothing had changed after more than two years since the divorce papers had been finalized.

"Get out of my chair," Trudi said when she flipped on the lights to her office. This little place was her one-room, PI sanctuary. She wouldn't have it fouled without a fight.

Samuel grinned and slid his feet off the desk. He nodded toward the room across the hall. "Sorry, but it looks like my office has been turned into a storage shed or something."

He looked good. The pig.

His skin was nicely tanned, almost like a loaf of pumpkin bread pulled fresh from the oven. *Been somewhere with sunshine,*

54

she thought to herself, *which could mean either a beach resort in Spain or a desert somewhere.* His eyes were smiling, eyes that always reminded her of cookies, a light chestnut color with slivers of chocolate sprinkles scattered satisfyingly through the pigment. Trudi stopped herself there. *Why do I always think of him in terms of baked sweets?* she wondered.

She swept over him again, disciplining herself to think in facts, not foodstuffs this time. She noted that he'd kept his hair reasonably short—not a military cut, but nothing lower than his ears either. He wore a suit coat over a collarless shirt that favored his lean, muscled torso, and denim jeans. And as always, worn black boots finished his ensemble. He looked ready for either business or pleasure, and Trudi knew from experience that was always the case with Samuel Hill.

She wanted to ask how he'd managed to break into her office before working hours, but she knew that was a stupid question. For a guy like Samuel, locks and office hours rarely meant more than a minor inconvenience. So instead she asked, "Why'd you stay?"

He stood and moved out from behind her desk, surrendering the prime real estate without a fight. This time.

"You called me, Tru-bear, remember?"

Trudi wished for the hundredth time she'd never revealed that childhood pet name to him. Her daddy had called her that, rhyming it with Christopher Robin's nickname for Winnie the Pooh in A. A. Milne's classic children's stories. It had been sweet for Samuel to call her that when they were married. Now it was just another scrape across the chalkboard of her heart.

"Yes, I did," she said. "And a week later, you're here in living color."

"We aim to please." He gave a mock bow.

"So why are you still here? You broke in before office hours, knowing I wouldn't be here, knowing my receptionist wouldn't be here." She glanced at her watch: 7:51 a.m. "Judging by the creases in your jacket, I'd say you sneaked in about two hours ago. Give or take."

"Good. Always the detective. Nice. But I didn't break in." He dug into his pocket and produced a key chain. So, he still kept a memento of their failed business partnership. She wondered if he also kept a key to her house.

"My desk is undisturbed," she continued, "except for these unsightly boot prints next to the telephone. But the books on my shelf"—she nodded behind her as she took the seat at her desk, dropped her briefcase to the floor, and faced him—"are a bit jumbled. Couldn't remember the exact order after digging through them, sweetums?"

She saw his eyes betray him first. A flash that reminded her of an adorably naughty boy caught on the couch with his girlfriend on the one day when Mom comes home early from work. She grinned to herself. That was a look she liked on him. She was on the right track.

"You were looking for something and you didn't find it, and that's why you stayed."

Samuel eased himself into one of the guest chairs and threw his hands up in mock surrender. "As I said, Tru, you called me."

Trudi repeated in her mind the message she'd left on Samuel's voicemail nearly a week ago. *Hey, it's me. I had a visitor today, asking about a Ford F-150 for sale. Since I don't own a Ford of any kind, I figured he must be looking for yours. So call me.* Then she'd marked it "urgent" and hung up, knowing that if he didn't call back in the next five minutes, there'd be no telling when he'd respond. And, of course, he didn't call back.

"All right then. Why didn't you call back?"

"I was out of the country. On business."

"For one of our government alphabets this time, or out on a freelance gig for some other international power?"

He let an amused grunt escape his lips and then leaned back in the ornate metal chair.

"If I told you," he said with a grin, "I'd have to kill you."

Now it was her turn to snort. "You could try. We both know how that would end."

She didn't know for sure if she could take him in a fight, but she did train regularly in mixed martial arts so she felt fairly confident in that regard. And she knew he had a soft spot for old lovers. He'd hesitate before delivering the final blow, and that's when she'd strike without mercy. It almost made her feel warm inside to think about the possibilities.

"I think we digress," he said. "I got your message. I came to see what it was about." He glanced around the room. "Are we clean in here?"

She nodded and rolled her eyes. Bug checks were a standard part of her business. The room was clear and had been for the entire two and a half years since they'd been divorced. Apparently she didn't anger people as easily as he did.

"All right," Samuel said, ignoring her petulance. "I assume we're talking about Truck. So what happened?"

She told him about the old man who had visited, about the picture, and about his mention of Samuel before he left.

Her ex-husband looked thoughtful, then asked, "Did you save the video? Can I see this man?"

Just then Eulalie Jefferson poked her head through the door. "Mornin', Ms. Coffey! I brought crumb cake and—oh! Sorry, didn't know you were in a meeting."

Samuel stood at the sight of the receptionist, so Trudi stood as well. "No worries, Eulalie. Please, meet my ex-husband, Samuel Hill." *The pig*, she finished to herself. "Samuel, Eulalie Jefferson."

Eulalie dimpled and shook his hand. "Nice to meet you, Mr. Hill." She exchanged a knowing glance with Trudi when she said, "Ms. Coffey has told me a lot about you."

"Well," Samuel said, still holding her hand, "don't believe everything you hear, Ms. Jefferson."

He winked, and even from behind the desk, Trudi could see Eulalie's cheeks flush underneath a shy smile. Trudi almost groaned out loud, but instead said, "Thanks, Eulalie. Crumb cake sounds great. Just give me a few more minutes with Mr. Hill, please. Thank you."

Eulalie pulled her hand away from Samuel and said, "Of course. I'll be out front." Trudi caught Samuel checking out the receptionist when she turned to exit. Three years ago, that would have made her angry. Today, it just reminded her of the sadness she felt when she finally knew their marriage was over. She sat heavily back into her chair, tired of the little games that she and this man constantly seemed to play with each other.

"Is that Eulalie Jefferson?" Samuel said to the door. "From your church? Wow, she's really grown up, and . . ." He turned back to his ex-wife and let that thought go unfinished.

Trudi tapped the mouse on her computer and in short order had pulled up the surveillance footage of the mysterious Dr. Smith. She didn't bother speaking, she just twisted the monitor so her ex-husband could see it. She ran it once, and then a second time before he finally spoke.

"I don't know this guy," he said, and the way he said it made her believe it.

"Well, he knows you. Says his name is Dr. Jonathan Smith and has ID to back it up. He also knows you're connected to Truck, and he was very interested in uncovering Truck's current whereabouts. So now you've been warned. I've done my duty, both to you and to Leonard Truckson. Now, if you don't mind, I've got work to do."

She pulled the monitor back toward her and began busily tapping the keyboard, hoping he'd take the hint and just walk away. Again. For however long it would be this time.

Samuel stood up, but he didn't move toward the exit, not yet.

"Say, Tru," he said, "you remember Christmas a few years back, I gave you a book for a special present?"

"Collector's edition of the *Complete Tales and Poems of Edgar Allan Poe*. Yes, I remember."

"You think I could borrow that, just for a day or so?"

Finally. She suspected that was what he'd come for, why he'd broken in to his old workplace. Her shuffled bookshelf was testimony to that. It was a small victory that he admitted it at last.

"Couldn't find it on the shelf this morning, huh?" she said.

Samuel said nothing, but his silence confirmed the accusation.

"Get a copy from the library," she told him. "I don't have time to dig it up today."

"Tru," he said. "I need your copy. You know that. Why not make it easy on both of us and just give it to me. I promise I'll return it, tomorrow at the latest. Okay?"

Trudi glowered, but she knew it was time to give in. Besides, she still had a secret or two up her sleeve. She reached down to her briefcase and produced the thick, hardbound edition of Poe's complete works. It was a beautiful tome, really. Fashioned with old-style precision that included lavish ink illustrations, a sturdy, sewn-in binding, and quarter-inch-thick cover plates on front and back. Trudi would have loved the book even if Samuel hadn't given it to her. She loved it more because he did, for a while, then after he left, she just loved the book and memory-moment it brought back to her.

She held the book out for him. He reached for it, brushing her fingers when he took the spine. She couldn't tell if that fleeting touch was for his sake or for hers.

"Thanks," he said quietly, then he smiled. "You still read it?"

In response, she started reciting her favorite of Poe's poems.

"It was many and many a year ago, in a kingdom by the sea, that a maiden there lived whom you may know by the name of Annabel Lee; and this maiden she lived with no other thought than to love and be loved by me . . ."

She choked involuntarily on the last words, tried to cover with a cough, but couldn't stop just a little moisture from leaking at the edges of her eyes. There was a familiar tenderness in Sam's face when he leaned over and kissed her cheek.

"I was a child," he recited softly in her ear, "and she was a child . . ."

He straightened and caught her gaze, and there was a singular silence between them, an aphasic moment that neither felt like breaking, not yet at least. She loved his eyes, she decided. Not just the chocolate flecks sprinkled in the amber settings, but the fact that his eyes knew her, saw her soul, even now, even years after. She missed those eyes.

But not enough.

She finally broke the moment, looking first toward the ceiling, then down at her desk.

"Thanks, Tru," he said quietly.

She waved him away, and he left. She switched the surveillance monitors to the reception area, then to the camera outside, watching as he wished Eulalie a cheery good-bye, then walked out the front door, across the parking lot, and off into the day.

After he was fully gone, Trudi sat at her desk, just breathing. *In-2-3, out-2-3,* she counted the breaths to herself. *In-2-3-4-5-6-7-8-9-10.* She let one long exhale finish, then reached back into her briefcase.

First she pulled out the morning edition of the *Atlanta Journal-Constitution* and dropped it on her desk. Next she recovered a silver key and a small half sheet of paper with enough wrinkles to indicate it had been carefully folded twice and placed flat in a quarter-inch-thick hiding place for a number of years. Hidden, she knew, sometime before that Christmas day when her husband had given her an expensive Poe collectible edition as a "special present."

Eulalie Jefferson stepped into the office carrying a stack of phone messages along with a nice slice of cinnamon crumb cake.

"So that's your ex-husband," she said warmly. "Handsome fella. Bet he's something of a lady-charmer, that one."

Trudi smiled in spite of herself. "Yeah, he is that," she said.

"Still, I'm guessing you wouldn't mind seeing him come around time and again. A girl always appreciates looking at pretty things, right?"

Trudi slipped the silver key and half sheet into her top desk drawer, then looked absently toward the surveillance monitor.

"Don't worry, sweetie. He'll be back. You can bet on that."

8

ANNABEL

Date Unknown

When I woke up, I found I'd somehow slid my head and body down onto the hard floor. I'd also managed to give myself a royal pain in the neck that brought shooting sparks into my shoulder when I tried to twist my head too far to the left. Lying there on the nubbed carpet, I didn't want to move 'cause it hurt to do it. I found I had a perfect view of the underside of the table and of Truck's dog across the room.

They was a drawer . . . no, that's not right. I am an educated girl. Not no illiterate redneck. Truck says I got bad habits from living in Alabama all my life, surrounded by rednecks who're proud of being illiterate. But that I shouldn't let that be me.

So I mean to say, *there* was a drawer on the underside of that table, a wide, shallow space on runners. I hadn't noticed it before, in all the ruckus.

It felt stuffy in here now. An uncomfortable heat that seemed

62

to be comin' down on me from the ceiling. The floor where I lay was still cool, but the air around me was like when somebody turns the furnace up too high during a cold winter day.

I took a deep breath and inhaled the smell of stale carpet and dried vomit.

Oh yeah. Sooner or later I'd need to clean that spot by the door. I felt a burning in my stomach, reminding me that I still hadn't eaten since . . . yesterday? Today? Before my last awake time.

I snuck a peek at the dog and saw it was watching me, waiting. It was still lying in the same place where it had been when I went to sleep. Its face looked pained, if a dog's face can look like that. I saw the dog wiggle uncomfortably.

Suddenly I really needed to pee. Was there a bathroom in this place? There had to be something, right?

The dog gave a short whimper. Not a begging type of sound, more like a "can I have your attention, please" kind of noise. I sat up, and it raised its head to keep my eyes in line with his.

This dog want something from me? Why didn't the animal just take it?

Its body was tense, hind legs pulled up tight beneath its torso. The tail swung, just once, and held still.

"What?" I said out loud. "What you want from me, Dog?"

In response, the animal gave that same whimper.

"Fine, go 'head on and do whatever you got to do." At this point, I needed to pee so bad, I was almost ready to let go right in my denim jeans. I didn't want to have to mess with this dog any longer.

But the dog just stared, waiting. Waiting? Oh, waiting!

I tried to remember my German vocabulary again, and it was easier now that Truck wasn't pressing my knuckles into the face of a beast. Let's see . . . well, duh. Some words are the same in English and in German.

I looked hard at that dog and said, "Okay."

It sprang up so fast it made me jump, sprang up like it'd been tied to that spot on the floor and I'd just cut the twine that held the dog in place. It started pacing and sniffing at the walls and floor.

Great, I thought. *Now I'm gonna have to clean up big doggie urine.*

Then the dog trotted into the wall opening nearest to me. It disappeared in there, and a few seconds later I heard the sound of animal spray. It lasted longer than I would have thought possible. Apparently old Dog really needed to go.

Well, at least it didn't go on the table.

I stood up and was rubbing at my neck when it came out of that opening. The dog sniffed the air, then trotted over to the main entryway and settled comfortably beside that door. It watched me again, but this time it was calm, almost disinterested. No growling, no bared teeth, not even tensed muscles.

I realized I was sweating.

I followed the dog's lead and walked over to the opening on the wall. When I peeked in, I heard the sound of rushing water much more clearly, and saw a small area with a broad, wooden slab built right into the concrete floor. There was three holes in the wood, just about the size of a man's rear end. Around the first hole was a little splattering of dog urine, but not much really. And down by the third hole was a wooden stick attached to a small base to hold it upright. There was two rolls of cheap toilet paper slid over the top of that stick.

An outhouse.

Truck had managed to build an outhouse here in the deep and left it ready for use. I didn't have to stick my face in one of those holes to hear that there was an underground stream runnin' beneath this outhouse. Pretty ingenious, really. Drop your mess down one of those holes, and that hidden stream would sweep it away clean as indoor plumbing. Swirling air above the stream even cleared out the stink in this outhouse, keeping the air in here fresh as outside.

Hearing that water rush beneath me was too much. I dropped my drawers and let my bladder have its sweet release. When I was done, I took some of that toilet paper and cleaned off the leftover dog mess on the first hole.

Pretty smart dog, if you think about it, I said to myself. *It found the toilet before you did, Annie-girl. And knew how to use it.* Clearly Truck had brought that dog down here before, maybe lots of times. I wondered what else that dog knew that I didn't.

And I wondered why it felt like this whole place was getting hotter and hotter by the minute.

When I came from the toilet room, the dog was still by the door, resting, it seemed. Its eyes opened to watch me move, but the head stayed comfortably on its front paws.

Now that I knew what the one wall opening led to, I figured I should check out the other one. I stepped across the room and into the other door-shaped space on the far wall. Inside there was a smaller space than the toilet area, just a cramped square closet with a counter attached to the wall and—smack dab in the middle—what looked like a round, brick chimney built into the floor. They was a rope secured into the top of the chimney, with a large metal loop attached at the end. In here, the sound of runnin' water was louder, closer. I didn't have to see the bucket on the shelf to know what this was.

"Uncle Truck done built a well down here, in this closet," I said out loud to nobody. I felt relief. Having this well meant fresh water as long as the underground stream kept flowing. The cool air pumping up from the stream felt good and moist, like freshness in the morning.

Suddenly I was terrible thirsty. I grabbed the bucket and started feeding it down into the well when another thought hit me.

Was I fixing to drink the same water I'd just used as a toilet?

Surely Truck would have thought of that, I said to myself. But just to make sure, I stuck my face into the well and tried to get a sense of what was going on down below. Judging by the rope, the underground stream was about eight feet down. I couldn't see it—couldn't see a thing down there in the darkness below. But I could hear it, and I could feel the coolness of the air flowing above the water and onto my face. After a few minutes, it was clear the water was flowing into this place from my right, then outta here to my left, where it would then become a toilet downstream. As long as the stream didn't get backed up or something, the air and water on this side would be clean, situated upstream from the toilet and any other waste I threw down there.

That was a relief.

I pulled up a bucket of water and drank hungrily, then splashed some on my face as well.

Why was it so hot in here?

I left the well and went back into the main room, where I saw the dog, sitting on its haunches, still beside the door. I immediately felt guilty. The animal had been here as long as I had, and it was covered by a thick coat of fur that had to be hot as well. I hesitated. If I really wanted to kill that dog, I could just let thirst and hunger do the job for me. But Truck's words was still fresh in my head.

Trust the dog like you would trust me. Understand? Yeah, I guess I understood.

"You thirsty?" I said to the dog. As usual, it just stared at me.

I didn't see any dog dishes or anything like that, so I decided just to use the bucket. I dipped it again and brought it out. I set the bucket by the table, then stood back and waited.

The dog licked its lips at the smell of water and turned toward the bucket but didn't move away from the door.

"What you waiting for?" I said. "Go on and get you some."

The dog didn't move. It looked me dead in the eye, just waiting.

This animal won't take a drink until I give it permission, I thought. *Amazing. When did I become its boss?*

I thought back to that moment when we first come into this bunker, when Truck pushed my hand into mortal danger. He'd been commanding the dog in German and then suddenly switched to Greek.

Was that it? Was Greek a language for assigning things and German a language for doing things? That thought made me chuckle. If it was true, this dog understood more languages than most grown-up folks I knew.

I'd have to find out later what *prōtos* meant, but for now it was pretty clear the dog was waiting on my permission before quenching its thirst. What a strange power to have over a beast. I wondered how long it would last.

"Okay," I said, looking the dog straight in the eye.

The animal reacted immediately, trottin' over to the bucket and lapping up moisture for a full minute before finally returning to its place by the entryway door. It lay down and looked almost peaceful.

I suddenly became aware that I was standing next to one of the bunk beds and that I had sweated through the armpits of my shirt. I raised my hand above my head and felt the warmth of the room increase. I lowered it down and tucked it under the bottom bunk. It was definitely cooler down there, though the whole room was filling up with heat I couldn't explain.

I looked at the dog. It had figured out the bathroom. It knew German and Greek and English. What was there to lose?

"Listen, Dog," I said. "Why's it so hot in here?"

The animal didn't answer.

9

TRUDI

Trudi Coffey let herself remember the first time she'd ever met Leonard Truckson.

It was her wedding day, what, ten years ago last May? She almost felt pity now for the twenty-year-old kid she'd been back then. A junior in college—English literature major, of course—and deliriously in love. So much so that she'd talked herself into getting married while still in school, ready for happily-ever-after with Samuel Hill to begin, even if that included a few final exams along the way.

They were in the reception hall after the wedding ceremony when she met Truck. It was a church wedding, something she'd only recently realized was important. Samuel was disinterested in the setting—he couldn't remember the last time he'd been in a church. And anyway, his eyes had room for only one thing that day: Trudi in her mermaid-style organza and satin dress.

Everyone was dancing and drinking and enjoying the moment with Trudi and Samuel, a moment that was supposed to last forever.

Sam had brought him to Trudi from the dessert table and introduced him as "my old friend, Truck." Trudi had wondered how anyone could tell this man's age enough to call him old or young or somewhere in between. His face was smiling behind clear blue eyes, but Trudi knew even then that this Truck was more than he let others believe. She took in his taut physicality, his nondescript dirty blond hair, and the fact that he didn't seem to like wearing a tie, not for this occasion or any other.

But he was friendly, interested in her, and an easy conversationalist. He found out she was a fan of Edgar Allan Poe and demonstrated his own enthusiasm for the Master of Macabre by quoting every line from the poem "Annabel Lee." Trudi was impressed.

He made a toast to the happy couple, then checked his watch and made some excuse to leave. On the way out, he said "Enjoy your honeymoon" and pressed an envelope into Samuel's hand. When they opened it, Sam and Trudi found a wedding gift they couldn't believe: Cash in the exact amount they'd budgeted for their entire honeymoon.

"How did you and Mr. Truckson get to be friends?" she'd asked in awe.

Samuel shrugged, and she noticed that he glanced quickly up and to the left before saying, "Oh, you know. Did some odd jobs for him in college. You remember."

No, she didn't remember.

She only knew that Samuel spent his summers down in Houston working as a roustabout on oil rig crews, and that he always came back with enough cash to carry him through the rest of the school year. Two years older than Trudi, he'd just graduated from the University of Georgia with a degree in political science. This summer he was forgoing the annual roustabout gig so he could stay with Trudi in Athens, Georgia, until she graduated, and then they planned to move to Atlanta and get their lives together really under way. For now, he planned to work as an assistant at some distant uncle's private law office in Athens. Trudi was disappointed by that choice; what was the use of having a political science degree if all you did was shuffle papers for Uncle Lawyerpants? But Samuel said it was fine, it was only temporary, had flexible hours, and besides, there was plenty of time for politics and such in the future. So they settled into Athens, making a life for themselves and enjoying every minute.

Over the next two years, Truck appeared from time to time at the newlyweds' household with other "odd jobs" for Samuel, odd jobs that almost always meant he was out of town for a few days, or a week, but never more than two weeks. Uncle Lawyerpants never complained, and Samuel always came back adrenalized—and with a wad of cash in his pocket.

Then she graduated and Sam had an amazing job offer from a firm in Atlanta that was looking for a research associate—someone who ferreted out information and helped lawyers prepare for trial. Trudi had wondered how a "research associate" at a law firm could make so much money, but Samuel said that Truck had put in a good word for him, and that was enough. They moved to Atlanta.

She didn't see Truck much after that but was disappointed to discover that Samuel's research work often took him away on business trips similar to the ones that Truck had furnished for him while she was back in school. She needed to fill her time, so she started looking for a job as well.

There wasn't a big market for English literature majors (with a minor in world mythology and religions) in the Atlanta metropolitan area, so she was actually grateful to get a job as a receptionist for a small-time private investigator located in Sandy Springs. Turned out, she was a natural at the work and soon was apprenticing as a PI under her boss.

Trudi and Samuel had been married five years when Samuel got laid off from the firm. That was when he came home with "a great idea."

"Look," he'd said, "most of my job is investigation work. And the same with yours. So why don't we stop working for other people and start working for ourselves? We can open our own little agency, make a little money, and get to see each other every day."

It was tempting, sure, but Trudi was hesitant. How could she ever leave her boss and then immediately become his competition? That seemed a betrayal of sorts.

Until six weeks later, when her boss announced he was closing the business. He'd come into an unexpected inheritance and had decided to take early retirement. He gave Trudi two weeks' severance and moved out of Georgia, he said to California, but Trudi had never been able to find him there when she went looking a few years later.

Regardless, suddenly both she and Samuel were unemployed.

Coffey & Hill Investigations was up and running in three months, inhabiting rented office space in a strip mall in Atlanta's West Midtown neighborhood. Situated between a classy-looking florist and a skeevy-looking insurance agency, it was less than ten minutes away from their home on Center Street NW, which was surprisingly convenient. Samuel took credit for that. And, thanks to a few referrals from Truck, CHI had solid business right from the start. Trudi had thought her prayers had been answered, her dreams had come true. But dreams rarely happen the way one wishes they would, and Trudi found that out the hard way.

It took almost two years after they went into business together before she added everything up, put it all together, and finally understood that Coffey & Hill Investigations was a cover operation for Samuel Hill's real job as a nameless, title-less field operative for the CIA.

That was in August.

They fought for days, for weeks and even months, about it.

Samuel denied everything. Then admitted one small thing and denied everything else. Then admitted one more thing and denied the rest. And then, finally, just before Christmas, and five months before their eighth wedding anniversary, Samuel had started cursing at her in Arabic. Apparently cursing her cowheaded stubbornness. Her parentage. Her extended ancestry. And even himself. Then he admitted everything.

Those summers as a roustabout? Spent mostly in Langley, Virginia, and a few of the world's political hot spots, where he'd learned the tricks of the spy trade from his handler, Leonard Truckson, and a host of others.

Uncle Lawyerpants in Athens? A retired CIA agent giving Samuel cover for clandestine activities under Truck's remote supervision.

That "research associate" job at the law firm in Atlanta? More training and a cover for Samuel's active operations for the CIA and a few other unnamed international alphabets. Samuel had been sent worldwide on various espionage missions but most frequently found himself planted somewhere in the Middle East, running guns, chasing terrorists, collecting intel, and more.

When he'd finally said he wanted out, that he wanted to spend his life with his wife, they'd offered him a compromise.

They would set him up with Coffey & Hill Investigations,

bring his pretty young wife into the new business, let him live mostly in this mildly interesting life. And he would, from time to time, continue to do "odd jobs" for Truck and the CIA, or the FBI, or some other governmental alphabet. It would be the best of both worlds. Supposedly. So Samuel said yes, and they made it happen, just like they promised. And Trudi had been generally happy.

Except for one minor glitch. At least twice a year, Samuel had to fabricate a reason to return to the Middle East, and it was carelessness in the planning for one of those trips that cost him Tru's love once and for all.

In addition to her, Trudi found out, Samuel Hill also had a part-time wife hidden away somewhere in Saudi Arabia or Jordan or Yemen or someplace else like that. And he was father to at least one child with her, a child growing up Arab, way out in a lost part of the world. Samuel refused to say whether the child was a boy or a girl, only that one existed.

"It was a mistake," he tried to explain to Trudi's tears. "I met her on an assignment, saw her again on a few other trips. We hit it off, and I was lonely. It didn't last long, a few months at most. I wanted to end it with her, but when she became pregnant, I couldn't leave her to face the punishment of Sharia law. Try to understand, in the Muslim culture, I'm all she has. Without me, she would've been abused as an adulteress. She would've been a criminal under Sharia law. They would've been brutal to her. Flogged her at the least or killed her by stoning as a legal punishment. And if they'd let her live, without a husband in that society, she'd have been cut off both economically and socially. Left to starve or isolated into poverty. I had no choice then, and I still have no choice now."

And so, at last, it was over between Trudi Coffey and Samuel Hill, all at once, all more quickly than it had begun.

He left.

The paperwork was filed.

On March 6, Trudi Sara Coffey signed her legal name.

It was done.

In just under eight years, Trudi had gone from innocent twenty-year-old lit major married to the man of her dreams to twenty-eight-year-old PI, divorced, disillusioned, and forced to make a new life alone. She often wondered if it would have been different if she and Samuel had had kids first, if she'd been the one to get pregnant. But there had never seemed to be a good time for that, always a new excuse to put off starting a family.

And she wondered if her own faith journey had contributed to the rift between them. She'd always been a "spiritual" type, interested in the unseen world, curious about God. In fact, that was why she'd chosen to focus her studies on world mythology and religions. For her, it had all boiled down to two questions: (1) Is there a God? and (2) If there is a God, who is he?

The first question had been remarkably easy for her. Yes, she felt certain the evidence tilted in the direction that a God of some sort did indeed exist. The second question had taken more thought, and she'd pursued it with dedication. Her studies at UGA enlightened and augmented her quest for an answer and, finally, after a long journey that ended about a year into her marriage to Samuel, she'd had to face the one person she'd been avoiding. Jesus, she'd decided, was more than just a good man, more than just a miracle worker, more than just a historical figure. He was, and is, God. And she wanted to know him.

It was a quiet conversion—no miracles or fireworks, but a change that permeated every aspect of her being. She was constantly surprised to find that Jesus was not just a story but a real, divine presence who made himself known in her life, regardless of her shortcomings. She started wearing a silver cross on a steel chain as a physical reminder of her spiritual reality. She never took it off except to clean it.

Samuel had not embraced her newfound conviction, but he'd not opposed it either.

"Whatever offers you comfort is enough for me," he'd said.

He remained a contented agnostic, not sure if God existed, not willing to rule it out but not terribly interested in searching out an answer either. Despite their love for each other, Trudi wondered if her devotion to God had somehow made him feel less loved by her, if perhaps he felt she had cheated on him first by meeting Jesus.

That thought made her angry all over again. A verse flashed through her mind: *Watch out that no poisonous root of bitterness grows up to trouble you* . . . She sighed. She knew that the guilt she was feeling was undeserved, and she was grateful that God continued to console her in moments like this, but it was never easy, not anymore. Suddenly the anger she felt simmered down into its more normal state: persistent sadness, hidden away, but ever-present nonetheless.

No root of bitterness, she prayed. *Gonna need your help on that one, Jesus.*

Now, two years and some months after the divorce, she was halfway through her thirtieth year, single, childless, and still trapped in the cycle of Samuel Hill's lies.

Trudi pulled open the low drawer on her desk, then adeptly popped up the false bottom inside. She looked at the key and the note that still lay in there. Tokens from Truck, she was sure. Tokens that Samuel had disguised as a present for her and left in her safekeeping. Well, she'd kept them safe, all right, even from her beautiful, lying, irresistible, pig husband.

She checked the clock.

Any time now, Sam would open the collector's edition of the

Complete Tales and Poems of Edgar Allan Poe. He'd gently pull away the thick end papers inside the back cover of the book, remove the thin cover to the false bottom hidden there, and peek inside for his little treasures hidden years ago. And when he looked into that tiny compartment, he'd realize that she also had found that hidden place, that she'd taken that precious key and half sheet of paper out of the book and secreted them away to somewhere else.

Then he'd be back, and she didn't know why that made her both happy and sad. So she just looked at it as cold, hard fact. He'd be back, and their little dance would go on once more.

She sighed. She was in no mood to start real work yet, not with the knowledge that any minute now her ex-husband would fill her doorway once more. So, she spilled open the day's *Journal-Constitution* and, as was her custom, looked first in the classifieds section of the paper.

She scanned the personals until the familiar advertisement came into view. It was only one line, easy to miss. In fact, she almost did miss it this time, because whoever the anonymous ad buyer was, the message sent out to the world this day was just a little bit different. Just a little bit changed.

Trudi forced herself to look at it a second time, unable to believe her eyes, unsure that it was the same one she'd read for so many months. But yes, there it was, written plainly in black and white for all the world to see. Only this time, for the first time, it read *Unsafe.*

10

ANNABEL

Date Unknown

When I close my eyes and listen hard to the world around me, sometimes that world explains itself to me in ways I can't describe.

Uncle Truck calls it a "gift of faith," meaning it's something he don't understand but has learned to trust about me anyway. It's not a thing I can make happen, or even control, but sometimes it works, and when it works it helps me figure out whatever is the problem I'm facing at that moment.

Truck first caught me doing it when I was learning Creole, when he was quizzing me hard on phrases like *"Ki jan lwen soti isit la Port-au-Prince?"* I was only about six years old. I took a moment to close my eyes and think about it, and the words just kind of lined themselves up in my head, first a row in Creole, then rows in English, German, and Italian. So, with my eyes closed, I read 'em all back to Truck.

"*Ki jan lwen soti isit la Port-au-Prince?*" I said. Then, "How far from here to Port-au-Prince? *Wie weit von hier, um Port-au-Prince? Quanto dista da qui a Port-au-Prince?*"

When I opened my eyes, Uncle Truck was just staring at me with his mouth hung slightly open. "We're done for today," he said. Then he got up and left me chanting Creole nursery rhymes while I played with my dolls.

After that, I heard him start telling folks I was some kind of supernatural at languages. I didn't tell him that it wasn't just languages that explained themselves to me sometimes. It was just the world itself that opened up for me, almost like a book telling secrets on itself. Anyway, Truck didn't care. He was just stuck on learning me how to talk in different parts of the world. He was pretty smart with languages himself, and I guess he wanted me to be like him.

Pretty soon, he insisted that twice a week, sometimes more, he and I would sit down and study some kind of foreign tongue. He said it'd come in handy someday, so I followed his lead and tried to learn. Actually, I enjoyed it. Truck was a good teacher, and I was a fast learner. It was a good combination.

Some days he'd read me a fairy tale in Arabic and then ask me what happened. And sometimes, just by listening to the rhythm and inflection of the words, I could tell him at least part of it.

In my mind's eye, I'd see a sheik or a jinn or a beautiful, sand-skinned maiden having an adventure out somewhere in a desertlike place, so I'd tell him what I was imagining inside my head. He liked it when I could tell him what he was saying, even when I didn't actually speak that language.

Then he'd crack down and make me learn lists of boring things like verbs and nouns and tenses and such. Some days he'd speak to me only in Creole, or only in Arabic, and expect me to figure out what he was saying. Most times I'd get it by the end of the day, even if I was slow at it in the morning.

The week of my eleventh birthday he spoke nothing but German to me for seven whole days. Just started jabbering at me first thing in the morning, with no warning whatsoever. When he finally came back to English on the eighth day, it was actually hard for me to transition back. I'd spent so long speaking German that I'd started to think in German. I had to translate backward for a day or so before it came natural to me again.

I learned a lot about languages from Truck, I know, but it was always easier for me to understand a language than it was to speak one. And growing up in southern Alabama ruined me for English anyway. Truck said it was because I was surrounded by ignorant farmhands who spoke nothing but redneck. I guess that means sometimes I talk redneck when talking American, but the foreign words I say right 'cause I learned 'em right. Whatever.

Even with the foreign stuff it was easy for me to forget those lists of verbs and nouns when they didn't seem important. Really, growing up on a farm in Alabama, when does it seem important to remember a list of common Haitian kitchen nouns?

But sitting in this hotbox of a bunker during my second awake time, I was wishing I'd paid better attention to all those times Truck drilled me on German verbs. I was wishing I could remember something more than just how to tell that dog to be still or sit down. I was wishing I could make that dog talk to me—in any language—just so I could hear another voice besides the scared little one in my head.

"Why's it so hot in here?" I said to the dog again. And once more, it just stared at me without moving away from its post by the front door.

Truck must've been heatstroked when he told me to bring a coat down here, I thought.

I was tempted to strip down right to my skivvies, it was so hot, but somehow that seemed disrespectful to my uncle, so instead I just took off my shoes and socks. I tossed them, along with that useless coat, on the top bunk of one of the sets of beds. That felt better. The floor was actually cool to the touch, which was helpful.

I splashed some water out of the dog's drinking bucket on my face and hands and looked around. I kept thinking I should clean up that vomit spot by the door, but that dog didn't look like it'd be happy about moving, not just yet. I decided to let it go, as now I was actually used to the smell enough not to notice it. It was pretty faint by this time anyway.

I looked hard around the room but couldn't find any kind of temperature control anywhere. Truck must've figured it wouldn't be necessary, socked down here in the earth like I was. But something had to be warming up the room, and I needed to figure out what it was.

I put my hand on the wall behind the bunk beds. Warm, but not blazing. I climbed up on the top bunk and felt the temperature rise in the air around me. I put my hand on the ceiling.

Hot. Not enough to burn my hand, but definitely hotter than the wall and floor below.

I closed my eyes.

At first, nothing happened. Then I imagined I was seeing heat waves like little squiggly lines in the air. It seemed like they were dropping, fire-red and burning, from the ceiling like snowflakes, or whatever the opposite of snowflakes would be. As they dropped through the air, they'd cool a bit and change until they met little blue, cold squigglies floating slowly up from the floor.

I opened my eyes. I couldn't be sure, but my best guess was that something upground, something on the surface above me, was sending those red squigglies shooting through the earth and toward this room.

That couldn't be good.

I started imagining what it might be like if that ceiling above me broke under the weight of all those red squigglies, if it collapsed right on top of my head. The thought of it almost panicked me again. I felt myself chopping at breaths. *That's a good way to pass out, Annie-girl*, I thought to myself. I tried to concentrate on taking in air like a normal person. I wasn't perfect at it, but at least I wasn't chopping oxygen no more.

I ain't much of a praying girl, leastways not enough to be on a first-name basis with any fine deity out there. I mostly think of myself the way Truck describes himself, agnostic. I ain't convinced that there is a God, but I ain't willing to bet much that he don't exist neither. Still, whenever I get into a fix that I can't worry through, I almost always feel the urge to ask Somebody out there for a little help. I figure that's something I'm going to have to deal with sooner or later. I think later.

I caught my breath and let it out, unaware that I'd been holding it in so long. And I let that breath be a prayer, one without words, 'cause I didn't know who to talk to or what to ask exactly anyway. Nothing happened, except that I started to breathe more normal, at least for now.

I splashed more water on my face, but by now the bucket was so lukewarm it hardly made a difference. I thought about dropping the bucket back in the well to get fresh water. That'd be colder, right? But the heat and the weight of the red squiggles was weighing down on me something fierce. It felt like something that was just sapping all my energy, all my strength, right outta my bones. I sat on the bottom bunk of one of the beds. I wanted to cry, but there was no tears available to spill outta me. I licked my lips and felt dryness forming at the back of my throat.

Before I could notice what was happening, that dog was standing beside me.

I jumped up and succeeded in bumping my head on the bunk above me. I started breathing funny again, but the dog just stood there. It wasn't snarling, wasn't growling, wasn't showing me his teeth.

"What you want, Dog?" I asked.

The dog took a quick step toward me and nudged me with his nose. I seen it was careful to keep its jaw locked near my hanging hand. The dog nudged me again.

German shepherds, I heard once, got their name from what they did, shepherding sheep all over the German countryside. Maybe the way they shepherded them sheep was by growling and snarling . . . and nudging strays from the herd with a big black nose.

I followed the nudge, took a step to the right. The dog seemed happy about that. It jumped onto the bottom bunk behind me and nudged again, this time on my shoulder, pushing downward on me with the bottom of its chin. I couldn't think of anything better to do, so I squatted down to my knees. It nudged my shoulder again, so I leaned in lower, and when I did, I felt coolness a-comin' off the floor underneath the bed.

"You want I should get down under here?" I said.

The dog jumped off the bunk and now pushed its side against me, pushing harder like it was trying to cram me under the bunk, like I was dirty laundry it was trying to hide. I ducked my head and rolled down under until my back touched the wall. The wall down here was gratefully cool, and the floor still gave off a mild chilly air as well.

"I get it," I said to the dog, who was now sniffing its nose at me under the bunk. "Cool air is getting trapped down here, low to the ground and covered up by the bottom bunk." I laid flat on the floor and welcomed the relief it brought. It wasn't quite like sitting in front of a window air conditioner, but it was certainly better than standing in that invisible oven out in the middle of the room.

The dog let out a sigh and placed its body down on the floor beside the bunk. At first that panicked me a little. Then I realized the animal was taking the hot spot, using its body to block red squigglies from following me under this bed.

"I guess you's a pretty smart dog after all," I whispered. *Or maybe some God out there answered my prayer.* I didn't dare say that last part out loud, 'cause I didn't know what I'd do if it was true.

My stomach growled, and my body felt dehydrated. I'd have to eat something soon. I guess I'd have to feed that dog something too. But for now, I was just gonna lay here and let the world cool off just a little bit before I did anything else.

I closed my eyes. A wash of vertigo passed over me, so I closed my eyes tighter.

I got no idea how long I slept after that.

11

THE MUTE

Sunday, September 6

Some people hated Denny's restaurants.

They said they were generic and tasteless and a perfect example of everything that's wrong with America's cookie-cutter corporate mentality. But The Mute liked these places. Liked the basic, starchy food. Liked the antiquated atmosphere that tried so hard to be modern. Liked watching average American families swallow down plate loads of pancakes and Lumberjack Slams and burgers and country fried steaks and milk shakes and whatever else was bad for you that they found on the menu.

He didn't even mind the mildly racist reputation that dogged the restaurant chain and was (mostly) undeserved. Sure, sometimes here in the South, an older waitress might frown at the sight of his coffee skin, might let his eggs get cold before dropping them at his table. That stuff happened everywhere, and it was nothing compared to what his mama had faced growing up during the age of segregation, or what his great-grampy had lived before, during, and after the Civil War. And besides, Denny's really did make the best grits anywhere in the nation besides Mama's kitchen. As far as The Mute was concerned, a good helping of steaming, Southern-style grits covered over a multitude of sins.

That's why he didn't find it an awful chore to come into the Denny's on Daniel Payne Drive in Birmingham four days in a row. The only thing that really bothered him was that, for the fourth day in a row, no one had shown up to meet him.

Truck's instructions had been the same for years. When Fade thirteen had to go into Plan B, The Mute was to send out the "unsafe" notice, go to Birmingham, and wait for the meeting. At Denny's. Sergeant Truck had thrown that in as a favor to The Mute. And so, every day since last Thursday, The Mute had entered Denny's at 9:00 a.m. He'd sat at the same table, ordered the same steak, eggs, grits, and black coffee, and waited a full hour for someone to arrive. He didn't know who it would be or even whether the person would be male or female. He just knew that Truck had said someone would come. So he waited.

"Table for one again, honey?" the hostess said when he entered the restaurant. She was one of the nice ones, though familiarity had made her a little flirty. The Mute nodded. "Well," she said with a grin, "I'm off tomorrow, so maybe I'll come in at nine and get us a table for two then."

She laughed at her own proposition and let a hand stray down his left bicep. He smiled appreciatively but didn't give any other encouragement. He hoped that was enough.

"This way, sugar," she said cheerily, leading him to the booth by the window he'd now claimed as his own. "Delores will be your waitress this morning, and she'll be right over with the coffee."

The Mute pretended to study the menu when he was actually checking out the clientele this Sunday morning. A few families at tables in the back. A young guy by the counter, hugging his coffee cup and looking just a little hung over. A middle-aged woman reading the newspaper and eating by herself. No, check that. A middle-aged couple, evidenced when a man, recently out of the bathroom, slipped in across from her in the booth and reached for the sports page. And that was it.

The Mute peeled off his jeans jacket and laid it on the seat beside him. Today he was dressed to blend in. T-shirt touting some world tour of a now-nostalgic 1980s band. A light blue overshirt, unbuttoned and untucked. Denim jeans. The only thing some might find out of the ordinary were the army boots tucked under the pant legs of his Levi's 501 blues, but this was Alabama. Even white kids from farm country wore army boots like tennis shoes in this part of the world.

"The usual today?" Delores asked, turning over his coffee cup and filling it with black, steaming liquid. She didn't bother to ask whether he wanted cream or sugar. The Mute nodded, and Delores said, "Have it for you in a jiffy."

The Mute sipped the bitter brew Delores had left behind and gazed at the door. Without really thinking about it, he tapped the ring on the middle finger of his left hand against the warm cup in his right hand. He glanced down at the insignia etched into the heavy silver band and felt a familiar flush of pride. It was two silver arrows, crossed with a silver dagger, and laid upon an encircling black ribbon. Written on the ribbon were the words *De Oppresso Liber*, and together they made up the emblem and motto of the Army's 1st Special Forces Regiment.

De Oppresso Liber, he thought. *To liberate the oppressed*. He hoped that was what he was still doing. But in order to do that, someone had to show up at Denny's. Soon.

He cursed to himself.

At 9:15 a.m., Delores dropped off his steak and eggs and grits—still warm from the kitchen—and left a bottle of ketchup nearby out of habit. The Mute picked up a fork and, just for a moment, let the food feed both his soul and his body.

At 9:17 a.m., he saw a man walk into Denny's and knew right away this guy didn't belong here—not at this hour at least. Maybe later, around noon, when the washed masses migrated from church to mealtime. But right now, this man was out of place.

He was tall, over six feet at least, and thick like a man familiar with the free weights section of a gym. He had dark hair, cut stylishly short, and a tanned face. He wore a navy-colored two-piece suit, a white shirt, a red tie, and black dress boots that actually made The Mute feel just a little jealous. He carried a book in his hands and nothing else.

The Mute took a mouthful of grits and chewed.

He watched the man scan the restaurant. He did it quickly, pausing only when his eyes passed over the drunk at the counter and again when they fell on The Mute.

The Mute avoided his gaze.

When the hostess greeted him, the man smiled genuinely and pointed toward the booth by the window. The Mute heard a muffled conversation that sounded like, "Not necessary. I'm just here to meet my friend over there." A moment later he was standing at the table's edge.

The Mute ignored him.

The man hesitated just a split second, then said quietly, "Truck sent me."

The Mute greeted him by lifting up his ringed finger and taking a loud slurp of coffee.

The man almost let his eyes roll but contained himself. "Nice to meet you too. Can I sit?"

The Mute raised his ringed finger higher, until it was about six inches from the man's nose.

"Seriously?" he said. "Right here, right now?"

The Mute ignored him.

"Fine," the man said. He dropped the book onto the bench seat across from The Mute, then stripped off his suit coat and tossed it onto the seat as well. From the way his shirt hung, The Mute could tell he'd removed a gun holster from inside his coat before entering this restaurant. Apparently he didn't want to risk scaring the locals.

Next, with an uncomfortable glance around the Denny's floor, the man began rolling up his left shirtsleeve. A moment later he stuck the inside of his forearm in between The Mute and his coffee cup. Just below the elbow joint, tattooed in silver, were two arrows, crossed with a dagger, and laid upon an encircling black ribbon.

The Mute leaned back in his chair and smiled, gesturing for the man to sit down. Delores was right behind him.

"Getcha something, honey?" the waitress said to the man.

"I'll have whatever he's having," the man said pleasantly.

"Steak, eggs, and grits, coming right up."

When she was gone, the two men allowed a moment to pass while they sized each other up. The visitor let his gaze rest obviously on the scar that decorated his host's neck. Then he extended a palm.

"I'm Samuel Hill," he said, "and I'm guessing you're the one Truck always called The Mute."

The Mute took the hand, and then let go.

"I got Truck's message," Hill said. "Just last Thursday. I would have been here sooner, but, well, Truck never said which Denny's in Alabama I was supposed to go to."

The Mute almost laughed, well, he would have if he could

make that noise. That was Truck. Never give anyone all the information. Spread it out, in bits and pieces, so everybody has something but nobody has everything. Except Truck, of course.

"Turns out there are exactly seven Denny's restaurants in Alabama. I went to the one in Auburn on Friday, and the one south of Montgomery yesterday. If I hadn't found you here today, I was headed up to Cullman tomorrow."

The Mute was starting to like this guy. But that didn't mean he had to be nice to him. He held out a hand and flicked his fingers in the universal "give it to me" gesture. Hill reached across the table and placed the book in his hand.

Complete Tales and Poems of Edgar Allan Poe.

The Mute smiled to himself. It figured.

"So," Hill said, "now what?"

The Mute pulled an ink pen from his pants pocket and scrawled a note on a napkin: *What do you know?*

Hill leaned back in his seat and let the fingers of his right hand tap absently on the space beside him.

"Well, let's see. About ten or eleven years ago, Truck called me out to Kuwait, told me he needed a favor."

So, Truck had involved this guy right from the beginning. Interesting.

"He worked out a system to send me a message, which seemed strange, because anytime Truck needed me, he usually just called. Anyway, he said when I got a certain message, I was to come to Denny's in Alabama, where one of his boys would meet me, and that together we were to pick up something valuable for him. He said to keep it hidden and safe until he came for it."

The Mute waited, thinking.

"Then, about five years ago, Truck showed up with that book"—Hill motioned toward the Poe collection—"and said it was a gift for my wife." He grimaced. "Well, now my ex-wife.

But that's another story. Anyway, he said it was a gift for my wife, but that if I ever had to come to Denny's in Alabama, it'd be a good idea if I brought it with me." Samuel Hill spread out his hands, palms up. "And that's it. That's all I know."

Just then Delores returned with a fresh plate of steak, eggs, and grits. "Enjoy," she said blandly, and then she was gone. Samuel Hill didn't even fake an interest in the food, just pushed it to the side and continued the conversation.

"So what's the big deal about the book?" he asked.

In answer, The Mute wiped his steak knife clean on a napkin and then opened the back cover of the book. His eyebrows frowned slightly at what he saw there, but he continued nonetheless. He slid the blade of the steak knife into the edge of the endpaper, twisting carefully to loosen the glue that held the paper to the inside of the back cover. Once the knife was inserted, he let it glide around the edges until three sides of the paper were no longer attached to the quarter-inch-thick cover board.

He gently lifted the paper up, and now his frown moved down to his eyes and mouth. The secret compartment was there, all right, but in place of a key there was just a pink slip of paper with the monogrammed initials "T. S. C." emblazoned at the top. He read the note and let an annoyed sigh spurt out of his lips.

"What is it?" Hill asked. In response, The Mute shoved the whole book back toward the visitor.

Samuel Hill picked up the pink notepaper and groaned. It read:

My Dearest Ex-Husband,
 Now you know what it's like when someone you trust betrays you.

 See you soon,
 Tru

How could Truck have ever trusted this bungling lothario? The Mute's mind started racing. He had to find the girl, and this book was supposed to lead him right to her and provide the key to set her free. He didn't even want to think about what would happen if he were unable to find her in time. Maybe she'd just die out there, wherever it was that Truck had hidden her. If he couldn't find her, that'd be the best thing, really. A mercy on her, even though she might not understand it.

"All right." Samuel Hill was standing now, lips flat and angry, sliding his suit coat over his shoulders. "Looks like I've got an errand to run. Meet me here again tomorrow?"

The Mute shook his head. He'd wasted enough time waiting for this clown. It was time to go hunting by himself.

"Fine," Hill said. "Then just tell me this: What is it that I'm supposed to keep safe for Truck? Did he pilfer something from Iraq? Fine art? Jewelry? Diamonds? What?"

The Mute thought for a moment, pictured the face of that lost little girl. Then he reached for the pen and napkin again.

Two emeralds. He wrote. *Priceless.*

"All right." Samuel Hill looked really angry now, both at the betrayal by his ex-wife and at the thought of traipsing around just to track down some of Truck's lost jewelry. But he didn't question the order, or Truck's command, so that was something. He was an idiot, but maybe not totally useless.

"Tell Truck I'll have his emeralds within the week," Hill said, then he turned to leave.

The Mute reached out and grabbed his arm. When Hill turned back, The Mute shook his head. He flashed the Special Forces ring again and then drew a finger across his throat.

It took Hill a second to understand what The Mute was saying, then realization fell heavy across his face. He sat down on the bench.

"Truck's dead?" he asked. The Mute nodded. "Wow. I didn't think that old man could ever die. Too much vinegar in his blood. Too mean-spirited. Too important."

The Mute nodded, grateful at last to share his misery with someone who understood the complex nature of Sergeant Leonard Truckson.

"Man was more than a father to me," Hill muttered to nobody.

The two men sat silently for a moment, then Hill let out a sigh. He stood, pulled out his wallet, and dropped some cash on the table.

He looked toward the door, then paused and turned back to The Mute.

"I've recently become aware of a man," he said evenly. "An older gentleman, Caucasian. Dresses well. Carries a cane." His eyes narrowed slightly. "I now find myself very much interested in locating this man. He goes by the name of Dr. Jonathan Smith. Do you know this name?"

John Smith? Couldn't get more generic than that. Still, The Mute read meaning in the big man's question. He suspected this Dr. Smith was somehow involved in the attack on Truck's farm.

The Mute shook his head.

Hill nodded slowly in acknowledgment, looking thoughtful. Then he shook The Mute's hand as a good-bye, a solemn gesture that almost felt like a salute.

"Okay," he said.

There was a silent moment between the men, then Samuel Hill walked out of the Denny's restaurant on Daniel Payne Drive in Birmingham, Alabama.

12

TRUDI

Monday, September 7

Trudi watched the security monitor from her desk chair, and she felt like cursing. She didn't, though. She didn't say anything.

Her ex-husband didn't bother hiding his car this time. He pulled into the small lot outside the storefront that held the offices of Coffey & Hill Investigations and slid his silver Ford GT in between a shiny black Mercedes and a dirty Toyota truck right by the front door. He looked a little tired, clothes a little rumpled, like he'd been on the road for a day or two, but otherwise none the worse for the wear. He seemed pleased to find the offices of Coffey & Hill unlocked, and he went inside.

Trudi switched the camera view to follow Samuel as he walked through the empty reception area. Eulalie had the day off, of course. At least that was one good thing.

Trudi's ex-husband barely hesitated when he found the front office empty and stretched his long legs onward, moving quickly toward Trudi's office in the back. He actually smiled when he first saw her, a smile of relief, Trudi thought, like he was worried she might not be here after all.

"Well, most folks take Labor Day off—" Sam started to say when he entered the office. Then he thought better of it and fell silent.

Apparently, feeling the nub of a handgun pressing at the base of his skull was a conversation killer.

Now Trudi did curse, but softly, under her breath. Idiot, she thought. He knew better. You never walk into a room without giving it at least a cursory visual check.

This time it played out just like the movies. Bad guy hides beside the doorjamb, pressed against the wall, gun at the ready. Then when the good guy walks in, the bad guy steps behind him with the gun pressed into service. Just like that, Trudi's best weapon—the unexpected arrival of her ex-husband—was neutralized.

"You're just a big, dumb, pretty donkey, aren't you, Samuel?" She said it sweetly, by way of greeting.

He smiled at her again. This time he seemed genuinely amused.

"Sorry, sweetheart," he said blithely. He raised his hands above his head. "I didn't realize you had company."

Trudi shook her head. The goon with the gun shoved at Samuel, motioning for him to sit in one of the two ornate metal chairs across the desk from Trudi. At that point, Dr. Smith stepped out from the other corner of the room.

"Hands on the arms of the chair, please," he said to Samuel, "where they are always in plain view. See, your wife is modeling the appropriate posture for you already."

"Ex-wife."

Trudi was sorry as soon as she said it. It was enough that

Samuel had been caught unaware. She didn't need to rub in the failure of the relationship as well, at least not right now.

Samuel complied with comfortable ease, but Trudi saw that he positioned his legs with the right foot back and left foot forward. Prepared to spring out of the chair in a split second if the opportunity arose.

"Honey," he said to her, "maybe you should introduce me to your friends."

Trudi grimaced at him. "The bearded wonder holding the gun I've just been calling Ugly Goon #1. The old guy with the cane, well, that's the one and only Dr. Jonathan Smith."

"It's truly a pleasure to make your acquaintance, Mr. Hill," Dr. Smith crooned. "You are a hard man to find."

"Sugarsweet-Plumberry," Trudi said to Samuel. "Old meanie here is looking for a friend of yours."

"Actually, my dear," Dr. Smith corrected, "we've already found Steven Grant, although he was going by the name of Truckson when we caught up with him. Sorry, I should have mentioned that to you earlier, back at your house."

Samuel's eyebrow furrowed at the mention of Truck. Trudi recognized that expression. It was a look that could kill.

"Maybe I should catch you up on things, Snicker-Muffin," Trudi interrupted. Inwardly she hoped her husband—ex-husband—was counting. She'd already laid out the count number for him and now was closing in on the trigger point.

"Dr. Smith and Ugly Goon #1 here showed up at my place for breakfast. Sadly, they didn't find anything they liked in my kitchen, so they went looking all over the house for something special. They spent nearly all morning in their little search. When they didn't find what they wanted at the house, they insisted that we come here to the office so they could make another awful mess for me."

"On a federal holiday?" said Samuel. "How uncouth. Some people have no manners."

Time for the code. Trudi hoped her ex was following the script.

"Well, you know how it is, Lightning-Bear. We came right over here and were just getting started when, lo and behold, you pulled up in the parking lot."

"I think that catches everybody up," Dr. Smith said.

Trudi saw Samuel shuffle his feet, shifting his left foot backward and his right foot forward, indicating he was now ready to take out the silent, gun-wielding goon on his left.

Good. He remembered the clues.

Trudi felt her body relax even as her mind seemed to tense up. Many years ago she and Samuel had worked out this little code sequence just for circumstances like this. In a hostage situation, one of them would first rattle off a number of adjectives in a row—two or four or whatever. When Trudi had called Samuel "big, dumb, pretty . . ." she was establishing a count for him to follow. In this case, three adjectives meant a count of three.

Next she'd start calling him idiotic pet names, except that the third pet name would actually be the code name of one of their defense plans. This time she'd decided to go with the Lightning-Bear attack. It would be fast and effective—if she could get Dr. Smith to sit down. She let her mind race toward opportunities.

"Now, Mr. Hill," Dr. Smith said, "I believe you may have something that belongs to me. A book. I'm sure you know what I'm talking about."

Samuel looked surprised. "You told them about the book?" he said to Trudi. "You didn't tell them when the time-lock opens, did you?"

Trudi took the bait.

"Of course not, you idiot! But now they know about it. Why can't you ever keep your mouth shut?"

Dr. Smith grinned. "I see," he said. "You've hidden the book in a time-locked safe. Very well, where's the safe?"

Samuel looked angry. He shut his eyes and leaned forward in his chair, but he said nothing.

Dr. Smith sighed. "Samir," he said, "perhaps you could encourage Mr. Hill to be more cooperative?"

The goon stepped forward and smacked the back of Samuel's head with the barrel of his gun. Samuel groaned and shuddered. Samir raised up for a second blow, and Trudi jumped out of her chair, concern creasing her face.

"Wait!" she said breathlessly. "Okay, fine. I'll tell you. Just don't hurt him anymore."

Samuel let out a piteous groan and gripped the metal arms of his chair. Trudi resisted the urge to roll her eyes. Her ex-husband always was an overactor.

"Ms. Coffey?" Dr. Smith said, clearly beginning to grow impatient. He motioned for Samir to step away. The goon moved backward until he was leaning gently against the wall, arms crossed and a satisfied look on his face.

"Fine," she said again. She motioned to the chair next to Samuel. "Please, Dr. Smith, sit down. The safe is here in my office, underneath this desk. The time-lock releases once a week, every Monday at . . ." She looked at the clock. It was 11:22 a.m. How long would be just long enough? She made a quick decision. "Exactly 11:51 a.m." She slumped down into her chair, hoping she looked defeated. "The book is in there. You can get it in twenty-nine minutes."

Dr. Smith smiled.

"Thank you, Ms. Coffey." He turned to his companion.

"Samir," he said in acknowledgment of a job well done. Then he eased himself down into the second office chair, ready to pass the next twenty-nine minutes comfortably.

"There is one other thing," Samuel said quietly to the room.

"And what is that?" Dr. Smith said, turning toward him.

"Brace yourself."

On the word *brace*, two things happened almost simultaneously. First, Samuel leapt from his chair toward the Ugly Goon Samir, and second, Trudi slapped the small black button hidden on the underside of her desk.

In only seconds, Samuel had pinned the goon's gun arm against the wall and delivered a vicious head butt on the crown of Samir's nose. Blood spurted out like a fountain, and to add injury to insult, the back of the goon's head cracked hard against the wall behind him. He collapsed almost immediately.

At the same time, in response to Trudi's pressing of the button, an electrical current flashed through both guest chairs in the office. The volts crackled through the exposed metal parts of Dr. Smith's chair and held him in their grasp. After a few seconds, Trudi released the button and watched Dr. Smith sag into a heap, now sitting partly in and partly out of the chair.

Trudi was a little worried that the electric shock might have killed the old man, but Samuel didn't hesitate.

"Let's go," he said. "Now."

She heard a long gasp escape Dr. Smith's opened mouth as gravity and inertia finally pulled him all the way to the floor.

"One second," Trudi said.

She pulled open the lower desk door and unhooked the false bottom inside. She scooped out the hidden key and half sheet of paper, then quickstepped her way toward the door. On the way out, she heard the Ugly Goon moan. She glanced back long enough to see Samuel kick him, hard, in the side of the head, and heard her ex-husband mutter, "That's for Truck. And believe me, there's more where that came from."

She saw Samuel hesitate, standing over Dr. Smith's limp body. He started to reach down for the old man's collar, then caught sight of Trudi standing in the doorway. "Another time, then," he muttered. He rose and spoke to Trudi. "Go. I'm right behind you. I'm coming."

Then she was outside, and Samuel was standing next to her, barely breathing hard.

"Let me get that for you."

He said it like they were just two lovebirds out on a date for the Labor Day holiday. With a slight bow, he unlocked and opened the passenger door of his GT.

"Always the gentleman," she murmured as she got inside.

Moments later they were speeding west on Interstate 20, neither one talking, neither one ready to start a conversation, at least not yet.

Still, Trudi couldn't help but notice that both of them were smiling.

13

ANNABEL

Date Unknown

I don't know how many sleep times and awake times I spent shuttlin' back and forth underneath that bottom bunk. Maybe a day. Maybe a week. I really can't tell.

In a place where there is no night, where battery-powered overhead lights never dim or brighten, you can't gauge the way time passes. Do I feel sleepy because I need a nap? Or because it's nighttime? Or because I just don't know what else to do with the time? Am I awake because it's noon? Or is it really midnight and I'm suffering insomnia? Did I sleep eight hours or twenty minutes? Was I awake all day, or just a few hours this time?

After a while, you quit trying to figure it out. You just assume that today is always now, and tomorrow, well, who knows when tomorrow is?

I do know that at some point in time, that dog stopped trying to herd me back under the bunk every time I came outta the potty room. And I know there was a moment when I realized this bunker weren't quite as hot as it was the last time I noticed it.

Then, eventually, it actually felt too chilly to keep crawling under that bottom bunk to sleep. Before long, unrolling one of them sleeping bags seemed like a good idea. And eventually I seen why Truck insisted that I bring my coat down into this empty bunker. Buried deep underground like I was, with no heater to speak of, the ground around me was working as insulation from nature's sweet sunshine. And yes, much as I'd complained about the heat before, now I lodged a few protests at the cold.

To nobody, of course. Just to that dog.

I wish Truck'd told me to bring extra socks. Guess he didn't think about that.

I don't remember exactly when it was, but I did at last explore every inch of this hidden place. Truck was right, there was plenty of food for me and that dog, though no way to cook nothing, no stove or hot plate or microwave. Guess that's for the best, but Wolf brand chili cold outta the can just ain't—isn't—as great as you might think.

I made the mistake of feeding that dog a can of chili one day. I figured it was good enough for me, it was good enough for a dog. I repented of that decision when the animal started passing gas a few hours later. Yeah, sure, I was gassing it up a bit too, but as they say, a person don't mind her own brand, if you know what I mean. Doggie digestion, on the other hand, ain't—isn't—nothing to take lightly. After that, I got smarter about feeding that dog. Vegetable soups. Bread and crackers. Beef jerky. That kind of stuff. The dog eats anything, so that's good. But seeing that animal masticate its munchies also makes me want to be careful it don't never get too hungry.

I also checked out that shallow drawer built into the table in the middle of the room. Inside it were two spiral notebooks, blank. Three ink pens. And a Walther PPQ semiautomatic pistol. Loaded. With two extra clips nearby.

A man's gun, I thought, hearing Truck's voice as I said it in my head.

There was a time, late last year, when Truck took me gun shopping with him way over in Atlanta. He always liked a good gun.

"Someday, Annie-girl," he'd said to me, "sooner rather than later, we're going to need to get you a gun of your own. Would you like that?"

I remember being excited about that idea and letting him know it in no uncertain terms. He took me to a warehouse-looking place where there was an old woman in a wheelchair showing off product. She had skin the color and texture of coffee grinds. And she had a nice, motherin' smile, like she'd be fine takin' to me if I decided I wanted to take to her. Truck talked to the woman like she was an old friend. Trusted. That was enough for me.

He let me handle a few of the pistols on display, but not one of the Walthers. "That's a man's gun," he said to me. "Too big for you. Here, try one of these."

I spent the next twenty minutes or so toying with smaller pistols and deciding that any of the Beretta shooters would be my favorite.

"I'm feeling mighty affectionate toward this one," I said, admiring a Beretta Model 21 Bobcat. It felt warm and comfortable nestled in my hand.

"Put it on your birthday list," he'd said with a grin. And then he bought something for himself and we left.

Looking at that Walther now, I see what he meant when he said it was a man's gun. It seemed large, heavy. Hard for a young girl's tiny fingers to handle. But it would fit nicely into Truck's oversized palm. I could see that just looking at it. *This must be Truck's gun*, I tell myself. *And whatever Truck intended down here, he wasn't gonna take any chances about who was in charge.*

I took a notebook and pen out of the drawer and placed them on top of the table. I left the gun in the drawer.

Today, whatever "today" means, I studied the books Truck left on the shelf for me.

It wasn't what I'd expected. There was a "collegiate dictionary" there. A Bible too, which was unusual given Truck's silent arguments with God/no God. Maybe he expected to be down here with one of his religious buddies. I heard Kenny and Rendel talking about church from time to time, so maybe he brought it down for them. But then again, maybe he left it for me, just in case I was ready to get 'round to reading it. I held the book in my hands and flipped through the pages. Seemed long. I rifled the pages again, and a bookmark fell out. I stuck my thumb on the page where it fell from and saw text highlighted in yellow.

And he entered again into the synagogue; and there was a man there which had a withered hand. And they watched him, whether he would heal him on the Sabbath day; that they might accuse him. And he saith unto the man which had the withered hand, Stand forth. And he saith unto them, Is it lawful to do good on the Sabbath days, or to do evil? to save life, or to kill? But they held their peace. And when he had looked round about on them with anger, being grieved for the hardness of their hearts, he saith unto the man, Stretch forth thine hand. And he stretched it out: and his hand was restored whole as the other.

"Well, ain't that something," I said out loud. But it didn't mean much to me. Truck ain't the Bible-reading type, and even though Rendel used to have me quiz him on Bible-memory verses sometimes, I can't say I ever spent much time in the Good Book neither. But I heard about who Jesus was, and sometimes Kenny'd tell me stories too. I never heard this one, though. A man with a withered hand? What was that exactly? And why was people so up in a tizzy over him getting a little healing? I didn't have no answers.

Something to read again later, I told myself as I returned the bookmark to its place. Then I went back to studying the shelves.

In addition to the dictionary and the Bible, there was also some books on history and philosophy, mostly stories of wars and such, including *A History of the English-Speaking Peoples* and *The Art of War.*

The last book on the shelf almost made me cry with happiness. It was a paperback edition of the *Complete Tales and Poems of Edgar Allan Poe*—a twin to match the copy I keep on the dresser in my bedroom. It ain't much, I know, but this is *our* book, Truck's and mine. He told me I got my name from his favorite poem in here, a poem called "Annabel Lee." I think I read that poem a hundred times, even after I memorized it, even after I could recite it word for word with my eyes closed. Whenever Truck gives me a "safe" code, he pulls it from my poem, so I can always remember it.

There's some scary-good stories in here too, one about a beating, undead heart, another about a woman buried alive in a haunted house, stuff like that. I used to read those stories, with Truck in the room, for the thrill of a good scare, but now that I'm down here in this underground box by myself, I think I'll stick to the poems and some of the shenanigans of Detective Dupin instead.

The important thing is, this book is here and there's no way Truck would've put it here but 'cept for me. For some reason, that makes me feel special.

There's one other book I found down here, but it wasn't on any shelf.

I was sleeping on the bottom bunk of a bed, wrapped up in a sleeping bag. When I woke up, out of habit, I kept my eyes closed and just listened to the world around me. Everything was very still. There was a slight hum comin' from the battery lights, so slight I mostly never notice it. I could hear my own heart beating steady inside my ears. And I heard a stiff, staccato breathing comin' from beside me on the floor.

I held my breath and suddenly felt my heartbeat pick up. My hand was hanging off the bed. Something warm and gritty-soft was moving underneath it, bumping lightly on my palm, then brushing delicately away every few seconds.

I opened my eyes and froze from my toes to my curls. That dog was lying beside the bed, pressed up against the wood plank that held the bottom bunk. And my hand . . . my hand . . . my hand was resting, almost touching, the animal's side while it slept.

Every time the dog would breathe deep in, its ribs would expand just enough to brush dirty fur against my fingers. It hit me then, that I was never safe when I was sleeping. That dog had been sniffing my hand while I was out, liked it so much it'd crawled underneath it and put itself to sleep with my hand right in bitin' distance.

I jerked my arm away, making a fist and tucking it deep underneath the sleeping bag. The dog stood up almost immediately, looking first at me, then at the door, then back at me.

"*Geht*," I said to it, but my throat was dry from sleeping and it came out more like "*Gegg.*" I swallowed hard and tried again.

"*Geht!*" I said. *Go!*

The dog dropped its head and trotted away from me over to the table. "*Sich hinlegen,*" I said shakily. *Lie down.* The dog did as it was told, but my heart was still beating like a rabbit caught in a hollow when the coyotes is near.

I decided that from that point on, I'd only sleep in a top bunk, out of reach of a finger-sniffing animal that might like the taste of me too much to resist it. When I climbed to the top bunk, I felt a lump underneath the mattress. I dug under there and pulled out what I found.

It was a book. Not a normal book like you buy at a store. More like a diary, or a journal. It had a blank, black cover, no markings on it at all. A fat rubber band held the thing shut. I snapped off the rubber band, and inside, in crisp, clear handwriting, someone had filled most of the blank pages with words. They wasn't English words, though. It took me a minute to get a feel for them. The first line read:

Die persönliche Rechnung Marelda Gregor, Psychiater, Biologen, Mystiker.

They was German words, and I knew some of them. I looked hard at 'em, trying to call back into my memory the vocabulary lists Truck had made me memorize at one time or another. I started picking at the words.

Biologen. I knew that one. It meant biologist.

Marelda Gregor. That had to be a name, somebody's name. That had to be the name of the person who owned this book and filled it with German words.

Mystiker. I heard that in a fairy tale Truck told me once. About an evil emperor who used a . . . a *Mystiker* to cast spells on a kindly prince. Was it magician? Sorcerer? No, wait.

Mystiker. Mystic.

Someone who studied books of spells and stuff. Who believed in demons and magic and tried to control 'em.

Weird. How could this Marelda Gregor be both a biologist and a mystic? That didn't seem to fit right.

I studied on the first line long enough until I could translate at least most of it into English: "The personal account of Marelda Gregor, *Psychiater*, biologist, mystic."

I closed the book, thinking.

I ain't got nothing but time down here in this empty tomb. And I am a smart, educated girl. Sure, I don't remember everything Truck taught me right yet, but I know myself well enough to know that, if I work at it, it'll come back to me. I never truly forget anything. I just forget where I hid it in my head sometimes.

So I made a decision. I'd start working at remembering more of the German language that Truck pressed into my brain. I'd keep working at it until it made sense to me, until I could read and understand the writing in this little black book I'd found.

And now I'm holding this book, looking at the words, waiting for the puzzles to resolve themselves in my brain. For some reason, it feels like this Marelda Gregor lady is gonna be important to me.

14

TRUDI

Monday, September 7

Trudi watched the countryside flash by through the passenger window of Samuel's Ford GT. Sitting inside the silent car made everything happening outside seem like a movie with the sound on mute.

She felt the adrenaline rush of attraction, of being back on an adventure with her strong, handsome partner, and then immediately tasted again the bitter disappointment of their failed relationship. She turned to look at him and despised herself just a bit for still loving him. But she'd been through that wringer before; she didn't feel like going through it again.

"So," she said at last. "Where are we going?"

He glanced over and smiled, a familiar expression that felt uncomfortably intimate to her. "Birmingham," he said.

"What's in Birmingham?"

"I'm hoping we can catch up to someone there. Someone who might be able to give me a few answers. And maybe some help."

She nodded slowly. "I don't know if you noticed or not, Samuel, but I've got nothing. No clothes, no money, no cell phone, not even my purse."

"Ah, but you still have those movie-star good looks. A woman can go far with that nowadays."

She hated it when he was charming.

"Seriously, Sam, if I'm going underground for a few days, even in Birmingham, I need more than a flirty smile and sexy makeup."

"Don't worry," he said, smiling. "I'll make sure you have everything you need."

Trudi bit her lip. Samuel was a professional liar and a cheat, but he could also be trusted in an emergency. He'd proven that more than once.

"Okay," she said, still thinking.

"Okay," he said, smiling at her again.

"And what about you? There's blood on your shirt."

He cursed. "Why do they always have to bleed?" He took stock of his clothing. "At least there's nothing noticeable on my coat. Well, no worries. I've got a bag in the trunk. Let's get some miles between us and Atlanta, and then I'll pull over and change."

They let a few mile markers go by in silence, then Samuel glanced her way and said, "This is nice."

"What's nice?" she snapped. "The part where I was kidnapped by some weirdo and his goon? The part where they trashed my house? Or the part where I electrocuted an old man and ran away from my home, my business, and my life?"

"All of it," he said with a chuckle. "Any of it. Whatever it was that let us spend some time together again without . . . you know. Just us being a team again. Being your partner. I like that. It's nice. So sue me."

Trudi felt like slapping her ex-husband, and like hugging him too. The pig.

"Well, maybe next time we could do it without the kidnapping."

"So you're saying there might be a next time?"

"Shut up, Samuel. You never know to quit while you're ahead, do you?"

"Right," he said. "Shutting up." He paused, then raised his hand as if asking for permission to speak.

"What is it?" she said.

He dug into his coat pocket and fished out a cell phone. "Is there anyone you need to call before you disappear?"

"You're thinking of Eulalie, aren't you. Figures. She's pretty, I agree, but a little young for you, don't you think?"

Samuel ignored the jab. "You don't know how long you're going to have to stay out of sight. And you don't know if—or when—Dr. Smith is coming back. Do you really want Smith and that goon of his to find sweet little Eulalie sitting at her desk next time he pays a visit?"

She sighed. "I guess I have to fire another assistant. Which is really annoying, because she was a good one."

"Hey, it happens. Might also want to call 911 and anonymously report a break-in at your office. Maybe they'll catch Dr. Smith and Ugly Goon still there, and we won't have to worry about them for the time being."

"Fine." She took the phone. The 911 call was easy and over quickly. The one to Eulalie Jefferson was not so much. The assistant was clearly disappointed but also distressingly sympathetic.

"I understand, Ms. Coffey," Eulalie said on the other end of the call. "I appreciate that you gave me a chance with your agency."

"No, really, you've been great, Eulalie," Trudi said, "and when I get back, I'll be sure to give you a glowing letter of recommendation. It's just a little family emergency, and I have to shut down the office for a while. It's nothing personal, I promise."

"Thank you," she said. Then, "Are you okay? Is there anything you need? Do you want me to pick up your mail for you or anything?"

Stupid, thoughtful people, Trudi thought. They can never make my life easy, can they?

"Oh, hey," Trudi said, "that's really nice of you. But no. Everything's fine."

"Okay," Eulalie said. "Well, I'll be praying for you. And if you need anything, or you know, if you're ever looking for a new assistant . . ." She laughed nervously.

"Yes, you'll be the first person I call. Thanks, Eula." She hung up and felt awful.

"Wow," Samuel said, "you really stink at firing people."

"Shut up."

Trudi leaned over and turned on the radio, pushing the search button until it landed on music, any music, and then turning up the volume. It was the eighties duo Hall and Oates singing the lullaby-ballad "Sara Smile." Trudi cursed softly and reached to change the station.

"No, leave it," Samuel said. "It's okay. It's just a song. And it's a good song."

She nodded, and let her head fall back against the headrest.

Trudi felt suddenly tired, emotionally worn out. She closed her eyes. When Samuel had first discovered that her middle name was Sara, he'd picked this song as "their song." Whenever he wanted to cheer her up, he'd launch into a slightly off-key rendition of "Sara Smile," and no matter how bad, or how mad Trudi was, it always made her smile. Now it just made her sad.

"You're an idiot, Samuel Hill," she said through closed eyes. *You had everything*, she thought. *We had everything. And you threw it all away.*

"Yeah, I still love you too," he said. She glared at him, and he shrugged. "But I know where we are now, and I know why. My own fault, I get it. But it doesn't mean I stopped loving you. Not ever."

"Sheesh," she said, "you must really want that stuff Truck left in the book."

He laughed. "Well, I am curious about it," he said. "What was it, anyway?"

"Oh no," she said, glad that she'd managed to change the subject. "That stuff is mine. You gave it to me for Christmas, remember? You're going to have to at least buy me dinner before you get anything."

"Saving your life from kidnappers wasn't enough?"

"For the record, I had everything under control, and technically, I saved your life. You didn't even see those guys until one of them stuck a gun to your head."

"Agree to disagree."

"And besides, if I hadn't given you the book, I wouldn't have been in trouble at all. I could have just given them the *Complete Tales and Poems of Edgar Allan Poe* and been done with it."

"Not while you kept whatever Truck hid in the secret compartment. They'd have come back for that within twenty-four hours."

"That raises another question, Mr. Hill. What took you so long to come back?"

"Ah, so you wanted me to come back? That's nice."

"No, I—oh, just answer the question."

"I had to take a meeting. And then I was distracted."

"Distracted by what?"

Samuel Hill's face slid into a stare, eyes flat and looking inward. Trudi felt the playfulness drain out of his body. "I don't know if I should tell you," he said. "I think it might be better, might be safer for you, if you don't know."

"Look," Trudi said, "I've already been kidnapped once because of you. And now I'm on the run from who-knows-who, hiding out with no one to count on but my ex-husband. I can't even go home, not yet, not until I know Dr. Smith and his cronies have been taken care of. So I think I'm already in this mess, whatever it is."

Samuel nodded but said nothing. Trudi waited.

"Well," he said finally, "okay. I guess you're right. What do you want to know?"

Trudi let her mind loose to think like a detective again. It felt good.

"Let's start with the meeting."

"Okay," Samuel said. "When I got back to the States, I got your message, but it wasn't the only one. I also got a message from Truck, sent coded in a newspaper. It was a trigger word telling me something Truck was guarding was, well, unsafe."

"Unbelievable."

"What?"

"You're the safe/unsafe couple in the *Journal-Constitution*? You and Truck?" The romantic in Trudi felt a sense of loss at this realization. She liked it better when she didn't know who was behind the ad.

"How do you know about the *Journal-Constitution*?"

"Technically, everybody who reads the *Atlanta Journal-Constitution* could know about the safe/unsafe ad in the personals section."

"Yeah, but how do you know what it means? And why would you read the personals section—are you dating someone?"

"I didn't know." Trudi answered the first question and ignored the second. "Until now. How was that supposed to work, anyway?"

"Truck made arrangements for someone to send out the message to me every day. As long as it said 'safe,' everything was good. But if the message ever was changed to 'unsafe,' that meant Truck needed me. I was to get the Poe book and, well, take a meeting."

"So you got Truck's message that said 'unsafe.' What was he guarding?"

"I don't think I should tell you that."

"Okay, fine. So you got the message and then went to meet Truck, is that it?"

"Not exactly. I met one of Truck's people."

"And?"

Samuel didn't answer at first. His eyebrows narrowed and his jaw tensed. Then, finally, he said, "Truck's dead, Trudi. And best I can figure, this Dr. Jonathan Smith had something to do with it. So before I could get back to your place, I had to spend some time calling in a few favors, trying to find out what I could about Dr. Smith."

Trudi let the news of Leonard Truckson's death sink in a moment. This situation had suddenly gotten much more serious. And, if possible, more dangerous.

"What did you find out?"

"Not much yet. But I've got a few people working on it."

"And you think whatever this thing Truck was guarding has something to do with Dr. Smith, and maybe that's why he was killed?"

"Maybe."

"So, if they got to Truck, how do you know they didn't get what he was guarding?"

"Because Dr. Smith was at your place. Because he was still looking for what was hidden in that Poe book. Because what's hidden in that Poe book is a clue to where Truck hid the whatever-it-is we're now looking for. And if he still wants that clue, it means he doesn't have what he's looking for. So we need to find it before Dr. Smith does."

"We?"

Samuel shrugged. "You got anything better to do this week?"

Trudi didn't answer at first.

If Dr. Smith had killed somebody already, and if that somebody was Leonard Truckson, then he was no one to be taken lightly. She was glad now she'd run a few volts of electricity through him. But she also knew that her close call with Dr. Smith and the way that she and Samuel had escaped him meant that, from this point on, she was more than just an incidental obstacle on Smith's way to the hidden thing. She had now, like it or not, earned the role of an enemy. The enemy of a man who had spent more than a decade tracking down Truck in order to kill him. Until she was out of the picture, Dr. Smith would keep looking. For her. For Samuel. And for whatever it was that Truck had hidden so well for so many years.

"So," she said at last, "how long until we hit Birmingham?"

15

TRUDI

Trudi and Samuel ate dinner at the Denny's restaurant on Daniel Payne Drive in Birmingham. This was against Trudi's wishes, as she'd seen an Olive Garden near the freeway that looked like a much better choice. But Samuel was insistent, and when she saw that the young blonde hostess—her name tag read "Shailene"—greeted him like an old friend, she figured she knew why.

"Welcome back," perky Shailene said. "Always nice to have a repeat customer."

"Two please," Trudi interrupted. She didn't have time for this little girl's flirty game.

Shailene led them, cheerfully, to a booth in the corner and promised, perkily, that Angela would be over shortly to take their order. When Angela turned out to be a busty brunette working her way through college at Samford University, Trudi decided that she hated all men. And all women under the age of thirty. And Samford University, just for good measure.

They gave Angela their orders, and to his credit, Samuel didn't let his eyes follow the waitress's curves as she walked away from the table. Trudi decided to forgive her ex-husband, for now at least, for inheriting a Y chromosome. It was time to get down to business instead.

It hadn't taken long to make the trip from Atlanta to Birmingham—less than two hours, actually. They'd gotten a room under assumed names at the DoubleTree Hotel on 20th Street. The clerk had been a little surprised when "Mr. and Mrs. Alec Smart" requested two double beds instead of a single king-sized bed, but professionalism prevented her from saying anything about it. Next they stopped in the hotel room long enough for Samuel to drop off his clothing bag and for them to each empty a travel-weary bladder. Then "the Smarts" stepped out to do a little shopping.

By the time Samuel had outfitted Trudi with a few pairs of jeans, some shirts and cotton sweaters, a requisite amount of undergarments, satin pajamas, a new purse, a pair of slip-on shoes, one light coat, and a sassy pair of red suede boots Trudi couldn't walk away from, she was ready to be done. But on the way back to the hotel, Samuel made one last stop, pulling into the parking lot of Macy's department store.

"Wait here," he'd said. "I'll only be a minute."

He was gone closer to twenty minutes, but when he returned, he carried a stylish red suitcase, just about the size of an airline carry-on bag. He tossed it heavily in the trunk with Trudi's new clothes and they went back to the hotel. She showered first, careful to keep Truck's key and half sheet of paper with her. Samuel hadn't asked again about those things, but she knew the time was coming. First things first, she supposed.

When he took his turn in the bathroom, Trudi found a stunning red evening dress in the closet. It was size 6, a sleeveless bodycon style with ribbed fabric and crisscrossing straps in the back. There was a red slip and ruby shoes in the closet as well. She was tempted by the gesture, but in the end decided to stick with jeans, a cotton sweater, and comfortable shoes for the night.

When Samuel had emerged from the shower, he was dressed in tan pants, a collarless shirt, and a sport coat. Although he tried to be discreet about it, Trudi noticed the Glock 36 pistol peeking out of the shoulder harness inside his coat. She wished she'd been able to bring along her own Beretta, but Dr. Smith's untimely visit had prevented that from happening.

Samuel didn't let on whether he was disappointed or not by her choice of evening wear. He simply grinned and said, "Ready for dinner?"

Trudi sat on the bed and took him in. He had a natural charisma about him, that was true, and just enough gentlemanly charm to keep a girl guessing.

"That's a pretty dress hanging in the closet," she said.

He shrugged.

"Seems a bit small for you, though," she said.

He laughed in spite of himself. "I thought you might want at least one nice outfit," he said. "You never know, we may need to go to a cocktail party or two before this affair is over."

She winced inwardly at the word *affair* but tried not to let it show. He'd done something thoughtful for her, and she didn't want to be ungrateful.

"Well, thank you," she said.

"There's a pair of earrings in the top drawer of the dresser too. If you want them."

She rose and opened the drawer. Diamonds. Dangly diamonds just like she favored. Was he flirting with her? She resisted the urge to put the new earrings on right then.

"Twenty minutes in Macy's and you come up with all this? I'd love to see what you could do with a full hour."

He gave a mock bow.

"The earrings are beautiful," she said. "And the dress. Thank you."

He put out his elbow for her. "Dinner, Mrs. Smart?"

"It'd be a pleasure, Mr. Smart," she said.

Of course, then he'd brought her to Denny's, where apparently the entire Samford University cheer squad was working the night shift, so that had dampened the mood just a bit. But it was fine. The food was hot, and there was plenty of table space to talk things over. When his plate was empty and hers was nearly so, Angela refilled their coffee cups, and Trudi could tell Samuel was starting to fidget.

"So, who wants to go first?" she said.

"I'm hoping you will," he said. "I've already told you everything I know."

"Not everything," she reminded. He nodded in deference.

"I've already told you *almost* everything."

"All right," she said. "I suppose you've waited long enough, though I don't know that what I have is going to be of great value to you."

"Try me. What did Truck hide in the Poe book? And how did you know it was there?"

She decided to answer his second question first.

"Well, I came across it by accident, right after the divorce. I was sorting through all the things to keep and all the things to throw out, and I came across the book. I know you. You appreciate Poe, but you're not what anyone would call a real fan. And I started wondering how you'd even thought to get me the book, and how you'd been able to come up with such an expensive collector's edition. It didn't take long for the clues to point to Truck."

"Fine, he gave it to me and said I should give it to you. You're a brilliant detective. Happy?"

"Well, once I knew it had come from Truck, I got suspicious. From there, it was only a matter of time before I figured out where the secret compartment was. And when I found it, I knew that someday you'd come looking for it. So I took out the contents and left you a note, and that's where we are today."

"I see. Nice touch with the little pink note, by the way. Was quite a surprise when we found it."

Trudi wondered who "we" was in her ex-husband's words, but he didn't seem aware that he'd let that slip. So he'd opened the book with someone else, which meant that he probably had been unaware of the secret compartment until the other person showed it to him. She started to worry a little. What if Samuel was just a bit player in one of Truck's large schemes? What if he didn't really know what he was up against or what he was doing?

Before they left Birmingham, she decided, she definitely needed to get a gun.

"Anyway, whatever it was you found in that compartment is going to lead us to whatever it is that Truck has hidden all these years. So maybe we should get moving on that?"

Trudi nodded and reached into her new purse. She pulled out the silver key and the half sheet of paper.

"I don't know what the key goes to," she said, "but I'd guess some kind of dead bolt lock, which could be anywhere in the world. As for the paper, all that's on it is some kind of math problem."

She unfolded the half sheet and let Samuel take a look. It read:

AL
9:6-11
31.
111
975,
-86.
809
845

Below the numbers were three geometric shapes. Two rectangles of roughly the same size, situated at a 90 degree angle from each other. Inside the rectangle on the right was a large square, drawn right in the middle.

"Does that make any sense to you?" Trudi asked.

"Some," Samuel said. "I think. I'm not sure about the math problem, but given Truck's initial instructions and where we are now, 'AL' is most likely a reference to Alabama. Also, the shapes on the bottom are a map."

"Seriously?" she said. "Two rectangles and a square? That's a map?"

"If you know what to look for, yes, it is."

"So what should I be looking for?"

"A hiding place."

Trudi fell silent.

"But this other stuff doesn't make any sense."

"Yeah," Trudi said, "Truck must've been strung out on LSD when he wrote this. Why don't you just tell me what you know?"

"Right, okay," he said. "Let me see what I can explain for you." He turned the half sheet so it faced her.

"The rectangles," he said, "are a property map. Like a diagram. Apparently there are three buildings on this property, here, here, and here." He pointed in turn to the two rectangles and the square. "Now, what's tricky about this is the square building."

"Right," she said. "If this really is a map, then it looks like the square building is smack-dab inside the rectangular one."

"If it were a smaller square, I'd agree with you. Then it could be a secret vault, or a hidden safe, or something like that inside the big building. But this square structure is too big for that."

Secret vault. Hidden safe. Trudi was starting to get a picture of what they were searching for. Samuel continued.

"Meanwhile, I can't tell you exactly what the numbers mean because, well, I don't know. I don't even know if the numbers run in order or if you're supposed to loop through at intervals or plot them geometrically on a graph or something, if you know what I mean."

"No, I don't know what you mean," Trudi snapped. Then she decided to set the bait. She pointed to the first number on the sheet. "Is that how many diamonds we're supposed to find?"

"No, there's only two—aw, man. You always do that to me. Why are you able to do that to me? I'm supposed to be a professional."

"Two what?"

"Come on, Trudi."

"If we succeed in this little mission, I'm going to find out sooner or later. Just tell me now. Two what?"

Samuel sighed. He reached into the inside pocket of his coat and pulled out a wrinkled napkin, which, Trudi noticed, matched the style of napkins used right in this Denny's restaurant. On the napkin someone had written: *Two emeralds.*

She leaned back in her seat, thoughtful. Samuel held the silence for her, waiting. Finally she spoke.

"All right. That's easy then. Listen, Samuel. I don't know why Dr. Smith is going to such lengths for a few random jewels, but there aren't any emeralds in the world that are worth risking our lives. Let's just leave them where Truck hid them. Let's just let greedy old Dr. Smith have them. Gems are worth even less than money; you can always buy more gems. So let's just walk away. I'll hire security back home, keep a watch for Dr. Smith types. You go back to chasing bad guys around the world. Everybody's happy, right?"

Samuel frowned. Trudi recognized his stubborn face coming to the surface.

"Right. Yes," he said. "You're right. That makes perfect sense. For you. In fact, here." He reached in his pocket and pulled out the keys to his GT. "Take my car. Keep it. Go home, get a bodyguard, and be safe. But me, well, I made a promise, and if Truck wants me to secure two emeralds for him, or two pink slippers, or two cow turds left over from the 1996 chip-tossing championship, then I intend to do it."

Trudi was suddenly angry. She felt the heat well up within her until it spilled out of her mouth and across the table at her ex-husband.

"For what, Sam? For what? Because you made a promise to your CIA handler ten years ago? Because you're a man of your word or something? Well, I've got news for you, cowboy, you've broken a lot of promises to a lot of people. You're good at it, in fact, and I've got the divorce papers to prove it. So what, now you're suddenly a man of conscience? Now you're a rogue of virtue? Save it for the flea market, baby, 'cause I ain't buying that load of junk."

They were silent for a long time, neither wanting to say anything more but neither willing to get up and leave either. The other patrons at Denny's gave them sidelong glances, and the family in the booth next to theirs decided to take the rest of their meal home in Styrofoam. Still they didn't speak. Finally, Angela came wandering cautiously over to their table.

"Everything all right over here?" she said gently. "You folks want some pie or something?" She looked at Trudi with sympathy in her young eyes. "On the house if you'd like it, honey."

"No, thank you, Angela. Just the check please."

They drove back to the hotel in the same silence they'd invoked at the restaurant. They got in separate beds, and Trudi waited to fall asleep. She listened for Samuel's breathing to turn light and even, and soon realized that he wasn't sleeping either. Finally she slipped out from under her sheets. She stood for a moment in the tiny aisleway between his bed and hers. He didn't move.

In the faded darkness, she couldn't see his face, but she could make out his stomach rising and falling gently. She watched it settle and firm up for a moment, then heard a gust of air blow out from between his lips. She watched his stomach filling up with air, deflating, filling, deflating. Still he didn't move.

She wanted to slip her body under the sheet and press herself next to him, feel his arm slide over her again, feel the warmth of his chest burn hot against hers. But she knew the rules. She knew those days were long gone.

"All right," she whispered toward him. "We'll go get the emeralds. But I'm doing this for you, not for Truck, not for any stupid promises you made, not for anybody or anything else. For you. That's it. You understand?"

He didn't say anything. Trudi nodded to the darkness and returned to her bed, alone. She wondered, for probably the thousandth time, if she would ever again feel like she was home.

16

THE MUTE

The Mute walked gingerly across the blackened ground, careful to avoid any potential hot spots left over at ground zero of what the news media was now calling the Great Conecuh Fire. He'd had to ditch his Jeep Wrangler Call of Duty MW3 Edition about five miles south, well out of sight of the fire authorities and volunteers still fighting the blaze some four miles west and north of here. The hike to the center of Truck's old farm had been surprisingly, and thankfully, boring.

Once, he'd run into a volunteer cleanup crew, maybe two miles in. The men and women on that crew looked tired and unwashed, hands and faces bearing streaks of soot, clothes smudged and in need of a good laundromat. And they'd looked proud, satisfied, as though working miles behind the lines, here in this awful, ashened desert, was a privilege and they were the elite few allowed in. The Mute felt slightly patriotic just watching them

125

dig and turn, tossing detritus left from the fire into a few heavy pickup trucks parked nearby. He watched them shrugging off the heavy burden of loss with first steps toward rebuilding, with first hopes of a better, brighter future. These people were signs of life, proof that even disaster can't kill the human spirit, not completely.

One of the men had saluted when he saw The Mute trudging through, mistaking his blue work gear and sturdy hiking boots for a fireman's tools, assuming The Mute thus embodied the heroes still on the ground to the northwest of here. The Mute returned the salute, paused to appraise their work and nod appreciatively. Then he'd moved on quickly through the cleanup site and toward the ruins that once were Truck's home.

There was nothing but rubble on top of more rubble, splintered wood, baked brickwork, fallen foundations. It spread across the land in jagged memories of what once stood, wind blowing pieces out of proportion, everything crushed and crumbled again underneath the fiery fist that had pounded the earth in this place.

The Mute knelt beside what had once been steps to the porch of Truck's main house. He couldn't help but smile. Even in this mess there was still life. A grasshopper sparked and flew from one dead ember to a patch of blackened grass. Somewhere in the unseen distance he heard a resonant knocking and realized a red-cockaded woodpecker had found at least one place to work its percussion upon nature.

Without warning, a thrushing sound arose behind him. He turned quickly, hand at his back, resting on the Kahr handgun stashed just inside his waistband. *Unbelievable.* He wouldn't have supposed it possible if he hadn't seen it with his own eyes. A lean and lithe bobcat peeked in his direction then skittered away into the distance, perhaps still hunting for a white-tailed deer caught unexpected by the fire and trapped on this side of nowhere.

Signs of life. He breathed them in, breathed the hope he felt by seeing them. It had been more than a week since the attack on Truck's property, since the girl with the emerald eyes had been hidden somewhere out of sight. At first The Mute had worried, had ground his teeth in frustration at the Great Conecuh Fire that prevented him from searching the heights and plumbing the depths to find her. Then, even in the rubble, he found life in crazy places, life that survived and would in some ways thrive as a result of this devastation.

If a grasshopper could endure the fiery furnace and still not perish, then that pretty little girl could do it too.

So he waited, and watched, and counted the moments until the fire had finally progressed enough, finally moved far enough away to take its heat, and the heroic workers who faced that heat, far enough away to allow him to return. To allow him to listen to the wind, to follow the clues, to track the footprints left in the air.

The girl was alive. He believed it, and so it was true.

The girl was safe. He trusted that Truck would have made that happen.

The girl was waiting. Waiting. Waiting.

The Mute started digging in the sooty refuse that surrounded Truck's old porch. It seemed as good a place as any to look for some new clue. Maybe something there would flash a hint, would give him at least part of the map he was supposed to have gotten from that inept CIA agent Samuel Hill.

Maybe, if he worked hard into the night, if he never stopped believing . . . maybe he could still find the girl.

Maybe he would even find her in time to save her.

Again.

17

TRUDI

Sunday, September 13

Trudi heard a soft knocking at the door of the hotel room and involuntarily put her hand over her mouth. She recovered quickly, though, and dabbed the mute button on the TV set, straining to hear anything more.

Had she just imagined it?

She held her breath and rolled silently off the bed, then tiptoed her way to the room's window. She looked out at the parking lot, searching for Samuel's car somewhere within the yellow lines that marked off the cement below. She couldn't find it.

Samuel had gone out to get dinner about half an hour ago. Was it too soon for him to be back? And if he was back, why was he knocking? Why not just use his key?

She stared at the back of the door, not sure what to do next.

If this were a movie, she told herself, then Jonathan Smith would be waiting outside that door. He'd have already disabled—

maybe killed?—her ex-husband. He'd be standing there, leering toward the peephole, holding a weapon. Waiting to pounce on her as soon as she opened the door.

She really wished she had her gun. Or that she'd gone out to get dinner with Samuel, but after the way their week had gone, that seemed to be unwise.

On the morning after the first night here in Birmingham, she'd awakened before him, staring at the ceiling feeling both whole and broken. It had been wonderful to reunite, at least somewhat, with her ex-husband. It had almost been a healing of sorts. But there, in the pale light of morning, all the memories came back to her. All the reasons why they'd split up in the first place. The knowledge that he had a child with another woman. That now, Trudi herself could possibly be "the other woman."

He roused slowly in the bed beside hers, sat up on an elbow, and looked at her in the face. He read the message there, and now it was his turn to sigh.

He rolled back onto his bed. "Tru," he said. There was a plea in his voice.

She turned her back and went to the bathroom. She turned on the water in the shower but let herself sob for a moment outside the spraying water first. Then she collected herself and went through her morning routine. When she came out of the bathroom, he was up, shirtless, sitting in a chair, staring out the window. He looked toward her when he heard the bathroom door open.

They shared a silent moment and both understood. They were still ex-husband and ex-wife. They still had crazy killers on their trail. And they still had to run some stupid jewelry-store errand for the recently deceased Leonard Truckson.

Samuel waited in the chair. His eyes looked tired.

Trudi took a deep breath and did what she had to do.

"I'm going to get breakfast," she said formally. "Want me to pick up something for you?"

He let his head dip forward toward his chest, now staring deeply at the floor.

"Just coffee," he said. "Black."

He didn't move from the chair. Trudi nodded, even though he couldn't see it. She turned and exited the hotel room. And it was done.

When she returned to the room, he was dressed and looking through files on his laptop. "Thanks," he said when she handed him the coffee. It was all business after that.

"Still nothing definitive on our elusive Dr. Smith," he said to her, "but I've got at least one contact who places him somewhere in Iraq near the beginning of the second Gulf War. So that may be something."

She nodded.

"I'll go back to Truck's math problem and see if I can figure anything there."

That's how they'd spent the rest of the week, taking turns searching out clues on Dr. Smith and working out logarithms to try to decode Truck's note. And they'd fallen into the habit of not eating meals out together. One would go out for food and bring back something for both of them. It was a distance created, and needed, a separateness to help redefine each day the limits they now lived under. So when Samuel had offered to go get dinner tonight, she was obligated to let him go alone. She hadn't really given it a second thought until now, until that indistinct knocking at the door had suddenly caused visions of movie-style madness flashing through her head . . .

There was silence outside the door now, not even the sound of footsteps or voices in the hallway. Nothing. Had she imagined—

Another knock. A little louder this time. Three quick raps on the outside of the door.

She knew that Samuel always carried two guns, no matter where he went. Even at her mother's Thanksgiving table several years ago. Two guns. That's just what he did. After their first night here in Birmingham, he'd stopped trying to conceal the Glock 36 in his shoulder harness. But she still hadn't seen where the other gun was hidden. Maybe he'd stored it here in this room? Maybe she could find it before—

She took a deep breath, said a silent prayer, and slid her feet toward the door. She held the breath in her lungs while she peeked into the peephole, knowing that her head would briefly dim the yellow pinhole of light that flickered on the other side of the hole, but also knowing that if she didn't, she'd never be able to open a hotel room door again in her life. She refused to be a person who let fear take charge.

The Lord is my shepherd, she told herself. *Even though I walk through the valley of the shadow of death, I fear no evil, for you are with me.*

She let out her breath in a deep sigh. On the other side of the door was her ex-husband, holding a soda in each hand, and in his mouth he clenched a large white bag with a Chinese emblem on the front. He was frowning, trying to lean in and use his elbow to knock again on the door. Trudi opened the door before he had to knock again.

"What took you so long?" he asked after Trudi relieved his mouth from the burden of carrying their dinner. "I was starting to get worried."

"I need a gun," she said.

"What?"

"I need my gun. It's only two hours back to Atlanta. Let's go get my gun."

"No."

Trudi frowned. "So, what, you're kidnapping me now? You're telling me what I can and can't do? Because you tried that little trick a time or two before, and we both know how that worked out for you."

Samuel set down their drinks and waved his palms in mock surrender.

"No, of course I'm not telling you what you can and can't do. I'm just saying . . ." He paused, then apparently chose to reword what he was going to say next. "Okay, why don't you tell me why you think you need a gun?"

Trudi felt like fuming at him. She didn't need a reason for anything with him, not anymore. She didn't have to ask his permission either. But she took a breath and decided that, if the roles were reversed, she would want him to treat her with a similar kind of respect.

"Just now, when you knocked on the door, I realized that we've been here almost a week—long enough for anybody really looking to find us. And when you didn't identify yourself, I had no way of knowing whether or not it was safe to open the door. I was in here all alone, unarmed. A sitting duck."

She noticed him give a quick rub across a small scar just in front of his right temple. It was an involuntary movement, she was sure, but it made her feel good anyway. She'd once cracked the bone outside his right eye when he thought it would be funny to jump out at her from a dark closet. She'd responded instinctively, with a sweeping roundhouse kick that finished with a trip to the emergency room for Samuel. He'd never tried to scare her like that again.

"I see. Okay, I understand. But it's unwise for you to go back to your home or your office until we know that Dr. Smith isn't waiting. And it'd be next to impossible to buy you a gun here, what with waiting periods and identity checks and such."

"Waiting period? Identity checks? Seriously? With your contacts, a little thing like a waiting period for a gun shouldn't be much of an issue. Or is this just about the fact that you're a man and you think only a man should have a gun? That you feel some macho need to protect a poor li'l helpless *gurl*? Is that it, you big strong man, you?"

"Well, just be patient, Tru. And think about it with a level head. You know I can take care of you. Why would you need a gun if I'm with you?"

Trudi felt fury building up inside her. This guy really was a pig sometimes.

"Why do you need to be such a domineering mule?" she spat. "I take care of myself, Mr. Samuel Hill. I've done it my whole life. I don't need you, or any man—or any woman, for that matter—to be my own personal protector. If you wanted that job, you never should have . . ." She stopped herself from saying the really hurtful part and took a deep breath before continuing.

"No, right, I know—" He tried to get a few words into the break, but she wouldn't let him.

"And I certainly don't need your permission to take my own self to my own office to get my own gun."

"Trudi, listen—"

"No, you listen. You think you always know what's best. Why do you always have to be right, even when you're dead wrong? I need my gun, Samuel. Now, either do something about it, or try to stop me. What'll it be, cowboy?"

"Come on, Trudi, be reasonable." He put his palms out and up, pleading for some kind of truce. "We can't go back to Atlanta. It's not safe. You know that. Even the 'Independent Woman' version of you knows that. We'll just have to work out a different plan."

"Fine. Give me one of your guns."

"What, so you can shoot me if I happen to lean too far out of the closet? I don't think so."

Trudi crossed her arms.

"Look, all we really need is a safe code. Some phrase that lets you know it's me on the other side of the door."

"What if it's you, but you're being coerced by some thug with a gun?"

"Okay. Right. Sure, that's good thinking. So we'll have both a safe code and an unsafe code. I say the safe code and everything is hunky-dory. You open the door. I say the unsafe code, and you know to jump out the window and run. Fair enough?"

Trudi fumed but couldn't think of anything better to say at the moment.

"What safe code are you thinking of?" she said.

Samuel gazed around the room until his eyes fell on the Gideon Bible beside the telephone. "How about something from that?" he said, pointing. "You're always telling me I should learn about stuff in there anyway."

She thought about it for a moment, then nodded. "Okay," she said. She flipped open the book to Psalm 23 and read the words she'd just recited to herself. She showed it to Samuel. "For the safe code we'll use the first line of this Psalm."

He nodded. "Good," he said. "And for the unsafe code we'll use the last line: 'I will dwell in the house of the Lord forever.' Can you remember that?"

She was tempted to say something snarky, to remind him that agnostics weren't likely to dwell forever in the house of the Lord. But instead she nodded. She didn't feel like having that argument again, at least not right now.

Samuel clapped the Bible shut, satisfied. "Okay, then," he said. He started unpacking egg rolls from the bag of Chinese food.

Trudi hesitated. It was good to have a safe and unsafe code, she knew. But she also knew she'd feel better if she had a gun. If she had *her* gun. And she was still angry at Samuel's patronizing attitude.

She stared at him while he unpacked the food and let her mind run through scenarios for a moment. Then she made a decision.

"Okay, those will be our codes, if we need them," she said, realizing as she said it that now it was almost an afterthought.

"Good," Samuel said, smiling. "Would you rather have sweet and sour chicken or broccoli beef?"

To herself she said, *I'd rather have my Beretta 3032 Tomcat.* But to him she said:

"I'll take the chicken."

18

ANNABEL

Date Unknown

I'm starting to see things that ain't there.

Ghosts mostly, I think, or something else like that. People who are plain in sight but missing substance of some kind, almost like a Hollywood special effect you'd see on a midnight movie around Halloween.

I am surprisingly calm about this new development.

I'd have thought it'd make me scared, but the dog seems untroubled as to their presence and somehow that makes me feel more comfortable with the situation too. Honestly, I think I'm likely just imagining them. It's as if my brain is so bored by this undecorated purgatory that it's decided to have a little fun at my expense, keeping itself busy by inventing invisible companions that pop in and out of existence. Keeps me on my toes, I'll say that.

'Course, it also could be I'm going squirrel-nuts from this

solitary confinement. But I think crazy folks don't know they's crazy, so I might be okay on that front. At least that's what I been told.

I suppose there is one more possibility, but I don't like to think too long on that one.

It's possible these gauzy visitors really are ghosts, somehow left behind, somehow drifting through an afterlife. Maybe they's something like me, hidden and lost, waitin' to be found. But if they really are ghosts, then that means there really is an afterlife of some sort, and if there's an afterlife, then every human has an immortal soul. How to explain that mystery? Only reasonable thinking is that some kind of God made it so.

If that's true, then I may have a reckoning to face someday, and I'm gonna be honest: that scares me a little. So I've decided not to worry on it, not now at least. Someday maybe, when it don't have to be so close at hand. When I can pick it up like a pretty flower or shiny rock, inspect it good and hard, and decide whether it's worth keeping inside or leaving out in the meadow.

Instead, I've just been watching these ghosts, or solitary-cell hallucinations, or whatever they are, trying to see what stories they gonna tell.

The first one I seen was a youngish guy, light-skinned and light-haired. I was on the bottom mattress of one of the bunk beds, trying to remember a song about sunshine, when I suddenly noticed a boy was sitting 'cross the way from me on the floor.

He was wearing all black clothes, some kind of combat outfit, I think, and sitting cross-legged in front of my outhouse. His left arm hung limp beside him, and his right palm pressed hard against the left side of his ribs. He was rocking back and forth, just a little, and ever so often he'd pull out his right hand and look at the fingers, almost like he expected to see blood, but there was nothing there that I could make out. His eyes would wince and then go wide, and he'd press against his chest again, rocking and rocking.

"You hurtin', mister?" I said out loud, but he didn't hear me, or didn't want to hear me. "What's your name?" I said. Again, just looking at that palm, a-rockin'.

I don't know how long I watched him, a few minutes, maybe an hour. And then he faced up like he was looking at me but could only see through me. He got a little hiccup in his eyes, some awful realization finally making sense to his brain. Then he sagged forward, both arms drooping, then onto his side, eyes still wide open.

He quit moving.

And I suddenly had to pee. Real bad.

I kept thinking that now was when ghosts should disappear, when his image should kinda dissolve and drift away. But I seen that guy lying there so long I was tempted to pee in the water bucket and pour it out later. It seemed wrong to cross the outhouse threshold if it meant I had to walk right over that dead boy. And then, finally, he just wasn't there no more, and I couldn't tell when he showed up or when he took gone. I couldn't tell if I'd been awake or maybe dreaming, or if maybe I was dreaming while I was awake.

I looked over at the dog lying by the front door, and saw it was watching me as hard as I'd been watching that dying boy. I felt cold, even wearing my coat. I think I shivered, and I wondered when was the last time I'd actually taken a breath.

The dog stood up and took a step, looking hard at me, looking almost like it was afraid of me. It stepped again, and pretty soon it was standing directly in front of me. The animal sighed heavily, then dropped itself down at my feet. A minute later, its eyes were closed and its legs was twitching, dreaming of battle, I suppose. Or maybe talking to that ghost.

I don't know.

I don't see imaginary things all the time. Just sometimes. Boys with grim faces. An old woman looking like she was so thirsty she 'bout couldn't move. Once I thought I saw Truck's boy Kenny, grinning at something happening back behind me, but he was here and gone so fast I just couldn't tell.

Then, when I wasn't expecting it, Truck was here.

He was sitting at my table, both hands out, palms down on the surface. And unlike the other "visitors" in my mind, Truck stared right at me. He didn't look happy.

"What's goin', Truck?" I said softly. "You comin' to get me at last?"

He just frowned. And stared.

"Truck," I said. "I ain't got nothing here. You got to come get me now. I think I might be going nutcase down here. You ain't . . ."

I felt suddenly angry at myself for my lazy nature. Truck used to chastise me for being a Southern girl, for taking on bad habits in the way I talk. I done learned all the wrong ways to talk just by hearing everybody around me talk that way, but I was still smart enough and educated enough to know the difference. Leastways, I shoulda been.

Looking at Truck sitting there at my table, frowning at my face, I understood what he was tryin' to tell me. Here in this shelter, I'd let my education slide. I guess that happens when I get nervous or scared. Still, I'd never be this lazy if Truck was here. So I tried again.

"You *aren't* gonna leave me here to die, are you, Truck?"

A horrible thought crossed my mind.

"Truck," I whispered. "Truck . . . you ain't dead, are you? *Aren't* dead? Are you?"

The creases in my uncle's forehead turned soft, and his eyebrows eased back to normal. He didn't move, he just kept his hands a-laying on that table, kept his eyes looking dead-on at mine.

I blinked.

And Truck was gone.

Resting on the table, in the place that would've been between his outstretched palms, there was that black book, that journal from Marelda Gregor. Waiting where I left it, sitting where I got lazy 'bout trying to understand it.

"I get it, Truck," I whispered at last. "I got work to do."

Sitting here feeling sorry for myself was gonna drive me crazy. Them random ghosts was proof of that. I got to keep myself busy.

I got to make myself a plan.

I got to get my head back into my German studies, learn whatever it is Marelda Gregor set down in those clean, handsome letters.

But first, I got to keep myself sane.

I got up from the bunk bed and walked over to the table. I opened that drawer and moved aside the gun. When I had a spiral notebook and one of them pens ready, I sat down to write.

This would be a book, my book. A collection of letters to myself, telling me who I am and what I am. Reminding me of what I been through, of things that seem far away, telling my soul that I have a soul.

I thought for a moment and brushed my hand across the first page in the spiral. Then I set that pen to work.

Uncle Truck keeps a German shepherd on his farm that'll eat human fingers if you feed 'em to him just right . . .

19

ANNABEL

Date Unknown

I cut my hand.

I was opening a can of sirloin burger soup when it happened, taking a break from my work because I'd forgotten to eat earlier when I woke up.

I'd rolled off the bunk thinking of Marelda Gregor and, instead of eating, just sat down at the table and continued where I'd left off after my last awake time. I was thinking I'd grab me a bite in a minute or two. I don't know how much time went by, but I know it was more than a minute because I started feeling light-headed and cranky from the burning in my gut. I figured it was time to feed the body so's I could get back to feeding the mind without being distracted by a growling stomach.

I was in a hurry, twisting on the manual can opener and actually liking the canned meat smell that seeped out with every turn. Then I heard that dog snort in my direction, like it was hoping I'd share the soup. Like it was really hoping not to have to share with me.

We'd been getting along lately, sort of. It kept its way and I kept mine. I don't know when exactly I started to trust it, but at some point I'd finally decided it wasn't gonna eat my hands as long as I kept it fed, and it seemed to have agreed to that arrangement as well. Anyway, at that point, I didn't want to be bothered by nobody unless it was Uncle Truck at the door hollering the safe code, come to let me out of this prison room.

I looked toward the dog and said *"Geht."* It turned toward the bunks and slid into a spot on the floor next to one. I just wanted to stuff a few bites of food in my mouth and get back to Marelda Gregor's journal, but when I checked to see where that dog was, I took my eyes off what I was doing with the opener. The can slipped. The razored edge of the half-opened lid sliced hard into my right index finger, just above the knuckle, spilling warm cranberry blood into my soup can.

I said a bad word in German, because it hurt like a rat bite. Then I figured that was kind of a good sign because it meant I was beginning to think in German. Except now I'd ruined my soup and was also casually dripping blood into a small pool on the carpet below me. I swore in German again, just because it seemed like the thing to do. Then I grabbed a napkin and pressed it hard into my hand, trying to stop the bleeding.

Funny thing about this bunker. It's got all kind of supplies, even some rough toilet paper in the outhouse room. Books and food and knives and forks, all manner of things a body would want and need during a hideout. Only thing I could never locate here is a first-aid kit, which seems like a mighty oversight to me. I mean, seriously, did Truck think no one would ever find need of Tylenol or a Band-Aid? So I just kept pressing a napkin into my finger, waiting for the blood to start drying up over the cut.

Then I noticed the dog.

It was sittin' up now, sniffing the air, very interested in what was going on over here in my neck of the woods. It took a step toward me and sniffed harder.

"No," I said, "the soup is ruined. Give me a minute and I'll open up another can for you."

The dog just kept sniffing.

I figured I'd better start cleaning things up before the animal sneaked dinner out of the spoiled can. I squeezed the napkin between my thumb and finger, then scooped up the soup can and dumped it down one of the holes in the outhouse. I hated to waste a whole can of food like that, but there was plenty more on the shelf, and for some reason, I didn't think I'd have to be in here before I got to the end of things up there.

When I came out from the outhouse, I froze.

The dog was over by the shelves, sniffing close to the little pool of my blood getting sticky on the carpet. It hit me that this dog was no stranger to human blood, that it'd probably eaten it before. That maybe it liked the way blood tasted.

I felt like I should say something, give it a command to *aufhören* or *geht*, to *cease* or *go*, but I couldn't open my mouth. It was like watching an accident that's about to happen, knowing you should be doing something, knowing you should be stopping it, but being helpless to do anything but watch and hope you ain't part of the carnage.

The dog sniffed again. Then it looked over at me. There was a second or two while I could see its mind working things over a bit. Then the animal dipped its head and licked at the red on the carpet. It licked a second time, then swung its head quick-like toward me again. It licked more, and kept licking until most of the blood on the carpet was gone.

I felt like throwing up, watching that dog slurp up my blood, wondering if it was getting a taste of me that it liked enough to want more of someday. But I couldn't do anything to stop it. I couldn't do anything but squeeze on the soiled napkin in my hand, trying hard to stop myself from bleeding, to stop myself from watching that dog eat the life that had only recently been flowing through my body.

When it was done feasting, the dog looked at me again, waiting. "*Geht*," I croaked. "*Geht.*"

The dog obeyed without hesitating, trotting back over by the bunk beds where it lay down, blinking.

I felt my arms trembling just a bit, but I tried to act like nothing was out of the ordinary between me and that dog. I got a wet towel and used it to dab up the rest of the blood from the carpet. I didn't want that dog comin' back for seconds when I wasn't looking.

I knew I should eat something, but I also knew that if I did, the grasshoppers flitting in my stomach would just hop it back out again. I decided to let my insides grumble just a little longer.

I went back to my seat at the table and tried to do my work. Truck always used to say, "A man needs a purpose," and I figured that meant me as well, even though I'm just an eleven-year-old girl. But I'd found a purpose down here in this purgatory, and I wasn't yet ready to give it up, even when a bloodthirsty German shepherd was eyeing me with unnatural curiosity.

The dog kept staring, but it didn't move, didn't growl or show any real emotion at all. Just kept its muzzle aimed in my direction, blinking slowly, watching.

I turned back to my notebook and allowed myself a little review. After Truck's ghost, or whatever that was, had come a-calling, I couldn't just eat and sleep and wait anymore. I had to do something, had to fill my time with more than emptiness. So I made it my calling to translate the journal left behind by

Marelda Gregor. After that, I spent my time in two collabora-
tive pursuits. Education and interpretation.

When I'd first wake up anew, after eating and taking care
of bathroom business, I'd sit with a notebook on the table and
begin making vocabulary lists just like the ones Truck had made
me memorize. At first it came slow, like pulling taffy that'd
cooled and hardened some in your hands. But with practice and
persistence, the language began to submit itself to my memory.

I made a list of verbs, kept adding to it until it numbered
more than fifty, then seventy, then one hundred. As I made the
list, I circled words that might come in useful, say, to control
a German dog. I practiced a few, discarded the ones that got
no response, kept close to mind the ones that turned that dog
this way or that. One or two of those verbs I didn't say out loud
because I was a little scared at how the dog would respond. But
I kept 'em circled anyway.

Next I started lists of nouns. Household items. Office equipment. Kitchen appliances. Proper names of body parts and
locations.

Then I tried to remember German sayings, slogans, and little
wisdom nuggets unique to that part of the world. *Was Hänschen
nicht lernt, lernt Hans nimmermehr.* What Johnny doesn't learn,
Johnny never learns. *Unverhofft kommt oft.* The unhoped for comes
often. *Ein Mann, ein Wort.* A man is only as good as his word.
That kind of thing.

After a while I caught myself talking foreign in my head,
holding entire conversations with myself in German. That's
when I knew it was time to go back into "the personal account
of Marelda Gregor, psychiatrist, biologist, mystic." So I done it.

The clean, crisp words written on the pages of Marelda
Gregor's journal are much less mysterious to me now, though
sometimes it takes a little thought to work 'em through just

right. I feel like a young'un just past learning how to read, finding the way but needing to work a bit before the letters unlock themselves.

And so, to take my mind off the dog's eatin' habits, I now begin to translate, listening to Marelda Gregor's voice unspool before me.

> *The personal account of Marelda Gregor, psychiatrist, biologist, mystic.*
>
> *It is October, the month of revealing, and for the first time I begin to have second thoughts. I feel this child moving within me; she hiccups and it tickles my insides, makes me smile. She rolls and kicks. She presses on my bladder, and even that fills me with an unnatural zuneigung, a fondness for what is hidden to all but me. I long to hold her in my arms and smell the sweetness of newness in her skin.*
>
> *Johannes Schmitzden is a genius. A dazzling mind. Yet Dr. Schmitzden would never understand what I am feeling right now. Never allow it. He has*

There's a sound that pulls me away from Marelda Gregor, distracts me from her voice speaking in my ear.

Choking. Coughing? What is it?

I glance up from my work and find the dog looking my direction, eyes glazed, staring but unseeing. It coughs again, like a chicken bone has got stuck in its throat, like it needs to get that bone out or it'll choke to death right here on this floor.

"Dog?" I say. It don't hear me.

I see the animal's body tremble, starting in its neck and shuddering all the way back to its hind legs. Another tremor and it hacks again, choking harder on whatever is choking it.

My hands feel sweaty. My heart thumps hard inside my chest.

It never occurred to me that I might be trapped in this bunker with a German shepherd carcass for a roommate.

"Dog," I say. *"Komm her."* My voice sounds thin in my ears. *Come here.* I don't know what else to do, what else to say.

The dog cocks its right ear my direction. Its eyes seem filmy and blank, pupils dilated. But its ears still seem to work. It recognizes my voice and struggles to move.

"Komm her," I say again.

It trembles to its feet, unsteady, looking almost woozy like it's drunk alcohol and is now feeling the effects. A strand of drool slips from the back of its jaw, lingering in space for a magnetic moment, then breaking off and disappearing into the carpet.

A tremor hits. The dog stands, unmoving, as the shaking takes over; its head dips downward. A slight whimper escapes. Whatever this is, it hurts the dog.

I'm caught in uselessness, frozen to my chair, unsure of what to do, unable to do anything I can think of to do.

"Bitte, komm her." I whisper it this time, pleading. *Please, come here*, I think, and I realize it is a prayer of sorts. To that unnamed deity I keep turning to when I'm afraid or overwhelmed. *Please let it come here.*

The animal moves. One shaky step. Another. Its hind legs seem to have difficulty working, like they's now just two sticks of wood attached to the back of its body. Another rope of saliva drips, and this time I see blood mixed with it. *Is that the dog's blood, or mine?* A step, its living front legs pulling the dead back end of itself toward me. Pulling again.

The dog is beside me now, the entire back half of its body frozen in crippling disuse. Another tremor hits, and it lowers its head pitifully into my lap. It closes its eyes while its muscled frame shakes and shivers. A soft whimper slips through its clenched jaw.

Its head is heavy on me, heavier than I expected.

The dog is helpless before me. Something I never knew was possible.

I feel the vibrations of its seizure tingling into my own bones. The soft hum of battery-powered lights reaches my ears. I wonder if Truck promised a triumphant return for this dog too. I wonder what Truck would do with this dog at this moment. What Truck would do *for* this dog.

I'm trembling myself now, but I do what's next anyway. I rest a hand against the animal's cheek. I stroke around his blinded eyes, behind his ear. I take his face in both my hands, then lean close to wrap an arm around his neck.

"*Es ist okay,*" I whisper to him. "*Du bist okay.*"

His body feels like trembling stone beneath my touch. He don't move his head from my lap, don't move at all except to tremor and shake.

"*Du bist okay,*" I say. "*Es ist okay.*"

The dog remains captive to his own body.

But, for now at least, he stops whimpering.

20

THE MUTE

Wednesday, September 16

It took nearly a week before The Mute discovered the tunnel entrance behind what used to be Truck's red barn.

To say it was covered in rubble and refuse would be an understatement. To say he could have dug for weeks and still might have missed it was to state the obvious. To say he knew he would find it, he knew faith would win out, well, that was something more of a stretch. But he hoped the hiding place would show itself to him sooner rather than later, and that hope endured through long days and short nights of digging, aching, planning, working, digging more, laying out grid lines in his head, and most of all, refusing to give up.

When he found the opening, the sun was just entering twilight before another night swept through southern Alabama. At first he wasn't sure what it was. From where he stood, it looked like a piece of scrap metal buried under wood and rock and blackened dirt. But the corners were still noticeable, and unlike other rubble in this area, it still lay flat to the ground. So The Mute picked his way over to that spot and began uncovering what lay beneath. When he was done, he found a flattened, scorched square of lead fused to what he guessed used to be a small hydraulic system. In his mind, he rebuilt an image of this spot from before the fire.

The doghouse, he said to himself. Underneath the doghouse.

It took a little time, and a crowbar he'd hauled over from his Jeep Wrangler two days before, but The Mute finally got the metal cover off. Down below, he could make out narrow steps that jutted inside a tunnel, going downward deeply and quickly to a wide landing area. From there the tunnel floor ramped down, curving off and around to the right. In spite of everything that had happened aboveground, pale yellow lights still glowed underground, at regular intervals in the tunnel, giving it an almost haunted appearance.

The Mute felt new energy flowing through his weary bones. Had he found it? Had he found Truck's hiding place?

Was the girl still alive?

There was only one way to find out. He stepped into the tunnel.

The air down here was dry, with hints of stale smoke, but generally usable once you got used to it. He stepped carefully through the curves that wound out and down and back in again, breathing shallowly, listening. He heard no sound except the soft scrape of his boots on the path below him. He noticed that the temperature lowered slightly the farther down he walked. Partway down, he stopped.

What if Truck had booby-trapped this place?

That wouldn't be out of the ordinary for a man like Sergeant Truckson. He was terribly protective of his secrets.

The Mute scanned the walls in the dim light around him, then turned his attention to the floor below. There were still prints on the path, messy and sometimes indistinct, but prints nonetheless. He knelt low to the ground and followed the story they told. One pair of large feet. One pair of smaller feet. And animal tracks. All had been running toward the low end of the tunnel, with wide spaces occurring between each footfall. Only one pair of tracks showed a return trip, walking briskly, but not as much space between them, not running.

So, this was it. Truck had brought the girl, and apparently the dog, down this tunnel. To where? To what end?

Judging by the pace of the tracks, The Mute figured that Truck had been in too much of a hurry to set traps this time. That he'd probably been more concerned about getting in, getting out, and facing down the attackers headed toward his farmhouse.

The Mute felt his stomach clench suddenly. *Nervous? You?* he thought. And he had to admit that he was. It had been two weeks since the attack on Truck's farm, two weeks since Leonard Truckson had finally been pulled, kicking and shooting, off the face of this earth. Two weeks since a little girl had been deposited deep underground with, The Mute knew, a very dangerous animal.

If I keep going, he thought, *what will I find?*

He took a breath and stepped forward. Then another step. Then he broke into a light jog. Two weeks was long enough for any little girl to have to wait for a rescue.

A moment later, he found his way blocked by a narrow metal door. Reinforced and built into rock. Impenetrable without heavy digging equipment or small explosives. Of course, explosives in this tunnel could bring the whole place crashing down.

No place left to go.

The Mute stood very still and listened. Maybe he could hear signs of life on the other side of that door. He held his breath and waited, but there was nothing. The only sound that filled his ears was his own heartbeat. He pressed the side of his head against the heavy steel and still heard no sounds whatever.

Dead? he thought, but quickly dismissed that notion, simply because he didn't want to believe it. *Sleeping,* he decided. *Resting.*

He began inspecting the door more closely. There were three dead bolts situated strategically along the edge, and that made The Mute start cursing the stupid Samuel Hill character all over again. Besides the one Truck himself kept, there was only one other key for those locks, he knew. It had been hidden in the collectible book of Edgar Allan Poe works, and Sam Hill had managed to lose it in the angry wash of a woman scorned.

The Mute ran a hand along the edges of the doorframe and was surprised to discover it was an airtight construction.

On the one hand, that would be good for keeping toxic fumes—like, say, smoke and ash—out of the bunker on the other side of the door. On the other hand, how would anyone inside get clean air? Was that part of the plan? Had Truck intended for his girl to either be rescued or, if that weren't possible, to slowly suffocate down here, deep underground?

Maybe there's an underground stream pulling air and water into this place, The Mute thought. Then he had to face the obvious. *Or maybe not.*

The Mute knelt down in front of the door, forcing himself to be patient, to think.

He considered simply banging on the door, hoping to get the attention of the little girl inside, but he soon dismissed that notion. If Truck had locked his girl in this place, he'd given her strict instructions about getting out. She was a smart kid, The Mute knew that. She probably wouldn't answer unless she heard

Truck's voice accompanying the pounding. And even then she'd demand a safe code, even from Truck. Being unable to speak was a distinct disadvantage in that regard. How to call out a safe code through a steel door when heavy breathing was the loudest noise your throat was able to make? If the edges of this door weren't airtight, he could've written the safe code on a slip of paper, slid it underneath the door when he knocked, as a means of allaying the girl's fears. But that too was not an option, and that meant banging on the door had to be ruled out as well.

No, he thought, *pounding on the door would just scare the child. Possibly make her do something desperate, or dangerous, or both.*

He needed the key, the one that Truck left specifically for this purpose. The one that Samuel Hill was supposed to deliver.

The Mute placed a hand on the Kahr handgun strapped to his thigh and briefly entertained the idea of simply blowing a bullet through each of the three dead bolt locks, but that too he dismissed quickly. For starters, if they managed to burst through the locks, there was no telling where the bullets would end up on the other side of the door. One could just as easily lodge itself in the girl, or the dog, as it could in a wall or floor. Also, a quick study of the satin nickel plating on these heavy dead bolts made The Mute suspect that Truck had had enough foresight to use bulletproof door locks for his bunker. The Mute didn't want a slug ricocheting off the door and back into the tunnel where he was kneeling.

He let his head drop. This was starting to seem hopeless, impossible. Truck should have known better. Should have sent someone better, someone who at least had a voice to speak with.

In his head, he heard one of Truck's lectures from back during their time in Iraq together. Truck always grinned when he gave those lectures, an expression that gave both encouragement and a challenge. He saw Truck's face grinning at him now.

If it were easy, anybody could do it. But you're not just anybody, and nobody can do what you can do. So stop crying for Mama and get the job done, soldier. That's an order.

The Mute felt like crying anyway, not because he couldn't break down the door, but because he remembered what a difference that ornery old man had made in his life. Saving him, and resaving him. Making him more than he thought he could ever be.

De Oppresso Liber.

Truck had lived by that motto, and he'd taught The Mute what it meant to do that day by day, hour by hour.

Cursed old man. The Mute grinned at the memory. *Cursed, wonderful old man.*

He settled back on his heels and took new stock of the obstacle in front of him. He knew where the girl was hidden. He knew she had the dog with her, a risky move, but also one with a potentially high upside. That dog, under Truck's command, was as much a soldier as any man he knew. And that dog was smart. Smarter than a lot of men. If Truck had taught the girl how to control the dog, then she had a powerful ally beside her in this bunker. Plus, she was in a place that would be nearly impossible for Truck's attackers to find, let alone break in to.

For the moment, she was *safe*.

The Mute stood, never taking his eyes off the door.

He needed the key, so he would get the key. Samuel Hill's ex-wife had it. It would be short work to find out who that woman was, where she lived, where she worked. So instead of waiting for the key to come to him, he would go to the key. He'd find Ex–Mrs. Samuel Hill and convince her to give it to him.

He turned and began walking back up the tunnel, making plans for how to disguise the entrance once more, to hide it from others who might be trying to find it. And then he had an uncomfortable thought.

Others were trying to find this hiding place, and that meant that eventually their search would lead them to the key that Ex–Mrs. Samuel Hill had stolen from her husband. What if they got to her first, got to the key first?

The Mute frowned.

Then he started to run.

21

ANNABEL

Date Unknown

I can't sleep, not while that dog is still sleeping. Not while he refuses to wake up.

After the final tremors of the seizure finished with him, the animal sunk his head off my lap and slid into a heavy mess on the floor. He breathed hard a few times, then scootched next to my chair and curled to keep warm. The dog's eyes were opened now, focused on me, blinking slowly. He made no sound.

I thought about gettin' up, gettin' one of them sleeping bags, and covering the dog over with it, but he kept looking at me like it was a comfort that I was near, like he just wanted to rest but didn't want to have to worry about me or what I was doing. So I just sat there and watched him breathe. Some minutes later, the dog's eyes shut tight and stayed that way. The tenseness in its forepaws and shoulders loosened, and it slept. He slept.

No, he didn't just sleep. This time that dog went away in

sleep, like he was knocked out or drugged or absent from the body that kept him.

I got up from my seat and, by accident, bumped the animal with a leg of my chair. Thumped him right in the middle of the rib cage curled outward while he slept. I expected he'd jump up, alert, ready to attack, ready to find out what had so rudely smacked his side while he was sleeping. But the dog didn't budge, didn't even respond. It was as if he didn't feel the intrusion, or if he did, he weren't capable of doing anything about it.

Normally this dog sleeps so light that just about anything makes his head pop up to survey the circumstances before he returns back to sleep. Normally all it takes is the rustle of my clothing or the clink of the water bucket or sometimes even just the sound of me turning a page in a book. But not now, not this time.

"Dog." I said it out loud, normal voice. He didn't move.

"Dog!" I shouted it this time. Same result.

"*Geht!*" I said. Then "*Komm her!*"

But the dog was dead to me, dead to the world, lost somewhere in the between-places that happen when you sleep. And now I knew that something was seriously wrong with that dog. The seizure was frightening, yes, but this inanimate animal scared me more. Was he in a coma? Was he gonna die?

Had my blood poisoned my dog?

I finally did go get a sleeping bag, finally did cover it over the dog just to keep him warm in this cool place. Then I sat on a bunk and pulled a sleeping bag over myself too, waiting, watching to see what would happen with that dog. But he didn't move, didn't even seem to dream. No twitching. No flickering behind his eyelids. No low growls lost in some nighttime vision. If I hadn't seen the slight rustle of the sleeping bag each time he took a breath, I might have thought he was forever gone already.

What do I do if this dog up and dies on me? I thought.

That was something that Truck surely hadn't prepared for. How long would it be before a dog carcass would smell up this room, before it would make me sick just to be near it?

I almost laughed at that thought. Honestly, wearing these clothes for as long as I had, living in this place with no shower or bathtub, I was pretty sure I wasn't no sweet daisy perfume myself. But again, you get used to yourself and your own smells. And I tried to keep things clean as I could with just a bucket of cold water and a few rags.

It could be worse, I decided. *I could be knocked out in a coma like that dog.*

So I waited. So I still wait. Hoping that dog don't die, and surprised that I'm hoping that. It wasn't too long ago I was wishing death on him rather than having to be locked up in here with a crazy animal. Now I'm having second thoughts.

Thinking on that brings Marelda Gregor back to mind. She's always nearby down here in this lost place. I've done translated a good patch of her journal so far, and it seems like I'm doing it right, but some things she talks about are still confusing.

Blood-Eaters, for instance. Stem cells and physiatrical superintendence. Sacred relics. A man with a withered hand. DNA supra-actualization and neuroregenesis. That kind of stuff.

She talks about the Order of Heinrich von Bonn like everybody knows what it is, but I ain't never heard of that religion. Apparently, Dr. Johannes Schmitzden was the leader of it, and she was his follower. But Dr. Schmitzden, like Marelda Gregor, was also a biologist of some kind, so I can't figure whether these two was in a cult of some unknown flavor or if they was just research scientists. Maybe they was both. I'll have to keep translating to find out more, I guess.

I think about getting up and working more on Marelda

Gregor's journal, but I still can't stop watching that dog. Worrying.

It's funny how you can get worn out just doing nothing but sitting on a bunk bed watching a near-dead dog. I guess it's the hours of fretting that get to you, make you feel tense and bothered, make you start wishing you could just relax and close your eyes, just for a minute or two.

With my eyes shut, I can hear the soft hum of the battery lights and the shallow puffs of breath slipping out the dog's nose at regular intervals. I start counting the puffs like counting sheep.

One.

Two.

Three . . .

Forty-eight . . .

Ninety-six . . .

When I open my eyes again, the dog is sitting on his haunches, right next to the bed, staring at me.

"So I guess we both slept," I say through a yawn.

The dog just looks at me, and I remember that it has now been hours and hours since either of us has eaten anything. Almost as if on cue, the animal licks his lips.

I give him a good, hard look. He seems downright normal again, like nothing ever happened. Eyes bright and attentive. Intelligent. Body sleek and muscular again, not uncoordinated and ill. Whatever happened, he appears to be over it. And he appears to be hungry.

"Right," I say. "Food. Got it."

A moment later, the dog is wolfing down canned tuna and a row of crackers, eating like he hasn't had food in weeks. He finishes so fast, I go ahead and give him my can of tuna too, and I head back to the shelf for an MRE with mystery meat and vegetables. The dog digs into the second helping of tuna and then freezes, mid-chew, swinging his heavy head toward the door.

"What's on, Dog?"

The dog swallows his current mouthful and looks over at me. I can see a snarl forming on his face, teeth just getting tempted to bare themselves at something.

Dog abandons his tuna and turns toward the door. No growl, just full attention, fangs slightly showing, tail standing at high alert. I start to say something, then figure I'd better take a cue from the guard animal. I keep still and silent.

Is that a noise outside the door?

There was a brushing sound, or at least I think there was. It happened so fast and quiet, I can't be sure, except that my dog responded to it. My animal steps quickly toward the locked metal entryway and leans into a crouch, tail vibrating, ready to attack.

For several minutes, nothing happens, no noise, no movement. Then the dog finally lets his tail dip to half mast, relaxes a bit, and steps closer to the door. He starts sniffing, trying to discern something with just his nose.

"Dog," I whisper. He ignores me.

Was someone here? Was someone finally here? Just outside that door?

"Dog." I whisper it again, more forcefully. He turns toward me with a question mark in his eyes.

"*Komm her*," I say softly. For some reason, it don't feel safe with the dog so close to the door right now. My animal responds immediately, trotting to my side, where he sits back on his haunches, ears pricked high, eyes still focused intently on the steel door.

Should I open the door? I think. *Unlock the bolts and take a quick peek outside? What if it's Truck out there, finally comin' to get me?*

But my uncle's last words to me stick in my head.

Don't open that door for anybody, you got it? Not even me, not unless you hear me say the safe code.

There's a moment more of heavy breathing on my side of the door, then without warning, my dog suddenly relaxes completely. His ears flick backward and his muscled torso returns to rest. He lies down on the floor beside me and even lets his tail swish once, side to side.

Whatever it was that got him all alert and interested ain't an issue no more.

I feel a pang of loss, like I might've missed an important opportunity. That's quickly replaced by a pang of fear, like I might've just missed something awful and dangerous. But it don't matter, because there ain't nothing but me and that dog in here. Just us two, nothing more.

I feel myself release a sigh. The dog looks up at me, then at the leftovers of his dinner. He licks his lips.

"Okay," I say. *"Nimm futter."* Eat your food. That dog don't wait for a second command. He leaves my side and returns to his business with the tuna. I don't wait for him to finish before returning to my own meal, but it's tasteless to me. I only eat it because I know my body needs it, because my stomach is burnin' for it.

There was something out there, right? Something that brushed up against my door and set off all kind of alarms in my German shepherd's head. Was that right? Or was it just my desperate imagination at work again?

I put away the refuse from our meal, dumping cans and such down one of the holes in the outhouse. But my mind keeps working the puzzle.

Maybe it was nothing. Probably it was nothing.

Maybe it was just some woodland animal. A squirrel or skunk

or something, just accidentally scraped outside my door, lost in this tunnel, trying to find its way out again.

Maybe there wasn't no noise at all. Probably that was true.

Probably I just imagined it like I imagined them random ghosts. My mind using my senses to play another mean trick on me.

Or maybe . . .

Maybe I'm gonna be trapped inside this bunker forever.

22

TRUDI

Sunday, September 20

It was a few minutes before 2:00 a.m. when Trudi pulled Samuel's Ford GT into the parking lot of the strip mall where Coffey & Hill Investigations kept its offices. The only other car in the lot was that same beat-up Toyota truck that had been left there for a few weeks now, obviously broken down and abandoned, for the time being at least.

Still, Trudi sat in the car for a moment before risking the first step out. Things were always well lit in this neighborhood, something she was suddenly grateful for. She waited, checked her mirrors, looked for any sign of Dr. Smith or one of his goons in the vicinity. The offices that shared this little lot with hers—a florist, an independent hair salon, and an insurance agency—were all dark, closed. The parking lot at the Tire South shop next door to her strip mall was empty, as was the Express Oil Change on the other side. Behind her, in the large

Kroger parking lot across the street, Arby's was closed. Taco Bell had lights on but was also unpopulated. There were a few cars scattered in the rest of the Kroger lot over there, but that place too seemed relatively abandoned for the night.

Safe, she said to herself. *No worries. Stop being paranoid, Tru-Bear, and get out of the car.*

She popped the lock on the GT and stepped onto the pavement. No shots rang out. No bad men jumped at her from behind the thick shrubbery that landscaped the bank side of this strip mall parking lot. She was alone.

She sighed in spite of herself and headed toward the office door. She was annoyed when she discovered that it was unlocked, then remembered that she'd left it that way when she and Samuel had made flight for Birmingham. She stepped in the door and locked it behind her. She wouldn't be long, but she didn't want anyone sneaking up on her through an unlocked opening anyway.

She paused inside the reception area, checking for other signs of entry, just in case she wasn't alone in here after all. Everything seemed clear, just as she'd left it. She did the routine, checking and clearing of each room in the office before venturing to relax. Only when she was certain the place was indeed empty did she allow herself to sit at her desk, to relax, and to get organized.

It had taken almost a week before she felt ready to escape from Samuel Hill's clutches.

Well, *escape* was probably a strong word—it's not like Sam was holding her prisoner. But it helped her to think of it that way when she was planning this little detour. Really, all she wanted to do was get here to her office, pick up her gun, and then get back to the hotel in Birmingham before Samuel had a chance to wake up and realize she was gone. But in order to do that, she had to spend time studying her man again, familiarizing herself with his routines and weaknesses, understanding his personality quirks and then deciding how to use them to her advantage. Fortunately, thanks to nearly eight years of marriage as background work, she was a quick study.

Samuel was a smart and capable person, but he wasn't her jailer. In fact, he didn't even feel the need to keep an eye on her when she left the room or stood right behind him, looking over his shoulder at some obscure fact he'd ferreted out online. Trust, that was his weakness. In spite of everything, he still trusted her. He assumed that she was still his partner, that she would never betray him or go rogue without warning him.

At night, when he came back from picking up takeout dinner, he simply dropped his car keys on the desk near the hotel room door and forgot about them until he needed them next. And each night when Trudi was the one to go out and pick up dinner, she did the same. One night she told Samuel she had a craving for grilled quail (and really, didn't he want a rib eye steak instead of a burger for once?) from Highlands Bar and Grill on 11th Avenue South. He agreed, so she preordered their dinner, then casually picked up his keys and left on the errand.

What she didn't tell Samuel was that, on her way to pick up the quail and rib eye takeout she'd called in, she stopped at the tiny locksmith shop on 14th Avenue and had a spare key made for Samuel's GT. She also bought a magnetic hide-a-key container there. She put the new key in the container and stuck it under the front bumper of the car, ready for her whenever she needed to make her move.

Step two was a little harder. It involved getting a pair of jeans, a sweater, and slip-on shoes hidden under the seat of the car, hidden in a way that Samuel wouldn't accidently discover them. She finally settled on rolling each clothing item into a tight cylinder, and then wedging them under the passenger seat, high and toward the front. She figured Sam would never ride in that seat and so he wouldn't move it forward or backward to accommodate his long legs. If the seat didn't move, neither would the clothes. She was ready.

And so, last night, Saturday night, she put on her satin pajamas, just like every other night they'd spent in this hotel room. She'd retreated to her bed and tried to sleep, wanting to actually rest a bit before driving all night long. She'd heard Samuel watch the news on TV, then heard a bit of one of the late night sports shows before he finally shut out the light and went to bed. She checked the clock. It was 11:22 p.m.

She heard him let out an extended sigh, a cleansing breath that usually preceded the time when he would fall asleep. She heard his breathing slacken, become shallow and even. In the darkness, she peered toward him and tried to tell if his legs were twitching yet. At 11:31 p.m., she was fairly certain he was out, but she waited until 11:45 p.m. just to be sure. If he wasn't asleep, he was putting on a pretty good act.

She slid out from under the covers on her bed and moved toward the door. She slipped a hotel room key card into the waistband of her pajamas but didn't bother with anything else. She was in the hallway as silently as a cat, holding down the room's door handle so the latch wouldn't make a "click" when she brought it to a close. Then she waited. If Samuel was aware of anything, he'd come out that door within the next two minutes, so she started counting the seconds backward.

One hundred twenty. One nineteen. One eighteen.

Down the hall she heard a door open and shut. She decided to ignore it. A tired-looking businessman stepped into the hallway, tapping on the end of a pack of Camels.

Ninety-seven. Ninety-six.

The businessman stopped when he saw her, did a double

take, then relaxed into a light grin. He nodded approvingly in her direction.

Eighty. Seventy-nine.

Out of the corner of her eye, she saw him dig in his pocket and come out with green paper. He walked in her direction, flashing a $20 bill. She rolled her eyes.

Fifty-two. Fifty-one. Fifty.

He pressed the money into her hand as he walked by. "When you're finished here," he whispered in what she assumed must've been his sexy voice, "come on down to room 321."

Trudi said nothing, and the man took that to be approval. He walked on past, letting his non-cigarette-hand stray across her pajamas as he moved down the hall. Trudi wanted to kick him in the groin and leave him groaning on the freshly vacuumed hotel carpet, but she resisted. *Perverted, lonely guy sees a woman standing in the hallway in satin pajamas. Of course he'll assume sex worker,* she told herself. She didn't look like a nun, she knew, but it still made her angry. Why couldn't a woman just be a woman? Why always a sex tool? She tried to shrug it off and focus on the task at hand.

Twenty. Nineteen. Eighteen. Seventeen.

After two full minutes had lapsed, Trudi figured it was time to go. She hurried down to Samuel's car, getting an odd look from the night clerk when she passed through the lobby, but gratefully avoiding the skeevy gent from room 321. At the car, she rescued her hidden key and then discreetly changed into the jeans and sweater in the empty parking lot. She was gone by midnight. Two hours later, she'd pulled up to her detective office in Atlanta, ready to get her gun.

Now Trudi settled into the chair behind her desk and felt complete, at least for the moment. This was where she belonged, where she'd felt most comfortable in the days, weeks, years since

Samuel left. Her home was nice, no doubt, but also an empty space with too many reminders that it was supposed to be filled by a family. This place, though, her office, her desk, had always been just hers. Even when Samuel had worked here, he'd been banished across the hall to what was now just a cluttered store-room of miscellaneous junk.

She inhaled and felt the old familiar thrill of the room. It was the wee hours of the morning, but just sitting here made Trudi want to get back to work.

They'd made progress on two fronts over the past ten/eleven days in Birmingham's DoubleTree Inn, but still nothing that rang of finality. At first, they tried to share Samuel's laptop, but that had gotten old, fast. So after a few days, Trudi's ex-husband had gone out and bought her an off-the-rack HP machine from the nearest Office Depot. It wasn't as powerful as the one she kept here in Atlanta, but it worked well enough to be useful. She set up a remote office in their hotel room and joined Samuel in the work.

She surveyed her own desk now, her real desk, and smiled inside. She was tired of working on that Office Depot laptop, sitting in a stale hotel room, always aware of Samuel doing similar work so close by that it was annoying.

Most people were surprised when they found out how boring detective work really was. It was more drudgery than excitement by a factor of ten or so. Hours, sometimes days, spent picking line by line through a phone record. Expanding eons doing nothing more than tracking down city real estate tax records or combing through ancestry records on the internet, trying to figure out who was related to whom, where they last lived, and who might have been in some kind of contact with the object of your search.

Having Samuel Hill on your team certainly made a difference, because he knew people who knew people, and because he himself was "people" with a range of access to otherwise private documents. So that helped, but still, when it came to Leonard Truckson and Dr. Jonathan Smith, the going was slow.

At this point they'd uncovered one very good lead in regard to Truck but only hearsay and rumors about Dr. Smith.

As for Truck, they'd tracked down one of his men from the time he was stationed in Iraq, a southern boy named Rendel Jackson-Fife. A name like that might have been a badge of character in the Deep South, but it was like a lighthouse beacon in the stormy seas of private investigation. Name like that was hard to hide, hard to take off the grid.

They'd tracked young Rendel from Fallujah to Fort Bliss in Texas, to an honorable discharge, to a post-military career as a roughneck in the Port Arthur area of the Texas Gulf. Samuel had recognized the oil company that employed Mr. Jackson-Fife; he'd worked for that outfit himself during summers at college. Now they just had to track down Jackson-Fife's whereabouts after he left the roughneck world and disappeared into society about four and a half years ago. A good lead.

As for Dr. Smith, the rumors were hard to sift. The best they could arrive at was a cloudy history behind the Iron Curtain, where he'd been educated as a medical research scientist, possibly doing work in stem cell studies. After the end of the Cold War, after the Berlin Wall came down in 1989, his whereabouts got fuzzy until sometime in the mid-1990s. Then he turned up in Iraq as a bureaucrat at a research hospital that was somehow remotely associated with Fallujah General Hospital and had blurry ties to Abu Ghraib prison. The name of the research hospital, and Dr. Smith's name, showed up in some classified records that Samuel dug up, but the address or exact nature of the research done there was still a mystery to them. For now.

Trudi restarted her desktop computer out of habit, then stopped herself.

It was 2:20 in the morning. Samuel was a predictable riser. With or without an alarm clock, his bladder usually got him up right around 6:00 a.m., and that was when he started his day. With that in mind, Trudi figured she needed to be back in her DoubleTree Inn bed by 5:00 a.m. at the latest. It was a two-hour drive from Atlanta to Birmingham. That meant she'd have to get out of here before 3:00 a.m., and really, she ought to leave by 2:30 a.m. to give herself some leeway in case something unexpected happened.

She turned from the computer and slid open the drawer that held her Beretta 3032 Tomcat pistol. She loved this little weapon. Contoured tang. Notched rear sight and blade front sight. Lightweight yet powerful. Easy to conceal. It was every-thing she needed and wanted in a gun.

She paused a second to choose between her ankle holster and the hybrid hip holster before finally settling on the hybrid. It fit snugly and comfortably behind the back waistband of her jeans, without bulging too noticeably on the outside or pressing too deeply into her skin on the inside.

She slid the gun in the holster, secured the holster inside the back of her jeans, and stood. She'd gotten what she came for; now it was time to go. She let her eyes sweep the top of her desk in one last, longing look.

Then she frowned.

When Dr. Smith and that goon Samir had abducted her from her house, she'd had to leave her cell phone at home on the kitchen counter. She was certain of that.

So why was that selfsame cell now sitting prettily beside her desk phone, as if placed there like a vase of flowers, waiting to be appreciated?

She glanced at the clock on the wall and decided to risk a few minutes more.

Trudi passed over the cell phone for the moment and instead brought up the archived video surveillance footage from the past few weeks. She quickly searched through the files until she came to the one marked "Monday, September 7."

She clicked play.

23

THE MUTE

Trudi Sara Coffey.

That was the name of Samuel Hill's ex-wife. Once The Mute had the name, it was fairly easy work to track her down to Atlanta, Georgia. She had a modest but reasonably nice home in an old neighborhood on the northwest edges of the city's center. She kept an office in a small strip mall less than three miles from her home. She ran a small detective firm, Coffey & Hill Investigations, out of that office. When The Mute saw "Hill" in the name of her business, he figured Samuel Hill had lost more than just a wife in his divorce. He almost felt sorry for the grunt.

The Mute had arrived in Atlanta late Friday night. He'd thought about getting a hotel but knew he'd feel better sleeping in his Jeep Wrangler with his guns and supplies in close reach.

He kept his SIG716 sniper rifle under the seat, with ammo in the glove box. He'd brought along both live rounds and rubber bullets for the SIG on this trip. In an urban setting, it was often better to subdue with rubber bullets than to kill with real ones. Hard to move a body, and with security cameras everywhere, hard to avoid being seen with the gun that killed the body. But if you just scared that body, bruised it, and let it leave the scene under its own power, then the shooting hardly ever got reported to police, which meant authorities almost never checked that ubiquitous surveillance footage and saw that you were the guy with the gun.

Also in the glove box was his .22 short mini-revolver with spare ammunition. It had been uncomfortable to drive the freeway with it stuck inside his boot, so he'd put it in the glove compartment. He kept the Kahr handgun nearby but had taken it out of the leg holster and instead tucked it inside the side waistband on his pants. His knife, as always, hung low inside his shirt on a thick metal chain wrapped around his neck.

The first thing he did in Atlanta was stop at a Burger King and get something to eat. There he called up the address for Trudi Coffey's home on his military-issue portable GPS device. It looked to be a small house on Center Street Northwest, in the West Midtown section of Atlanta. He studied the surrounding area, checking entry and exit arteries and noting nearby landmarks. He also correlated it with the woman's office on Howell Mill Road Northwest, diagramming routes, estimating traffic, memorizing the whole map in case he needed to have it at hand in a hurry. Then he drove around to the Coffey home to scout out the neighborhood.

He cruised straight through first, getting a sense for the layout and the general tenor of the area. It appeared to be a basic residential honeycomb. Judging by the abundance of mature trees growing everywhere, and the quaint, efficient architecture of the homes, The Mute guessed this neighborhood had been built sometime in the 1930s or 1940s, endured a decline, and then been slowly renovated over the decades. Now it was a simple, homey, middle-class enclave in this big city. Most houses were darkened for the night, and plenty of family cars were parked up and down the street. The only vehicle that seemed out of place here was an expensive Audi TT RS sports car parked just around the corner, at the end of Coffey's street.

A midlife crisis car for some suburban dad? The Mute wondered at first.

Then he noticed that the car was parked uncomfortably close to the stop sign at the corner. He soon surmised that the parking spot its driver had chosen would be mostly out of sight from the front of Trudi Coffey's house but would keep her painted-red front door and slightly creaky porch swing still in view of the driver. When he saw the glowing red dot of a cigarette butt flash hot and then fade in the darkened car, his suspicions were confirmed.

Somebody out there, probably the same somebody behind the attack on Truck's farm, was keeping an eye on Trudi Coffey. Or staking out her home, waiting for her to return. That made more sense, considering the outcome of the raid that killed his commander.

The Mute drove out of the neighborhood, then circled back in until he was obscured from obvious sight lines inside the Audi but still able to watch that car from his own vehicle.

When you can't find the hen, he thought, *you follow the fox that's hunting the hen.*

He settled in behind the steering wheel and let his mind drift toward blankness. Spending long days and nights at Truck's security outpost, he'd learned how to almost sleep-wake, letting his body relax into a near-sleep state, staying just focused enough to come alert at any sign of trouble or any movement that was out of the ordinary. That was the talent he used now, giving his body rest in the night while also staying just watchful enough to be of use in this impromptu stakeout.

Around 6:00 a.m. on Saturday morning, a slate gray BMW 7 Series car pulled slowly into the neighborhood and parked behind the Audi. The BMW driver got out and walked to the window of the other car. The Mute watched the two drivers talk for a minute or two and then saw the Audi start up and pull away. The BMW driver got back in his car and nudged forward until he took over the prime parking spot.

So, Trudi Coffey isn't here, The Mute told himself, *and she's been gone long enough that they have a stakeout rotation working on the home. Likely there's a similar stakeout at her office. So which location should I be watching? And for how long?*

He decided to wait through this day in this place to see what might happen. Then he let his eyes close for a nap. The hours passed uneventfully, with a few breaks for food and bathroom duties. The Mute was always careful to leave and enter this neighborhood out of view of his quarry and made sure never to park in the same place twice. Suburbanites like the folks in this block might be the suspicious type.

It had been just after 8:00 p.m. Saturday night when The Mute finally saw something worth waiting for. A black Mercedes GL-Class SUV had rolled into the neighborhood and parked right next to the BMW.

I know that car, The Mute thought. He sat up for a closer look, eventually taking the scope off his sniper rifle to use as a telescope. Things were getting interesting.

Sure enough, through the rifle sight, The Mute made out a familiar face. A Middle Eastern man, with an Americanized style. Muscular and well-dressed. The same bodyguard who had surveyed the aftermath of the attack on Truck's farm alongside the old man with the cane. Above the Arab's neatly trimmed beard, The Mute could make out bruises under the eyes and a small, X-shaped bandage taped across the bridge of his nose. If it wasn't broken, it had almost been.

Wonder what the other guy from that fight looks like? The Mute thought absently before focusing on the man's eyes. Despite the wounded nose, the eyes were clear, alert, and busy.

The Arab spoke sharply to the driver in the BMW, and it was clear the Arab was in charge. After a moment, both cars pulled away from the curb and headed out toward the main roads.

The Mute moved into action, following the mini-convoy from a distance, trying hard to keep them in sight without letting himself be seen. After only a minute or two, at one indistinguishable point, the BMW split off from the Mercedes, leaving The Mute to decide which car was worth following and which one wasn't. He took a peek at the GPS map in his head and realized that the Mercedes was on a route toward Trudi Coffey's office building. He followed the Mercedes.

It was only about five minutes more before The Mute and the Arab both arrived at the Kroger grocery store on Howell Mill Road Northwest, situated across the street from Coffey & Hill Investigations. The Mercedes was not as careful about staying out of view, and parked itself at the edge of the grocery lot, next to an Arby's fast-food restaurant, where it faced toward the front door of Trudi Coffey's office across the street. Whether that position was from carelessness or arrogance, The Mute couldn't tell. But it was obvious that if Trudi Coffey came to her office, the Arab would see it happen.

What the Mercedes wouldn't see, might not ever notice, was the Jeep Wrangler that followed it into the Kroger shopping center. There was a Taco Bell located just north of the Arby's in the grocery lot, so The Mute parked his car behind the burrito palace, out of sight of the Mercedes but still able to keep a nice, side-angle view of the tiny parking area in front of Coffey & Hill Investigations.

A few moments later, the man inside the Mercedes never knew when The Mute, wearing dark jeans and a sea-green jean jacket, exited his Wrangler and used parked cars to cover his movement in order to get a closer look. When he was only about ten yards away, The Mute paused and stared through the darkness into the Mercedes, reading movements, studying gestures.

It was the same Arab, all right. He was watching Coffey & Hill Investigations with a singular focus, unaware that other people were in the parking lot around him. The Mute guessed he could probably walk right up to the man and never be noticed until he'd fired a bullet right into the man's skull.

Guy deserves worse than that, The Mute told himself, *after desecrating Truck's body like he did.* But The Mute knew he wouldn't do it, not here, at least. Not where surveillance cameras from the nearby fast-food restaurants would see him commit the crime. Not in a place where the body would be found and explanations would be demanded.

The Mute circled back to his Jeep without being seen. He popped inside Taco Bell and bought a XXL Grilled Stuft Burrito and large Mountain Dew to go, then returned to his parked car and settled in for the night.

He pulled the sniper rifle out from under the seat, keeping it low and out of sight of random passersby. Without looking, he loaded the SIG with rubber bullets, then returned the gun to its home beneath the bench. He might not kill this arrogant bodyguard tonight, but he might have a chance to hurt him a little, to scare him. Maybe add to the pain that somebody caused when they broke the man's nose.

That thought made The Mute smile. He reached into the

Taco Bell bag and chomped down on a few bites of his burrito. It was good and helped him unwind. He chewed slowly and let his mind relax, let his senses savor the moment. He would wait and watch. Maybe something would happen in this place, here, tonight.

It was just a few minutes before 2:00 a.m., in the wee hours of Sunday morning, when The Mute saw a silver Ford GT sports car pull into the parking lot of the strip mall across the street. The rest of the world around him was silent, empty, unmoving. Nothing happened for a moment or two, and then the car door opened on the GT.

The Mute sat up in his seat, eyes taking in the prelude to drama happening on the other side of the road.

A woman got out of the car.

24

TRUDI

The emotional part of Trudi Coffey wanted to just pick up that cell phone and begin inspecting it to see why it had been left here for her to discover. The intellectual side of her knew that was a bad idea. As her old PI mentor had taught her, it was always better to get background on anything unusual rather than just diving in and seeing what happens. So her first act was to try to put this telephone thing in some sort of context. She let her mind run through the sequence of events from recent days, following the mobile phone on expected paths.

The last person to see this cell had to have been Dr. Jonathan Smith, she said to herself, *at my home, in my kitchen, while I was otherwise occupied with his stupid goon, Samir.* So that was where she intended to start.

She cued up the surveillance footage from Coffey & Hill cameras on Labor Day and then began scanning the video. It wasn't long before she saw herself enter the office, captive of

Dr. Smith and his goon. She fast-forwarded through the elec-trocution; she'd seen that firsthand already. Then, after seeing her and Samuel run out of the office to safety, she set the video to normal speed once more. She studied the two unconscious men left in her office, waiting to see what had happened next.

After only a moment or two, Dr. Smith started twitching, and then he sat up creakily on the floor.

The old man was tougher than she'd thought. Trudi couldn't tell if she was impressed or disappointed by this new fact. She decided to be both.

A moment later, Samir came up suddenly, shouting. It looked as if Samuel might have broken his nose. Trudi hoped that was the case. The Arab was apparently angry at the treatment, and angrier at having been beaten so easily by her ex-husband.

"This guy hates to lose," Trudi whispered to herself. "Have to remember that in case I meet Dr. Smith's goon again sometime in the future."

Whatever it was the old man said, it calmed his associate down long enough for him to go to the little bathroom in the office and clean himself up a bit. While he was gone, Trudi watched Dr. Smith recover his senses. He stood and made his way—albeit unsteadily—around until he was behind Trudi's desk. She noticed that he seemed to need the cane this time. That made her feel slightly pleased.

He didn't touch anything, but she could see her visitor's eyes inspecting the setup from her side of the desk, figuring out exactly how she'd prewired her office to run electricity through the guest chairs. After a moment, he looked around the corners of the room until he spotted the surveillance camera. He nodded toward the camera with a slight tilt of the head, as if tipping a hat in her direction.

When Samir returned, he looked better but now had two

black eyes forming and a bandage on his nose. Trudi squinted at the man and realized he'd reset his nose all by himself while in the bathroom. "High tolerance for pain," she muttered. "Another thing to remember about this guy."

There was a moment when the two men seemed to be arguing. From what Trudi could tell, Samir wanted to trash the office, but the old man wasn't ready for that, not yet. When they'd reached an agreement, the old man sent Samir out into the lobby.

It was then that Trudi saw Dr. Smith reach inside his coat pocket and produce her cell phone.

She saw him begin checking out the contents and cursed herself for turning off lock mode on the phone when she was at her home. *Bad habit*, she told herself, but it was too late, the damage was done. Still, she always kept in mind that a mobile phone was easy to lose, so she deliberately kept only the barest minimum of information on there. What would he find, really? Speed dial to Menchie's frozen yogurt? A grocery list on her note pad? Her Wordament high score?

After only a moment, Dr. Smith seemed to arrive at the same conclusion that Trudi had just reached. There was nothing of value to be found on this little piece of equipment. He looked up into the camera again, then he reached down and picked up the landline telephone sitting on her desk. He dialed a number, and Trudi saw her cell phone flash to life.

He's calling my cell, even though it's right there in his hand?

Dr. Smith never took his eyes off the camera while he spoke into the voicemail box that eventually answered her mobile phone. She tried to read his lips, but that was a skill she'd never mastered. After he was done with the message, Smith hung up the desk phone. Then he held the cell phone where the camera would clearly see it and made a show of shutting it off and then placing it carefully on the desk next to the landline.

Just then, Samir reentered the scene, swirling his fingers and pointing toward the door. The old man nodded, and in a moment they were gone.

"Must've heard the police coming," Trudi said to herself. When uniformed officers entered the scene a few minutes later, she knew she was right. She switched off the video and let it revert to real-time images. She could guess what happened next. Atlanta's finest had checked through the office, found nothing out of the ordinary, took a few notes for a report they'd have to file later, and then went on their merry way.

Trudi looked at the cell phone still sitting placidly on her desktop.

"So, you left me a message," she said to the now-invisible Dr. Smith. "Interesting play."

She reached for the cell and held it in her hands. She powered it on and tapped it to bring up the home screen. She was just about to hit the voicemail button when something on the computer caught her eye.

In the real-time surveillance image that flicked on the screen, she saw movement outside. It took a moment for the face to fully register, and then it came to her like a bolt.

Samir the bodyguard was striding angrily across her parking lot and toward the front door of Coffey & Hill Investigations.

25

THE MUTE

The Mute watched the Arab crossing the street in front of him and decided it was time to act. He reached under the bench seat of the Wrangler and retrieved his sniper rifle, unlatching the safety without bothering to look at it.

He exited his vehicle, never letting his eyes stray from the figure now walking away from him, carefully choosing appropriate targets on the back of the man's body. With rubber bullets, he wanted to hinder this guy, not murder him. But it would also have to be enough to stop the threat to the woman. He identified spots that would hurt and temporarily disable but not cause the Arab to lose consciousness.

Kidneys. Back of the neck. Rib cage. Knees.

In the end, he settled on the right kidney, pulling it easily into his sights. He noticed the Arab nearing the front door of Coffey & Hill Investigations, saw the man reach inside his suit coat for what The Mute could only assume was a gun in a shoulder harness.

He fired, one silent crack of thunder that sent a rubber bullet toward its mark.

The Arab responded almost immediately, lurching forward and losing his gun in the process. He dropped to one knee, right hand pressed on his kidney where the bullet had struck. His eyes searched the area but never came in contact with his attacker. The Mute saw him measure the distance to his gun, now on the pavement about three feet away from him, so The Mute fired another shot.

The Arab's gun sparked and flew down the sidewalk, now well out of reach. The man rolled away from the shot until he was under the cover of the bumper on the silver GT in the parking lot.

Now the question was only this: did this Arab carry two guns or just the one?

The Mute waited. He saw his quarry steal a look out from behind the car and then dart back into cover. The idiot still hadn't identified where his attacker was stationed.

Amateur, The Mute muttered inside his head. *And if he's an amateur, chances are good that was his only gun.*

As if confirming that suspicion, the Arab lunged from behind the car, running toward the handgun on the pavement. The Mute almost laughed. He fired again, one shot into the hand outstretched for the gun on the ground, a second rubber bullet driven into the wobbly knee that tried to retreat after the failure of reaching the gun.

The Arab yelped and collapsed to the ground, where he immediately began crawling until he was safely back under the bumper of the GT.

The Mute heard a stream of profanities fly from behind the

car. Then, "Okay, you win! If you wanted me dead, you would have killed me already." There was a pause, and then hands raised above the sight line of the car. "I'm coming out."

The Arab stepped unsteadily into view, clearly favoring the left knee that was so recently abused by a rubber bullet. He looked out and around, still unsure where to find his attacker.

The Mute stood, rifle raised, and began crossing the street. When the two men were about ten feet apart, he stopped.

"Very nice shooting, American," the Arab said. "Rubber bullets?"

The Mute nodded, and the Arab returned the gesture.

"Now that we've moved from hot war to cold, Mr. America, is it okay with you if I put my hands down?"

The Mute didn't respond. The Arab held his pose for a moment, then slowly let his arms drop to his sides, watching for any objection. When none was given, he let his shoulders fully relax while reaching back to rub his bruised kidney. He tried a grin.

"Military man, clearly," he said with a friendly manner. "Army? Navy? Marines?" The Mute didn't answer, and the Arab shrugged. "I'll never understand why a man like you would fight for a country that enslaved your people like this one did. Still, there's no accounting for taste, right?"

Has just enough of an accent to give away his heritage in the Middle East, The Mute told himself, *but still speaks English well*. This was clearly an educated enemy, probably with a college degree from some university in Massachusetts or New York, and a student visa in his trash can back home.

"Well," the Arab said, "we can't stand here all night. What's your business, American?"

The Mute tilted his head toward the door of Coffey & Hill Investigations.

"Ah, the woman. I see." No one spoke for a moment, then,

"Well, while I appreciate your skill with that pop gun, I have business with that woman as well. I'm afraid my business must take precedence over yours. But I will make it worth your while."

He reached toward a pocket. The Mute prepared to fire another bullet. At close range, even a rubber bullet could do real damage, but if this guy was pulling a weapon, then The Mute didn't have much choice. The Arab saw the precariousness of his position and froze.

"No, no. No gun. See?" He slid only two fingers into his pocket and came out with a money clip. "How much is the right price, American? One thousand? Two?" He grinned lasciviously, then tossed the money clip at The Mute's feet. "Here, take it all. Ten thousand American dollars, plus a gold clip worth another thousand. All for you. And all you have to do is turn around and walk away from here. Easy, right?"

The Mute kicked the money clip under the Ford GT. Now the Arab frowned. No more pretense of friendship.

"You don't know what you are doing, American boy." He emphasized the word *boy*. Apparently he'd also studied American history. "Do you know who I am?"

The Mute shook his head.

"I am Samir Sadeq Hamza al-Sadr. Perhaps you know of my family, of my uncle? Yes, I see you know of us. Perhaps you learned of us firsthand when you and your country failed in Fallujah?"

The Mute felt like spitting.

So, this piece of work was part of the Sadr clan, part of Muqtada al-Sadr's Mahdi Army that had terrorized Iraq after the American invasion.

Muqtada al-Sadr's incitation to violence and aid to insurgents in Fallujah and Najaf had extended the war in Iraq by years and cost many innocent lives. Yet the man and his clan remained a strong political force in that country—and a ruthless power broker in the back alleys of that nation. The 2014 blitzkrieg of the Sunni-based Islamic State in Iraq and Syria had weakened al-Sadr's influence some, but the canny leader still was a force to deal with.

Fueled by steady streams of cash from Iran and by fiery, extremist rhetoric, the Mahdi Army had infiltrated Iraq's police forces and governmental infrastructures, which meant al-Sadr and his followers still held influence in many Shiite strongholds of Iraq. That included Baghdad proper and especially the slums of Sadr City, where a million or so Shiites revered him as a patriot and holy man.

"Now, take the money and go," the Arab was saying, "before I lose my patience with you. You have performed well. There is no shame in this."

Samir Sadeq Hamza al-Sadr took a step forward.

"The woman is necessary to me, to my family. She must suffer for insults to our great name." He paused to grimace and trace the outline of his broken nose with a long finger. Then, "Go, it is nothing to you. Go, American. Don't force me to make you suffer too."

The Mute lowered his rifle and watched as Samir's paternal frown relaxed into a smile.

"Yes, you know—"

To his credit, Samir didn't cry out when the butt of The Mute's rifle cracked across the bridge of his nose. He simply dropped to one knee, silent for a moment. Then he looked up through angry eyes and spat out a curse in Arabic. He stood.

"I should kill you, American," Samir said. "Maybe I will anyway."

The Mute fired a bullet at the man's ankle. Samir buckled but stayed upright. "What are you—"

The Mute fired again, this time near the other foot, then a second shot at the ground, causing Samir to leap into an impromptu little dance.

"American, you—"

The Mute shifted his stance, effectively quieting the Arab for the moment. Then he spun the rifle off his shoulder and let it clatter to the ground. Samir's eyes glittered.

"A man your size against little me?" he mocked. "How embarrassing for you when I slit your throat."

The Mute grinned. He felt pretty certain he could break this Samir's neck in hand-to-hand combat, but that wasn't in the plan, not tonight. He reached down to his hip and pulled out his Kahr handgun. He leveled the weapon at Samir's midsection.

The Arab was speechless for a moment, then he nodded appreciatively. "I see, I see," he said softly. "You speak loudly for a man of no words." He nodded toward the Kahr. "This one doesn't bother with rubber bullets. I see."

There was a thick moment of shared silence while Samir considered his options. The Mute watched his eyes track from the gun, to the GT, to his Mercedes across the street, and back again.

"It is not wise to make an enemy of me, American. I am a powerful man. I can reach inside your dreams to take from you anything that matters to you."

The Mute raised the gun to strike him in the face again, but Samir covered and cowered before the blow came. He moved backward two quick steps, then sneered.

"Yes, you win this time, American boy. I see it as plainly as you. But you must know this. I will not be left unfulfilled."

He began walking in a wide circle, with The Mute as the origin of the circle, pointing himself away from Coffey & Hill Investigations and toward the Mercedes that waited for him across the street.

"I will find this woman again. I will take her, but for your sake, Quiet One, I will not kill her." He paused and stepped out toward the street. The Mute followed his movement with both his eyes and his gun.

"In fact, I will make sure she doesn't die. You see, I can use a woman like this. You know what I mean by *use*, yes? I thought so. There are many ways to use a woman, many ways to give yourself pleasure while giving them pain. I know this. I like this. A woman like the one you protect today? Young. Beautiful. Strong. She has special virtues for agony, and I will explore them all. Long before I'm done, she will beg me for the mercy of death. When that happens, I will tell her of you, of your contribution to her life. And for your sake, I will feast on her more, refusing her death until death comes of its own accord. You have secured that for her, friend. Let that be your memory of me, of this encounter tonight. That she will live in my grasp until I no longer find pleasure in her company. That's what you have accomplished tonight."

The Mute felt his eyes going red with rage. The muscles in his neck stiffened to the point of pain. His mouth bent into a snarl. If he were capable of growling, it would have spilled from his mouth in this moment. He was an animal, ready to tear this man apart with raw vengeance.

I will exterminate him now, The Mute thought, *and rid this earth of his disease.*

Surveillance cameras, body extraction complications, none of that mattered. It was time for Samir Sadeq Hamza al-Sadr to die.

The Arab saw it happening. His nose flared and dipped. A new light flickered into his widening eyes. Fear, a sudden impulse for flight, something that seemed an unfamiliar emotion for this man. His mouth opened slightly, but no words came out. He stumbled backward.

As if uncontrolled by his own mind, The Mute felt his arm extend and his eyes take aim. It was nothing new to kill a man. And it would be satisfying to kill this animal. His finger began to tense upon the trigger of the Kahr handgun.

Before he could complete the action, though, the sound of an engine hummed into existence. A car, heading this way. The Mute checked his fury long enough to let the gun slide to his side. A second later a silver Camry came into view on Howell Mill Road, quickly arriving and then passing by. Random nighttime traffic. Maybe a kid on his way home from a party, completely unaware that his presence had just forestalled a murder—or justice.

Samir breathed heavily. He didn't delay any longer. He'd been closer to death than a mouse's whisker, and apparently that was something that finally got through to him. He turned and ran away from The Mute, ran as fast as his bruised knee and feet could carry him, toward the safety of his Mercedes SUV. A moment later, the Arab was gone, leaving The Mute standing alone in the little parking lot outside Coffey & Hill Investigations.

Now that it was over, The Mute felt his muscles shaking with the flow of adrenaline. He wondered if it had been a mistake to let that man get away from this place alive. He wondered what the consequences of that decision would be. And then he took full control of himself again.

He was here for one reason: to save Truck's girl. And he needed Trudi Coffey to do that. Needed her map. Needed the key she'd stolen from Samuel Hill.

He turned to face the front door of the detective office.

It was time to meet Samuel Hill's ex-wife.

26

TRUDI

Trudi was transfixed by the scene as it unfolded on her surveillance monitor.

When Samir the goon had finally turned tail and run away, she felt herself exhale deeply. Only then did she realize she'd been holding her breath.

That big marine was going to kill that man.

Trudi was a little unsettled by that truth, especially in her stomach, where a delicious grilled quail dinner was threatening to revisit her. Sure, she'd seen dead bodies before, and yes, she'd fought in more than one skirmish over the years. It came with the territory. But she'd never had to take someone's life and never seen a life stolen away either. The thought of it left her trembling.

Trudi stared at the monitor, unsure what to do next.

Samir was obviously bad news, clearly someone to be avoided. But what about this military man? Was he a friend of Samuel's?

Or from some other faction? Was he an enemy or an ally? Or neither?

Trudi dared to look at the clock on her wall. It was now 2:38 a.m. If she didn't get out of here soon, she'd never make it back in time to fool Samuel. But could she risk going outside with that man still out there?

She turned back to the monitor and saw the man standing in the middle of the parking lot. Even from here, he looked imposing. She guessed his height at six-foot-three or something close to that. He carried a thick, muscular frame that reminded Trudi of some of the defensive linemen she'd seen wreaking havoc as part of the Atlanta Falcons football team. His hair was cropped short, like he'd just come out of basic training for the army. He wore dark Levis, a sea-green denim jacket, and military boots. And right now, he was carrying a wicked-looking handgun and a long sniper rifle.

He stood and stared for a while at the front door of her offices, and Trudi wished he would do something. At least if he busted through the plate glass in the door, she'd know he was an enemy.

Finally he turned and walked over to Samuel's Ford GT. He laid the sniper rifle on the hood of the car and then placed the handgun next to it. Before she knew for sure what it was, he also reached inside his shirt and pulled out a long knife on a chain. He set that next to the guns. Then he strode away from the car to an open area in the parking lot. He sat down cross-legged on the cement and waited.

Trudi bit her lip.

I think that was an invitation, she said to herself. *Do I want to accept?*

She looked at the clock again. It was now 2:44 a.m.

Well, I can't stay in here forever.

She stood up from her desk. For comfort, she patted the back of her jeans, where the Beretta was safely stashed. She took a step toward the front door, then stopped. She reached back over her desk and scooped up her cell phone, stuffing it in her pocket. She still wanted to hear that message from Dr. Smith, but it would have to wait until later. Right now, it seemed, she had a date.

When she opened the front door of Coffey & Hill Investigations, the man was still sitting on the ground, waiting. She shut the door behind her, unsure if she should lock it or not. If things went badly, would she be able to get back into the office and lock the door behind her before this large man could stop her? She decided it was worth the chance, and left the office unlocked.

The big man still made no attempt to move, apparently waiting for her. She took a step off the sidewalk and halted there to take a closer look at her visitor. One thing she hadn't noticed on the security camera was the large, dark scar that crossed his neck. She winced at the sight, in spite of herself. Then she spoke.

"Well, you got rid of that goon Samir, so you must be good for something."

The man smiled at her. To her surprise, the smile seemed genuine.

"Do you work for my ex-husband?"

The man grimaced and shook his head, clearly insulted at the idea of being Samuel Hill's employee.

"So who are you?"

The man said nothing but instead reached his right hand over his left and removed a ring from his finger. He held it up.

"Go ahead."

He flipped the ring into the air, aiming it in Trudi's direction. She caught it in one hand and gave it a quick inspection.

"Army Special Forces," she said. "I see. So are you a friend of Samuel's, then?"

The man hesitated, then shrugged.

She started to toss the ring back at him, then hesitated. She decided to hold it just a minute or two longer.

"Okay, you can get up, but do me a favor and stay away from those guns." She gestured toward the arsenal atop her car.

The man stood, unlimbering himself easily and with a quickness that made Trudi worry. This guy was obviously a fighter. Despite her martial arts training, she didn't think she could take him. Didn't think it would even be close. Better to stick with diplomacy instead.

"So you're Special Forces, but you don't work for Samuel Hill. Who do you work for?"

The man glanced around them and then pointed toward the abandoned Tacoma parked not far from her car.

"You work for Toyota?"

Now the man really did smile.

"Right, I get it. You work for Truck." She hesitated. "Do you know he's dead, I mean that he's been killed?"

The smile faded, and the man nodded.

"I suppose you want the Edgar Allan Poe book. That's all anybody seems to care about nowadays. Well, I don't have it. I gave it to my ex-husband."

The man nodded and then pantomimed opening a book. When he knew she understood, he pantomimed removing something from inside the back cover of the book.

"Ah, I see," she said. "You want the secret stash."

The man nodded, then pantomimed a sheet of paper and a key.

"So you know what was in there," Trudi said thoughtfully. "How do you know that?"

The man held up four fingers, then pointed to himself.

4 me, Trudi interpreted. *For me*. She quickly understood that he was saying Truck had left those things in the book for him. And now he was here to claim them.

She frowned and looked hard at the scar on the man's neck. "Are you . . ." She hesitated, then pointed at the scar. "Are you, um, mute?"

The man looked relieved. He nodded. He tapped his fists together and then let his fingers fly in a mock explosion.

"War wound? Iraq?" Trudi asked. The mute man nodded. "I see," she said. She took a step closer and held out his ring, which he placed back on the middle finger of his left hand.

"I don't have the map or the key," she said bluntly. "I'm sorry. I gave them to my ex-husband."

The mute man's face fell.

"I can tell you what was on the map, if that helps."

He nodded, interested again.

"Well, it said 'Alabama' at the top. Then it had a string of numbers and a map of three buildings at the bottom. Best we can figure, the map is for some kind of property Truck had, a place with three buildings."

The mute man held out his palm and pointed downward into it. Trudi took a minute to understand.

"Underground? Is that what you mean?" The mute man nodded. "Yes, one of the buildings on the map was underground. We only figured that out about two days ago, so that shows how slow we are. It looks like a main building, an outbuilding, and then something built underneath the outbuilding."

The man smiled and nodded. *So we were on the right track*, Trudi thought. *That's a good thing, I guess.*

The man took two fingers on each hand and crossed them in front of Trudi, questioning her with his eyes.

"What? I don't know what that means."

The man looked frustrated, but he tried again. He held up one finger.

"One?"

He nodded. He held up two fingers, then three, then four.

"Two, three, four? Oh, I get it." She made the crossed fingers sign back at him. "Numbers. You want to know the numbers on Truck's map?"

He nodded, pleased.

"Right, well, I should have them memorized by now." She started reciting. "31. 111—"

He held up a hand to stop her and pulled a GPS device out of the pocket of his jacket. He waved his hand, and she started over.

31.
111
975,
-86.
809
845

He tapped the numbers into the GPS, and Trudi felt suddenly foolish. *Of course*, she said to herself. *Latitude and longitude. How simple. Sheesh, and I call myself a detective.*

The mute man held the GPS toward her, and she saw the spot on the map. 31.111975,-86.809845. It was farm country, down in southern Alabama. A spot just outside the Conecuh National Forest.

"That's Truck's place?"

The man nodded. He started pantomiming again. From what Trudi could tell, first he was milking a cow, then hoeing a field. He was so earnest about it that she didn't laugh at his work, though it did look a little foolish for a big army ranger to yank at invisible cow teats in the middle of the night.

"It's a farm?" He nodded. "So the aboveground buildings are what, a house and a barn? Samuel will be glad to know this. He says he's to pick up something for Truck from that place."

The mute man frowned. He pantomimed opening a door.

"The key, yes. Samuel has the key." Trudi could see him thinking. "Don't worry," she said, "we'll do right by Truck."

The man looked deep into her eyes, and Trudi felt a little uncomfortable, but all she said was, "I promise."

The mute man held her gaze a moment longer, then nodded. A decision made. A course of action chosen.

He turned back to the GPS device and tapped on it for a moment. Then he looked back at Trudi. He sighed.

He pantomimed striking a match. "Fire?" Trudi said. He pointed to Truck's farm on the GPS device.

"Yes, I heard about that. The Great Conecuh Fire. But they're starting to get it contained, right? And this spot where the farm is should be miles away from the hot spots now."

The mute man nodded slowly, then pointed again to the GPS. Trudi saw he'd marked a second spot on the map, about two and a half miles from Truck's farm. She followed the roads and saw what he was telling her. She pointed to a main road.

"Blocked by the fire's path?"

He nodded. He put his finger north of the second spot on the map, checked to make sure she was paying attention, then traced down a few Alabama back roads until his finger stopped at the second location.

"You're saying we should drive to here to avoid the fire's aftermath, to avoid fire fighters in the area? Then what?"

He nodded and handed her the GPS. He put up both hands, palms out, then pointed to himself. He repeated the gesture, adding the number *4* just before pointing to himself.

Wait—4—me, Trudi interpreted. "Wait for you here?" She pointed at the spot on the map.

He smiled and nodded.

"Wait for you here, and then you can take us in to Truck's

farm by foot. I get it." She hesitated. "I'll have to run it by Samuel first. You've met my ex-husband, right?" A nod. "Then you know he can be stubborn about things, especially when Truck is involved. If Samuel is opposed to this, it won't happen. You'll be stuck there all by yourself. We won't be coming. I won't betray him just to make you happy. You okay with that?"

The mute man grinned and nodded his agreement. He extended a hand, but Trudi held off on shaking to finalize the deal just yet.

"Okay," she said. "I'll go get Samuel—"

He pantomimed opening a door again.

"Right," she said, "I'll go get Samuel—and the key. And we'll meet you here." She pointed to the second location on the GPS. "When?"

The mute man looked at a watch, and Trudi caught that it was now about ten minutes after 3:00 a.m. *I'm going to be late getting back to Birmingham. Maybe I won't get caught speeding.*

The mute man looked at her and then held up seven fingers.

"Seven o'clock. Today? Tonight? Tomorrow?"

The man shook his head. He pointed down.

"Seven o'clock tonight?"

He nodded. He smiled again, then put out his hand again. She shook the hand once, firmly.

It was done, then. They had a deal. She would go back to Birmingham, pick up Samuel, and take him to the rendezvous. They'd meet the mute man there at 7:00 p.m. tonight and hike into Truck's farm. There, the two men could argue over who took control of Truck's emeralds, and she'd finally be finished with this whole Leonard Truckson business once and for all. Well, except for the whole Dr. Smith and Samir wanting revenge thing. But that was a problem for Future Trudi. Right now, she would focus on one thing at a time.

She started to return the GPS device, but the man shook his head.

"I'll keep this, then?" she said awkwardly.

He nodded, then gave a longing look toward the weaponry atop her car.

"Yes, of course, by all means," she said. "I've got to get back on the road anyway."

The big man collected his guns and knife, then turned to leave. He gave her a short salute before jogging across the street back to a waiting vehicle. When he was gone, Trudi returned to her car and began the two-hour journey to Birmingham. Her mind raced with aftershocks of this unusual encounter, but at least she felt like there was a plan in place now, a way to reach the beginnings of a conclusion in this matter.

One thing still bothered her, though. She'd learned what the math problem was on Truck's map. And the "AL" at the top of the map, well that had to mean "Alabama," didn't it? After all, that's where Truck's farm was.

But just below "AL" on Truck's map was the notation "9:6–11." That part was still unexplained. At first, she and Samuel had thought maybe it was a reference to a Bible verse or a Sura in the Qur'an, but after looking through both books a bit, they'd ruled that out. Now it struck her that even the mute man hadn't known about it, and that she'd left it out when talking to him.

So what did 9:6–11 mean? She didn't take Truck for a man to put that in the map unless it meant something. She let her mind wander in the direction of that problem while the mile markers passed quickly by.

Trudi had driven about seventy miles away from Atlanta when an unwanted truth finally interrupted her thoughts.

"Oh man," she said to the empty car. "I forgot to lock my office. Again."

27

ANNABEL

I finally done it.

I shucked off all my clothes, skivvies and all, and ran 'round this big room screaming bloody murder. I kept running and screaming until I was panting and out of breath, red-faced and pink-bodied with exertion. I think it was the first time I actually scared that dog. At first he jumped and nipped at the air when I ran, then he backed himself up into a corner and sat there a-watching the crazy naked girl runnin' and runnin' until she couldn't run no more.

When I was done, I thought I'd feel better, but it just made me sad, and I don't know why really, but I started to cry. Hard crying. The kind that seeps out your nose and your eyes both. It was awful, but after I was done, after I'd wiped my face and rubbed my eyes, then I felt a little improvement. So I guess it was worth something.

Truck didn't put no washing machine down here, nor did he

include a shower. But by now I was feeling sticky and sweaty on top of who-knows-how-many-days of body odor and dirty clothes. I decided to take advantage of the moment.

There wasn't no soap down here, but there was plenty of water. I spent some time hauling up buckets from the well, squishing my clothes in the cold freshness, then wringing them out over the toilets in the outhouse. There wasn't no clothesline in here neither, so I just laid 'em out flat on the floor to dry. By the time I was done, I was shivering from the cold, but it felt good to know my clothes would be sorta clean and dry in just a few hours.

I wrapped myself up in two sleeping bags and perched on a top bunk of the bed. That was a time ago. And now the dog finally comes out of his corner to start investigating.

From up here, he looks kinda funny. I actually feel like laughing.

"What you looking at, Dog?" I say to him. "Ain't you never seen a body go crazy before?"

He sniffs at my clothes, then turns away in disinterest. Me, I'm thinking now about how it's foolish to put clean clothes on a wretched body, knowing that means sooner or later I'm gonna have to toughen up and use that ice-cold well water to scrub my personal hide. I shiver just thinking about it, and it makes me laugh out loud.

It feels good to laugh.

Seems like years since I last knew how to do it. And that makes me get all teary-eyed and weepy again. Maybe I am getting bat-crazy in here.

After a time, my body is warmed up enough to make me feel like venturing out of this cocoon of sleeping bags. I flip open the blankets and feel cool air skitter across my skin.

Too soon, I decide. I wrap back up in the sleeping bags and wait some more.

My dog has taken his usual position at the side of my bed, resting comfortably, ready to spring into action at any moment.

"Hah!" I shout.

Just testing the limits.

The dog raises his shaggy head up to look at me, but his eyes appear unconcerned. His look seems to say more "You want something, Girl?" than "What's goin', Girl!" Guess by now he's getting to know me a bit, and I'm getting to know him too.

I'm still a little flush from my naked runnin's, so I say to him, *"Es ist ein guter Hund."* *It's a good dog.*

Spark my lighter if that dog don't stand up now and start to wag his tail just a little, just one swish or two from side to side.

"Es ist ein guter Hund," I say again, then I add a little correction. *"Du bist ein guter Hund."* *You're a good dog.* Sure enough, that tail wags again.

Is this the first time I ever said something nice to that dog? At least so's he could hear it? The animal looks at me with expectation in his face, and it strikes me that when Truck said things like that, he probably gave this dog a treat. I'm not sure how my dog will react if he gets praised and don't get a treat as part of the bargain, so now I'm in for it.

Like it or not, I'm gonna have to shrug off this warmth and skip through the coldness in my altogether just to get that dog a snack. Next time I'll know better, but now I'm under a stern obligation. So off I go.

Dog seems happy with the beef jerky I toss his direction, so that's good. And now that I'm out here, I figure it's time to face the job at hand. The well water is worse than ice on my bare skin, but just a little rubbing with a wet rag reveals to me how greasy and dirty a girl can get while just sitting in a clean room. Even I'm disgusted by what appears on the rag after swashing it under my arms. I grit my teeth and complete the work.

When my skin is finally scrubbed pink and raw, I drop the rag in the bucket to soak. I'll wash it out later, when I can feel my fingers again. For now I leap back under the sleeping things and try to get warm.

I'm surprised at how nice it feels to be clean again. Clean is something you never miss until you can't get it easy, I guess. But for now, blood is pumping happy in my veins and even the air around me seems to smell better. I tuck my wet head under the sleeping bag and let hot breath fill the space until I start to get a little claustrophobic and have to crack the edges to let fresh air in.

The world around me is quiet. Apparently that screaming girl has calmed down a mite. I feel myself relax and know it will be easy to go to sleep again. I don't know if it's nighttime or just nap time, only that sleep sounds nice.

When I wake up, I'm still buck-skinned, but cozy and warm under the covers. I want to just stay here, to keep in this womb-like place for as long as possible, but I make the mistake of letting my hands rest on my belly. That reminds me quickly of the bodily demands, so I sigh and make my way to the outhouse.

Afterward, I check the clothes and find my shirt and underwear are dry, but my socks and jeans are still a little damp and cold. I brave up and get dressed anyway. My body heat will dry the clothes quicker than this cold floor.

I feel a little sad as I pull on the last sock, like I had a little vacation there for a minute but now it's over. Like for a short moment in time, I was free again, a girl again, having fun with life and the world around her. But now I'm back in my prison clothes, seeing the four walls around me and knowing I ain't going nowhere, no matter how much I run and scream and cry.

I look over at the dog and see that, in his own way, the animal must also feel the same. Cellmates. I guess that's what we are.

A couple of jailbirds just waiting for freedom to come knocking on our cage, shouting the safe code to let us out.

"Where the heck are you, Truck?" I say to the walls.

As usual, they don't answer.

On the table before me is Marelda Gregor's journal and my own notebook. We've had an interesting journey so far, Marelda and me. But she always leaves me with more questions than answers.

I look at my notebooks on the table, waiting for me to return to them again. I suppose it's time, so I sit down to work once more . . .

> *Die persönliche Rechnung Marelda Gregor, Psychiater, Biologen, Mystiker . . .*
>
> *It pains me that this baby still has no name.*
>
> *It's been two months now. The child deserves a name. But Dr. Schmitzden won't allow it. He says that giving the prototype a name will humanize it in the eyes of the workers, and that it will negatively impact their ability to do their jobs.*
>
> *I see the wisdom in his words; I know he is right. And still, is this child not already human? Is she not already a living, breathing thing?*
>
> *She is weak, even Dr. Schmitzden sees that. Her cries, once full-fisted and fraught with power, now echo damply, like whimpers from a sickened animal. The drainings have been too frequent. They sap her of strength and life. She's too young, too new to endure that kind of treatment. Dr. Schmitzden knows it just as plainly as I do. When he gave her to me for nursing six days ago, even he acknowledged the obvious.*
>
> *"Feed her well, Frau Gregor," he said. "She needs her strength."*
>
> *He could see in my eyes the questions that came. He let his hand caress my shoulder, a gentle touch, one I remember.*
>
> *"Don't worry, dear Marelda. I will not let her die. She is too valuable to me."*

"Yes," I said.

He smiled. "Perhaps we will wait a week before the next draining. Perhaps that will ease your worries, yes?"

I nodded, and he said, "A week then. It's settled." He gave me a light squeeze. "Now, feed her well."

"Yes," I said, and he left me to my work.

She barely ate at first, she was so limp and frail. But I was patient, and she has a strong will, this one. After a time, she took her fill. Each new day her body grows to match her will.

I feel her warmth pressed against mine. She who lived inside me has come to know me again. Come to trust me. She sleeps now and I see the beauty of the stars in her face.

I know I should not do it. I know it is unwise. But she is my child, and despite her future, despite her place in the work we have begun, this baby deserves a name.

Yes, of course I understand what we are doing. It must be done. The Order of St. Heinrich von Bonn demands nothing less than everything, this child included. I knew that when I dedicated myself to this life, to this cause.

And still . . .

She is just a child, and every child is worthy of a name.

Sleep, little one, sleep in your mother's arms tonight. Rest. Be strong.

Tomorrow is one week since your last draining. Tomorrow will be hard for you. But tonight, you may sleep in safety. This is my promise to you, and I swear it by the name I give you now.

Sleep, my Raina Aemilia Gregor.

Sleep, my little life. Tomorrow will be bitter for you, but not tonight.

No, not tonight.

I swear it.

28

TRUDI

It was 5:18 Sunday morning when Trudi pulled Samuel's car into the parking lot of the DoubleTree Inn in Birmingham. She cursed her feeble mind for not thinking to block the parking spot when she left. Now there was a Dodge Avenger in the place where Samuel would expect to find his GT. Well, nothing to be done about it now. She'd have to make sure she was the one who went out to get "real" coffee at breakfast. That would give her an excuse for having moved his car.

She parked a few spaces down from the back entrance and was frustrated to discover that some of the hotel patrons were already up and tossing luggage into their cars, smoking cigarettes by the back door, and generally going about their business in conspicuous ways. After being up through the night, all Trudi wanted to do at this point was simply sneak back into the hotel room on the third floor and try to force a few hours of sleep before having to be up and on call to Samuel's demands for the day. After all, he would expect that she'd slept through the night in the bed next to his. He would expect business as usual.

Trudi sighed.

She changed back into her pajamas inside the car this time, hoping for at least a little privacy. She was pretty sure that one man smoking by the back door caught sight of what she was doing, but at least that guy was polite enough not to gawk. Next she rolled up her jeans and sweater, gun and GPS device stowed safely inside, and stuffed them back under the passenger seat along with her slip-on shoes. She'd have to retrieve those later. Maybe when she went out for coffee. Now there was nothing to be done for it but satiny pajama-clad exhibitionism.

She climbed out of the GT and made her way to the back entrance. She wished her satin outfit didn't give such a clear view of her braless-ness every time she took a step, but again, that was out of her control at this moment. She'd just have to endure the stares.

When she had trouble fishing her hotel key card out of her waistband, the smoking man smiled tolerantly and leaned toward the door.

"Let me get that for you," he said, swiping his own keycard in the reader at the back door. Trudi heard the lock click open and felt suddenly grateful for small kindnesses. Maybe there was at least one decent man on this planet. Of course, he was probably going to die a horrible death from lung cancer someday, but for now she'd take what she could get.

"Thanks," she muttered as she walked on by.

Trudi took the stairs instead of waiting for the elevator, so at least that was over fast. Then she was on the third floor again, thankfully with an empty hallway. She reached for her keycard and thought of the sex-starved man in room 321. She wondered how long he had waited up for her to come knocking on his door. She hoped all night, a long, frustrating night.

She slid the keycard in the reader on her hotel room and then gently opened the door, squeezing quickly inside in hopes of keeping the bright lights in the hallway from disturbing Samuel's sleep. She needn't have worried.

When her eyes adjusted to the darkness inside the room, she saw Samuel sitting in a chair by the window. He was shirtless but wore a pair of pants as if to indicate that he'd found her missing and done just enough searching to discover she was indeed gone from here. In his lap was his Glock 36 handgun. He looked weary.

Trudi stopped inside the doorway and waited. *Silence is always a powerful tool*, she told herself. She set her hotel keycard on the TV set. After a moment, Samuel straightened up in his chair and sighed.

"You get your gun?" he said.

"Yeah."

"Okay," he said. "I'm going back to bed."

He set the Glock on the dresser as he stood, then walked down the narrow aisleway between the beds and slid between the sheets.

Trudi thought for a moment about telling him what she'd learned from her little foray back into Atlanta. She thought about telling him the meaning of the "math problem" on Truck's map, and of their upcoming appointment tonight at 7:00 p.m. But his back was to her now, and she understood that he too had probably been up most of the night, worrying about her. She felt a twinge of guilt about that.

Mostly, though, she felt tired all the way down to her bones. That empty bed next to Samuel had never looked so inviting. She squinted her eyes and made an executive decision. They could both wait just a little longer to talk about things. They needed a few hours' sleep to restore good humor and proper manners. She let her shoulders relax and headed toward her mattress.

Trudi climbed under the covers and was off into dreamland barely seconds after her head hit the pillow.

When she awoke, it was already after 10:00 a.m., and the bed next to hers was empty. On the dresser was a tall cup of takeout coffee and a Styrofoam container that, from the leftover smell in the room, she assumed had scrambled eggs and some kind of now-cold breakfast meat inside.

She sat up and rubbed her eyes. Samuel was in his usual spot at the desk, engrossed in some random fact on his laptop. The man did have a good work ethic, she'd give him that. She let her eyes roam and saw the jeans and sweater she'd left in the car now unfolded and hanging over the back of a chair. In the seat of the chair, she saw her Beretta Tomcat, still in its holster, the GPS she'd received last night, and a fresh box of ammunition.

Good call, Sam, she thought. *A gun without ammunition isn't much of a gun. Should have thought of that myself.*

She stretched and leaned back onto her pillow. It felt good to take a moment and breathe, especially after the excitement at her office last night.

"Thanks for the coffee," she said to the back of Samuel's head. "And the ammo."

Her ex-husband waved a dismissive hand. "No problem," he said to the computer. He tapped the keys quickly once more, then swiveled his chair to face her. "Have fun last night?" he said behind a tolerant grin.

"You know it, cowboy." She returned the grin. "Girls just wanna have fun, right?"

He nodded, always a gentleman. He seemed ready to let the betrayal slide this time, and he changed the subject.

"So, when I couldn't sleep last night, I did some thinking about our good Dr. Smith. Finally it hit me: What if his name hasn't always been Smith? What if we're spending all our time tracking down the sketchy history of a Smith, when maybe his name was once Smithhouser or Smithereens or some other variation?"

"Good thinking."

"Anyway, I called one of my buddies in the State Department and came up with a few possible alternatives. One of the guys on the list appears to have been in Fallujah around the same time that we've put Dr. Smith and Truck in that area. I think it's worth pursuing. What do you think?"

Trudi smiled inside. She had to admit that she missed this, missed the daily give-and-take of having Samuel as her partner in an investigation. He was a good thinker, and someone with natural initiative. Then her mind wandered to his faults, reminding her of his, um, other entanglements in the Middle Eastern world. She felt suddenly tired again. And just a little bitter.

"I met a friend of yours last night," she said to the ceiling.

"What?"

She could hear the injury in Samuel's voice, the little boy who wanted some acknowledgment of doing good work while she was gone. It had to pain him that she'd completely ignored his latest findings, that she'd dismissed his revelations as if they were unimportant. She almost felt bad about it, until she pictured some stunning young Arab woman with the man she'd called her husband. Then it didn't feel bad at all, not even a little bit.

"Friend of yours. Met him outside my office last night. Said to tell you 'hey.'"

Samuel sighed and leaned back in his chair. Trudi ignored

him and instead headed to the bathroom, leaving him stewing in frustration. She did her business and then, out of spite, decided to go ahead and take a leisurely shower while she was in there. When she got out, she paused to stare at the cross necklace she always wore. The silver glinted in the foggy mirror, reminding her that she was more than just a bitter ex-wife, despite the way she felt at the moment.

More, she told herself. *This life is not all I have. There is always more to come, both today and tomorrow.* She sighed.

In the other room, she heard the TV set. It sounded like ESPN announcers pontificating on why this team or that was in dire straits, and how that player or this one was the greatest athlete ever to put on a uniform.

She pulled on her jeans and noticed then that although Samuel had found her handgun, he hadn't checked her pockets. In one she had a $20 bill. In the other was a mobile phone. She decided not to bring attention to those facts, at least not now. She continued dressing, adding a tight jersey tank top to her ensemble, then partially buttoning a plaid, long-sleeve "boyfriend" shirt over it all.

He turned off the TV set when she came out of the bathroom, said nothing while she secured the Beretta and holster inside the back waistband of her jeans. He just watched her, following her eyes with his. When she sat down to put on shoes and socks, he finally spoke.

"Going somewhere?"

"Got an appointment to keep," she said. She cocked her head and tried to sound playful. "You can come if you promise to keep your hands to yourself."

He sighed. "I get it," he said, "you're still mad about me keeping you from getting a gun. Well, you took care of that problem without my help. So what do you want from me now, an apology?"

"Sure. An apology would be nice."

He stood and bowed his head slightly. "Ms. Coffey," he said, "I was a jerk. A domineering male donkey. Please accept my humble apologies."

Sometimes he was too cute. Trudi hated that. She hated that she could love and hate this man in the same moment. Now it was her turn to sigh.

"Fine," she said. "You're forgiven."

"Thank you," he said. "Now, do you want to tell me what happened last night or do I have to do another dance for that song to be sung?"

She laughed in spite of herself. Samuel was not a good dancer. Enthusiastic, yes. Good? No.

"I met somebody who knows you. He showed up at my office in the wee hours of the morning."

"What's his name?"

Only then did it strike Trudi that she'd never gotten a name out of the mute man. *Didn't seem necessary at the time, I guess,* she told herself. But now it would've been useful to have that information.

"He didn't say."

"What did he look like?"

"Large. Dark skin. Muscular. Wore an army Special Forces ring and carried a lot of guns."

Samuel's forehead wrinkled. "This guy, did he have a thick scar across his neck?" Trudi nodded. "Congratulations," he said, "you are one of the chosen few who has met The Mute."

"The Mute? What an awful nickname. Seems mean, even for you army types."

Samuel shrugged. "Not a nickname, at least as far as I've heard. That's just his name. I hear Truck gave it to him, and he kept it." He looked at Trudi with a little concern. "Are you okay? The Mute has, well, a reputation."

"Stone-cold killer?" she said.

"Yeah. Among other things."

"I'm fine. Your Mute was a perfect gentleman." *With me, at least. Can't say the same for his treatment of Samir.*

"So what did he want? The map?"

"Yes. But he also told me what the math problem on the map is."

Trudi handed the GPS device to Samuel and showed him the coordinates saved on it.

"Man," he said. "We must be morons."

She shrugged. It seemed hard to argue that conclusion given the evidence. "It's a farm, down in southern Alabama. Apparently there's a main house, a barn, and then an underground structure built beneath the barn. We'll find Truck's emeralds down there."

"What's this other spot on the map?" he asked.

"Our rendezvous point. I told The Mute we'd meet him there at seven tonight, take him to the emeralds, and be done with this whole business."

She waited for Samuel to object, for him to complain that he was responsible for the emeralds, not The Mute. She expected him to argue about it, but instead he said, "Good plan. My guess is The Mute knows that area like my cousin Freddie knows how to cook up bacon."

Trudi snorted at the reference. She'd met Freddie. He ran a gourmet barbecue joint in Texas, and judging by his weight, it was safe to say he often sampled his own cooking.

Samuel looked more closely at the GPS map. "Why don't we just go straight to Truck's farm and—oh, never mind. The Conecuh Fire. Did The Mute say anything about that?"

"Well, he didn't *say* anything."

"You know what I mean. Guy can't speak, but he still gets his message across."

"He said roads were blocked up to the farm, but that we could hike in from the rendezvous spot."

Samuel tapped on the GPS screen. "It's about two hundred miles from here to Peachtree, which looks to be about twenty miles from Truck's farm. So maybe a three-hour drive? Maybe three and a half since we're going into backcountry after we get past Peachtree."

"Okay," she said. She looked at the clock. It was now a few minutes after 11:00 a.m. She took a sip of cold coffee and peeked inside the Styrofoam container. She found cold eggs and sausage inside. She wrinkled her nose and dropped the whole container in the trash. "So we've got time to eat lunch before we head out?"

Samuel looked at his watch. "Sure," he said. "You want me to go out and get something for you?"

There was a slight hesitation, then Trudi shook her head.

"No, we can go out together. We might as well check out of the hotel too."

He nodded.

They spent a few minutes packing up their things, and Trudi found herself feeling disappointed that she'd never had a chance to wear the red dinner dress and diamonds her ex-husband had bought for her. He caught her staring at the dress before packing it away.

"Another time." He shrugged. "It'll still look great . . . whenever."

"Another time, then," she said. She sighed and folded the dress into the suitcase.

They were down at the front counter by 11:30 a.m.

Trudi almost laughed when she saw the guy from room 321 also at the front counter, arguing over a charge for some pay-per-view movie that had "accidentally" come on his TV set at 3:30 a.m. He looked up long enough to recognize Trudi and shoot her an annoyed look. Then he saw Samuel Hill. His eyes widened, and he seemed suddenly impatient to leave the premises, even without settling the issue on his bill. Samuel saw the exchange and gave Trudi a questioning look.

In response, Trudi pulled a $20 bill from her pocket and placed it in her ex-husband's hand. She nodded toward the other man.

"Samuel," she said, "be a dear and return this to that man over there. I, um, borrowed it from him last night."

Her ex-husband looked at the money, at Trudi, and over at the man now desperate to settle his bill. The corners of his eyes narrowed.

"Be glad to," he said.

Samuel turned toward the man. He flipped open his brown bomber jacket, just wide enough for the guy to see the Glock pistol now holstered inside there. He took a step in the direction of his intent, but he was too late. The other guy was already running out the door.

Sam turned back to Trudi.

"I think I'll keep this," he said, raising the $20 bill.

Trudi laughed out loud.

"Honey," she said, "you definitely earned it."

29

ANNABEL

For better or worse, tonight begins the real adventure.

I feel cold. And never more alone than right now.

For better or worse . . .

It's not a cold that comes from outside in. The cold sits inside me. I think it may stay there, even when—even if—I ever return to sunshine.

Tonight begins the real adventure.

I keep thinking of Edgar Allan Poe's horror story, "The Pit and the Pendulum," the way it begins: "I was sick—sick unto death with that long agony; and when they at length unbound me, and I was permitted to sit, I felt that my senses were leaving me." That's the way I feel right now.

Sick—sick unto death.

Bound and senseless.

For better or worse, tonight begins the real adventure.

It's the last line of Marelda Gregor's personal account. Now that I've translated the entire slim volume, I wish I'd left it stuffed under that bunk bed mattress. I wish I'd never found it at all. Better to live stupid than to live awful. But Truck always told me he wouldn't allow no stupids in his house.

"It hurts me, Truck. Hurts me inside."

Of course, no one hears. Not even that dog. He's sleeping by the door, legs twitching.

I can't cry, not no more. No reason for it. Marelda Gregor is gone. She's been long gone. I know it, otherwise why would Truck have this journal? Why would Truck have me?

"Was you gonna tell me, Truck? Was you ever gonna tell me?"

My uncle was always good with confidences. Why would I assume he didn't keep any secrets from me?

It strikes me now that I've seen Marelda Gregor's plain black notebook before. Years ago, when I was 'bout seven or so. I forgot that. I forgot it even existed. But it must've been her book. Nothing else makes sense now.

I was bored, waiting for Rendel to finish cooking dinner. I wandered 'round the house and ended up in Truck's study. Sitting here now, wrapped up in sleeping bags, I can almost see the moment in my head, see it clear and clean like it was a picture in a photo album.

Uncle Truck is at his desk, head down, concentrating hard on something. He's got a pencil in his left hand, and his right hand is pressing down on a page in a book that sets on his desk, pressing it open so's he can see it more clearly.

"What's goin', Truck?" I'm saying. "Will you read to me?"

He looks up but don't smile.

"No time now, Annie-girl. How about after dinner?"

I start to pout, and he sighs. With his right hand, he closes the book on his desk. It has a blank, black cover, no markings on it at all.

"Come on, Annabel. Aren't you getting a little old for that attitude?"

It's a warning, and I'm old enough to know that it's best to heed Truck's warnings. Still, I'm feeling hungry and bored. I try to prolong the conversation.

"What you reading, Truck? Can you read that to me?"

My uncle looks unhappy. After a moment, he shakes his head. "Not today, Annie. Maybe someday." He takes a thick rubber band and wraps it around the black book, sealing it tight.

"Why not, Truck?" I skitter into his lap like I belong there. "I'll sit real still while you read it. I promise."

The book sits on the desk before us. Black and closed to my eyes.

"Tell you what, Annabel," he says, and his voice sounds solemn and serious. "When you turn thirteen, on your thirteenth birthday, I'll let you read this book for yourself."

He slides the book into a drawer on his desk and then shoves me off his lap. "Now go help Rendel with dinner. I've got work to do, and I'm not getting it done with curious little girls making all kinds of interruptions."

He smiles at me, and I know it's time to go.

It's just one of a million memories my mind holds, one easily forgotten. One I did forget until just now, this moment, when it suddenly had new meaning and demanded to be recalled.

I look over at Marelda Gregor's book on the table. I know it was her book Truck kept from me, her book he was saving for my thirteenth birthday. I guess I see why, now. Thirteen is gonna be an important number in my life. If I ever get to it.

When I was done reading "The Pit and the Pendulum," I

had nightmares for a week. Rats chewing at my clothes. Falling down a deep, dark, endless hole. Being tied to a wooden beam. That kind of thing. It got to where Truck forbade me from reading any more Poe stories for a while, to the point where I was sorry I'd ever read that story. Now, looking at the personal account of Marelda Gregor sitting on the table, I feel the same way.

I have so many questions. And I'm afraid to find out the answers. I see the Bible peeking at me from the top shelf across the room, but I don't have the courage to read that highlighted page again. Not now, not knowing what I do now.

I finally get unwrapped from my covers and walk over to the table. I put the black journal into the desk drawer, along with my own notebook and writings. And I see something else I forgot.

There's a Walther PPQ semiautomatic pistol still in this drawer. Loaded.

I know how to use a gun. I never used one as fancy as this one, but a gun's a gun. Aim and click. Brace for the kick. Let the bullet do the work.

I reach inside the drawer. The pistol feels heavy in my hand.

The dog is awake now, watching me from his spot in front of the door.

I wonder if I should kill the dog first, or myself.

One bullet, that's all it would take. It would be easy. Killing me would be easy.

I look at the dog.

Killing the dog would be hard. It would hurt like reading Marelda Gregor's diary.

I put the gun back where it belongs, back in the drawer under the table. It's Truck's gun anyway, and he'd be mad if he knew I messed around with it.

I sit down on the floor beside the table. It seems like years since I was sleeping warm in my own bed, since I was complaining that it was too hot up there in my third-floor bedroom. I wonder if my stuff is still up there. For some reason, I miss the wallpaper. Bluebell flowers against a cream background, sprinkled floor to ceiling on three walls. The fourth wall is blank white, behind the head of my bed. In my dreams sometimes I heard them bluebells tinkling like wind chimes in my head. I miss them little bluebells now, even though I never thought to appreciate the painted flowers while I had 'em at easy distance.

I'm lying on the floor now, and I feel the coolness seeping up into my body. *If I lay here long enough*, I think, *I won't need no gun to kill myself. The cold in my bones will do it for me.* And I realize I've made myself a plan. I can't live no more like this anyway. It's too much for me, too much for an eleven-year-old girl.

It ain't nothing for me to strip off my socks, my shirt and pants. Now the chill beneath me makes my bare thighs quiver. Now my shoulders and arms. Don't know if it's minutes or hours, but now my teeth is chattering like skeleton bones on Halloween. I force myself not to move. I welcome the cold, wishing for it to spring death on me.

I hear when you freeze to death, you just eventually fall asleep and die. So I try to fall asleep. My feet and fingers feel numb, and my spine is hurting from the shivers on this hard cement floor. I close my eyes tighter. All it takes is a strong will to die. And Truck always said I was the most self-willed child he ever seen.

My ears feel like someone is pinching at 'em and poking into the flesh with toothpicks. Somebody groans, and only afterward do I realize it's me.

Let me die.

I don't know what God I'm praying to, but he always seemed to answer before when I needed him most.

Make me die.

I don't hear no answer. I try to sleep. If I sleep now, I think maybe I won't wake up. *Sleep. Go to sleep.*

I try to think of a lullaby, but for some reason no song comes to mind. I try to cry, but tears won't come neither. Only groans. *I'm so cold.*

The shock of the dog's body against mine causes me to jump. I open my eyes and see him crawling in close to me on the floor, pressing his furry warmth against my left side. His eyes lock onto mine as he nuzzles in next to me.

"What you doing, Dog?" I chatter at him. He just presses his cheek against my ribs.

Now I am crying, not from sadness but from anger.

"*Geht!*" I shout at him. "*Geht.*"

He whimpers slightly, fidgets, but he don't leave my side. Instead, he lifts his big, shaggy head and lays it like a blanket across my icy belly.

"It ain't gonna work, Dog," I say through chattering teeth. "You ain't no fur coat. Just leave me alone."

He looks at me from the corner of his eye, but he don't move. We are at a stalemate, that dog and me. Me trying to freeze myself and him trying to warm me back to life.

"You're a stubborn hound," I say softly. He just blinks at me. Slowly I raise my arms and wrap them around that awful head. He sighs and nuzzles into my touch. I start to worry that maybe the dog is right, that maybe freezing to death ain't my only option. And besides, is it really cold enough in here to die from it? Probably not. Probably I'm just suffering for no reason.

I'm a stubborn girl too, though. So I continue to lie on the floor a while longer, shivering, aching, suffering. Maybe that's what I need anyway. Maybe it's the suffering that redeems me. I think the Catholics in Peachtree call it penance. So I choose to suffer, even if I can't die.

In the end, it's human biology that defeats me. A long sigh and I finally push the warmth of the German shepherd off my belly. He stands nearby, tail low, watching.

"It ain't no thing, Dog," I mutter. "Nothing to worry about."

I stand up and move toward the outhouse, feeling the pressure rise inside my intestines, no longer able to ignore it.

I knew I shouldn't have eaten that whole can of chili.

30

TRUDI

The forest was quiet when Trudi and Samuel pulled the Ford GT into the clearing at the rendezvous point. She didn't have to check her watch to know that late afternoon was turning into early evening.

"So, I guess we're a little early," she said. "Got some time to kill until The Mute shows up. Want me to tell you a story?"

Samuel smiled, and Trudi knew he was remembering the late nights during college when she'd regale him with obscure mythology and history she'd picked up from her literature studies. That thought made Trudi smile inside as well.

They were now situated at a plateau of sorts on the edge of the Conecuh National Forest. It was a flat clearing that had somehow avoided the worst of the fire. Trudi guessed it had been cleared with tourists in mind because a wide hiking trail into the forest spiked off from one end. She could envision people parking their minivans here and then taking off for a day's trek inside the wilderness. It was nice.

Samuel stretched his big frame, cracking his spine and his knuckles in the process. He looked toward the sky and then surveyed their surroundings.

"How much more daylight do you think we have?" he said.

Trudi made a judgment call. "A few hours, give or take."

"So The Mute wants to take us on a night hike?"

"I guess so. What's it matter to you? You worried about not being able to keep those emeralds?"

"No." Samuel let his eyes stray past the scenery and onto his ex-wife. "Honestly, The Mute was supposed to get the emeralds anyway. I was supposed to give him the map and the key, and then he was supposed to take care of the rest."

"So why are we out here in the nothingness of Alabama on a cool autumn evening? If this is your idea of a date, it's not so great."

"Now I just have to know why Truck was so concerned about two little gemstones. I mean, Leonard Truckson was not a man without means."

Samuel's use of a double-negative grated at the English major in her, but Trudi tried not to think about it. Samuel always got defensive when she corrected his grammar.

"Curiosity killed the cat," she quipped.

"Good thing I'm not a cat," he said. "But seriously, there must be something more to this. Something important. I want to see it through to the end. I owe that much to Truck. I owe him that much and a lot more."

Trudi nodded. It was hard to argue with a man when his reasoning went along emotional lines like that. Besides, she was here now, and honestly, she too was curious to see these all-important emeralds.

The light, cool breeze around them was a welcome blessing. The smell of smoke still lingered, and the sky still held black marks created by the fire. But word on the news was that workers now had it 70 percent contained. The Great Conecuh Fire should burn itself out within the next week or two.

Her mind wandered to earlier in the day, when they were eating lunch at the Homewood Gourmet restaurant on 28th Avenue South in Birmingham. She'd waited until Samuel excused himself for a bathroom break before digging the cell phone out of her pants pocket. The battery was still over 60 percent—plenty of life left as long as she didn't overuse it.

Trudi tapped the touch screen and held the phone to her ear. There were fourteen messages waiting for her, but she was only interested in the first one. Dr. Smith's voice was clear and crisp, despite his recent encounter with an electric chair.

"Mary had a little lamb," he said, "its fleece was white as snow; and everywhere that Mary went, the lamb was sure to go. It followed her to school one day, which was against the rule; it made the children laugh and play, to see a lamb at school. And so the teacher turned it out, but still it lingered near, and waited patiently about till Mary did appear. 'Why does the lamb love Mary so?' the eager children cry; 'Why, Mary loves the lamb, you know' the teacher did reply."

The message ended, and Trudi hung up her cell.

What in the world?

Was that old man really bonkers? Why had he called and left a nursery rhyme on her voicemail? She'd half expected some kind of threat, a promise of vengeance, maybe a clue to what he was planning next. But "Mary Had a Little Lamb"? Seriously? It made no sense.

She cued up Dr. Smith again but then had to stuff the cell phone back into her jeans midmessage when Samuel returned from the bathroom. She hoped he hadn't seen it, was glad when he didn't ask questions about it. Then they'd made the drive down here to Peachtree and the Conecuh National Forest. Several times on the way, she'd been tempted to tell her ex-husband about Dr. Smith's phone call, but it seemed like such a silly message that she never could bring herself to do it.

Now she watched Samuel begin exploring the rendezvous spot, peering down the trail and checking other entry points into the forest. She started to feel suspicious.

"Come here and keep me company," she said. "I want to hear more about your thoughts on Dr. Smith."

He ignored her. Instead he consulted the GPS device, then continued inspecting the countryside, getting his bearings.

"Samuel." She could almost see the thought balloons forming over his head. This guy was too predictable sometimes.

He waved her off, and seemed to be counting something in his head. Finally he turned to her.

"Listen, you wait here," he said. "I'm going down to Truck's farm. I'll bring the emeralds back in a flash. Give me an hour, maybe an hour and a half." He held up the GPS. "I'm going to take this, if you don't mind. Just in case."

"Samuel," she said, "just wait. The Mute'll be here soon, and we can all go in together."

"Not necessary," he said cheerily. "I can get everything done in the time it takes for him to get here. Easy-peasy. You just relax. I'll take care of everything."

"Come on, Sam. Do you really think it's wise to go gallivanting off on your own in this unfamiliar territory? Use your head for once."

"Yes, you're right. The pretty chirping birds might turn into dangerous monsters inside the forest. I'm willing to take the chance."

"You're insufferable."

"And you're so pretty when you pout."

He stuffed the GPS into his pocket and headed away from the clearing. She noticed he was deliberately avoiding the wide hiking trail that was so pleasantly marked out for visitors. He disappeared into the line of trees. Trudi cursed and started jogging after him. She caught up with him after only a minute or so.

"You know where we're going?" she said grumpily. "Or are we just on a pleasure tour?"

"Well, it is a pleasure to go on a hike with you, if that's what you're asking. And yes, I do know where we're going." He pointed southwest. "Really, all we need to do is walk that way for about two or three miles, and we're there. But we'll keep an eye on the GPS to make sure we don't get lost."

Trudi didn't admit it, but it was kind of nice to tramp through this forest with her ex. The farther they went into it, the more signs they saw of the fire's impact and aftermath, but there were also signs of life sprouting from the ashes. And Samuel seemed genuinely happy to be out in the world again.

He always was an annoying outdoorsy type, she said to herself. *Me, I prefer the comforts of civilization. Camping for me means a stay at Motel 6.* But the moment was good, and so she kept her thoughts to herself. Besides, walking was always good exercise, and a woman her age needed to stay in shape.

Evening had fully arrived when they reached Truck's farm, and Trudi saw the devastation that fire can cause. The place was a ruin. No signs of life, nothing to cheer the human heart. Just rubble and blackened debris.

They came in from the northwest corner of the property, and when the full area was in view, Samuel let out a low whistle. Trudi didn't say anything at first, but she agreed with his sentiment.

"Maybe we should have waited for The Mute after all," she said. "How are we going to find an underground entrance in all this mess?"

Samuel was undeterred. "It'll show itself to us. We just have to get the right vantage point. Come on."

He stepped over a burned branch and headed toward the center of the property. Trudi followed. Samuel kept walking until he stood in the road on the other side of the structures, now situated on the south side of everything. Trudi stood next to him, and they both took in the scene.

The demarcations where the two main buildings had stood were still visible to the naked eye. "That must have been the main house," Samuel said, pointing toward a burned-out porch. "Which means that"—he pointed to the other leftovers of a building—"was the barn."

"Okay," Trudi said. "So we know the underground structure is below the barn. What do you think, is it a bunker of some sort?"

"Probably."

They stared intently toward the rubble left of the barn, looking for clues. Trudi saw nothing. It was frustrating, but Samuel seemed to be making sense of the scenery, so she kept quiet.

"There," he said. She followed his line of sight and saw remnants of a chain link fence that ran intermittently behind the barn. "If Truck were making an entrance to an underground bunker, he'd keep it out of sight from the road, behind the barn. And he'd probably put some sort of obstacle there as well."

"Like a chain link fence? Isn't that a little obvious?"

Samuel shrugged. "Makes sense to me. Probably kept farming machinery or some other kind of equipment back there to disguise it. That would make it easy to explain why he'd keep the fence locked."

Trudi had to admit that Samuel's reasoning made a certain kind of sense. "Should we check it out? Daylight's almost gone, you know."

Samuel nodded slowly and began to step carefully toward

the barn. Trudi followed, looking for signs that would reveal an opening to the underground. When they stood next to the edge of the fence, she still didn't see anything to indicate they were anywhere besides a field of refuse. Samuel started working methodically from one end of the old barn to the other, staying on the backside of the burned-out structure.

Trudi decided to take a different tack. She climbed up on a large stone and tried to give herself a bird's-eye view. It was obviously a low-flying bird, but it helped. She raked the scenery with her eyes. It seemed undisturbed and secretive. Then her eyes flicked back to something they'd passed over previously. Down at the far end of the barn, near what used to be the back corner, something was wrong.

She jumped off the rock and went to check it out. For some reason, a *Sesame Street* song from her childhood chimed in her brain. *One of these things is not like the other* . . .

She let her eyes wander, relaxed her mind to hear what the scene was saying to her. A branch here. A rut in the ground there. Melted metal. Rocks. Small animal tracks printed in the ash. Rough cuts in the terrain and—there. It was there, plain to see if anyone was really looking.

Someone had been here, after the fire. Someone had swept this spot, erased human tracks, and all animal tracks in the process. Arranged the rubble like a work of art intended to imitate the surrounding area. There was a human touch in this corner. She saw it now. She moved in closer for a more detailed inspection, then started pulling at brush and debris. And she found it. A flattened, scorched square of lead fused to what looked like an inoperable hydraulic system.

"Samuel," she called out. "Over here."

31

THE MUTE

The Mute frowned when he arrived at the rendezvous.

He'd figured on getting there early, scouting the location a bit and giving the ex-couple a familiar face when they finally showed up at the appointed time. He hadn't figured that they would get to the rendezvous before him and take off alone.

Had they gone on to Truck's farm without him? Or had they been taken against their will?

A quick scan of the area showed no hint of mercenaries, but The Mute decided not to take any chances. He drove around the clearing and back out again, leaving behind the silver GT he'd seen Trudi driving very early that morning.

After more than a decade living in this place, The Mute knew every nook and cranny available to him both in and around the Conecuh National Forest. It took only about ten minutes for him to stash his Jeep in an inconspicuous place and then return to the rendezvous point on foot. He came back fully armed, with his SIG716 rifle strapped to his back, knife and Kahr handgun warmly in place, and even his .22 short mini-revolver tucked securely inside his right boot.

He stopped at the edge of the rendezvous and gave himself an unobstructed view of the clearing. He spent a minute or two watching, but he saw nothing more than a few woodland animals and a bird or two flitting through branches. He stepped into the open and walked cautiously to the GT parked at one side.

His eyes stayed active, never resting in one place too long, wary of unseen dangers. But the world seemed quiet and at peace.

The Mute leaned over the driver's side of the silver Ford and saw it had been left unlocked. He opened the door and peered inside. Everything seemed undisturbed. He began checking the area around the car, found two sets of footprints but no sign of struggle. He sighed and leaned against the side of the vehicle.

Idiots, he thought. *They went in without me.*

The question now was whether he should follow them in, maybe meet them coming out with the girl, or whether he should simply stay here and wait to meet them as they'd planned previously. Likely, if he waited, he'd be rewarded by Coffey and Hill coming to the meeting with the girl in tow. Of course, that assumed they'd be able to find the entrance to the bunker, even after he'd worked to disguise it. Still, maybe they were that good. He might have to come back in a day or two and retrieve a few things left behind, but that could wait. The important thing was the girl. He supposed that having them bring her to him was just as good as him picking her up himself. But it still irked him.

The smell of smoke from the Great Conecuh Fire still lingered in the air, but he was glad to be back in this place anyway. It felt like home, like a safe moment in a very dangerous world. He looked around and found a great oak tree that had survived the fire reasonably well, still thick with branches that grew toward the sun. It took only a moment to climb into the cover those branches provided, to situate himself comfortably with a nice view of the ground below. If he had to wait, at least this was a good place to do it. He let a breath slide through his lungs and settled in.

The first real sound he heard was not one he wanted to hear: the hum of ATV motors.

The Mute sat up in his perch and eased the SIG rifle over his head.

A moment later six Kawasaki ATVs rolled into the clearing. Three of the ATVs carried one man, the other three carried two. The Mute didn't need to see the black-clad fighting uniforms to know who these guys were. He recognized some of the faces from the aftermath of the battle at Truck's farm.

Not a good time for this, he told himself.

He counted the men: nine. Only nine. Based on his last observation of this crew of mercenaries, there should have been twelve. Where were the others? Already in the forest? Staking out Truck's farm, looking for people like Samuel Hill and Trudi Coffey to come walking in unaware?

The mercenaries left their vehicle and gathered in a group. Two of them detached and went to check out the Ford GT, then returned with a report for their comrades. The Mute couldn't make out exactly what they said, but it appeared that they expected to find that car in this place. That knowledge made The Mute even more uncomfortable.

If they know Coffey and Hill are here, he thought, *does that mean they also know that I'm here?*

He didn't have long to worry on that, because mere seconds later he heard the engine of another vehicle, a car this time. His eyes slitted when he saw a black Mercedes GL-Class SUV join the ATVs in the clearing. It was the same car he'd stalked in the wee hours of the morning back in Atlanta, outside of Trudi Coffey's PI office. He wasn't surprised when Samir exited from the driver's seat. He leveled his aim toward that man.

One shot and it's done, he thought. *At least then I can take out their leader before I die.*

But he knew that was a foolish tactic, one that likely condemned Trudi Coffey, Samuel Hill, and the girl to death as a result.

Patience, he told himself. *The opportunity will come.*

Down below, three more mercenaries also exited the black Mercedes. *Ten, eleven, twelve*, The Mute counted. *Those are the last fighters. Everyone is here. That's something, at least.*

He watched the soldiers come to attention at the sight of Samir. The Arab started giving orders. He saw him make arcing gestures, assigning certain roundabout paths to certain men.

They're not going straight in, The Mute thought. *They're not going to risk missing Coffey and Hill by going in a straight line. They're going to surround Truck's place first and then close in like a fist, coming from all directions, cutting off all exits. Good plan. Wish they hadn't thought of it.*

After everyone had their orders, Samir got back into his Mercedes, alone, and drove away. The mercenaries didn't hesitate. Four of them took off running on foot, heading into the forest in a southwesterly direction. Three more mounted ATVs and drove away into the trees, apparently moving toward positions to form the circle around Truck's farm. That left five men in the clearing.

After a moment, two of the men in the clearing climbed on a single ATV and headed out on the road, following the direction the Mercedes had gone moments before.

Securing the back lines, The Mute assumed. *Making sure no one can sneak up behind them. They'll be back soon.*

For now there were only three soldiers below him, and he watched as they took up positions around the Ford GT. They were the welcoming committee should Trudi Coffey or Samuel Hill make it out of the forest and try to escape in this car.

It was time to act.

The Mute peered into the scope on his rifle, finding a target on the mercenary farthest away, the one standing near the trunk of the car, behind the backs of the other two. Chances were good the other two might not even notice their comrade was dead at first, and if they did notice, there'd be a few seconds while they turned to inspect his body. They wouldn't be able to find The Mute and react before he got off two more shots, and that would be all he needed.

The Mute took in a deep breath and let the image of Truck's body on the front porch of his own home fill his mind.

This is for Truck, he told himself.

He squeezed the trigger. The first mercenary collapsed without making a noise. The other two soldiers never even turned around.

This is for the girl.

The second shot felled the shorter of the two black-clad fighters. The remaining soldier let out a shout and fumbled for his gun.

And this is for me.

It was over in seconds. Three shots. Three dead men. The Mute had learned long ago not to think about it more deeply than that. A sniper had to keep his work compartmentalized. Eliminate the enemy and move on. And The Mute was good at his work. He never let an enemy suffer with a mortal wound that took hours to accomplish its goal. He used kill shots only. One bullet and the job was done.

There were seventeen shots left in the twenty-round detachable box magazine on the SIG rifle, but he knew he wouldn't have opportunity to use them all. Didn't matter. He would only need two more for now.

He waited with the patience of a hunter, unmoving. It was thirty-two minutes before the two mercenaries on the ATV came rolling lazily back from the road and into the clearing. The Mute didn't give them time to discover the bodies of the other soldiers. He took out the driver first, then the passenger, and did it all before the ATV had a chance to crash into a tree.

The Mute inhaled and let a moment of stillness inhabit the world around him. He hoped that when he finally fell to an enemy's bullet, his foe would give him that same small courtesy someday. After the silence, he strapped the SIG rifle across his back and climbed down the tree. He checked his watch.

It was late. If Trudi Coffey and Samuel Hill weren't here by now, they weren't coming. He took a step toward the trees and stopped.

A crack of lightning thundered through the woods, followed closely by a second explosion.

Two gunshots.

He waited but didn't hear anything more.

Two gunshots, he told himself again. *One for Coffey and one for Hill? Or from them?*

He hesitated only a few seconds before picking a pathway. It appeared that he was needed inside the forest.

The Mute began jogging toward the thunder.

32

ANNABEL

I wake up to the sound of voices.

My mind feels foggy and clumsy. I'm not sure where I am or what's going on. It takes me a second to remember my lot in life, my purgatory with a killer hound.

Where is my hound?

I sit up on the top mattress of one of the bunk beds. After my flirtation with suicide, my senses righted themselves and I gave up that line of thinking. Pretty quick-like, I realized I didn't really care to be half dressed and freezing my toes into ice cubes. I slid into all my clothes except my shoes and wrapped up in a couple of sleeping bags here on this top bunk. Then time disappeared again.

When I woke up just now, I was snug and warm inside the sleeping bags. And I was hearing things.

I peek out from under my covers and check the room for ghosts. It's been a bit since I last seen any, but who knows what kind of schedule folks in the afterlife keep to? Maybe they been on vacation or something, and ready to get back to work on me now. Except they was never talking ghosts before. Always silent-film actors. Appearing, doing their thing, and then disappearing like magic dust.

I don't see any ghosts this time, but I do see my dog. Apparently I ain't the only one hearing things.

The dog is staring hard at the steel door, staring and hinting at baring his teeth. Like before, he don't growl. He just gives his full attention, fangs slightly showing, tail standing at high alert.

There's a soft rumble on the other side of the door, and now I know my mind ain't playing tricks. Somebody's comin' down that tunnel, close enough already that they can probably see the door. Maybe even already standing just outside.

I strain my ears, listening. A man's voice. Not Truck's. And a woman? There's a man and a woman out there?

The words they're saying are still muffled, hard to make out.

"Mdsf just because ydasff . . ."

"Wrfyfg must you alwffsys . . ."

Dog lets out a low growl.

"Ruhig sein," I hiss at him. *Be quiet.*

Dog don't look at me, but he does stop growling. He skitters a bit, searching for a better position from which to attack the door.

I drop off the top bunk and, just because it seems the proper thing, lace on my tennis shoes and put on my coat. Them voices are closer now, and if I listen hard, I can hear soft syllables slipping through the metal.

"You're just jealous that I found the tunnel and you didn't." It's the woman. "Whatsamatter, big boy? Don't like getting beat by a *guuurl?*"

"It's not a competition," the man says. "And besides, it doesn't matter who found the tunnel first. What matters is that I've got the key."

I hear something insert itself into the top dead bolt on the door. I hear a tinny "click" as the lock inside flips to the open position. I cover my mouth to keep any sound from accidentally popping out. The dog is growling again, low and even.

"What's that noise?" The woman.

"I don't hear anything. You must just be *a-skeered* down here in the darkness." His voice is teasing.

"No, seriously. I hear something. Wait."

I don't want to make any noise, so I risk placing my hand on the dog's head. He gets the message and stops growling but stays tense and ready next to me.

It's silent outside for just a drumbeat or two, then the man speaks.

"I don't hear anything at all, except my own breathing. Are you sure you heard something, Tru?"

"I don't know." Another long pause. "I guess not. I guess it was nothing."

A key enters the second dead bolt on the door. I hear it snap open with a sharp *tap* inside the casing.

"Is Truck the kind to leave booby traps lying around?" the woman asks.

So these two know Uncle Truck, I think. *But are they friends or enemies? Truck seems to have plenty of both.*

I can't stop my heart from racing. I can feel adrenaline pulsing into my hands and feet. My head pounds, but not in the same way as a headache. More like a countdown clock, ticking inside my earholes, taking me to a moment I'm not sure I want—but a moment I also desperately want to come.

"Well." The man draws out the word, like *we-eh-ell-ll*, like he's thinking on it before answering. "Yeah, generally speaking. But I don't think we have anything to worry about here. If Truck had booby-trapped this place, we probably would have hit it back at the tunnel entrance."

"Okay."

Now the key is in the third lock. I can't think what to do. Truck told me never to open that door unless he was on the other side, unless he was shouting the safe code at me from that tunnel. He said he give me the only key, his key. He never told me what to do if somebody on the outside just came a-barging in with another key—and without an invitation.

I see my dog bend low, ready to attack. It strikes me that if this dog is about to do some harm, then maybe I'm standing a bit too close to mayhem.

I step back, back, bump into the table, then move around and behind it.

The third dead bolt snaps to the unlocked position.

"After you," the woman says. "But we'd better hurry so we're back in time for the meet."

"Right."

The heavy metal door shudders, then scrapes wide. A large man is on the other side, hand on the knob, shoving it open. He's got short black hair and a thick, athletic build. He's wearing jeans and a brown leather bomber jacket. A woman stands behind him. Pretty. Long hair, and also athletic-looking. I can't make out much else about her because the man blocks most of her from view.

There's only one second from the time the door opens until my dog attacks. The animal makes no growls or barks to warn of his comin', just lunges directly toward the big man's throat. It's hard for me to look. The woman makes a choking sound, like she wants to scream a warning but knows no matter what she says it'll be too late.

The man is fast, faster than I expect him to be. In what must be a fightin' reflex, he ducks low under Dog's snapping jaws, ramming his shoulder into the animal's chest and shoving him backward. Dog is barely set off by that, finding new purchase for his footing and lunging again. This time the man is ready. He grabs the door handle and tugs, slamming the steel into the jamb before the dog can get close to him again. Dog claws at the door, growling and snarling, but there's nothing he can do. The hellhound's quarry is safe on the other side, in the tunnel.

After a moment, the dog stops clawing. It sniffs busily at the edges of the door and then comes over to my side, breathing hard and angry. I kneel beside him.

"*Guter Hund*," I whisper. *Good dog.* "*Setz dich.*" *Sit down.*

On the other side of the door, I hear them two talking. And I hear the bottom dead bolt snap back into a locked position.

"What was that?" the man says.

"Looked like a booby-trap to me," the woman says. Her way of saying "I told you so," I guess.

"That animal tried to kill me."

"Maybe," she says. "Or maybe it was just protecting the girl."

"What?"

"That little girl behind the table. Maybe it was just trying to protect her."

"What girl? There's no girl in there. Is there?"

"How could you not see the girl?" There's exasperation in the woman's voice. "She was standing there plain as hallway twins in *The Shining*, looking straight at you all calm and collected. Wearing a blue coat. You didn't see her?"

I feel an irrational flush of pride. *The woman thought I was calm and collected? I was scared to the nibs. But she didn't know that. Nice.*

"No, I didn't see her. I was otherwise occupied with a rabid, fanged beast that wanted to eat my throat. Maybe that distracted my attention?"

"Right. You're right. Thanks for fending off the attack, by the way."

"We aim to please." I hear him smiling in his words.

"So," the woman says, "what do we do now?"

There's a moment that passes, then the man speaks. He's apparently leaning close to the door, trying to make himself heard.

"Little girl?" he says. "Little girl inside the bunker? Can you hear me?"

Dog starts growling. I don't say nothing.

"Little girl?" he says again. "We come in peace."

Even I roll my eyes. I hear the woman.

"Idiot," she says. "Why are all men idiots?"

"Little girl—"

She interrupts him. "Stop calling her little girl. Clearly she has a name."

"Well, we don't know her name, do we?"

Now the woman is close to the door.

"What's your name, sweetie? My name is Trudi. The handsome idiot with me is Samuel. Will you tell us your name?"

Something in me wants to answer this woman. But I'm not ready to tell her my name. Not yet.

"What you want?" I say.

I hear the woman shushing the man.

"Truck sent us," she says.

"How do you know my uncle?" I say.

"Uncle?" It's the man. "Leonard Truckson is your uncle?"

I don't answer. I hear the woman talking to the man again. "Will you keep your mouth shut for just five minutes? Please?" Then to me she says, "Samuel used to work for him. For your uncle."

Something's not right with that answer. I ain't never seen this guy 'round Truck's farm. 'Course, Uncle Truck traveled a lot. He could have hired this guy from anywhere. But that wasn't the problem at this juncture.

"What do you mean, 'used to'?" I say.

They don't respond right away. Then the woman speaks.

"Honey, I don't know how to tell you this. Your uncle is, um, well, he's dead. He was killed in a raid on your farm here. I'm sorry."

Baby girl time again. I can't stop tears from choking through me. The dog stands and walks a circle around me, then sits again, pressing his side against my hip.

Truck's dead? That would explain why he ain't never come to get me. But it don't explain why I feel so suddenly lost in a foggy sea.

I hear whispering on the other side of the door, and finally the woman hisses to the man, "Just give her a minute. She just lost her uncle. Give her a little courtesy, okay?"

I'm starting to like this cranky woman. I sit in the chair at the table and let myself heave out a few sobs. It don't take long, just long enough. When I'm ready, I call out to the door.

"What you want? There's nothing in here but me and this dog."

"Honey." The woman's voice sounds almost like family. "Are you okay in there? Do you need anything?"

"Tell her to call off the dog so we can go in," the man says. She ignores him.

"Have you eaten? Do you need some food?" she says.

"Tell that man I can't let him in," I say. "I can't let anybody in unless they know the safe code Truck give me."

The man curses. I think he thinks I didn't hear him. "Could you make this any harder, Truck?"

"Okay," the woman says. "That's okay. But can you at least tell us your name, honey. And if there's anybody you want us to call for you?"

Rendel, I think. *Curtis. Kenny. The Mute. Any of Truck's boys, really.* But I don't say that out loud. If they don't know Truck's boys, I won't give 'em away.

"Annabel," I say at last. "Annabel Truckson."

There's a little commotion on the other side of the door.

"Wait a minute," the woman says. "Is your name Annabel *Lee* Truckson?"

I feel a shiver. She knows my name?

"Yes, ma'am," I say. "Annabel Lee Truckson."

There's whispering on the other side of the door. I get up and move closer so's I can hear it better.

". . . the map. Don't you see?" It's the woman. "Truck didn't mean 'Alabama' when he put 'AL' on that map. He meant Annabel Lee. He meant the poem, and his niece."

"I don't get it," the man whispers. "How does that help us?"

"Give me a second," she says. Then I hear her begin to recite my poem. "'It was many and many a year ago'—Line 1. 'In a kingdom by the sea'—Line 2. 'That a maiden there lived whom you may know'—Line 3. 'By the name of Annabel Lee'—Line 4."

I find myself reciting alongside her.

> And this maiden she lived with no other thought
> Than to love and be loved by me.
> I was a child and she was a child,
> In this kingdom by the sea . . .

She stops, and I hear her counting. "Line 9," she mutters, "words 6 through 11 . . ."

I step back from the door. Dog is by my side, snarling at the steel before us.

"Annabel, honey," the woman says to me. "Love that was more than love."

I feel something release inside me, a gratefulness that I just can't describe.

So, Truck didn't leave me all alone out on that sea. Truck had a backup plan, and that plan is standing outside right now.

"*Geht!*" I say to the dog, motioning toward the outhouse. When he stands at the door to the toilets, I tell him "*Ruhig sein.*" *Be quiet.* "*Sich hinlegen.*" *Lie down.* "*In Frieden.*" *Be at peace.* Dog obeys me, but he don't seem happy about it.

"Ma'am," I say, "I'm gonna open the door."

33

TRUDI

Trudi tried to move in front of Samuel so that she'd be the first thing the girl saw when she opened the door, but her ex-husband would have nothing to do with that. The memory of the attack dog was too fresh, apparently. He jutted out his arm and took two steps backward, forcing Trudi to do the same.

It was only a moment before she heard the bottom lock click and the heavy steel door begin to scrape. The girl was not as strong as Samuel, so it took her a few tugs to get it to open wide enough for a clear view.

She was a pretty little thing, with a face that was much too serious for a child at her stage in life. Trudi guessed Annabel was twelve or thirteen, but she couldn't be sure. She had chestnut hair that dipped past her shoulders, and a lean but healthy frame that looked used to chores on a farm. Trudi gazed into her eyes and felt a dawning realization.

In front of her, Samuel stood carefully aloof, trying not to scare her and thus incite the ire of the guard dog. He searched the room before saying anything, making sure he knew where the dog was stationed, making sure he was ready in case of another attack. When it became clear that the girl had subdued the German shepherd in an open-air doorway across the room, he turned his attention to the child.

He knelt down partway until he was about eye level with her, and he extended his hand. "Ms. Truckson," he said, "my name is Samuel Hill. It's a pleasure to meet you."

The girl flushed a little in her cheeks, but her expression remained serious. She shook his hand gently. "You can call me Annabel," she said.

Samuel held her eyes for a moment, and Trudi could see that he'd made the same deduction she had. He sighed ever so slightly, and nodded. "You have beautiful green eyes, Annabel," he said. He let his gaze drift sideways up to Trudi. "Like two emeralds. Priceless."

So Truck hadn't hidden gemstones in this underground bunker. He'd hidden his niece, his priceless niece. Someone he desperately wanted to keep safe.

Trudi stepped forward and also extended a hand. "I'm Trudi," she said. "May we come in?"

Annabel vacated the doorway to let them enter. Over by the wall, the dog sat up on his front legs and started growling.

"*Aufhören!*" the girl said sharply. "*Ruhig sein.*" The dog responded immediately. He licked his lips nervously but stopped growling and baring his teeth.

"*Aufhören,*" Samuel said genially. "I think that means 'stop it' or something like that, am I right?"

"Cease," the girl said. "You speak German?"

"Only a little." He grinned. "Only when Truck was yelling at me and expecting me to know what he said."

The girl gave a small smile. Apparently she and Samuel had had similar experiences with Leonard Truckson.

"*Ruhig sein*," Samuel said. "I don't know what that means."

"Be quiet," Annabel said. "I told him to stop growling at you."

Trudi and Sam both nodded. Trudi began to take stock of the surroundings. Food on shelves. Bunk beds. Water in a bucket on the floor. And a table in the middle of the room with four chairs around it.

"How long have you been down here, sweetie?" she asked.

The girl shrugged. "I kinda lost track of things."

"I can see how that could happen," Trudi said.

"Miss Annabel," Samuel said, motioning to the table, "may we sit down and talk to you for a minute or two? I think we all have some things to figure out."

Annabel nodded and took a chair at the table, sitting on the far side, facing toward the steel door. Samuel and Trudi occupied the seats on her right and her left.

"Where are you from, Annabel?" Samuel asked.

"Right here on Truck's farm." She looked at Samuel like he'd just asked a stupid question.

Samuel cleared his throat and tried again.

"I mean, where are you from originally?"

"Alabama."

Samuel looked mildly frustrated.

"Where were you born?"

"Peachtree, I guess. Or maybe Mobile." She shrugged. "Truck never said what hospital exactly I was born in."

A light sigh escaped Samuel's lips.

"I mean, where are your parents from?"

"What's the big deal with where she's from, Samuel?" Trudi interrupted. "Give her a break. She's from here. She lives with her uncle. Isn't that enough for now?"

"No, Trudi, that's not enough," Samuel said evenly. "You don't understand what's going on here, so just let me do my job. Okay?"

"What's going on, mister?" Annabel said.

Samuel leaned back in his chair and stared at the ceiling as if asking for patience. Or wisdom. Or both.

"What do you know about your uncle's work?" he asked at last. "Did he ever talk to you about that?"

"You mean the work here on the farm? Or . . . or the other stuff?"

"The other stuff."

"No. He never talked much about that. Nothing specific, at least."

"What are you getting at, Samuel?" Trudi asked. She was losing her patience. "Just lay it out and stop playing spy games. We're in a bunker ten feet underground where we found a little girl and a rabid dog. We've got strange people chasing us, maybe wanting to kill us, and a mute assassin waiting for us at a rendezvous point. I think we're well past whatever you think is 'classified' at this point."

"She's a Fade, Trudi." Samuel sounded remarkably calm. "I'm just trying to find out why and where she came from. I've never known Truck to Fade a child before, so you'll forgive me for not having all the answers right now, okay?"

Trudi felt like her ex-husband was speaking a foreign language, or that they were speaking a language where all the words had different meanings.

"What in the world is a Fade?"

Samuel turned to the girl. "Do you know what a Fade is, Annabel? Did Truck ever talk to you about that?"

She shook her head slowly. The girl was trying to keep up with the conversation but was clearly just as confused as Trudi was.

"Did Truck ever talk to you about leaving this farm, about leaving Alabama?"

Annabel shook her head, then paused. "Well, he said that when I turned thirteen he was planning to take me on a trip to see the world. Something like that."

Samuel nodded. "Okay," he said. "That helps. That probably means you are a Fade Thirteen, meaning you are to stay Faded until you turn thirteen and you can reclaim. How old are you now?"

"Eleven," Annabel said. "I'll be twelve on December 13."

Trudi felt as confused as she imagined the girl to be. She tried not to sound annoyed.

"Samuel," she said. "I don't know about Annabel here, but I'm lost. Can you start at the beginning and explain this to me? What's a Fade?"

Samuel looked at Trudi, then back at Annabel.

"Okay," he said, "here it is. In a nutshell. Truck was a professional Fader. That was his main job with the CIA."

"Uncle Truck was CIA?" Annabel sounded genuinely surprised. Samuel nodded.

"What does a professional Fader do?" Trudi asked.

Seemingly unaware that he was doing it, Samuel rubbed a spot on his forearm. Trudi noticed the place he rubbed was where an Army Special Forces tattoo was inked into his skin.

"A Fader helps people escape from, well, impossible circumstances. He hides them away until it's safe for them to come back."

"Like the witness protection program?"

"Similar, but not exactly. With witness protection, the person disappears into a completely different life forever. With a Fade, the subject is just hidden for a time, and any assets the subject has are kept in trust or hidden until the end of the Fade when they can be reclaimed."

"If that's what Truck was doing, then why did you think he was keeping gemstones in this bunker?"

Samuel looked a little embarrassed. "Well, it's kind of expensive to implement a Fade. And Truck was never shy about getting paid."

"I see," Trudi said. "So Truck was allowed to steal from the people he Faded. To skim off the top of their bank accounts and valuables for himself."

"The CIA called it his 'commission' for services rendered." Samuel shrugged. "I never said Truck was a saint. Anyway, a Fade may last years, but in the end it's always temporary. That's why I need to know where Annabel came from, what her life was before she came to Truck. So she can reclaim her life. That's what Truck intended."

"I been with Uncle Truck for longer than I can remember," Annabel interrupted suddenly. "Since I was a baby. He told me my parents was killed in a war." A hesitation, like she wasn't sure she should reveal what came next. "I think maybe the war in Iraq. Truck said my mother give me to him to take care of."

Samuel looked thoughtful. He leaned over the table and looked deeply into Annabel's eyes.

"You should know," he said, "that Truck never personally watched over a Fade, not that I ever knew of. The fact that he actually made you a part of his family and stayed with you all these years means you must be something special. Your mother too."

The girl looked grateful at Samuel's words. There was a thick moment of silence among them, then she asked, "What happened to Uncle Truck?"

Trudi looked to Samuel, who hung his head slightly. "I don't know all the details, Annabel, I was just told that he'd been killed. Told by someone close to him."

"Who."

It wasn't a question, it was an assumption that Samuel would tell her whatever she wanted to know.

"Well, I don't know his real name." Samuel actually looked a little flustered. "He's one of Truck's old army boys. He goes by a nickname."

"What nickname?"

Samuel shrugged. "Well, Truck always called him The Mute."

Trudi started to roll her eyes at her ex-husband, but then she saw a flicker of recognition cross the girl's face. Was that hope in her eyes?

"The Mute," Annabel said. Her face brightened considerably. "The Mute. Is he here? Is he with you?"

Trudi and Samuel exchanged a glance.

"You know The Mute?" Trudi asked. The girl nodded.

"Is he with you?" she asked again.

Trudi got the feeling that once this child asked a question, she never let it go until it was answered. *Kind of like* The Little Prince, Trudi thought, *in the classic book by Antoine de Saint-Exupery.* Then, in a moment of randomness, *Wow, I should read that book again . . .* Trudi pushed that thought aside and forced her mind to return to the present moment.

"No," she said to Annabel, "The Mute's not here with us now. Not yet, at least."

"But he is in the area," Samuel said. "He's very concerned about you and your safety. We're supposed to meet him. Soon."

"If you want," Trudi said, "we'll take you to him, honey."

Annabel nodded. "If The Mute's here, he'll help me. He'll help us. He has to."

Trudi and Samuel exchanged a glance. *Stone-cold killer is a friend of this little girl's?* Trudi thought. *There's definitely more to this child than meets the eye.*

"Why is that?" Samuel asked.

"He's my godfather. Truck made him so. He's bound to me. He'll help me."

"Godfather?" Samuel snorted in surprise. "Don't you have to be Catholic for that? I don't know that Truck ever found religion, did he?"

Annabel shrugged. "My uncle never said. But The Mute's my godfather either way."

"All right then," Samuel said. "The Mute is your godfather." He looked around the bunker again, and his eyes fell on the dog. "Is it safe to travel with that dog?"

The girl turned and faced her pet. There was genuine confusion on her face. "I don't know," she said at last. "I never took him anywhere."

Samuel's hand brushed nervously at his sternum. If possible, Trudi thought she saw the dog grin at that. But of course, that wasn't possible. Samuel peered through the open doorway and down the tunnel.

"Does The Mute know your dog?" Trudi asked. "Does the dog know The Mute?"

The girl nodded. "He helped Truck to train him a few years back."

The girl's eyes flicked to the floor, then toward the dog in the corner. Trudi noticed that she stuffed her hands underneath her thighs in her chair. The girl seemed uncomfortable at the thought of the dog's training but didn't say anything more.

"Okay, then," Trudi said. She turned to her ex-husband. "Why don't you go get The Mute and bring him here, Samuel? My guess is he's already got a plan for traveling with both the dog and the girl." She turned back to the child. "I'll stay here with Annabel. We'll tell stories to each other to pass the time until you get back."

Samuel hesitated. He nodded toward the dog. "Will she be safe in here with your pet?" he asked the girl.

Annabel looked from the dog to Trudi and back again. "I'll make sure he behaves," she said. The girl said it with conviction, but for some reason Trudi felt like she was trying to convince herself as much as she was Samuel.

Trudi's ex-husband checked his watch.

"Go," Trudi said. "If you leave now, you'll get there just in time to meet him. Bring him back here and we can all be on our way."

"Are you sure this is a good idea?" he said.

"Sure it is," Trudi said. She walked over to Annabel and took her hand. "We'll have fun. It'll be like girls' night out."

"I'll protect her," Annabel told Samuel, and she said it with such seriousness that even he stifled a chuckle.

"Yes, I think you will," he said at last. "Okay, I'll go. I'll get The Mute and bring him back here, and then we can all go someplace safe to talk about what happens next."

Samuel reached into his pocket and produced his key to the bunker. He handed it to Trudi. "You lock that door as soon as I close it, and you keep it shut and locked until I get back. Promise?"

"Of course," Trudi said. "But you'd better get going or you'll be late. We'll be fine. Just go."

Samuel nodded toward his ex-wife. Then he knelt down in front of the girl. "I'm glad we met, Annabel. I'll be back soon. And someday you've got to remind me to tell you some great stories about your crazy uncle."

The girl at last let her face relax into a real smile.

"I look forward to hearing you tell them stories, sir," she said. He patted her quickly on the shoulder.

"You can call me Samuel."

"Okay."

He stood and pointed at the steel door. "Don't open this door again until I get back. Until you hear me say Annabel's safe code from the other side. Got it?"

Trudi and Annabel both nodded. Satisfied, he turned and walked into the tunnel, pulling the heavy door closed behind him.

"Trudi?" he called through the steel.

"I'm doing it, I'm doing it," she said, jumping toward the door. Only after Samuel was convinced all three dead bolts were locked in place did they hear him jog away from the door and down the tunnel.

Trudi turned to the girl and smiled. "So, nice place you got here. What's the neighborhood like?"

34

ANNABEL

It don't take long for me to decide I like this Trudi lady.

She's nice, for starters. And she laughs easy. But mostly I'm impressed at how comfortable this woman is in front of that dog. She shows absolutely no fear, barely even looks in the animal's direction. The dog seems to have figured that out too, because after a time he quits watching her and just lays his head down on the floor, over by the outhouse where I'm making him stay.

After Samuel Hill leaves, Trudi glances around and then sits comfortably on the bottom mattress of one of the bunk beds.

"Want to tell me a story?" She smiles.

I shrug. I can't think of any good stories at this particular juncture.

"All right," she says. "How about a game? You ever play the Question Game?"

I shake my head.

"It goes like this. We take turns asking each other questions until we get to know each other enough to become friends. Do you want to go first?"

I shake my head, but I also walk over and sit on the bed with her. Out of habit, I pull a sleeping bag over my legs to keep warm.

"Okay, I'll go first," she says. "What's something everybody should know about Annabel Lee Truckson?"

"I am an educated girl," I say without thinking. I'm surprised at first by my response, then I realize that fact is important to me, that I want this lady to know that about me.

"Really?" She says it with genuine interest. "I would have guessed. Where do you go to school?"

"No schools," I say. "Truck says that's a waste of time and taxpayer dollars. I learn stuff from Truck."

"I see," she says. "What kind of things did Truck teach you?"

"Math. Reading. Geography. Languages. That kind of stuff."

She laughs lightly. "I'm pretty good at English, but I was never much with foreign languages. *¿Dónde está el baño?* That's about the best I ever got with Spanish."

Where is the bathroom? My mind translates it automatically.

"I can speak some Spanish," I say. "But I'm best at German and Creole."

"Amazing," she says. "Four languages, and you're only eleven years old?"

I shrug. Truck spoke more than that, but I guess four or five languages ain't bad neither.

"So you really are an educated girl," she says to me, and I hear admiration in her voice. "You are something special, Annabel. That's for sure."

"Is it my turn to ask a question now?" I say.

"Of course. Ask away."

"Are you an educated girl?"

She dimples. "Well, yes, but in a different way than you. I went to college at the University of Georgia. That's where I met Samuel."

"What you learn there?"

"I studied English literature and world mythologies."

That sounds like a lot of gobbledygook to me, but I try to look appreciative. She laughs at my expression.

"Mostly that means I spent my time reading a lot of great old stories and poems and tried to understand them."

I decide right then that if I ever go to college, I'm gonna study English literature and world mythologies. Spending long days and nights reading stories in old books sounds like heaven.

"Is that why you knew my poem?"

"Well, I guess so," she says. "But, you know, I've always liked Edgar Allan Poe, especially his poetry. I've been reading his work since I was younger than you."

"So are you a teacher now?" I ask. "Do you teach people about all those old stories?"

"No, no I don't." She looks rueful. "Sometimes a person's education doesn't translate well in the real world, and for some reason, not many people want to hire a girl who spent four years reading stories and memorizing poems by Edgar Allan Poe."

"So what do you do?"

"Believe it or not, I'm a private investigator. I help people solve problems, kind of like a police detective, but I work on my own instead of working for the police."

"Telling stories sounds like a better job. Maybe you should try to be a teacher."

"Maybe I should, Annabel Lee, maybe I should."

"And Samuel?"

"CIA."

"Right. I forgot. He seems like the kind who should be a private investigator though."

"Well, he has done that too." I see her rubbing the empty ring finger on her left hand. "It's complicated."

That's what grown-ups always say when they don't want to talk about stuff, so I decide to let it drop. "What about this?" I ask, pointing to a thick, silver cross hanging on a steel chain around her neck.

"What about it?"

"Truck says that sometimes he thinks that's all a myth too."

"What do you think?"

"I ain't so sure."

"Mmm."

"Ain't it now when you start preaching at me?" I say. I've been in this kind of conversation before. She grins.

"I think," she says, "somebody else is already talking to you about this subject."

I nod. Maybe she's right. Maybe that's why I can't stop think-ing about that unknown God out there. Maybe he's already talking to me, deep inside, telling me to believe. I'm gonna have to deal with that possibility someday. Someday soon, I think.

"You have questions you want to ask?" Trudi says. I shake my head. No, not yet at least.

"All right," she says, and it seems like she's made some kind of decision in her head. "When you have a question, you let me know and we'll see what we can find out. Together. Mean-time"—she reaches up and removes her necklace—"you take this. It'll remind you that God sometimes comes calling when you least expect him. And, of course, it'll remind you of me too." She dimples, and I can't help but mirror her smile.

"Okay," I say, taking the necklace and putting it in my pocket. "Your turn."

"Do you like stories?" she says.

I can't keep myself from grinning. "The way a possum likes june bugs for breakfast."

Trudi laughs again, and I'm noticing that I like it when she laughs. She looks at her watch. "Well," she says, "we've got probably an hour or so before Samuel gets back here with The Mute. Want me to tell you a story?"

I nod and settle back under the sleeping bag.

"Okay," she says. I notice she's rubbing her legs with her hands. She's wearing a thin wool coat over jeans and some lay-ered shirts. Probably fine for upground, but maybe she's getting cold down here in the bunker. I lift up an edge on the sleeping bag. She looks a little surprised but then slides under it next to me.

"Thanks, honey," she says. "It is a little chilly in here."

I like the warmth of her next to me. It reminds me of when Truck used to sit me in his lap and read to me. It reminds me of family.

"All right," she says. "How about Greek mythology. Do you know the story of *The Iliad*?"

I shake my head, and she continues.

"Well, *The Iliad* is the story of the Trojan War. Bunch of men fighting over a woman, as usual. But a long time ago in the ancient world, the warriors of Greece sailed a thousand ships to fight the warriors of the city of Troy. One of the princes of Troy had married a beautiful maiden named Helen. Problem was, she was already married to one of the princes in Greece. So the Greek fighters came to steal her back.

"*The Iliad* starts right in the middle of that war. The Greek kings had banded together and taken over most of the cities and towns surrounding Troy, and now, every day the Trojan armies and the Greek armies fought battles to see who would win possession of the city of Troy—and of the beautiful Helen. Agamemnon was leader of the Greek kings, but the best warrior among the Greeks was Achilles."

"I've heard of Achilles," I say. "Wasn't he the guy that got stuck in the heel with an arrow?"

"Yes," she says, "that's him. But that comes later in the story. Right now he's still an unstoppable warrior, cutting down anyone and anything that dares to stand in his path."

"Okay," I say. "Go 'head on."

"Well, one day Agamemnon got jealous and demanded that Achilles give him a slave girl they'd taken captive in a previous battle. Achilles didn't like that one bit. He was furious at Agamemnon about it, but what could he do? Agamemnon was the *prōtos* among the Greek kings, the big bad king. And so—"

"Wait a minute," I say. "Wait. What was Agamemnon?"

"He was the main king for the Greeks, the leader in the kings' coalition and council."

"No, what'd you call him? Just now, what'd you call him?"

"Oh, I see. He was the prōtos."

"What's that mean?"

She leans back and looks at me in mock surprise. "What? Could it be?" she teases. "The remarkable Annabel, our finely educated girl, doesn't know what prōtos means? There's actually a language her mind has yet to unravel?"

I frown at her, but my eyes are smiling. "It's ancient Greek, right? I know that much. I just don't know what that particular word means."

"Prōtos." She says it loudly enough that my dog looks up from his spot by the outhouse. She don't notice this, but I do. "It means 'foremost,' or 'best of all.' First over everything."

"Like"—I think for a minute—"like chief dog in the pack?"

"Right. So when King Agamemnon gave an order, Achilles

and the others had to follow that order because he was the prōtos, the 'chief dog' in the pack of Greek leaders. Make sense?"

I look over at my dog, and he's got his eyes locked onto mine. It all makes sense now, Truck's words when he put me in this place. Truck was the prōtos for that dog. The boss, the chief of him. And when Truck left me down here, he transferred that position to me. In that dog's eyes, I became the prōtos, the one person the dog had to obey.

Truck gave me his own place in that dog's eyes. From the moment when he forced that dog to smell my fist and take me as his prōtos, this dog became my dog.

"You okay, honey?" Trudi has stopped telling me her story. She watches me closely, also now keeping an eye on the dog across the room from us.

"I'm fine," I say. "I just made sense of something I hadn't figured out before."

"Something to do with that dog?" she asks. I nod.

"Can we finish *The Iliad* in a minute, Trudi?" I ask.

"Of course," she says. Then she waits.

I get up and walk over to my dog. He pushes up on his front legs and sits tall, waiting for me to give a command.

"Du bist ein guter Hund," I say. *"Ein guter Freund."*

You're a good dog. A good friend.

The animal seems pleased. His tail swishes on the carpeted floor. I go over to the shelves and pull a strip of beef jerky out, giving it to my dog as a treat. To her credit, Trudi don't say nothing, she just watches. When Dog finishes his treat, I say "okay" and release him from the spot by the outhouse. Trudi don't respond, but I see in her eyes that she's suddenly concerned about having this dog loose inside this cooped-up space. I decide to do something about that.

I walk over to sit next to Trudi on the bunk bed, and I call to the dog.

"*Komm her.*" The animal steps warily over to us. He seems to sense that Trudi is not a threat, but he don't trust her neither.

I take Trudi's hand in mine and form it into a fist. Then I push it out toward the dog. Trudi don't resist. She trusts me, and that makes me decide to trust her as well.

The dog sniffs at her fist but don't bare his teeth or growl.

"*Schützen,*" I say to him.

The dog looks at me and then at Trudi. He sniffs her hand once more and then gives a light snort.

"*Schützen,*" I say again.

The dog pushes his nose against her hand, then trots to the door, where he lies down across the opening.

"Annabel?" Trudi says.

"It's okay," I tell her. "He'll protect you now. I told him to protect you, and I am his prōtos. He has to obey."

"I see," she says. But she seems unconvinced.

I climb back under the sleeping bag next to her and get comfortable.

"So," I say, "what happened next with Achilles and Agamemnon?"

Before she can answer, Dog jumps to attention. My animal stares hard at the steel door, baring his teeth. Like before, there ain't no growling. Just full attention, fangs slightly showing, tail standing at high alert.

There's an unexpected pounding on the door.

"Annabel," Samuel's voice says. "Are you in there?"

"I'm here," I call out just before Trudi claps a hand across my mouth. "Wait," she hisses in my ear. "It's too soon for him to be back. Quiet."

There's a grunt on the other side of the door. Did Samuel bump into something?

"Ooookay," he says slowly. He sounds disappointed. "So you're in there after all."

What's he talking about? He knows I'm in here. He left me here himself.

Trudi's whisper is so close it's almost inside my head.

"He shouldn't be here for at least another half hour," she says. "Ask him for the safe code."

"What's the safe code?" I call out. I hear a rustling sound on the other side of the door. Then he speaks again.

"I will dwell in the house of the Lord forever."

Wait a minute, ain't that the Bible? What's that supposed to mean?

Trudi reacts almost immediately. She pulls us both out of the sleeping bag until we're standing on the floor by the table. She kneels very close to my ear.

"He's not alone," she whispers. "It's not safe."

"Annabel?" he says. "Did you hear the code? I said, 'I will dwell in the house of the Lord forever.'"

"Tell him okay." Her whisper is still almost inside my head. "Stall. Tell him you're coming to open the door."

"Okay," I holler at the door. "Give me a second. I'll be right there."

"Good," Trudi hisses.

She reaches into the back of her jeans and comes out with a small pistol. It reminds me of the Beretta guns Uncle Truck showed me in Mobile, and I wonder, briefly, if he would've really gotten one for me when my birthday came 'round in December. But that thought quickly shunts away as I watch Trudi. She handles her gun like she's greeting an old friend.

"Take the dog and go hide in that room." She points toward

the outhouse. "I'm going to have to fight now, and I don't want to have to worry about you getting caught in the mess, okay?"

Dog still isn't growling, but he does skitter a bit, searching for just the right place for an attack. I walk over to him and put my hand on the nape of his neck. He divides his attention between me and the door, and somehow I manage to convey to him to follow me. We go into the outhouse. I put the dog inside, away from the opening, but I stand where I can see what's going on in the main room of the bunker.

I hear Samuel grunt again. Then: "Annabel? Are you still in there?"

Trudi nods at me.

"I'm comin'," I shout.

Trudi flattens herself just inside the doorway, against the wall. She raises the gun over her head with one hand. With the other, she takes out Samuel's key and begins unlocking the dead bolts, going from the bottom to the top.

Click.

Click.

Trudi takes a deep breath.

Click.

A moment later, the handle turns from the outside, and the door begins to push open.

My dog growls beside me, low and even.

35

TRUDI

Trudi felt herself take a deep breath and hold it. She was ready.

She reached across her body and slid the key into the last dead bolt, twitching it into the unlocked position. A moment later the handle turned from the outside, and the door began to swing inside the bunker. Trudi hoped that Samuel would be smart enough to get out of the way quickly, but after the door was open, nothing happened. No one entered.

Trudi was beginning to regret that she was holding her breath. She heard several feet shuffle, then Samuel's voice.

"Well, are we going in or what?"

"Quiet," another voice said, and she heard Samuel grunt. A blow to the ribs, she figured. She heard a radio frequency click open. "We've found the girl," the voice said. "Underground bunker."

Trudi looked across the room and saw Annabel peeking out from the doorway in the wall, staring straight at the entrance to the bunker.

"On the way," another voice answered through the radio.

Trudi couldn't place the accents. Were they German? She couldn't tell. She split her lips and tried to let air slide silently out between her teeth. *Come on, come on*, she fretted.

As if in response, Samuel stepped into the room. She saw his eyes catch sight of her in his periphery vision, but he didn't react.

"Come on in, fellas," he said jovially. "You afraid of a little girl or something?" He winked toward Annabel. Trudi saw that his hands were bound with a zip tie in front of him and that he was no longer wearing his jacket. Worse yet, the holster strapped to his side was empty.

So he'd been ambushed on the way to find The Mute. But what had happened to The Mute? A question for Future Trudi. Right now she had other things to worry about.

Samuel turned around and faced the doorway. He reached up and scratched his nose with two fingers.

Two bad guys, Trudi thought. *Thanks for the tip, Samuel.*

Samuel stepped backward as the first bad guy entered the bunker, drawing his attention away from where Trudi stood hidden beside the door. She was going to steal a page from Samir's playbook, but she needed to wait until the second goon entered.

The guy holding the gun on Samuel was thick and athletic. He wore a black military outfit that featured several weapons attached in various places and a radio Velcroed to the shoulder. His hair was dirty blond and short, cropped so close to his head it was almost nonexistent. His eyes surveyed the main room of the bunker but gratefully failed to check behind his back where Trudi hid.

The second goon was dressed similarly, but his hair was brown and fell down just over his ears. This was the man Trudi accosted.

When the brown-haired goon was two steps into the room, Trudi stepped forward and pressed the muzzle of her Beretta

Tomcat into the top of his spine, just where it entered the base of his skull. She also delivered a sharp blow into the man's left kidney at the same time, making sure her gun followed, and was felt, as he sank down in his boots.

"I'd keep still if I were you," she said. The man started to turn, so she cracked the meat of her pistol across the base of his skull. This time he sank to one knee and kept still.

The blond goon swung around at the sound of Trudi's commotion, and when he did, Samuel struck, sweeping his manacled fists into a double-barreled uppercut that landed squarely under Blondie's chin. The goon's eyes rolled up into his head and he crumpled to the floor.

"One shot and he's out?" Trudi said admiringly. "You been working out, Samuel?"

Samuel ignored the comment, but Trudi could see his eyes twinkle at the compliment.

"You won't succeed," the brown-haired goon said through a thick tongue. "We are many."

Samuel ignored him too. Instead he beckoned to the girl peering into the room.

"Annabel," he said. "You did great. Now, do you have a knife or something to cut me loose?"

"You should give up now," Brown Head said. "You—"

He didn't finish because Trudi smacked him in the skull with her gun again. "Thought I told you to keep still," she said. "That includes talking." The goon fell silent.

It took only seconds for Annabel to cut Samuel's bonds. It took a little longer to prevent the dog from biting into the flesh of Brown Head and Blondie.

"They ambushed me about halfway out," Samuel said, retrieving his Glock 36 from the now-groggy blond goon. Once he'd reholstered his gun, he also relieved the two goons of their weaponry. "They said they had mercenaries surrounding Truck's farm on all sides, and then they brought me back here. When they saw the opening to the tunnel, they forced me down here."

"He called for backup," Trudi said. "That means it's time for us to go."

"Gonna have to keep them from following us," Samuel said. He picked up one of the mercenaries and shoved him roughly toward the bunk beds. A moment later Blondie's hands were zip-tied around a wooden beam on the beds. Brown Head was quickly subdued in the same way.

"What about the guns?" Trudi asked. "Too many to take with us. But we can't leave them here either. They could be used against us later."

"I know what to do," Annabel said, jumping into motion. She loaded the weapons into her arms and disappeared into one of the openings in the wall. They heard the clatter of machinery, and then Annabel returned.

"Tossed 'em down the sewer," she said. "Gone."

Trudi was really beginning to like this kid.

Samuel turned to Brown Head. "How close are your buddies out there?" he said. "And how many?"

Brown Head sneered. "Eat worms and die," he said.

Samuel laughed out loud. "Wow, do you watch old movies or something? Keep working on it, bro. You'll come up with something better next time."

Brown Head braced for a blow, but Samuel just patted him on the head. "Kids say the darndest things, don't they, Trudi?"

Even Annabel chuckled at that. Trudi holstered her Beretta and tapped her watch. "Time to go, Sam."

He looked at the dog and then at the girl.

"What do you think, Annabel?"

"I think I can handle him," she said. Samuel nodded. Annabel turned to the dog and said one word. *"Geht!"* She motioned toward the open doorway.

The animal shuffled up beside her, nudged her with his nose as if to say, "Okay, but you come too," then he bolted down the tunnel. He was out of sight before they could breathe.

"How far do you think he'll go?" Trudi said, and she saw Annabel's face go white.

"I don't know."

"Then let's go find out," Samuel said.

The man and the girl started on a trot after the dog. Trudi paused long enough to pull the heavy steel door closed, then she followed. When she got to the end of the tunnel, she found Samuel and Annabel standing on the steps just under topside. The dog was nowhere to be seen. She gave a questioning look at Annabel.

"Gone," she whispered. "Somewhere out there." She pointed to the hole above her.

"Why aren't we out there?" Trudi asked Samuel.

"A guy with a gun is out there."

"Did he see you?"

"Don't think so. He showed up about thirty seconds after the dog ran out and was gone. He's right above us now. Looks like he's waitin' for some friends to join him."

Trudi leaned up close to the tunnel entrance, peering above her. Then, before Samuel could say or do anything, she leapt out the hole and into daylight.

The mercenary was caught completely unaware. He fumbled for his gun, but Trudi was too fast and too precise. She slammed her shoulder into his chin and tackled him like a linebacker blitzing a quarterback. He was dazed but not out. She rolled off his body and readied a side kick for his throat. But now she was too slow. Before she could let fly, Samuel was there, pressing a knee into the chest of the mercenary and hammering him with fists to the face. The man went limp.

"All right, let's go," Trudi said breathlessly. "Annabel," she called. "Let's go."

The girl was by her side in an instant. Samuel, meanwhile, was binding the mercenary with a zip tie.

"He was facing the south," Samuel said to nobody in particular.

"So what? Let's go, Samuel. No time to waste."

"That means the rest of the mercenaries are coming from that direction."

"Good. We'll be running the opposite way."

Samuel shook his head. He pointed toward a Kawasaki ATV parked a few feet away.

"They're on all-terrain vehicles. If they're as close as I think they are, they'll catch us before we're a mile away."

"Then let's get going."

"No." Samuel hefted the limp mercenary up and dropped him heavily on the ATV. The man groaned but didn't fight.

"What are you doing, Samuel?"

Trudi's ex-husband grinned, and in his face she saw a ten-year-old boy playing war games in the backyard. His eyes were bright, his body taut and excited. This was his playground; she knew it. This was why he'd stuck with Truck and the CIA for so long. It wasn't simply money or loyalty. This man enjoyed it. He enjoyed the strategy, the tactics, even the fisticuffs and gunplay. Something about being so close to death made him feel fully alive. It was a rush Trudi would never understand and something she could never compete with.

"You two start running." He pointed northwest into the tree line. "Get to The Mute at the rendezvous point and get out.

I'll take Junior here and lead the other mercenaries on a wild goose chase."

"Samuel."

"Done it a million times, honey." He clapped his hands in anticipation. "In lots of worse places than this. When the mercs show up, I'll get their attention, then take off on the ATV. If they get close, I'll dump Junior off the side. They'll stop to pick him up, and when they do, I'll ditch the ATV and hide in the forest. I can last for days in there. Easy as pie."

"Samuel."

He leaned close to Trudi until their lips almost touched. "I know," he said softly. "I love you too. But you've got to go."

Trudi searched his eyes, smelled his skin, willing herself to remember his face. She completed the distance between them and brushed her lips quickly across his.

"Okay," she said. She turned to Annabel. "All right, sweetie. You feel like going for a jog with your Aunty Trudi?"

36

ANNABEL

"Mercenaries," Trudi grunts to nobody. "I hate mercenaries."

We'd only been runnin' a short time before they caught us. When we left Samuel Hill, he was trussing up a soldier and getting ready to cause some manner of mischievous distraction. Trudi grabbed my hand and pulled me into the forest, setting a steady, jogging pace, watching me closely to see how I could keep up. But I'm a country girl. Runnin' comes natural to me. It makes me feel clean and strong.

Pretty soon she picked up the pace and we both settled into a good run. Behind us I heard shoutin' and figured Samuel was doing his job. Ahead of us was nothing but burnt-over trees and grasses, with open spaces sprinkled here and there along the way.

I'd guess it was about a mile away that the mercenaries caught up with us. We was just entering into a jagged space underneath the tree cover, almost like if someone plowed a short field into the shape of a lightning bolt and surrounded it with oaks. Trudi paused long enough to get her bearings, to make sure we was still headed the right way. Then just when we started up runnin' again, she saw the soldier pop out from behind a tree.

"Mercenaries," Trudi said to the ground. "I hate mercenaries."

"Hands behind your heads!" the bad guy shouts at us now.

Trudi stands tall and places her palms behind her head in surrender, so I copy what she's doing. The mercenary is wearing all black, with a police-style radio Velcroed to his left shoulder. He pauses to grumble something into that radio.

"Annabel, honey," Trudi says to me through clenched teeth, "I have to kick this guy into dreamland. When that happens, I want you to run behind him and use one of those big tree trunks to hide until I'm finished. Okay?"

"Okay," I whisper back. She seems unafraid, like it's no big deal to face down a bad guy with a gun. I figure I should at least act like I'm not scared, just to keep up.

The mercenary steps toward us, his gun aimed at Trudi's midsection. "On your knees," he orders. Trudi looks confused. She leans her head in his direction like she couldn't quite make out what he just said. He steps closer. Now he's just a few feet away, so close I can smell the sweat under his arms and see the red streaks in his irritated eyes.

"On your knees!" he says again. But he's too late.

Trudi moves so fast it takes me a full second to react, then to run away from the fray. I can't take my eyes off her, it's like she's runnin' a clinic on butt-kicking and I want to be sure to catch everything she does.

First Trudi lashes out with her left hand, gripping the inside wrist of the mercenary's gun hand and twirling like a dancer into his body. A shot fires, but it spits harmless into the space she's just emptied. He tries to club at her with his left hand, but she ignores it like it's nothing. Instead she presses her back against his chest and pulls his right arm into a mock embrace around her. He grunts like she's just dislocated his shoulder. Maybe she has.

In a heartbeat she's got both hands on him, sliding her left hand to cover the butt of the gun while her right hand wraps like a snake just below his wrist. Then in a blink, she smashes the soldier's wrist down, hard, against her upraised knee. It makes me flinch. Even from where I'm standing, I can hear the crack of bone breaking.

The man screams like an animal. He claws toward Trudi's neck and face with his good hand. The gun flies toward the ground while his broken hand hangs limp at the edge of his arm. It looks a little like an unstrung yo-yo, dangling and spinning in the air.

Now Trudi wings an elbow behind her ear and into the man-animal's temple.

He staggers backward as she turns to face him. Her eyes are narrowed, her body's taut and ready to spring. A roundhouse kick, up, then arcing through the air with increasing momentum until her boot connects with the mercenary's jaw. No one's screaming or shouting now. We're all just waiting for the final blow to land. It's almost like slow motion TV with the sound turned way low. The man collapses like a game of Jenga, falling limp, facedown into the burned and broken muck that covers the ground.

He tries to roll toward his lost gun, but it's a feeble, childish effort. Trudi stabs the heel of her boot into his temple, and he goes still.

There's nothing then, no sound but panting, no motion but Trudi leaning down, hands on her knees, to catch her breath and make sure it's over. Slowly, without taking her eyes off the broken man, she steps to the side and rescues his gun from the underbrush.

I'm mesmerized by this woman, by her courage and skill and intensity. So much that I don't even hear the other man comin' up behind me.

I got no idea he's there until he yanks my head backward by the hair and rubs the nub of a pistol too deeply into my right ear. He pulls on me so hard it almost raises me to my tiptoes. Then I smell sour breath as he growls into my left ear.

"Scream."

I try to swallow, to speak, but nothing comes out.

He pulls tighter, and I feel the sting of several hairs popping roots out of my skull.

"Scream," he says angrily. He shakes me like a rag doll. "Scream now."

And so I let loose my lungs. It comes out as a gargling yelp, sounds more like an inflated, high-pitched moan than a real scream. But it's enough.

Trudi's head snaps in my direction, eyes flecked with steam, like a big cat ready to pounce.

The man drags me forward, gun still in my ear. I feel his joy in this moment. It practically shudders like sweat off his body. The smell of it sickens me.

"Samir," Trudi says. It's a swear word in her language.

"Very impressive," Samir says, pulling more strands out of my scalp, nearly dangling me above the ground while I try to keep up by walking on my tiptoes. "For a girl."

Trudi grimaces. It's almost like she's more annoyed at this jerk's sexism than she is at the fact he's got a heavy firearm poking down the hollows of my head. She unrolls her arm and aims the barrel of her new gun at the head of the man on the ground.

"Let her go," she commands. "Let her go or your buddy here finally gets to meet God. I'm guessing it won't be a happy reunion."

Samir grunts, something I think he meant as a laugh.

"You think I care what happens to that pawn?" he says, still dragging me closer to where Trudi stands. I finally feel the pressure of his muzzle pull out of my ear, leaving the right side of my face stinging and a little hard of hearing.

"Here," he says matter-of-factly, "I'll do the job for you."

He takes quick aim and fires once, twice, into the head and chest of his fallen comrade. I suddenly feel like throwing up but am able to swallow it down before it spews out of me. Trudi jumps backward, out of range, a shocked look on her face.

"See?" Samir says. "You wouldn't do it. I can tell. You're a fighter but not a cold-blooded killer. So I did it for you. Now that's finished and we can move on to more important things."

The hot barrel is back in my ear, making me whimper, burning at my skin.

Trudi responds immediately, tossing her gun aside and placing her palms on the back of her head. "Let her go," she says calmly. "You're hurting her."

Samir looks absently at me, almost like he forgot I was there, like for the moment I was just another prop in his demented play.

I see now that he looks out of place in this setting. He wears an expensive suit, dark blue, and is wearing fancy black loafers too. Strange shoe choice for runnin' around in a forest, if you ask me. Maybe he didn't expect to have to do dirty work today. His face is a little puffy, and I can see that he's got traces left over from at least one black eye. A small bandage crosses the bridge of his nose. Lost a recent fight, maybe? Hard to tell. Whatever it was, he seems unaware that he still has a wound on his face. Like it don't hurt or it never mattered. This worries my head a bit. Some men like pain, both in themselves and in others. I think that this guy might be that kind.

He drops me, casually, and shoves me forward.

"On your knees," he says to Trudi. She looks confused, acts like she don't understand . . . but he's not buying it. Not this time. He reaches for my hair again, and Trudi quickly complies.

"Hands inside the front of your pants," Samir commands. Then he shrugs. "I left my zip ties in the car."

Trudi grimaces. She shoves her palms into the front of her jeans.

Samir is feeling good now, in control.

"I know, I know. You can still use those hands if you need to, but you American harlots wear your pants so tight that it'll take at least a second or two for you to get them all the way out. And you'd be amazed at what I can do with a one-second head start."

He takes a slow look at the surroundings, listening. He nods.

"It won't be long," he says. "That inept fool did at least radio out for the others. They'll be here soon. Ten minutes. Maybe fifteen at most. And they'll have plenty of zip-tie handcuffs. Meanwhile . . ."

He notices me again, looking at me with an expression that makes me feel like something less than human. Like a guinea pig or a rat in a lab. He shoves me, a palm-kick that feels like a punch on my shoulder. I stumble.

"You," he says to me, "facedown on the ground."

I look at Trudi and she nods, slightly, at me. She wants me to cooperate. For now.

I lay on my stomach, and Samir steps on the back of my neck, shoving my face into the ashen ground. His voice echoes around my head.

"You stay here, understand?" he purrs down at me. "If you move, first I kill her. Then I kill you, understand?"

I want to nod, yes, I understand, but I can't move my head with his foot on my neck. I can't speak either. His weight presses down on me, making it difficult to breathe.

"I kill you, understand?" he says again, emphasizing it with a shove of his heel.

"She gets it, moron," Trudi interrupts at last. "You don't have to say 'understand' thirty times. She's an educated girl."

Trudi winks at me, and I feel an unexpected flush of pride.

"I get it, moron," I echo, wiggling just enough to allow air back into my lungs. "Understand?"

Trudi smiles with pleasure. Samir looks annoyed.

He shoves at me again with his foot and then takes a step away, a step toward Trudi. He walks slowly over to her until he stands behind her, looking down at her.

"You are feisty," he says. "I like that."

"Bet you say that to all the girls," Trudi quips. To me she rolls her eyes and says, "You believe this guy?"

And now I get it. Samir isn't just an enemy. He's a bully. And the thing bullies hate is not being able to scare someone they're trying hard to scare. So Trudi's eggin' him on, making it clear she ain't afraid of him or anything he might do. Getting him flustered, waiting for him to make a mistake so she can make her move.

I figure I should add my two cents.

"No, I don't believe this guy!" I say. "Whatever, right?"

Even as I say it, I know it ain't poetry. I ain't never been great at trash talk, not like Figgy or Truck. They could talk smack like it was a natural-born tongue. But despite my deficiencies, my words have the right effect.

Samir glowers at me, then turns his attention back to Trudi kneeling on the ground with her hands immobilized, dug deep into her jeans. He leans in close to her, whispers something I can't make out, then he licks along her jawline and earlobe. It's disgusting and creepy, and I know that's what he meant it to be.

Instead of cringing like I am, Trudi laughs out loud.

"Is that supposed to be foreplay?" she says. "'Cause really, it just tickles."

He pushes her forward, angry, and now I have to admit I'm more than a little scared.

He wraps his gun arm around her neck, pressing the butt of the pistol against her left cheek. Then, without warning, he kicks her in the spine, knocking her facedown onto the ground. She rolls onto her back, still keeping her hands stuffed into her pants. I can see she has 'em in tight fists down there now.

She looks him dead in the eye and snorts like he just told a lame joke. His face looks inflamed with anger.

"Seriously?" she mocks. "You think you're the first psychopath ever to touch me? Clearly you've never met my ex-husband."

She laughs lightly, then nods in the direction of his bandaged nose.

"Oh wait, you have met him. I almost forgot. He gave you that busted nose and a good long nap to boot."

Samir is nearly gone with fury now. I wonder how much more he'll take before he snaps. I worry that Trudi's gone too far, that maybe we won't get out of this after all.

He starts shouting at her, calling her all manner of nasty names, both in English and in Arabic.

Still, she just grins.

In a sudden motion, he skids forward onto one knee and jams the barrel of his gun into her mouth. She gags, and I can see even she didn't expect this.

"When I'm through with you," he seethes, "you will beg me for—"

The black and gray flashes by me so fast that at first I'm not sure what I'm seeing.

My dog made no growls or barks to warn of his comin'. One

moment we was alone with the psychopath. The next, Dog is here, tearing toward him with teeth bare and muscles rippling.

Samir barely has time to pull the gun out of Trudi's mouth before Dog is onto him, biting, chomping. Crushing.

The man's hand is captured first within the fangs of my dog, gun and all. Samir screams, screams, screams. Dog clenches his jaws tighter, resets, does it again.

I can almost feel the bones in Samir's hand splintering. Like sonic shock waves rippin' at the air around me. The gun slides away, covered in saliva, and drops to the ground. Still my dog is yanking, slashing at the man's hand, refusing to release the prize it now holds captive in its jaws.

Samir tries to pull away, fails, and falls to the ground. Screaming. Cursing. Screaming again.

Dog jerks his head hard to the right, and Samir's eyelids flutter.

Dog steps back, jaw still snapping in anger.

There are fingers missing on Samir's right hand.

Four fingers gone. Only Samir's bloodied thumb is left, bone gashing out through the thin layer of skin that keeps it attached.

Trudi has regained her hands and rolled away from the fray. Even in her eyes, I see shock at the brutality of Dog's attack. She stands frozen, eyes wide, unable to do anything but watch.

Now Dog begins to growl. Samir is crying and moaning, begging for help, begging for mercy. My dog has none to give.

Fast as a viper he charges again. Smart as an executioner, he targets what he must know from Truck's training is a man's most vulnerable spot. Samir doesn't even scream when his manhood is crushed through his pants, when my dog grips and shakes that area so hard that, in spite of myself, I do throw up in the burnt grass in front of me. His eyes roll into the back of his head and the beast of a man goes limp like a torn pillow.

I wonder if he may be dead. He don't move, don't even twitch.

Dog worries the body some more, treating it like a brutal play toy, sinking teeth into this spot, then that one, dragging the body to the left and then the right.

"Call him off," Trudi croaks toward me at last. "Call him off, Annabel. Stop him."

Yes. It's over. It's more than over.

"Aufhören!"

I try to say, "Cease!" but my throat is too dry and sore. It comes out as *"Afghn."* I swallow once, twice, and try again.

"Aufhören!" I say.

Dog pauses, Samir's left hand now locked in his jaws. Dog looks at my eyes.

"Aufhören!" I say again, willing myself to be this dog's master, his prōtos.

Dog drops the psychopath's hand.

"Lass es." Leave it.

Dog steps away, back from the body. He's panting. There's blood in his teeth, on his tongue, already matting in his fur. The sickly stench of copper and bone cakes his nostrils, fills the oxygen in my breath, hovers in the pink-tinged air that surrounds us all.

Dog trots around the carnage and comes to where I am now kneeling in the burnt grass. He sits beside me, panting, licking, working to get the bits of flesh and taste of blood out of his mouth. Other than the licking, he's still and docile, a killer completely in my control.

Trudi follows the dog with her eyes until she looks at me. There's true horror in her face. And relief. She says nothing.

"I'm . . . I'm sorry," I say at last. "He was just protecting . . . Dog was . . ."

Trudi stands straight and stares deep into my eyes. She looks strong again, composed.

"Don't apologize, Annabel," she says grimly. "For anything. That dog of yours just saved both of our lives. Saved me from a brutal rape before being killed. Saved you from who knows what torture that evil man would think up. No, don't apologize."

There's silence between us, no sound except Dog, licking, licking, licking his teeth. Now it seems even he's disgusted by the violent act, like he's trying to clean away the awful deed.

I try to hold it in, but I can't any longer.

I start to cry, hard, hurtful tears. I feel them draining all of me, and I know I'm crying because I'm scared, because what I just saw was awful in ways more than words. But I'm also crying for Truck, for the man who scared me so much and loved me so much more. For my uncle who taught me, protected me, and even trained a dog to eat human flesh for me. *It's more than I can take*, I think—or am I praying? *More than anyone should have to take.* The tears burn me, inside my eyes and outside on my skin. I can't stop trembling. I can't find air to breathe, like I'm gonna suffocate, like I might be drowning and there's no one to save me. No one.

And then I feel her arms, her strength. She wraps me, holds me tight, spends herself to cover me and bring me back to sanity. I see that she's crying too, crying like me, crying with fierceness and anger and sorrow. Holding me, holding me. Saving me.

We stay like this for what feels like a long time. And then, as quickly as it started, it's over. She feels my body relax; she knows the time is done. She gently releases me, puts her hands on my shoulders, and looks at my face. And her face softens from sorrow into something sad but less severe.

"Sheesh," she says at last, "do I look as bad as you do?"

I laugh in spite of myself. "Yeah," I say. I wipe wetness from her face. She pushes hair out of my eyes. "No," I say after a moment, "you look worse."

She snorts and gives me a playful shove.

"It's okay, Annabel," she says. "We're going to be okay."

I nod. We both look at the world around us, a world that's changed forever, a world that lives and dies in colors more real than they were just one hour ago.

"What do we do now?" I ask.

She stands, and as she stands, we hear a pathetic groan. After all that awfulness, Samir, somehow, remains alive. Trudi looks his direction, pain in her lips and eyes.

"Ten minutes ago I hated that man more than any other," she says softly. "And now all I feel is pity for him. Pity and sadness."

She reaches behind her back and produces her gun. Somehow that Beretta kept its place inside the waistband pressed against the small of her back. I don't know how, but I'm glad it did.

"I guess even the worst of us deserve some measure of mercy," she says, to herself more than to me.

She walks to Samir, and he groans again, eyes unseeing, body unmoving. She raises her pistol and points it at his temple. One shot ends his misery. A second shot guarantees him that it's over.

I feel exhausted, like all of me has been pulled out of me. Then I remember.

"Trudi," I say, "he said there'd be more comin'."

She starts to swear, then stops herself, grimacing. She returns her pistol to its holster in the back of her waistband. She sits hard on the ground beside Samir. "I forgot that. I can't believe I forgot that."

She looks around at the burnt-out forest, at the two dead men in the grass, then at me.

"Annabel, honey," she says, "I think it's time for us to run again."

37

THE MUTE

The Mute saw the sun disappear on the horizon and realized too late that he'd left his night-vision goggles in his Jeep Wrangler. He wished for a full moon.

He checked his watch. Clearly they'd all missed the rendez-vous. He kept working methodically through the trees, targeting the direction he'd heard the gunshots come from. Twice he'd stopped, waited, unsure if there were mercenaries somewhere out of sight in the woods around him. Both times had proved to be false alarms, but they also reminded him of the necessity of caution. There were seven of them left, plus Samir Sadeq Hamza al-Sadr. He had to be careful none of those guys saw him before he saw them.

He kept walking.

Before long, he heard another gunshot. And a second shot soon after. It was closer this time, but north and east from where he was walking, behind and up from his current position. He gauged it was at least a mile away. Had he overshot? Walked right past them? Taken the wrong line to Truck's farm and missed them completely? Or had they been pushed off course by the mercenaries, forced to go deeper into the woods than they should have gone?

The Mute had no answers, and now he was split between two destinations. Should he follow the gunshots again, keep trying to find Trudi Coffey and Samuel Hill in these woods? Or should he make his way to the farm, try to find out if they'd been able to free the girl? What if the girl was now in the hands of the people firing the guns?

He paused and knelt next to a thick, blackened stump of a tree, listening. In the branches above him, a woodpecker tap-tap-tapped against a massive tree trunk. He paid it no mind. He listened for human sounds, more gunshots, shouting, crisp, burnt grass crunching under running feet. There was nothing, only the forest hums of small animals and leaves crinkling in the wind. He looked to the south and felt drawn to Truck's farm. But he'd already been there, and without the key, that was a dead end.

He looked to the northwest and imagined what might be there. Coffey and Hill? The girl? Black-clad soldiers on ATVs?

The easy choice would be to go to Truck's farm, check out the situation, wait for Coffey and Hill there.

He looked at the ring on his middle finger and knew he wouldn't make the easy choice. No soldier would be left behind in this fight. Not Samuel Hill. Not Trudi Coffey. And definitely not Annabel Lee Truckson.

Find your people in the forest first, he commanded himself. *Then find your girl in the bunker. Bring them all out. Dead or alive.*

The forest was quiet around him, except for the scrape of a woodpecker's bill across the bark of a tree. It might be slower going than it would have been with his night-vision goggles, but that would be okay. He was no stranger to the night or to the Conecuh National Forest.

He reoriented his sense of direction to focus on the last place he'd heard gunshots. *A mile*, he decided. *Go in a straight line this time*. He shifted the weight of the SIG marksman rifle on his back and resumed walking.

A pop registered in his ears, loud and insistent, as if that woodpecker had found a knot in its tree and wouldn't rest until it turned the wood into powder. Then more scraping, followed by a tap-tap. Suddenly he froze and listened more intently.

Woodpeckers don't scrape against a tree, he said to himself. *And they don't know Morse code either*.

The Mute felt his blood chill. He rolled to the right and took cover behind the nearest tree of decent size. He listened.

Tap, scrape. Tap-tap. Scrape scrape scrape. Scrape scrape scrape. Scrape, tap scrape.

L-o-o-k.

Tap-tap scrape. Tap, scrape scrape, tap.

U-p.

The Mute turned his head to the branches above him. A hand waved in the shadows, and he finally saw the "woodpecker" that was tapping a handgun against the tree trunk in Morse code. Samuel Hill was hidden in a dense thicket of partially burned tree limbs, crouching low and into the trunk, trying hard to get his attention.

Now was not the time for questions. The Mute stood and started to come out from his hiding place until he saw Hill wave his arms and motion with his palms down.

Hide.

The Mute slid down onto his belly and unhooked his SIG rifle. He locked eyes with Samuel Hill and saw the CIA agent point his gun in a sideways direction.

Over there.

The Mute didn't have to wait long. It was literally only seconds until the sound of an ATV registered in his ears, and only a moment after that when the vehicle came rolling into view. There was one black-clad soldier on the Kawasaki. Only one. He was moving slowly, following whatever signs he could read in the fading light.

The Mute raised his rifle and took aim.

Scrape scrape. Scrape scrape scrape.

M-o? What did that mean?

He looked toward Samuel Hill again and saw the man shaking his head. He tilted his gun away from the soldier on the ATV and raised three fingers.

M-o. As in there's mo' of these guys a-comin'.

The Mute let his rifle slide down. The soldier on the ATV sensed rather than heard the movement. He stopped and got off his vehicle, hand on his pistol, crouching and surveying the area around him. At that moment two more of the mercenaries came jogging into the area. It looked as if they just magically appeared. One minute there was no one, the next two men were standing between the trees about thirty feet away from where The Mute was hiding.

Had he been in Samuel Hill's perch, The Mute would have begun picking them off one by one like he did back at the rendezvous spot. But from this angle on the ground, success in that kind of strike would be hard to gain. He could get the first one, yes, but there were too many obstructions at ground level. The others could lose themselves before he'd get a second shot off, and then he'd be trapped here, unable to retreat without being seen—and killed.

He forced himself to breathe in shallow drafts, keeping his muscles frozen even while his hands gripped his SIG. Best-case scenario would be that these guys wouldn't see anything out of the ordinary. They'd keep walking, keep searching, keep moving away until he and Samuel Hill could start moving again as well.

The three men clustered beneath Hill's tree, and The Mute almost wished the CIA agent would start shooting. If he could take out one mercenary and confuse the others, that would give him time to fire two shots from the SIG and complete the task. But Hill had his gun tucked close to his side, his back pressed hard against the bark of the tree. He was waiting for the best-case scenario to unfold.

A moment later, a new mercenary took the wheel of the ATV and drove north into the woods. The other two men followed on foot. The Mute started counting in his head, listening for signs that the soldiers might return. When he reached a count of one hundred, he tried to make eye contact with Samuel Hill again, but the man in the tree was looking out into the forest, apparently trying to track the mercenaries' movements from his perch up above.

At a count of one hundred and twenty, The Mute let his limbs relax. He stood and started walking toward Hill's tree. He'd only taken two steps when the mercenary "magically" appeared between the trees to his right.

"Don't move," the soldier said through a thick European accent. "Don't even clench your teeth together or I put a hole inside your skull."

Not good, The Mute thought. *Not good at all.* He dropped his rifle to the ground and raised his hands in the air.

The mercenary took a step closer, and The Mute saw him staring hard at the scar on his neck.

"You are one ugly thing," the soldier spat. "Not the guy I was looking for, but you'll do. I recognize you from the description my CO gave this morning."

The Mute turned slowly to face the fighter who held the gun. Still too far away to make a move. The mercenary leaned his chin toward a radio transmitter on his left shoulder. "Cat caught canary," he said into the radio, "and this one's got a big scar across his—"

The crack of gunfire spilled past The Mute's ears, one beat behind the moment when the bullet entered the soldier's chest. The man gurgled and fell to the ground, eyes already going glassy in his head. The Mute jumped toward the mercenary to finish him off, but Samuel Hill had done his job. This soldier wouldn't last more than a minute or two longer.

Behind him, The Mute heard Hill sliding down the tree and hitting the ground with a thud. He turned in time to see the spook roll on his shoulder and then spring up to his feet.

"You're welcome," Hill said breathlessly. "Now, come on, we'd better get out of here before his buddies come back to see what's taking him so long."

A voice crackled through the radio on the dead man's shoulder. The Mute missed the first part of what it said because the accent was confusing. But he made out the rest of it.

" . . . girl and the woman surrounded. Forward on my mark. *Geht!*"

Hill heard it too. There was no need for either of them to speak. Hill pointed in the direction the other two soldiers had just gone. They both took off toward the party.

They'd been going for several minutes, trying to keep an angle wide enough not to miss the women in the woods but also trying to move swiftly toward their goal. Then there was a single gunshot, different from others they'd heard. Louder, more percussive, as if shot from a small cannon instead of an automatic pistol.

Both men stopped and took stock. The Mute listened to the

echo in the trees around him. He looked toward the sky and was grateful to see a bright, full moon shining through the burned-out branches of the forest. It was not the same as sunlight, but it did give more than enough illumination for the task at hand.

The Mute isolated the origin of the echo first. He pointed, and Samuel Hill nodded.

Dead or alive, The Mute promised himself.

No one left behind. I will bring them all out.

Dead or alive.

38

TRUDI

Trudi reached for Annabel's hand, pulling her toward an opening in the tree line to the west. But before they could break into a full run, she hesitated, listening. She finally squeezed Annabel's hand and came to a complete stop.

Trouble, she thought. *Now we're really in trouble.*

The sound of ATVs crunching through the blackened remains of the Conecuh National Forest barely preceded their appearance. Two machines popped up west, blocking the way to The Mute, to safety. A third emerged from the north. There were three soldiers total, one on each of the three ATVs. Trudi recognized the men on the second and third ATVs.

Brown Head and Blondie. Apparently they'd been freed by their comrades. And rearmed with automatic weapons.

For a moment, Trudi held hope in running backward, running south toward the bunker they'd just come from. If she surprised them, if she was smart, she might be able to run, hide, ambush, run-hide-ambush some more. Do something at least until Samuel could find them and lend a helping hand.

The pig.

He always was absent when he was needed. It was like his special gift to the world. Or to Trudi personally.

Then, appearing almost as if by magic from the thick woods, a fourth ATV hummed into existence behind her. It came from the south, blocking her retreat. And it carried the one man she didn't want to see.

"Dr. Smith," she muttered. "Of course."

Annabel's eyes widened. "Johannes Smith?" she asked. Trudi didn't answer. Instead she watched the older man unlimber himself from the ATV while the other soldiers aimed short rifles and handguns in their direction.

"*Gestellt, dass sich!*" He waved toward the mercenary in the north. "Dolt. You shoot her, you might hit me."

The dolt soldier lowered his rifle immediately and began moving to his left, to a place where his line of fire wouldn't encompass any of his allies.

"And you, Ms. Coffey," Dr. Smith said. "Would you kindly toss your weapon to the ground now? Thank you."

Trudi made up a new curse word inside her head, then unholstered her Beretta and sent it flying into the brush.

The old man carried no weapon, only his cane. In spite of everything, he still wore an expensive tailored suit and polished black boots that crackled the underbrush beneath him when he walked.

"Well," he said. "At last. It's good to see you again, *meine Tochter*." He nodded politely toward Annabel.

Trudi became slowly aware of the animal beside her. A low growl rumbled from its throat, vibrating the flesh and fur he wore. She glanced down and saw Annabel's hand resting gently on the back of the dog's neck, saw also that her hand was the only thing preventing the German shepherd from racing to attack the old man.

"Johannes Schmitzden?" The girl's voice was trembling, but she stood her ground. "Are you Dr. Johannes Schmitzden?"

Dr. Smith cocked his head to the side as if appraising Annabel anew.

"You know this name, yes?" he said. At the corners of his mouth, a smile played, and his eyes were alive with interest.

Annabel nodded.

The German shepherd took a step forward and bared its teeth. The girl involuntarily squeezed on its neck, and the dog responded, restraining himself but never taking his eyes off the old man.

"What of the name Raina Aemilia Gregor? Does that one speak to you as well?"

Annabel nodded.

"Who told you of these names? Steven Grant? Leonard Truckson?"

"My mother."

Now the old man's eyebrows rose. He appeared ready to say something more but decided against it. Instead he turned to his companions.

"Take the women," he ordered. Then his eyes fell on the dog growling at him. "Kill the animal. Make it suffer for what it did to poor Samir."

"Annabel," Trudi whispered. Her mind was racing. She couldn't let this ruthless man take the girl, but she didn't know what to do. So she said it again. "Annabel—"

But Annabel wasn't listening. She knelt quickly beside the German shepherd. She lifted her hand off its neck, and she whispered one word:

"Angreifen."

Trudi didn't need to understand German to know the command the girl had just given the dog. He didn't hesitate, launching into an instantaneous attack, barreling toward Dr. Smith like a hound of hell hungry for human blood.

The men behind her shouted. She could hear them running toward the old man. But Dr. Smith stood his ground, a new fierceness on his face. His left hand grabbed at the stem of his cane, separating it effortlessly from the handle. And Trudi now saw, as if in slow motion, the ornate handle of the cane was actually the butt of some kind of decorative handgun. The barrel of the gun slid out of the cane stem as if oiled, constantly at the ready.

Dr. Smith extended his right arm with a precise snap that was unexpectedly brisk for a man of his age. Then came the thunder, an explosion that echoed like a small cannon through the Conecuh National Forest.

The animal squealed, an agonizing yelp that followed the sound of bone cracking. It fell in a bloodied mess about four feet away from where Dr. Smith stood, unmoving.

The dog writhed on the ground, bullet imbedded deeply into its right shoulder, just below the socket. Blood seeped from the wound, turning the thirsty ground into a muddy patch. Below the wound, the dog's foreleg twisted in grotesque fashion.

Trudi heard Annabel's scream through a fog, as if the girl next to her was standing far away and all that reached her ears was the echo of suffering. A second later she felt the impact of a mercenary body that tackled her and pinned her painfully to the ground. Trudi tried to struggle at first but knew it was in vain. She could barely breathe from the unexpected collision, let alone struggle under the weight of the attacker who held her trapped on the ground. It was Brown Head, and this time he was taking no chances with her.

Annabel was too fast for Blondie.

She raced toward Dr. Smith, shouting in staccato breaths, "*Nein! Nein! Aufhören! Lass es!*"

The dog was still trying to get up, to finish the attack, unwilling to admit that the wound in his shoulder was mortal, that he was a mortal animal at all. Trudi heard the girl's sobs, loud at first, then muffled when she buried her head into the animal's neck.

"*Nein*," Annabel said softly now. "*Lass es. In Frieden.*" And then "*Bitte, bitte.*"

Dr. Smith towered over the girl now. "This dog means something to you, yes?"

"*Ja.*" Annabel didn't lift her head from the dog's neck. "*Er ist ein guter Hund. Ein guter Freund.*"

Trudi wasn't much on German, but she could guess at that last part. *A good friend.*

"*Ja*," Smith said. "I can see this was a good dog."

The German shepherd stilled itself at Annabel's touch, panting, an involuntary whine escaping only intermittently.

"What if I told you that you could heal this beast? You alone. What would you think then?"

"*Sie sind ein verrückter, dementen alten Mann.*"

The mercenary atop Trudi snorted at Annabel's words and shook his head in slight admiration. "Your child," he whispered into Trudi's ear, "just called him a crazy, demented old man."

Dr. Smith frowned and looked up. Brown Head responded immediately, digging a fist into Trudi's ribs. "Quiet," he growled, covering for his lapse. Dr. Smith turned his gaze back to Annabel.

"Take the girl," he commanded to Blondie, the soldier on his right. "Keep her bound. Your life is forfeit if she escapes. You understand?"

The mercenary nodded and reached toward Annabel. The

dog growled and snapped at him, trying to defend his charge even in his immobility. Blondie leaned in to deliver a kick at the bleeding dog, but Annabel stood between them.

"I'm ready," she said. "I won't fight. I won't escape."

The soldier nodded, grabbing the girl's arms and securing them behind her with a zip tie.

The dog growled and tried to stand.

"*Nein,*" Annabel commanded. "*In Frieden. In Frieden.*"

The dog sighed heavily and slid down to the ground, lying on its wounded shoulder, burying the pain in the ashen, blood-muddied ground.

Smart dog, Trudi thought. *The weight of the dog pressing the wound into the ground will help stop the bleeding.*

Next Dr. Smith moved to where Trudi lay pinned to the dirt by her captor.

"The question with you," he said, "is whether to kill you now or to try to extract information from you first."

"*Sie ein verrückter, dementen* old man." Trudi knew she hadn't gotten it perfectly, but she figured it would be close enough for Dr. Smith to understand the intent. She knew she was right when the man on top of her slapped the side of her head in response.

"Well," Smith said, "you need work on both your language skills and your manners."

He nodded to the mercenary, who quickly zip-tied Trudi's hands and raised her to a standing position. Trudi was annoyed to feel the tingling that overtook her feet and shins. That meat-head soldier had sat so hard on her that her legs had fallen asleep. Even if she were to try to kick her way out of this, it'd be a few minutes before she could put her legs to any good use. She was worried about simply balancing on her feet just now.

"You may be needed in Truckson's bunker," he said. "And you might be helpful with the girl." That seemed to be enough for now. Trudi was pulled roughly toward Dr. Smith's ATV and then zip-tied to the bar beside the passenger seat, forcing her to lean slightly off the ATV so that her right foot just barely avoided the ground. She saw that Annabel was similarly loaded onto Blondie's ATV as well.

A moment later the little convoy sped wordlessly through the trees, heading back toward Truck's farm and to the bunker that was hidden beneath the ground there.

Trudi worried about Samuel. Had he already been caught? Killed? Was that why he still wasn't here? And what of The Mute? Was he still waiting at the rendezvous point? Or had he been killed too?

Trudi caught sight of Annabel on the other ATV. Her tears had dried now. Her face looked calm, passive. Resigned to her fate. But in her eyes a fire was burning. Trudi watched the forest pass by and wondered what was going through the child's mind at this moment.

In the distance behind them, a dying animal howled.

39

TRUDI

Trudi marveled at the supreme confidence of Dr. Smith. Even though she was tethered to the ATV, she was still close enough to the old man to disable him with a kick. Surely he knew she was capable of that. Yet he evinced no concern whatsoever at what she might do.

She was tempted to kick his jaw just out of spite.

She didn't though, because she knew what he knew. No matter what she did, Annabel would be in danger. And as long as the girl was in harm's way, Trudi wouldn't risk anything that could get her hurt in the process or hurt as retaliation for Trudi's actions.

The old man had reason to be unconcerned. Apparently he knew his enemies well.

They rode in silence. Trudi scanned the surrounding forest, looking for, hoping for any signs of Samuel or The Mute. She was disappointed.

"I got your phone message," Trudi said finally.

"I know." Dr. Smith said it like they were old friends discussing the weather.

"What did it mean?"

Dr. Smith only smiled.

"'Mary Had a Little Lamb'?" she said. "You called my cell and left me a recitation of 'Mary Had a Little Lamb'? Maybe you are a crazy old man."

"You are not a fan of nursery rhymes?"

Trudi glanced toward Dr. Smith and saw Annabel riding on Blondie's ATV behind him. She was watching the old man intently, trying to follow the conversation.

"Not this time," she said.

"I see."

Trudi was frustrated by the smug silence that Dr. Smith ushered in at that moment. She tried to wait, but patience had never been her strong suit.

"So," she said. "What did it mean?"

"Nothing," he said.

"What?"

"It meant nothing. I could have just as easily recited Keats or the dictionary. It didn't matter what message I left, only that I left a message."

He flicked a look toward her, a reflection of triumph in his eyes.

What in the world is this guy talking about? she wondered. *I don't get it.*

"You must know, Ms. Coffey," he said, "that after our first meeting I made you a subject of no mild study. You had proven yourself someone of intelligence and certain physical resources."

"Surprised you with that electrocution bit, didn't I."

Dr. Smith nodded in acknowledgment. "Yes, that was . . . unexpected."

"So what did you learn about me in your studies?"

"You, Ms. Coffey, are a predictable personality."

Trudi felt herself getting unreasonably angry at that comment. It reminded her of a recurring fight she'd had when she and Samuel were married.

"In fact," Dr. Smith continued, "you even got a Wonder Woman tattoo on your hip just to prove to your ex-husband that you were not predictable. But getting that mark as a means of proving unpredictability was easily predictable by anyone who understands human nature."

Trudi was really annoyed now. Only four people in the world knew about that tattoo. Trudi, Samuel, her doctor, and the tattoo artist who had applied the maroon-and-gold "WW" symbol.

So, Dr. Smith really does do his homework.

"What are you, some kind of psychiatrist?" she grumbled.

"Psychologist," he said. "Similar, but different enough to warrant correction. And a physiologist. And a priest of the highest order."

Trudi was tempted to ask more about that priest thing, but she was still preoccupied by the phone message.

"So I'm predictable, so what? What's that got to do with 'Mary Had a Little Lamb' on my voicemail?"

Dr. Smith smiled at the countryside ahead of him. "Where is your cell phone now?" he asked.

"In my pocket."

"Exactly."

The crushing realization hit Trudi like a waterfall of guilt.

"You tracked my cell phone. You triangulated our position when I turned it on back in Atlanta."

"Of course, my dear. There was no need to hurry because you were transmitting your location to us at all times. All I needed to do was get you to turn on your cell and carry it with you. I believe 'Mary Had a Little Lamb' was successful in doing that."

"How did you know I'd keep the phone with me?"

"What is your occupation, Ms. Coffey?"

Trudi found this man's superior attitude maddening, mainly because it appeared he actually was intellectually superior to her. That was really annoying.

"Detective," she said through clenched teeth.

"And what do detectives do but solve mysteries? It's almost an obsession with people who go into that business."

"So you gave me a mystery, an inexplicable nursery rhyme phone message," Trudi muttered ruefully, "knowing I'd keep it close to me until I could solve it."

"And knowing that your possessive nature would prevent you from telling your ex-husband about it. But don't feel bad, Ms. Coffey, everyone is predictable if you know something about human nature."

"I could've turned off my phone at any time," she muttered.

"Yes," he said, "you could have. But you didn't. In different circumstances, you might have turned it off, yes. But you couldn't this time, not while the mystery still lingered inside there. That's not who you are. This is your neurosis, it is what makes you a good detective. So I took advantage of it. There is no shame in this for you. It is just the way of the world."

Trudi had no answer for that.

They arrived at Truck's farm in silence. Trudi struggled with the guilt of knowing that she was responsible for giving away their location to Dr. Smith, and also with the knowledge that if they were to escape alive, she'd have to get over that guilt and concentrate on the situation at hand.

Waiting at the entrance to the bunker were two other mercenaries and one more ATV. Dr. Smith left Trudi tied to the vehicle while he went over to talk to them. They seemed agitated about something, and Trudi noticed Dr. Smith frown. He left them and came back to the ATV. He motioned to his other soldiers. They cut Annabel loose and brought her to him.

"This one"—he nodded toward the girl—"will not cause us any more problems, am I right, *meine Tochter*?"

Annabel shook her head and looked at her fists. "I won't cause problems," she said. "Will you let Trudi go now?"

"Not yet," he said. "But it's nothing for you to worry about." He nodded toward Trudi. "Take her and secure her inside the bunker. Then return here to me." Brown Head and Blondie jumped to obey. They took no chances. One held her at gunpoint while the other cut her zip ties off the ATV, then tied her hands behind her back.

"Wait a minute," Trudi said. "Dr. Smith—"

He waved a dismissive hand in her direction. "Don't worry, Ms. Coffey. We still have much to discuss. But for the moment I must take care of other matters."

Trudi felt the world closing in. Once she was trapped inside the bunker, her options for escape would be next to nothing. She'd be lost underground, without hope.

"She was just trying to protect me," Annabel was pleading now. "Dr. Schmitzden, please, just let her go. She's not part of this. She doesn't even know."

"*Ruhig sein*," Dr. Smith said. "Quiet, child." He put a hand on her head, a motion that suddenly brought to Trudi's mind the image of Annabel restraining the German shepherd by putting a hand on its neck.

The two mercenaries started dragging Trudi toward the tunnel. Brown Head held her arms behind her, twisted to the point of pain, while Blondie remained a few feet away with his gun trained expertly at her abdomen. A thousand thoughts flitted through her mind, but Trudi couldn't come up with any reasonable plan of escape.

Is this it for you, Tru-Bear?

"Don't worry, Annabel," she called out behind her. "These goons can't do anything to me. Just be brave, okay? I'll be back in a minute."

Annabel didn't answer. Trudi strained her ears to hear, but the girl remained silent. As she neared the tunnel entrance, Trudi heard Dr. Smith speaking to the three remaining soldiers.

"Hill is still at large in the forest. He's been joined by another Special Forces operative, and they've already killed some of your comrades. Hunt them down until they are dead. Burn their bodies. *Geht!*"

Trudi glanced up to see the three mercenaries jog to their ATVs and prepare to leave.

So her ex-husband was still alive, and he'd met up with The Mute after all.

Samuel, she said to herself, *I hope you know what you're doing.*

40

ANNABEL

I'm watching them two soldiers drag Trudi down to my bunker, and I keep saying to myself, *Do something, Annie-girl. Do something!* But what can I do? I'm just a kid, an eleven-year-old girl. I ain't Truck. I ain't Dog. I ain't even Trudi Coffey.

Johannes Schmitzden barely looks at me, but I know he's not letting me out of his sight, not ever again. Especially not now.

"Hill is still at large in the forest," he tells his soldiers. "He's been joined by another Special Forces operative, and they've already killed some of your comrades. Hunt them down until they are dead. Burn their bodies. *Geht!*"

The Mute, I say to myself. *The Mute is with Samuel Hill. They'll help me. They'll help us. If they can stay alive.*

I shake away that last thought. The Mute's good at staying alive. It's what he does. He will come. I force myself to believe it.

When the mercenaries are gone, Dr. Schmitzden finally turns his full attention to me.

"*Sie sind eine harte Mädchen zu finden, meine Tochter.*"

You are a hard girl to find, my daughter. My mind translates it without trying.

"You're in America. Speak English."

"I see Steven Grant did not teach you proper manners."

"His name is Leonard Truckson."

"Was."

"What?"

"His name *was* Leonard Truckson."

Johannes Schmitzden is staring down at me with a curl in his lip. He wants to hurt me now, to prove he is my prōtos. I don't know what to say, so I say nothing. After a moment, he relents.

"You are a hard girl to find, my daughter," he says again. "But patience and diligence always win in the end."

The soldiers who took Trudi down into the bunker return. They stand nearby, waiting for orders. Dr. Schmitzden takes my arm and pulls me toward the tunnel. To the soldiers, he says, "Guard the entrance. I have work to do."

The soldiers don't question the command. They follow us to the tunnel and take up positions at the opening while we go down the narrow stairs into the shadowed underground. The air is dry now, still, with a smoky aftertaste. Dr. Schmitzden stands a moment at the base of the stairs, and I see admiration in his eyes.

"Your Leonard Truckson was a resourceful man," he says. "A worthy adversary."

"Uncle Truck was somethin' more than a person like you could even imagine," I mutter.

"Uncle?" Dr. Schmitzden raises an eyebrow. I don't say nothing. I think maybe I already said too much. When he realizes I'm done talking, he jerks his head forward.

"Let's go," he says.

There's not room for both of us to go through the narrow tunnel side by side, so Dr. Schmitzden pushes me forward and then follows barely one step behind me. We go down through the wide loops, winding down, down, down. I start to feel claustrophobic in here again, making it hard for me to breathe, almost making me long for the open space of the bunker ahead. Finally the dirt floor levels out and the path straightens. Twenty feet down, I see the narrow steel door, left open.

Home again, I say to myself. It almost makes me laugh.

Once inside the door, I see Trudi sitting on the floor next to the bunk beds. Her hands are zip-tied low around one of the beams on the underside of the bed. Her hair is mussed, and I think there's a new shiner forming around her left eye. She grins at me.

"Glad to see you could make it," she says through a cut lip. "Though you could have left your monkey at home." She wrinkles her nose like Dr. Schmitzden has a bad smell on him. A tiny laugh escapes me without permission. Dr. Schmitzden just frowns and pushes me toward the table.

"Sit," he says. "*Setz dich.*"

I take a place at the table, sitting on the far side so I'm facing the door. Dr. Schmitzden is looking around, taking stock of the bunker. He's clearly impressed.

"How long were you supposed to stay down here?" he says. I shrug. "A while, I think," he says, answering his own question. He walks slowly around the room, checking out the supplies on the shelves, pausing to look at the book titles there too. He taps at the Bible and nods. Then he peeks a head into the outhouse and comes out nodding. He don't bother going into the second opening in the wall.

"A well?" he asks me, pointing toward the other wall. "That's what I'd do." I nod, and he seems pleased. "A worthy adversary," he says to no one. "A shame your 'uncle' had to die before I could meet him properly."

"A shame that anyone had to die," Trudi says from the floor. "Maybe you can tell me, Dr. Smith, what is it about this girl that makes her so important to you? Makes you into someone willing to kill just to get her?"

Johannes Schmitzden lets his gaze settle on my face. There's a little smile at the corner of his lips, an expression that reminds me of a man from Peachtree who made his living selling collectible coins.

"He wants to eat my blood," I say to Trudi. "He's a Blood-Eater."

Dr. Schmitzden snorts. "I have been called by that crude name," he says, lips still smiling at the corners. "But I don't want to eat *your* blood, *meine Tochter*. Your blood is toxic when ingested orally. It must be mitigated with beta blockers and injected directly into a vein. Or didn't you know that?"

"What are you talking about?" Trudi says. "What does her blood have to do with anything?"

"He's a Blood-Eater," I interrupt.

"What the girl means," Johannes Schmitzden says amiably, "is that I am a high priest in the Order of St. Heinrich von Bonn."

Now it's Trudi's turn to snort. "The Vampire Sect? They're just a myth, a wild story used in the Middle Ages to scare German nobles into rebelling against the popes in Rome."

"Oh, Ms. Coffey," Dr. Schmitzden says, "I assure you the Order of St. Heinrich von Bonn is quite real, and it has been for more than a thousand years." Now he looks at me. "It's time, my dear. Please try not to cry out."

He extracts a black zippered wallet from his inside pocket. He opens it and pulls out a long syringe needle, along with an empty glass vial and a glass slide. Trudi looks confused, like she's trying to recall something she learned in college, something she thought was unimportant at the time but now wishes she'd studied more closely. Johannes Schmitzden takes my arm. His eyes dare me to struggle, but I know if I do, he will hurt me, or Trudi, or both of us. I close my eyes and brace for the needle. I avoid making a noise when he inserts it into my vein. I hold very still until he's finished.

"Okay," Trudi says, sounding alarmed. "This is just nonsense. What are you doing to her? The Blood-Eaters are a myth. A crazy cult. They supposedly were relic hunters and magicians, people who tried to work sorcery with bits of remains from ancient saints and such. You're saying that's you? And that Annabel here has something to do with that?"

"Impressive," Dr. Schmitzden says as he releases my arm. He presses a small cloth on the spot where the needle sucked my life. "You know more than most about our religion. But you must stop using that crude name. It's improper and derogatory."

Trudi is openmouthed. Dr. Schmitzden assumes a professorial air as he continues working with the vial of my blood. First he peers closely into it, as if trying to read a secret message in the dark, purple-red fluid.

"The Order of St. Heinrich von Bonn," he lectures, "has its roots in a Brandenburg monastery over a thousand years ago. It became a repository for holy relics, a place to keep fine artifacts of religious mysticism."

"Like what? Bones of saints? Splinters from Jesus's cross?"

"Yes, those things and others. Mostly, though, the reliquaries at the monastery contained bits of holy men. In 1096, the abbot of the monastery became ill. No amount of medicine or prayer could effect the head monk's healing. And so the brothers turned outside the church for answers."

"Druids." Trudi is apparently remembering her mythology studies.

"Druids." Dr. Schmitzden nods like a professor giving a gold star to a student. He now lays out a cloth on the table and puts the glass slide on the cloth. Next he reaches back into his black zippered wallet and pulls out another small vial, this one filled with a clear liquid.

"The Druids showed the monks how to harness the power of the relics in their care, how to unleash the spiritual world into the physical." Dr. Schmitzden arranges the glass slide to receive a drop of my blood.

"Relic worship? That's your thing? Isn't that missing the point? God is the miracle worker, not some dead man's bones."

The crazy man ignores Trudi, continuing his story as if uninterrupted.

"The head priest was cured. Of course, when he reported his cure to Rome, he was executed for witchcraft. And then, by decree of Pope Urban II, the Order of St. Heinrich von Bonn was condemned and ordered to disband. Rome sent men to kill the renegade monks, but they didn't send enough. With help from the Druids, the remaining priests stole away with the relics and continued to create their new religion in the forests of eastern Germany."

"So you combined mystic Christianity with relic worship and Druid sorcery, and bam! A thousand years later you need a little girl's blood? You are insane."

"And you are an ignorant infidel," he says.

"So I guess we're even?" Trudi says. "Oh yeah, except I'm not sucking blood out of little children for kicks and giggles, so maybe I'm still ahead."

Trudi winks at me, and I can't help but smile. I know this woman must be scared, but she's doing everything she can to keep me from being scared too. I find that I love her for this.

Dr. Schmitzden ignores her. Instead, he carefully lets two

drops of blood spill onto the glass slide, then he sits back and sighs.

"This girl's blood is more than you would believe possible."

He removes the stopper from the vial of clear liquid and lets a drop of that mingle with my blood on the glass slide.

"See for yourself." He says it breathlessly, like he's waiting for a miracle. On the glass slide, there comes a hissing, then a faint whiff of burning. It only takes a few seconds, and the chemical reaction of my blood and the clear liquid is complete, a combustible boiling that seems strange and otherworldly. In only a few moments, the blood and liquid have evaporated completely, leaving only a thick black stain on the glass slide. Even Trudi doesn't know what to say.

Dr. Schmitzden smiles and looks at me like he's found a chest full of pirate treasure.

"Good. Good!" he says. He claps his hands. "We are not too late."

He looks at me with hungry eyes.

Suddenly, I feel cold.

41

TRUDI

Trudi heard the blood burning before she understood exactly what was happening up there on the table.

Did that blood just ignite? she wondered. *This is getting crazier and crazier.*

She looked at Annabel and saw the girl's somber face return. The child shivered and wrapped her arms around herself.

Dr. Smith carefully deposited the glass slide in a poly bag. Then he raised the vial of blood to his face and sniffed it. He was apparently happy, and Trudi guessed that being happy made him conversational.

Just keep the old man talking, Trudi told herself. *Keep him talking until you can think of something to do.*

"What do you mean, 'We're not too late'? Too late for what? Are you going to eat her blood?"

"Of course not," he said absently. "Did you not see what just happened? This girl's blood is toxic if swallowed. The first person we tried that on nearly died. He convulsed into an epileptic seizure and then fell into a coma. We were never able to wake him."

This guy really is a Blood-Eater. Or at least he thinks he is.

"After that, we tried smaller doses. Same result, except that some of the later ones woke from their comas." He stared appreciatively at Annabel. "For the ones who awoke, the miracle happened."

Trudi didn't know what to say. She followed Dr. Smith's line of vision over the table until she came to Annabel. The girl was looking down, avoiding Dr. Smith's gaze. She caught Trudi looking at her in her peripheral vision.

"He thinks," Annabel said, "that my blood can bring miraculous healing. That it's somehow medicine for sick people."

Dr. Smith beamed. "Your mother told you this?" he said. Annabel nodded. "You must tell me how. Does she visit you in the night?"

Trudi wanted to interrupt but found she wanted to know the answer as well. Weren't Annabel's parents dead? Killed in Iraq, that's what she'd said. Isn't that why Truck adopted her?

"No," Annabel said. "She left me a book."

Dr. Smith's eyebrows zipped upward as if pulled by a fishing line. "Really?" he said to her. Then to himself, "Interesting."

Trudi decided she didn't like the direction this line of conversation was going. It seemed like Annabel was about to reveal a secret she didn't want to let out.

"What makes you think Annabel's blood is some miraculous medicine?"

Dr. Smith looked hard at Annabel. "Why don't you tell your friend?" he said.

Annabel shook her head. "I don't understand it, really. Just that it's something called neuroregenesis."

In response, Dr. Smith leaned back in his chair. He spoke to Trudi, but he never took his eyes off of Annabel.

"According to biblical history," he said, "a dead man was once tossed into a tomb that held bones of the prophet Elisha. When the dead man's body touched the bones, it experienced a miraculous neuroregenesis. The dead man came back to life. It was that story that first prompted the Order of St. Heinrich von Bonn to become relic hunters. And we've been very good at it over the centuries."

Dr. Smith paused long enough to make sure Trudi was listening, then he stood and walked over to the bookshelves. He pulled the Bible off the shelf and dropped it on the table. He flipped it open about halfway through.

"I see this one is marked," he said to Annabel. "By you?"

She shook her head.

"Truckson then," he said. "Leaving you more clues."

Annabel looked shamefaced, like she should have known that, like she should have memorized whatever it was that Dr. Smith was referring to.

The old man read aloud, "Mark 3:1–5. 'And he entered again into the synagogue; and there was a man there which had a withered hand. And they watched him, whether he would heal him on the Sabbath day; that they might accuse him. And he saith unto the man which had the withered hand, Stand forth. And he saith unto them, Is it lawful to do good on the Sabbath days, or to do evil? to save life, or to kill? But they held their peace. And when he had looked round about on them with anger, being grieved for the hardness of their hearts, he saith unto the man, Stretch forth thine hand. And he stretched it out: and his hand was restored whole as the other.'"

"Kind of an odd time for a Bible lesson, don't you think?" Trudi said. "So two thousand years ago, Jesus healed a man with a withered hand. That doesn't mean Annabel has sacred blood or something."

"As far as the Bible is concerned, that encounter with Jesus in the synagogue was the end of that story. Except it wasn't."

Dr. Smith's eyes glittered as he closed the Scripture book. He sat back down, across from Annabel, at the table.

"The healed man was so grateful," Smith said, "he became something of a missionary for Christ, traveling through as much of the world as he knew to spread the news of Jesus. And, in another miracle, that formerly withered hand became an agent of the supernatural. When the man touched the sick or the injured in the name of Jesus, they too were healed."

"Let me guess," Trudi said, "then some vampire weirdos from your cult did something weird to him. Did they drink his blood?"

Dr. Smith ignored Trudi's interruption, speaking only to Annabel.

"When the man died, his hand was severed and saved as a holy relic. By the time we got it a thousand years later, all that was left was the bone and lower joint of the index finger. My forefathers were unable to access the miraculous power stored in the bone, so they began to experiment. In the 1800s, they took what they knew of mysticism and began to combine it with basic biology and scientific process. In 1933, Hitler rose to power, with Joseph Goebbels as his Reich Minister of Propaganda."

"Goebbels was a Blood-Eater." Annabel filled in the blank. Trudi felt disgusted.

"Herr Goebbels was high priest in the Order of St. Heinrich von Bonn," Dr. Smith corrected. "And he gave the bone to his acolyte. My grandfather. Together they sought to unravel the mystery of power hidden in the bone. World War II was an especially fertile time for them, and they made many advancements."

"Human experimentation. Nazi atrocities against the Jews. That's your legacy?" Trudi said. She felt like spitting.

Dr. Smith didn't respond, but it was evident that Trudi had hit the nail right on the head. *So, this crazy man is descended from an entire family of brutal, scientific, cultic psychopaths.* Trudi pushed down the panic that threatened to overtake her.

"After the war, my family moved to Erfurt in the German Democratic Republic, where my father joined my grandfather in the work."

Communist East Germany, Trudi mentally noted. *Behind the Iron Curtain during the Cold War.*

"And when they passed away, Dr. Schmitzden took over." It was Annabel. Even she sounded disgusted. The old man nodded as if accepting a compliment.

"We had some difficulties in funding after the fall of the Soviet Union and the reunification of Germany. Until we found a sponsor in Iraq. After the first Gulf War, it seemed that Qusay Hussein was interested in, well, innovative methods of keeping soldiers fit for fighting."

"You were a stooge for Saddam Hussein's son in Iraq?" Trudi wished she could break her zip tie just so she could crack this old man's teeth.

"Possibly." He shrugged. "I was never told exactly who was in charge. But I was given a large laboratory and plenty of prisoners to use for my studies."

"What about my mother?" Annabel said suddenly, fiercely. "Was she one of your prisoners?"

"Ah, Dr. Marelda Gregor. No, she was no prisoner." Smith looked nostalgic, as if remembering a picnic in summertime or a family reunion at Christmas. "Your mother was a brilliant woman. A natural with languages—I think she spoke seven or eight fluently. Miraculous in that regard, really."

Annabel's face flushed.

"She came to me when I was in Erfurt," Smith continued. "She was young, beautiful. Startling green eyes, I remember that best about her. Striking. She was only twenty-five or twenty-six years old. Like me, she'd earned a PhD in psychology. And during her studies, she had discovered that the human mind is more than mass attached to the body. She found the impact of the spiritual world irresistible. She wanted to join the Order of St. Heinrich von Bonn as my disciple."

Dr. Smith shrugged. "I sent her back to school. Ten years later she returned with an undergraduate degree in biology and a medical doctorate specializing in stem cell research. She followed me to Fallujah, and we set out to unravel the mystery of power."

Alarms went off in Trudi's head at the mention of Fallujah. *That's where Truck was stationed during the war*, she thought, *and where he must have recruited Rendel Jackson-Fife to join him in this Fade for Annabel.*

"And then you came along"—he nodded toward Annabel—"offering the answers."

"In my blood." Annabel looked grim.

"In your stem cells."

"She was going to stop you. Did you know that? She was going to leave."

"Yes." Dr. Smith said it without emotion. "Her only fault. You. She couldn't do to you what needed to be done."

"What needed to be done?" Trudi hated asking the question.

"During Marelda's pregnancy, we implanted into the child's stem cells the last of the relic. We ground the tip of the finger bone from the man with the withered hand into fine powder and made it part of this child's DNA." He nodded toward Annabel. "Your mother almost died during the surgery. But she was strong. She was very strong."

"What was that supposed to do?"

"In my studies I discovered there are spiritual forces at work in biological functions. The reason no one had been able to unlock the healing power of the bone was because it had only been tested with adults. It needed an innocent. A child. Only in that purity could the healing miracles be released."

"That's why he's been so hot to find me," Annabel said. "When I turn thirteen, I won't be a child anymore."

"It is the age of accountability," Smith said matter-of-factly. "And, if my theories on mystical physiology are correct, her blood will be useless then."

"So, what, you're just going to drain her blood for the next year and half to mix your little potions?"

As soon as Trudi said it, she knew it was true. That was why Smith had spent more than a decade painstakingly tracking Truck and this girl. His great plan for her was to suck her dry and then discard her when she turned thirteen. The horror of that made Trudi strain on her bonds, desperate to break free and save Annabel from this mad scientist's plans.

"Things are necessary," Dr. Smith said calmly. To Annabel he said, "I can't promise that you won't suffer, but I do promise not to make you suffer needlessly. And in spite of what you may think of me, I never tell a lie."

Trudi let her mind swim past her encounters with Dr. Smith. He was deceitful and criminal, but he was right. He had never outright lied to her.

"You can't do this," Trudi said softly. "She's just a child."

"That's what her mother told me. It was not enough."

"Is that why you killed her?" she accused.

"No, I could never have killed Marelda Gregor. She was the incubator for my greatest achievement." He tipped his head toward Annabel. "That's why I arranged for her to be kidnapped by Iraqi insurgents. They would profit from her, and if necessary, they would kill her for me."

"She was going to leave you." Annabel said it with urgency, and Trudi saw her fighting tears. "Why couldn't you just let her go?"

"Because, *meine Tochter*, she was going to take you with her. I couldn't let that happen. Of course, I didn't count on your Leonard Truckson and his army Special Forces soldiers getting involved."

Trudi could guess what happened next. Truck and his men came to steal away Marelda Gregor, and bad things happened.

"She called for them to come," Annabel said.

"Yes," Smith said grimly. "She promised secrets about Qusay Hussein and Muqtada al-Sadr's Mahdi Army. Promised a windfall in intelligence for your American CIA interrogators. How could they resist her pleas for help?"

"Somehow she contacted The Mute," Annabel said. "Asked for help to escape from you. To get me away from you. And she waited for them. She said it was the beginning of 'the real adventure.'"

"The Mute?" The old man looked curious. "That was his name? Interesting. Regardless, this mute and your uncle timed it wrong. They didn't count on members of the Mahdi Army getting to Marelda before they could. To their credit, Truckson and his men did manage to liberate both your mother and you away from al-Sadr's fighters, but she was already wounded by the time they got to her. She died at the compound. Truckson left her body but took you away."

Raw anger flashed across Dr. Smith's face. It was the first display of real emotion Trudi had seen from the man.

"He stole what was rightfully mine," the old man said. "And he hid it in this backwater countryside for more than a decade. He deserved all that came to him."

"Her." Trudi couldn't help herself saying it.

"What?" Dr. Smith said.

"Her. You called Annabel 'it.' But Annabel is not that. She is a human being, flesh and blood. And spirit. An educated girl. *Her*."

Dr. Smith stood and walked to Trudi until he towered over her. He stared at her unblinking for a moment, then with unexpected fury, he smashed his knuckles across the right side of her face.

Trudi grunted. The force of the blow caused her to smack her head against the bunk bed on the other side. She closed her eyes at the unexpected pain. There was a moment of quiet in the bunker, and then underneath the unkempt hair and battered lips, Trudi's voice called out firmly, defiantly.

"Her," she said again. "Her!"

42

THE MUTE

Night was in full force when Samuel Hill and The Mute found the dog.

The German shepherd was lying in the brush near a dead mercenary and a mangled body that, upon closer inspection, turned out to be Samir Sadeq Hamza al-Sadr. The Mute refused to pity the Arab, and instead turned his attention toward the nonhuman form stretched out and bloodied on the ground.

At first The Mute thought the dead animal might be a small deer or a bobcat, perhaps caught in accidental gunfire, or maybe a casualty from some natural predator. Then he took a step closer and saw the full moon shining on the matted, furry body, and he knew what had taken the brunt of that cannonball explosion they'd heard before.

"Ah, no," Hill said. "Come on, not the dog."

Samuel Hill apparently knew that dog too. Recognized its importance.

"If they got the dog," he said softly after checking the dead bodies nearby, "then they got the girl, they got Annabel. And if they got to Annabel, they got to Trudi."

The Mute didn't move, watching the carcass of the dog, hoping for any slight movement.

"Do you think that they would've taken Trudi with them? Or would they have . . ." He trailed off and tilted his head toward the dog.

The Mute shook his head. He didn't know. But the dog, Truck's dog . . . Truck's soldier . . .

Hill began searching out the hidden places surrounding where the dog lay, hissing intermittently, "Trudi! Trudi, are you out here?"

The Mute could see pain and anxiety etched in the man's face. He would look for her until he dropped, or until her dead body appeared before him. And if he found her dead body, The Mute would pity any person who had anything to do with making her that way.

But the dog, was he still alive? Or had that cannonball of a bullet silenced the animal forever?

The Mute approached the German shepherd, focusing his vision on the shadowy spot that outlined his torso. Was that movement? Did the ragged rib cage rise and fall? The Mute moved closer until he was able to kneel down next to the animal, to touch his neck and side.

The eyes were closed, but The Mute could hear a rasping rale pass through the dog's teeth. He placed a hand on the animal's side and felt his chest cavity rise and fall and rise again, ever so slightly, but undeniably so.

Signs of life, The Mute thought. *The dog still lives. There's still a chance.*

For a moment, his mind was filled with plans of action. Carry the dog back to the Jeep. Pound on the door of Dr. Anthony

Packer, the vet that Truck had used on many occasions. Save the animal's life.

He gently reached down and rolled the dog off the wounded shoulder. The animal yelped and came awake growling, then he recognized the hands that held him. The Mute saw the dog's tail thump once, twice against the ground. One soldier greeting another in the theater of war. The dog's shoulder was smeared with blood and ash and mud, a dirty mess, but The Mute was relieved to see that most of the bleeding had been staunched by the red mud pressed under the dog's body. If he left now, if he didn't waste any time, this dog would live. The Mute knew it to be true, and that thought filled him with hope.

Then he heard Hill calling softly to the wind.

"Trudi! Trudi, are you here? Are you safe?"

A choice to make, The Mute realized. *The soldier or the girl. There isn't time to rescue both. But how can I leave either one behind?*

He sat frozen, watching the dog as it watched him, listening to his ragged breathing, seeing him struggle to stand and fail. It was a full minute before The Mute realized that Samuel Hill was now kneeling next to him.

"We've got to go," he said. "They're not here. From what I can tell, they took the ATVs and headed back toward Truck's farm. We've got to go there."

There was silence between them, and in the silence, The Mute heard the crunch of burnt grass, the melody of death in mercenary army boots.

He reacted instinctively. Without warning, he launched himself at Hill until they were both on the ground, rolling and chasing themselves away from automatic gunfire that ripped through the night. When the bullets paused, Hill crab-walked behind the stump of a large oak tree. The Mute lay stock-still in the burned-over grass and hoped he was out of the moonlight.

"Did you get them?" a voice shouted. "Are they still alive?"

"One got away, but I think I got the other one," another mercenary called back. "I'll go check. Cover me."

The Mute heard gunfire sail over his head, but he didn't move. A moment later one of the mercenaries was standing warily over him, keeping a safe distance.

"This one's—"

A burst of bullets cut into the air, slicing through and silencing the nearest mercenary. He fell to the ground like a sack of onions, blood already dripping from wounds in his forehead and chest. Behind him, the other mercenary let loose a volley of gunfire, aiming above The Mute's head and toward the tree where Samuel Hill now hid, crouched into a ball that The Mute would not have thought possible for a man his size. Under the cover of this distraction, The Mute slid his right hand behind his back and retrieved the Kahr handgun stashed there. When there was a break in the fire, he struck, rolling onto his back and firing two shots toward the mercenary in the dark. At least one shot struck home. He heard the man grunt and fall to the ground.

The Mute scrambled to his left and found cover behind another tree. He looked for Hill, but he was no longer in the hiding spot.

Was he shot? Had he run? Where was he?

The Mute waited, watching and listening. After a moment, he heard the sounds of a hand-to-hand battle, then one gunshot, then more fighting. A few minutes later, Hill reentered The Mute's view, dragging a mercenary who was wounded in the leg.

"Okay, you can come out now," Hill said. The Mute stepped out from behind the tree. "You hurt?" Hill asked. The Mute shook his head. "Good. This joker actually shot himself in the leg trying to get at me."

The mercenary insulted Hill's ancestry and suggested he perform a physically impossible sex act. His advice was ignored.

"This one," Hill said, "we keep alive. I think Homeland Security will want to have many long conversations with him."

The mercenary stopped talking, the reality of his situation setting in. This was the age of terror, after all, and anyone invading America with less than stellar motives could, and sometimes did, disappear completely. He didn't struggle when Hill hung his wrists from a thick branch on an oak tree and secured him there with zip ties.

His arms are going to hurt after an hour or so like that, The Mute thought absently. But he had more important concerns on his mind. He walked back to the wounded dog still lying in the woods. The animal's tail swept the ground at the sight of him, but he no longer attempted to stand and greet him properly. The Mute could see his life was fading, and with it strength was going too.

A choice to make, he told himself. *An awful choice.*

Samuel Hill jogged over to The Mute's side. "Come on," he said. "We're running out of time."

The Mute didn't respond; he couldn't take his eyes off the wounded dog.

"Mute," Hill said again, and this time The Mute looked up at him. There was new understanding in Samuel Hill's eyes. "This your dog, Mute? Annabel said you helped Truck train him."

My dog? he thought. *Yes, my dog. Raised by Truck's voice and guided by my hand. Truck's dog, yes. And mine.*

The Mute nodded slowly.

"I see," Hill said. He sighed. And then he made the awful choice.

Samuel Hill knelt down and gently slid his hands underneath the dog's carriage. The animal nipped at his arms weakly, but the big man ignored his feeble effort. He gave a light grunt and lifted the limp weight of the German shepherd until he held him securely in a standing embrace. The dog finally stopped fighting and let its head sag into the cleft between Hill's chest and shoulder. The man let out a long exhale. He looked across the dog's body and stared intently at The Mute.

"The woman," Samuel Hill said, and there was pain in his eyes. "My ex-wife. She is everything to me. More than everything. You understand?"

The Mute nodded. He understood. Of course he understood.

"If I do this for you"—he nodded toward the dog—"then promise me you'll do everything you can to save her. To save both of them, your girl *and* my ex-wife. Anything and everything."

The Mute nodded. *No one left behind*, he told himself.

He couldn't express the gratefulness he felt at Hill's act of sacrifice. Leaving his ex-wife's life in another man's hands while he tried to save an anonymous dog for no other reason than it was important to that other man. The Mute vowed not to let that act be in vain.

Samuel Hill searched the eyes of the soldier and found what he was looking for. "All right then," he said. "I'll meet you all tomorrow morning at 8:00 a.m., in Birmingham. Denny's, of course." He turned and began a light jog, heading back to the rendezvous point where his car was still parked and waiting.

See you on the other side, The Mute said to himself.

He watched Samuel Hill disappear into the woods, and then he turned toward Truck's old farm. He started doing math in his head.

Twenty-four mercenaries total, he said to himself.

Truck took out twelve during the attack on the farm. He'd eliminated five more at the rendezvous spot. Samuel Hill had saved him from one earlier in the night, and they'd found another lying dead next to the body of Samir Sadeq Hamza al-Sadr. Now they'd just dealt with three more here. That was twenty-two enemy soldiers, total, so far. He began trotting toward the south, only one thought filling his mind.

I must kill two more men tonight.

43

ANNABEL

"Her." Trudi keeps her head down, but her voice refuses to submit. "Her!"

Johannes Schmitzden backhands her again, then again, then a third time. His fingers fold into fists now, and he keeps them rainin' on her. She tries to ball up, to protect herself, but the awkward way she's strapped to the bedpost makes that nearly impossible. He keeps hitting her until she finally slumps to the floor.

Her nose is bleeding now, and she's beginning to show bruising under her right eye, a grotesque match for the work the mercenaries did on her left eye earlier. Finally Dr. Schmitzden's work is done. He steps away from her and turns toward me. He's breathing hard, but he looks satisfied.

He reaches a hand in my direction, and I flinch. I seen what he just done to Trudi. Is he gonna do the same to me? But he don't. He don't hit me at all.

He strokes my cheek gently.

Like a mother caressing a child.

He kneels down so our eyes are level. I see Trudi watching from the bunk. She's finally stopped eggin' him on, but I see the anger in her jaw. And the worry. He brushes a strand of hair from my face and looks deeply into my eyes.

"It."

He says it tenderly, but the force of the word hits hard just the same. To this man, I'm just an experiment. A prototype. A lab rat. Nothing more. He stretches to full height and returns to his seat across from me at the table.

"It won't be long now," he says to no one in particular. "Once my men have eliminated Samuel Hill and his companion, we will leave this place. We'll return to Iraq where"—he nods in the direction of Trudi—"you will have to be a peace offering to my employer. He won't be happy to know that you killed his nephew. But having your writhing body for revenge will do something toward appeasing him."

The old man's eyes sparkle with possibilities when his gaze returns to me.

"And, of course, having you back in our possession will keep the money flowing too." He looks at me, and I see a kind of hungry joy flooding his eyes. Like Christmastime when there's lots of presents under the tree.

"There is always some kind of war going on in that part of the world," he says, "and anyone who can perpetuate that war is valuable to certain men. Your blood will help us perpetuate any war. The vaccines we extract from it will keep the ranks of jihad fighters swelling, healing their wounded, demoralizing their enemies with endless numbers of men who keep coming back from near-death to fight again and again."

"It won't work," I say. I'm surprised my voice ain't trembling. "Your experiments are flawed. My mother saw it. She saw it, and that's why she wanted to leave."

"It will work." Schmitzden seems to be stating a fact, not trying to convince me or anybody that what he says is true. It's like he's saying the sun is hot or two plus two is four. As far as he's concerned, it ain't even a question of faith, it's just plain, hard fact. "Your blood, it's different. Special."

"Okay, yeah." I nod. "I know there's something different about my blood. Maybe it's from that stuff you mixed into my DNA. Or maybe it's just funny blood. Everybody has different things about 'em. That don't mean my blood makes miracles."

"*It* doesn't understand," he says to Trudi, daring her to contradict him again. She don't. Not this time.

"My mother understood," I say. "You said yourself she was brilliant. She said it wouldn't work. That she'd made a mistake. That it was all a mistake."

Schmitzden don't respond this time. He just looks at me, like he's trying to decide if I'm a space alien or a cow's udder turned upside down and put on display in a carnival madhouse. He leans forward, both elbows on the table.

"Tell me," he says after a minute, "what else did your mother say?"

"Lots of things," I say. *Awful things*, I think.

"These were in a book she left you, yes?"

"Yes." I don't know what Dr. Schmitzden is getting at, but I don't like the way he's suddenly interested in what I'm saying.

He holds out his hand. "Give me the book."

I'm frozen in my seat. It never occurred to me that he'd want to take the book from me. Something in me can't let it go. It's the only connection I have to my life. Truck's gone. My mother was stolen from me. How can I give up the plain, black book that whispers her words in my ear?

He slams a hand on the table, making me jump in my seat, and I see he's pleased by my reaction.

"Give me the book."

There's a threat in his eyes. He wants me to know that he'll beat it outta me like he just beat Trudi if I don't give him my mother's journal.

"Why?"

I'm stalling, I know it. But I can't think of anything else to do.

"It will provide important perspective on the beginnings of our experiment. Perhaps she kept some thoughts to herself that I should take into account."

She said it wouldn't work, moron! She said your whole experiment was bat-crazy! That God alone works true miracles, not men! I want to scream it, but instead I say, *"Bitte."* Please. "I want to keep it. *Bitte.* I need to keep it."

He looks annoyed. "It wants to keep Mommy's journal," he mimics. Then he resumes his demand. "This book belongs to me. Anything *It* has belongs to me. Give me the book."

"I don't know where it is."

He shakes his head mournfully. "You hear that, Ms. Coffey? It doesn't remember where the book is. Do you think It wants me to hurt It?"

"Give him the book, Annabel, honey," Trudi says. "Give the crazy man the book. We'll get it back from him later."

"I think," Dr. Schmitzden says, "the book is here, right here in this bunker. I think if I start looking for it, I will find it. What do you think?"

I want to look away from him, but his eyes won't allow it.

"Give me the book."

I feel walls crumbling inside me, fortresses that kept me safe, disintegrating under his gaze.

"It's in the drawer," I say at last, motioning to the table in front of me. "In here."

He extends his hand, waiting for me to bring out the book

and deliver it to him. I know it's over. I slide open the shallow drawer on my side of the table. When I look inside there, I see Marelda Gregor's journal, a few pens, my translation notebook, my own notebook journal.

And a Walther PPQ semiautomatic pistol.

A man's gun.

Loaded.

Barrel aimed straight across from me. Pointing directly at the midsection of Dr. Johannes Schmitzden. Aimed at the man who is responsible for my life, and for the death of my mother. And my uncle.

I look at Dr. Schmitzden. He's waiting. He frowns and shakes his hand toward me, tapping the palm of his right hand with the fingers of his left. I know he won't wait much longer before simply pushing me out of the way and taking the journal—and the gun—for himself.

I look to Trudi. She's watching me closely. Worried. Her right eye is almost swollen shut, but she don't seem to notice. *Give him the book*, she mouths. She's worried this old man really is gonna hurt me.

I see one of them ghosts suddenly reappear in this room. It's just a flash of light in the corner of my eye, but I see it clear as day. There's a man sitting at the table. Both hands out, palms pressing down on the surface. Neither Schmitzden nor Trudi see him.

In my head I hear a sound. It's an animal dying, howling after me, begging me not to leave him in the muck and ash of a burned-out forest.

Then the world collapses around me until there's nothing but me, my mother's book, the gun. And Dr. Johannes Schmitzden.

I take a breath, filling myself with oxygen.

I reach inside the drawer.

44

TRUDI

To Trudi's ears, the sound of splintering wood that followed the gunshot was actually more noticeable than the gunfire itself. The carbine explosion was surprisingly crisp and quiet.

Trudi recognized the sound of a silencer on the end of a pistol but couldn't tell at first where it had come from. She whipped her head toward the steel door that served as entry into the bunker, half hoping, half expecting to see Samuel Hill standing there, saving the day. But there was no one there. They were alone.

Trudi heard a second muffled explosion, accompanied by more splintering of wood, and now put things into place.

Dr. Smith jerked backward in his chair after the first shot, a look of true surprise crossing his face. He said nothing. His hand dipped off the table and down toward his midsection. He slumped.

The second shot appeared to hit the slumping man just below

the heart. He gave a grunt, then a sigh. He toppled backward and to the left, taking the chair with him to the ground.

Trudi heard a ringing in her ears, tried to shake it out, and finally decided to live with it.

"Annabel," she said. "Annabel!"

The girl turned and looked at Trudi with blank eyes. She pulled away from the drawer, and Trudi saw the big gun she held in both her hands. It looked heavy, like the expression on Annabel's face.

"Is he dead?" Annabel said. Trudi tried to look past the fallen chair to glimpse the old man. He didn't appear to be moving.

"I think so, honey."

Annabel nodded and carefully placed the semiautomatic pistol on the now-wobbling table. She sank back into her chair, eyes unblinking, lost in her own world.

"Annabel."

The girl looked up again. Trudi raised her bound hands as high as she could.

"Somebody may have heard those shots."

Annabel stared blankly, uncomprehending at first. Then a switch flipped in her head, and she nodded. She got up from her chair and went to retrieve a knife from the kitchen supplies. When she came to Trudi, she stopped and winced at the sight of her close up. She reached gingerly toward the bruised face.

"I'm sorry," she whispered. "I'm sorry he hurt you. Are you gonna be okay?"

Trudi tried to smile, in spite of the electricity it sent through her face. "Of course, honey. I've gotten worse than this just falling out of bed."

Annabel seemed relieved. She reached out with a knife and cut away the zip ties that held Trudi to the wooden beam. Free at last, Trudi tried to stand, then wobbled and sat hard on the bunk bed.

"Legs went to sleep down there on the floor," she explained. "Poor circulation, I guess. Give me a minute."

Annabel nodded. "Do you think anybody heard?"

Trudi looked down the tunnel and listened intently. She didn't see or hear any movement.

"I think we're safe for now." There was a pause. "That was a very brave thing you did, Annabel. Dr. Smith was insane and very, very dangerous."

"He was my father."

Trudi felt her jaw split, ever so slightly.

"What?" she said at last. "What did you say?"

"Johannes Schmitzden was my father. I read it in my mother's journal. They . . . they came together just so they could make me. So they could have 'an innocent' to use in their experiments."

"Honey."

Trudi didn't know what else to say, so she reached out her deadened and tingly arms and pulled Annabel into a hug. They didn't say anything for a minute or two, and then Annabel finally pulled away.

"Will I go to jail?" the child asked.

"No," Trudi said. "We'll find Samuel. And The Mute. And they'll make everything just go away."

Annabel nodded, trusting Trudi's words without question.

"I don't want to stay in this room no more."

Trudi still felt pins and needles throbbing in her feet and ankles, but she stood up anyway. "All right," she said. "Let's get out of here."

Annabel recovered her mother's journal from the table drawer and stuffed it somewhere inside her coat. Then she turned to Trudi. "What about them soldiers guarding the entrance to the tunnel?" she asked.

Trudi looked thoughtful for a moment. She reached over to the table and hefted the heavy Walther semiautomatic. She checked the clip and then turned back to Annabel.

"I think this'll even things out for us."

She kept the gun at the ready in her right hand and reached for Annabel's hand with her left. They began walking.

Trudi couldn't help herself, she started counting the round lights that dotted the dim walls of the tunnel. When she got to fourteen, she forced herself to stop counting, to stop noticing. *You really are predictable*, she scolded herself. *Obsessive-compulsive or something. Maybe that makes you a good PI, but it also makes you vulnerable to people like Dr. Smith. And it makes you annoying.*

It took only a few minutes before the narrow steps that led up to the outside came into view. Annabel looked pale, like she was about to have a panic attack from claustrophobia. When she saw the steps, Annabel released Trudi's hand and started running toward them, apparently desperate to be free from her underground prison.

"Annabel, wait!" Trudi hissed. She wanted to get a lay of the land, to gauge where the mercenaries were before they ventured aboveground. The child heard the call and slowed, then stopped, waiting at the foot of the steps. She was whitefaced and breathing hard, but she was fighting the urge to run, trusting Trudi's voice more than her own instincts.

Annabel turned back to face Trudi. At that exact moment, two black-clad mercenaries came tumbling down the steps, crashing into the child in a melee of shouts and screams.

Trudi joined the shouting, raising the Walther pistol, trying to get a clean look at either of the two soldiers. One of them had apparently already been shot multiple times, body limp, head lolling in unseeing finality. It took a few seconds before Trudi understood why. Brown Head had used Blondie as a human shield, protecting himself from gunfire by forcing his comrade's body to accept the bullets fired in his direction.

At first Brown Head cowered behind Blondie's dead form until he understood that the person tangled up in their mess of bodies was the girl, Annabel. With a sudden movement, he shoved his comrade's body in the direction of Trudi and grabbed Annabel with a forearm around her neck. He raised her high until she became a new shield blocking Trudi's aim. Annabel started kicking immediately, scratching at his arm with her hands. The soldier looked wildly down the tunnel, registering Trudi's presence, then back at the tunnel opening above him. He decided to take his chances with Trudi.

First he shook Annabel hard, then he tightened his grip on her neck. Trudi could see the color fading from the child's face.

"Tell her to settle down!" the mercenary shouted to Trudi. "Or I'll kill her right here and now!"

Trudi said nothing, still looking for a clean shot at the man's head, but Annabel let her body go limp in his grasp. He loosened his hold just enough for the girl to cough and sputter and start breathing again.

"It's over," Trudi said. "Dr. Smith is dead. Your partner is dead. Let the girl go."

The mercenary shook his head. "You don't understand. There is no going back. This mission was always success or death."

Trudi lowered her gun. "No," she said. "You don't have to die. Not today. Let her go."

Brown Head ignored her. Instead he put a foot on the lowest step and craned his head, trying to get a glimpse of what was going on outside.

"Your sniper is crazy." Fear tinged the mercenary's voice. "He killed Rolf with a single shot. Rolf was already dead, but he just kept shooting. Kept shooting. I think he was trying to make his bullets pass through Rolf until they hit me."

"I've got news for you," Trudi said, raising the Walther once more. "I'm a little mentally unbalanced myself today."

"Stay back! I will kill her—you know I will. I'm the one who finally took out her uncle, you know. I'm the one who ended the life of the great Leonard Truckson."

Trudi stopped advancing, but she didn't lower her gun.

"Annabel," Trudi said, "you doing okay over there?" The girl nodded, eyes locked onto Trudi's.

"Kill this worthless animal," Annabel said fiercely. She nodded again.

Trudi almost laughed out loud. This girl was a force to be reckoned with. Maybe Dr. Smith was right about there being something special in her blood.

Brown Head was nearing a full state of panic now. His gun flew wildly between Annabel's head and Trudi's torso, but his real attention was on the sniper outside the tunnel.

"American!" he shouted above him. "American! I've got your little girl!"

In response, a volley of automatic weapons fire sprayed across the top step of the tunnel. The mercenary crouched low, taking the child with him. Annabel started kicking again.

"If I die," he grunted at last, "you die." Then he yanked hard on Annabel's body and, carrying her as a shield, rushed to the top of the stairs.

"No, wait!" Trudi shouted, but she was too late. She ran to the base of the steps and saw Brown Head disappear from view, still holding Annabel. Trudi took the steps two at a time and peeked out of the tunnel, leaning her shoulders onto the ground just outside the entrance while leaving the rest of her body underground.

It took a moment for her to acclimate to the night outside,

but when she did, she figured out that Brown Head had now taken cover behind a parked ATV. He still kept Annabel captive, pressing her into the open gaps of the ATV. She tried to take aim but knew that at this distance, in this moonlight, she'd be just as likely to hit the girl as she would the man.

Should have taken the shot when Annabel told me to, she told herself.

"Let the girl go!" she shouted into the darkness. "You can still come out of this alive."

A strong hand covered her mouth.

It came from nowhere, appearing as if by magic out of the darkness, silencing her voice behind an impenetrable grip. Trudi tried to scream, tried to fight. She swung the Walther toward her attacker and then quickly found her gun hand pinned to the ground. She struggled to break free, astonished at the raw strength that kept her trapped and unable to move. Then a face was next to hers, staring hard into her eyes. And below that face, etched deep into the neck, was a thick, familiar scar.

"GheMutgtf!" she breathed. *The Mute!*

When he saw recognition in her eyes, The Mute released his hold on her mouth and hand.

"What—" she started to say, but he shook his head. He put a finger to his lips, and Trudi knew what he was asking. *Would you shut up and let me do my job?*

"American!" the mercenary was calling to the wind now, clearly unaware where The Mute was hiding. "Don't make me kill your girl! Surrender now and she will live! American, do you hear me! Answer! Answer!"

The Mute motioned for Trudi to move. She rolled out of the tunnel, staying low to the ground and letting him take her place. She watched him lean on his elbows, sniper rifle balanced like a pendulum in his arms.

"American!"

There was a single shot, and Brown Head toppled backward to the ground. Annabel pushed away immediately and came running toward the tunnel entrance. When The Mute saw her, he shunned his rifle and came out of the tunnel. He knelt on the ground.

Annabel crashed into him like a wave hits a cliff, wrapped herself around his broad shoulders, and buried her head deep into his neck. He stood, holding her in his arms, swaying gently, turning in a tight, slow circle, unwilling to let go.

"I knew you'd come," Annabel was saying to him over and over. "I knew you'd come for me. Like you did before. I knew you'd come."

Trudi said nothing, just sat in the dirt and ash watching the reunion. *It's over,* she thought. *It's finally over.* And then a worry creased her mind.

But where's Samuel?

The pig.

45

TRUDI

Monday, October 26

Trudi Sara Coffey brushed a darkened curl away from her eyes and, as was her custom, looked first in the classifieds section of the *Atlanta Journal-Constitution*.

She scanned the personals until the familiar advertisement came into view. It was only one line, easy to miss, but Trudi couldn't start her morning without checking to see if its invisible author still had the same message to send out to the world.

Safe.

She looked again at the four-letter word she'd grown accustomed to seeing, let a faint grin pass on her lips in gratefulness that it had returned, then contentedly turned back to the front page to begin her day in earnest. Half an hour later, she heard a knock on the doorframe to her office. The man who filled her doorway was tall, lean, and muscular, carrying a leather valise in one large hand. His chocolate eyes were smiling at her. His hair had been cut but still strayed longer past his ears than she remembered it last. He wore a gray wool trench coat over a collarless blue shirt and denim jeans. And as always, his favorite black boots bottomed out his outfit. He looked ready for either business or pleasure. As usual.

"Detective Coffey," he said formally, "there's someone here to see you. He doesn't have an appointment, but he's hoping that you'll see him anyway. Ma'am."

Samuel Hill flashed his teeth, and even though she knew he thought that was his "irresistible, boyish grin," she couldn't help being happy to see it.

"I would have buzzed in," he continued, "but it seems you still haven't hired a new receptionist."

"Who has time for interviews and such?" She shrugged. Then, "So, you're back in town. When did you get in?"

"Just yesterday. Can I come in?"

Trudi gestured toward the metal guest chairs in front of her desk. Samuel hesitated. "You'll keep your hands where I can see them?"

"Relax, you big chicken. I'm not going to electrocute you. Unless you deserve it."

The big man gave her a dubious look and then decided to risk it. He settled down comfortably. "You look good," he said. "Much better than the last time I saw you."

Trudi blinked involuntarily. It had been more than a month since she'd received a beating at the hands of Johannes Schmitzden. Her face had healed nicely. There were no physical mementos of her bruises and cuts, but it was harder to rid herself of the mental wounds. Time, she had decided at last, would heal the inner scars.

"Thanks," she said. *You don't look so bad yourself, cowboy.* She didn't dare say that out loud. Too much baggage. So she went another direction with the conversation. "How did the cleanup go back in the Conecuh Forest?"

"All done," Samuel said. He cracked his knuckles. "Sadly, it turns out there were a few dozen more casualties of the Great Conecuh Fire than first estimated."

"Yeah, I saw that on the news," Trudi said. "They indicated the additional bodies had been burned beyond recognition. No identification possible."

Samuel shrugged. "I guess that happens sometimes. Makes you think twice about hiking solo in a national forest, doesn't it?"

"Mmm-hmm."

There was a moment of awkwardness, but Trudi just waited. *Silence is a powerful tool in a private investigator's arsenal*, she reminded herself, *and in ex-husband/ex-wife relations*. Her patience was rewarded when he reached inside his jacket.

"Here," he said at last, "I thought you might need this. To replace the one you lost."

He placed a brand-new Beretta Bobcat handgun on the desk. *He's so cute sometimes*, Trudi thought. *He's practically blushing, like a little boy offering a flower to his favorite girl.* She didn't have the heart to tell him that hers had been a Beretta Tomcat, not a Bobcat, and that she'd replaced that little ditty within a week after her return to Atlanta. Oh well, having a backup gun would be a nice luxury. She'd definitely keep this one nearby too.

"That's very thoughtful," she said to him. "You shouldn't have."

He shrugged and tried not to look too pleased with himself.

"Oh, and I almost forgot," Samuel said, "I brought you something else too."

"What is it?"

He reached inside his brown valise and produced a book with a bow wrapped around it.

"An early Christmas gift," he said, "from a mutual friend." He emphasized the *mute* syllable of *mutual*.

Trudi took the book and removed the bow. It was an expensive illustrated gift edition of S. Morgenstern's *The Princess Bride*, by William Goldman. Hardbound and thick, it was a beautiful tome. Fashioned with an imitation of 1800s-style precision that included lavish, four-color illustrations, a sturdy, sewn-in binding, and quarter-inch-thick cover plates on front and back. Trudi resisted the urge to flip open the back cover and run her hands across the endpapers there. She knew that what she expected to be hidden there, she'd find. But for now, she didn't want to know anything else about it unless it was absolutely necessary. Unless something was *unsafe*.

"It's lovely," she said.

"He thought you'd like it. But maybe you should keep it in a safe place?"

"Of course." She set the book next to the telephone on her desk, then turned her attention back to Samuel. He fidgeted uncomfortably.

"Annabel sends her love," he said at last. "She's fine. Safe. And her godfather. He's fine too."

"Good to know," Trudi said. She let her mind drift back to their last meeting, on September 21.

It had been a hard parting when she and Annabel had said good-bye. The morning after the last stand at Truck's farm, The Mute, Annabel, and Trudi had met Samuel at Denny's restaurant in Birmingham. Samuel had brought two plane tickets, one for The Mute and one for Annabel.

"We still don't know enough about Dr. Smith and his freaky Order of St. Heinrich von Bonn," he said. "Best to keep Annabel in her Fade for a while, at least until she turns thirteen."

The Mute had accepted the tickets without looking at them. "Plane leaves Birmingham-Shuttlesworth around 4:00 p.m.," Samuel said.

Trudi saw The Mute frown at that news, but she didn't know why. *Not my business*, she'd told herself. *Something between him and Samuel.*

"Meanwhile," Samuel continued, "the CIA is actively looking into Dr. Smith's organization now. The boys in Langley aren't happy about losing a man like Truck. They beat Homeland Security to that last mercenary we left in the woods. They plan to question him while the fight over jurisdiction plays out."

A perky young waitress delivered their breakfast at that point, and following The Mute's lead, they ate mostly in silence. Then, too soon, it was time for good-byes.

Trudi followed Annabel until they stood beside a Jeep Wrangler in the parking lot. She noticed a few thick bags in the back-seat. Samuel and The Mute made some excuse to leave the women alone.

"I can't believe I just met you yesterday," Trudi said quietly. "I feel like we belong together already."

Annabel smiled and blushed. "Thank you, Miss Trudi, for coming to me. I think God might have sent you. I couldn't have made it without you."

"Nonsense." Trudi was blushing now. "You're a strong, educated girl. And besides, God tends to get things done with or without me."

They didn't say anything for a moment, and then Annabel leaned softly in and wrapped her arms around Trudi's waist. In spite of herself, Trudi felt her eyes grow damp. She imagined, just for a second, that this was what it felt like to be a real mother to a real child. She didn't want to let go. She knelt down and pushed her cheek into Annabel's neck.

"Why don't," Trudi said into her ear, "why don't you just stay with me, honey. I want you to stay. I'll keep you safe. I promise."

It was a long moment before Annabel responded. "I can't, Miss Trudi. The Mute, he's my godfather. Truck told me if anything ever happened to him, I was to go live with The Mute."

Trudi nodded and felt tears spring out despite her efforts to keep them in. "Okay, I understand." Trudi nodded again and stood, leaving a hand resting on Annabel's shoulder. "If you ever need me," she said, "no, if you ever just want me, you let me know. I'm bound to you now, just like The Mute. I'll always be there for you, okay?"

"Okay."

Trudi now wished she would have said the words she was thinking then, but she hoped the girl knew them anyway. *I love you, Annabel Lee Truckson.* She hoped she knew.

And then they were gone. Annabel and The Mute drove off down the highway. Samuel drove Trudi back to Atlanta, gave her the name of a bodyguard he trusted, then he was gone too, and it was left to Trudi to resume the life she'd run away from just a few weeks earlier. Before everything changed.

She'd never called the bodyguard; she didn't need to. No one came after her, and it was only a week or so before she was buried in her work again—background checks, insurance fraud investigations, asset locates, skip traces. It was predictable work, and she was liking it again. Almost . . .

"I have a postcard," Samuel said now, bringing Trudi back from her reverie, "if you want to see it."

"No," Trudi said. "It's better if I don't have any idea where she might be."

Samuel nodded. He stood and looked through the door down the short hallway to the reception area at Coffey & Hill

Investigations. Trudi stood behind her desk, trying to be polite while he left. Again. The pig.

But he didn't move toward the exit. Instead, he turned back to her.

"So," he said, "they're telling me to take a sabbatical."

"What?" Trudi didn't follow where he was going.

"The CIA. They want me out of the field for a bit. They say that the whole Annabel Lee situation makes me 'hot' overseas right now, and they want me to cool off stateside for a while."

"Wow, I'm sorry, Samuel. I know how that must be hard for you."

Her ex-husband shrugged. "At first I was a little upset about it. But now I'm thinking maybe it's for the best."

"Good for you."

Samuel gave a long look across the hall toward the cluttered storage room.

"I notice you still have an empty office here at Coffey & Hill Investigations." He placed an unnecessary emphasis on the *Hill* part of Coffey & Hill. "And, you know, I've got some free time ahead of me."

Trudi bit her lip. "What are you suggesting?"

"I'm suggesting that maybe I could come back."

"Samuel." Trudi sat down heavily. "You know we can't do that. Not after, well, everything."

"No, no," he said, "I understand that part. I understand we can't get back together that way, not as husband and wife. But, you know, we're a good PI team, Tru-Bear. We were a great team working on the Annabel Lee case. We can't be lovers, I get that, but why can't we be partners? It is called Coffey & Hill Investigations, after all. That's both our names on the sign out there."

Trudi didn't know what to say. She let the idea roll around

in her head. *It would be nice to have Samuel Hill around again*, she thought. He was a superb asset to any private investigation. Smart. Resourceful. Connected out the wazoo. And a girl always appreciates looking at pretty things, right? But still . . .

"I don't know, Samuel," she said at last. "It seems like it could be a big mistake."

"I know," he said, "it could be. Or it could be just the thing we've both been looking for since . . . since a few years ago."

"I don't know."

"How about this," he said, and she could see his eyes glinting. "What if I just clean out the mess in your storage room over there? How about I come in tomorrow morning and just do that? Then, after, we can talk more about other things. Sound fair?"

Baby steps, she said to herself, smiling. He was using the *What About Bob?* strategy on her. She knew it, and he knew she knew it, but he was trying it anyway.

"All right," she said at last. "Clean the storage room. Tomorrow is fine for that. Then we'll talk."

"It's a deal." He turned to go, but she called out to him before he reached the door.

"And Samuel?" she said. "One more thing."

"You got it, Tru-Bear."

"I need a receptionist."

He looked dubious. "I don't know that I'm cut out for answering phones," he said.

"No, not you." She waved him off. "But you made me fire my old receptionist. So you have to do one thing for me."

"What is it?"

She scribbled something on a sheet of paper, tore it off the pad, and handed it across the desk.

"Call Eulalie Jefferson and talk her into coming back. Be

charming. Offer her a raise. Tell her she can have your car. Just get her back here for me. Can you do that?"

Samuel Hill took the paper and let his fingers brush gently across Trudi's hand. He looked at the telephone on her desk, and his gaze flicked across *The Princess Bride* still sitting beside it. He turned away from the book and locked eyes with Trudi.

He smiled.

"As you wish," he said. "As you wish."

EPILOGUE

THE MUTE

Seven Years and Three Months Later
Tuesday, December 13

Even in midwinter, sunshine covered the Haitian marketplace of Port-au-Prince like a warm blanket spread out to welcome visitors.

The Mute sat at the edge of the economic melee, drinking in the warmth that tingled on his skin. He wore tan shorts and a cotton tropical-print shirt. Despite his best efforts, he also wore a straw hat that sheltered his face and neck from the worst of the sun. She insisted on that, and she could be pretty stubborn when she got an idea in her head. Just like her uncle.

He watched her walk through the open-air market and marveled once more at her. She'd grown into a beautiful young woman. Long brown hair, sun-bleached in just the right spots. Penetrating green eyes. A lithe, graceful figure that turned more than a few heads. A smile that made the world feel like a better place. If she were back in Alabama, the gossipy old women would call her a "man-killa" and try to fix her up with their grandsons.

Here in Haiti, after her thirteenth birthday, she'd given up the name Annabel Lee but had insisted on keeping her uncle's last name. Raina Aemilia Truckson, that was who she'd been for many years now, and who she intended to be until she died.

She turned, and The Mute saw sunlight glint on her collarbone. A silver cross hung there, kept near her heart, decorating a steel chain.

She never said where she got it, but she never took it off, not since she was twelve. After that birthday, she'd told The Mute she had some thinking to do, and she'd buried herself for weeks in a Creole translation of the Bible. She'd asked questions. He didn't know many answers and had directed her to others in Port-au-Prince. A missionary pastor. A voodoo priest. A Catholic church. Even an Islamic imam. In the end, she'd returned back to that Bible. She was patient but also determined.

One day she'd turned to him and, seemingly out of the blue, said, "The one thing I can't get past, can't dump off to the side, is Jesus. If he existed, he couldn't 'a been just a good man or some great teacher. He had to be more." She'd waited for a response, but The Mute just shrugged. She'd smiled and nodded. "I guess that's it then. I know who I am now."

She'd stood and kissed his forehead and then walked off into a new life. That was the day she'd started wearing that silver cross, a memento on the outside to remind her of what had happened on the inside.

Now, seeing her in the marketplace, that one-sided conversation came back to his mind. Watching his goddaughter grow into maturity over the past several years certainly made a good case for what she believed. As a result, The Mute had thought some about matters of faith and eternity but had never given it the sincere, searching treatment she had. *Maybe someday I'll have to do that*, he told himself. *Maybe someday soon.*

Raina stopped at one of the sellers, and The Mute watched her begin the obligatory dickering with a laugh and a warm greeting. She was a friend to everyone here, and everyone treated the pretty white girl as if she were a member of the family.

She turned to walk away. The Mute could make out her lips saying, "Twòp twòp bagay." "Much too much" in Haitian Creole. The seller came running out from behind his booth, wooing her, begging her to come back.

The three-legged dog resting beside The Mute growled at that sight, popping up into a tripod position. He was an old dog now, graying and slightly deaf. But the German shepherd never forgot who he once was, never quit trying to be protector for the girl he'd grown to love. The Mute let a hand fall on the animal's head, and he stopped growling, but he still never took his eyes off her.

And now the transaction was done, a trade made for an undetermined amount of *gourde* banknotes. The girl looked toward the edge of the marketplace and caught The Mute's eyes. She raised her prize: Barbancourt, Haitian Rum. A bottle to celebrate her nineteenth birthday today.

The Mute snorted. The girl didn't even drink, but she knew it was his favorite. She'd made sure there'd be something special for him at tonight's celebration. As if just spending time with her wasn't enough by itself.

He watched as she moved on to the fruit vendors.

They'd been in Haiti for seven years now, always talking about moving away someday but never bothering to make any plans for change. They'd never heard again from the Order of St. Heinrich von Bonn or any of Johannes Schmitzden's cronies. The Mute assumed that they'd lost track of the girl or been forced underground after the Islamic State rose to some semblance of power in Iraq. Then, since she'd reached age thirteen and beyond, she was no longer of any value to them. At least that's what he hoped.

On her thirteenth birthday, The Mute offered to return her to Germany, to end her Fade and let her reclaim her life and her mother's fortune. Apparently there was a home and a significant investment account waiting for her whenever she wanted to claim it. But she'd declined.

"Let's stay here one more year," she'd said. And so they did. And another year after that. And another. When she'd turned eighteen, The Mute tried again, but she'd refused.

"My home is Port-au-Prince," she'd said. "Yours too."

And that had settled it. They were Haitian in heart, if not in origin.

Now she was done with the fruit vendors. At home, a stew of rice, beans, and mutton was simmering. They would add the mangoes and sweetbread to the meal and have a birthday feast. Afterward, they'd make vanilla sponge cake, the Haitian style, and he'd sip at a glass of the rum while she opened her presents.

It was a good life.

Someday, he knew, there would be a young man who would steal her heart away from him. But today, on her nineteenth birthday, she was still his little girl, and he was still her Mute.

She smiled as she walked toward him. She whistled, and the dog beside him sprang to life, trotting out to meet her, making three legs seem just as easy to use as four. She paused to press her cheek against the animal's neck, and The Mute heard her saying in Creole, *"Ou se yon chen bon."* You're a good dog.

The Mute stood as she drew closer. *Li se yon lavi bon*, he thought for what he figured must have been the thousandth time. He felt unexpectedly grateful.

Even in midwinter, her smile covered the Haitian marketplace of Port-au-Prince like a warm blanket spread out to welcome visitors.

It's a good life, he told himself again, returning her smile.

Yon lavi bon.

Read an excerpt from the next
COFFEY & HILL MYSTERY

COMING
FALL 2016

1

RAVEN

Atlanta, GA
Downtown
Friday, April 14, 8:11 p.m.
16 minutes to Nevermore

My dad used to tell me the best way to stay out of trouble was to think about tomorrow before you act today.

Every Friday night in high school, just before I stepped out to go crazy with my friends, he'd look up from whatever he was reading—the Bible, a new Sharon Carter Rogers thriller, a boring book about Roman history, whatever—and he'd give me that same lecture:

"Son, ask yourself if 'Tomorrow You' is going to thank you for the circumstances you get him into tonight."

Of course he was right. Dad generally gave good advice—it was kind of his job, after all. And of course I mostly ignored him. I figured that was my job.

Right now, though, I'm kind of wishing Last-Night Me had

been paying attention to Dad's most famous lecture. Even if LNM had just made some kind of contingency plan or something, that would've been helpful. But, as usual, that guy was just winging it, hoping things would work out anyway, regardless of what he did.

Eternal optimist, I guess. That's me. Hope it doesn't get me killed today.

The timer app on my cell phone beeps to tell me there's only sixteen minutes left. I take in a deep breath and let it out slowly to calm my nerves. *Gotta keep my wits. No time to panic, not yet at least.*

The Big Dude in the wheelchair twitches and groans. I can see that his subconscious mind is fighting the drug that knocked him out, but there's nothing I can do about it right now. All I can do is punch the elevator button again, swear a little bit, and hope that sixteen minutes is going to be enough time to get done what needs to get done.

And then I see her.

Wow.

Trudi Sara Coffey pops through the door to the stairwell without hesitating, like she knew I'd be here, like she knew I'd be waiting for this stupid elevator on the sixth floor of the Ritz-Carlton Atlanta hotel.

She's cleaned up for the occasion, a rare treat, if you ask me. Sleeveless red dress, sexy but not trashy—I think they call it a bodycon style. It's sleek with ribbed material that hugs her hips until the fabric ends just above her knees. Below that is a pair of black ankle boots, flirty, with a gold buckle, metal sequins, and chunky heels. Stylish, but also convenient for running. Or kicking.

Her hair is thick and chocolatey, casually twisted and tacked up on her head in a way that just makes me want to kiss her neck. Dangly diamond earrings are her only jewelry, except for that long, black marble chopstick-thingy holding her hair in place. And stuck to her left hand is a little black purse—Mom would've called it a "clutch." The way she's holding the purse, with the snap undone, tells me what I would've expected from her anyway.

She wants to be able to get to her Beretta Tomcat quickly. Just in case.

I know she's just jogged up six flights of stairs, but she's barely breathing hard, like she could run up the next eighteen floors of this hotel without any problem. *She keeps in shape, this one.* Of course, one peek at that red dress reveals that secret. She pauses long enough to glance up and down the hall, checking to see if we have company. Then she turns her full attention to me.

"So, Raven," she says now. "This is interesting."

"Don't call me that, Trudi," I say, too quickly. "I mean, you don't have to call me that. You can call me—"

"Raven," she interrupts. "I can't help noticing you've got my ex-husband, unconscious for some reason, strapped into Mama's wheelchair."

I cringe at that. This could be hard to explain. I decide to postpone that conversation.

"You look great, Trudi."

I'm stalling, obviously, but I mean it too. My mom always taught me it's important to acknowledge a woman's efforts at looking pretty. Plus, if this ends badly, I'll never forgive myself for missing an opportunity to tell Trudi Coffey that I think she's just heartbreakingly beautiful. Seems like she doesn't believe that about herself anymore. And she definitely deserves to believe it.

"I mean, wow, Trudi. Spectacular. You should dress like this all the time. Are those Vince Camuto boots? Very nice."

"We're talking fashion now? That's where you want to go at this particular junction in your life?"

I shrug and try out what I think is my adorably sheepish grin. "I'm just saying you're dressed nice today. It's a compliment."

Her stupid ex-husband groans again, interrupting our conversation. She presses a hand to her hip and frowns. "This doesn't look good, Raven."

The timer app on my cell phone beeps again.

"What's that?" she says.

Only fifteen minutes left. I jab at the elevator button a few times. *What . . . is . . . taking . . . so long?*

"Raven." She says my name again, a little intensity building in her voice. She steps toward me, and I suddenly get a maddening whiff of Bvlgari perfume.

How's a guy supposed to concentrate when a woman like this is standing just two feet away? I cannot catch a break today.

"They already shut down the lifts in the whole hotel," she's saying now. "SWAT's going to be here any minute. So . . . you want to explain what's going on, or do I step out of the way and let them take you down? I'm giving you a chance here. Maybe you should take it."

I close my eyes and take in a sweet breath of violet, orange blossom, and jasmine. I try to make a mental list of my options at this point, and it's not very long.

In the end, though, all I can think is,

This is going to get really messy, really soon.

ACKNOWLEDGMENTS

I need to thank three strong-willed women for making this book possible.

But first I'm going to tell you a story that explains why I need to thank them. I'll try to keep it reasonably brief, but I'm not making any promises, so if you just want to know the names of those strong-willed women, go ahead and skip to the last paragraph of this section.

I've been writing professionally for more than twenty-five years now, mostly nonfiction and inspirational books, with a little theology thrown in for good measure. Some books were successful, some weren't. So it goes. Still, I've managed to sell close to two million copies of my books worldwide, so things seem to be working out okay. For now at least.

Anyway, a number of years ago, there was a night when I couldn't sleep. I was bored, so I spent the time making up the premise for a suspense novel. Afterward I figured, *Why not?* and I started writing it.

When it came time to pitch the novel to publishers, no editor would read it. My agent at the time explained it this way: "They keep telling me, 'Mike Nappa is an inspirational writer. He can't write suspense.'" So I did what any stubborn writer would do.

I erased my name completely from the manuscript and made up a pen name instead—a woman's name. I resubmitted the manuscript to one of the publishers who'd seen it (and not read it) a year prior. I told them the author was a homemaker in Florida, and that this was her first attempt at writing.

I had a contract offer on my desk in three weeks.

In the end, I wrote three novels under that pen name. All were well-reviewed (one even won an award!), but to be honest, none of them were hugely successful, so maybe those original editors were right not to read my first manuscript. (Boy, it hurts to say that.)

Still, back in 2009, full of hope and wonder, I started writing *Annabel Lee*. I thought it would be the fourth book for my pen name. I got about thirty pages in when, surprise! My publisher notified me that they'd decided not to publish any more books from my homemaker in Florida. My brief career as a suspense novelist was over.

Hey, I figured, *I gave it a good shot. Just didn't work out.*

So I went back to writing inspirational and theology books. In fact, I published two nonfiction books that I think are the best things I've ever written. Both of those books had first-class marketing and publicity campaigns attached, and both were projected to do very well in the marketplace—and *both books failed spectacularly*. One of them was such a financial fiasco that my editor told me to stop sending him new book ideas. Ever. He would, he told me in the most polite and respectful way, be laughed out of his publishing committee if he mentioned my name in there again.

Sigh.

About the time of that first big failure, my wife, Amy, started badgering me about "that story with the 'safe/unsafe' code in the newspaper." Why didn't I go ahead and finish that manuscript? She wanted to know what happened, and said it was kind of mean that I'd gotten her hooked with the first thirty pages and then left her hanging.

I told Amy, in the most polite and respectful way, that finishing *Annabel Lee* was an enormously stupid idea. Writing a suspense novel is really, really hard, I said. An awful, time-consuming, ego-shattering experience from beginning to end. And hadn't I already failed as a fiction writer? Why waste a year working on a new book that was destined to fail like the others?

Amy politely and respectfully reminded me that I'd also failed in my career as a nonfiction writer. So why not try failing at fiction again? At least then she could find out what happened.

Wives, right? (Insert eye roll here.)

I told her no. Final decision.

And that was that.

Sort of.

My wife has learned the secret to controlling her husband. "I'm praying that God will change your heart," she told me. And she started praying. Before long, she'd enlisted my pastor's wife, Jan Hummel, to pray the same thing. Yeah, they ganged up on me. Pretty mean, right? And they kept cheerfully reminding me every week of their prayers for my career success as a novelist. And before long, I kept having more and more sleepless nights where all I could think about was what might be happening with Annabel, Trudi Coffey, and The Mute.

I caved.

All right, all right, I told Amy and Jan. I'll write this book, and it'll be a big, time-wasting failure, and it'll be all your fault. So there.

They didn't feel any sympathy for me. In fact, they were happy about my impending misery.

Whatever.

So I let myself get lost in the world of Coffey & Hill Investigations. It took forever, but I found myself not minding that so much. When *Annabel Lee* was (finally!) done, around Christmas of 2012, I was exhausted. But at least it was over. I gave a signed copy of the manuscript to Jan for Christmas and let Amy read it on my computer, and then I tried to forget about it. Except that now both Amy and Jan started pestering me to get it published. Given my publishing history, I knew that was a silly pipe dream—but I also thought I'd better not let them start praying again. I began sending it out to publishers and tried to hope for the best.

A lot of editors simply refused to read it. After all, I was an inspirational author, not a novelist.

A number of editors read it, hated it, and felt like they should tell me all the reasons why they hated it as part of the humiliating rejection process. (I never understand why editors think they have to do that . . . but I digress.)

Several editors read it, loved it—and then told me they still weren't going to publish it even though they loved it. (I never understand that one either.)

One editor at a very large, New York City publishing house actually dangled a potentially lucrative contract in front of me. He loved *Annabel Lee*, he said, except for all that "supernatural" stuff. If I'd cut out the spiritual elements in the plot, he'd publish *Annabel Lee* for me. What could I do? I turned him down.

Then another publisher said she liked the book a lot, but it wasn't religious enough. If I'd go back through and beef up the spiritual elements of the plot, her publishing committee would likely be interested. What could I do? I turned her down too.

See, Amy and Jan? Writing Annabel Lee *was a complete waste of time. I told you so!*

Then, in 2014, Vicki Crumpton at Revell came along. And this was strange: She read the book (even though she knew I wasn't really a novelist). She *liked* the book. And she didn't demand that I rewrite the whole thing to make it fit her preconceived notions of what was or wasn't "spiritual."

Huh.

Well, I warned Vicki, I know some people on your publishing team, and they probably won't like hearing my name around the office. She just smiled and told me—in the most polite and respectful way—that doing her job was really none of my concern, now was it?

Long story short, Vicki won.

Next thing you know, here I am on a lazy Sunday afternoon, writing an absurdly convoluted story in the space where acknowledgments are supposed to go. But all that is to say . . .

Special thanks to three strong-willed, wonderful women who made this book a reality: my wife, Amy. My pastor's wife, Jan Hummel. And of course, my editor, Vicki Crumpton. All of you make my life better—even when I stupidly get in your way.

—Mike Nappa
Summer 2015

Mike Nappa is an entertainment journalist at FamilyFans.com, as well as a bestselling and award-winning author with more than one million books sold worldwide. When he was a kid, the stories of Edgar Allan Poe scared him silly. Today he owns everything Poe ever wrote. A former fiction acquisitions editor, Mike earned his MA in English literature and now writes full time.